"King . . . I shall make you more than this. What you dreamed of is dross beside my dream, long and long inside Dun Gol. King is only the beginning of it. Caer Wiell was ours once, like Caer Donn; but those were not the names. I shall teach you to call them. Of all Mankind only you will be left, my self, my very soul. You wanted Eald thrust aside; I shall cast it down, and make the world again what it was. And you will see, self, what wonders there are to see—of jewels like the sun and moon, of elegance and pleasure, of things so rare no Man has seen them. **We shall scour the world and own it.**"

Hugo-winning author

C.J. CHERRYH

has also written:

THE DREAMSTONE

DOWNBELOW STATION

SUNFALL

WAVE WITHOUT A SHORE

THE PRIDE OF CHANUR

THE "MORGAINE" TRILOGY

THE "FADED SUN" TRILOGY

BROTHERS OF EARTH

SERPENT'S REACH

HESTIA

HUNTER OF WORLDS

MERCHANTER'S LUCK

PORT ETERNITY

THE TREE
OF SWORDS
AND JEWELS

C. J. Cherryh

DAW BOOKS, INC.
DONALD A. WOLLHEIM, PUBLISHER

1633 Broadway, New York, NY 10019

FIRST PRINTING, AUGUST 1983

1 2 3 4 5 6 7 8 9

DAW TRADEMARK REGISTERED
U.S. PAT. OFF. MARCA
REGISTRADA. HECHO EN U.S.A

PRINTED IN U.S.A.

TABLE OF CONTENTS

Prologue

The Tale as Told

in

The Dreamstone

There was war in a certain land of Men, but that was not an unusual thing. It spawned outlaws, and that, among Men, was not unusual either.

Most of the outlaws of this land lurked about the fringes of the deep woods, particularly in the vale of the Caerbourne, where the trees were old and known to be unfriendly. Few even of the most desperate strayed beneath those branches, and most especially they did not come at night, when the shadows and the trees had powers they lacked by day.

Death hunted in that woods. The Keeper gave him leave. There were often other baneful things, some of which had once been Men, and most of which had never been.

But one night of many nights a Man came into the Ealdwood, and so trespassed in Faery, that being one of the aspects of this forest, old among forests of the world. This Man's name was Niall, and he was, to be sure, an outlaw, among other things; but he was so sad and weary a Man on this night that he touched the elvish Keeper's heart—or perhaps it was fey luck that was on them both, that Arafel found him quickly and sent him back across the river.

"Do not come again," she warned him, but for pity, perhaps again because of some luck that was on him, or her, this night, she told him where a refuge lay, a tamer, homelier place than her own, but a part of Faery all the same.

So he went to this refuge folded in the hills—a farm, a steading filled with various Men and beasts who had lost their way in the world and found peace in this valley so isolate from the harm outside. Niall learned more homely skills than swordcraft, and learned magic and truth—from the land, from all he met; and soon he stopped thinking about war altogether.

Nor was Eald so dreadful here. It peeped and pranked about the haymow in the wizened, hair-covered shape of the Gruagach, the Brown Man, who knew more games than malice. But it was Eald all the same, and it was due its respect.

There were children on the steading—like the urchin Scaga, thief and scoundrel, who mended his ways for Niall. There were men and women of all sorts, some of whom might also have known war, but no one spoke of that. It took luck to find this place, the last hope in all the world; and no one wished to lose it.

Outside the valley, of course, the world went right on being what it was, unjust, for the rightful King had been defeated in battle and murdered years ago; and now his kingdom was partitioned into the hands of rogues and brigands, who did as they pleased with it.

But this world touched the valley from time to time. For Niall it came in the person of Caoimhin the archer, who stumbled wounded and starving up the fencerow one harvest day.

"You must go back," Caoimhin pleaded with Niall when he had had a meal or two—for they were old comrades, from the days when Niall had been Niall Cearbhallain, the King's own champion. The old King had left an infant son—Laochailan was his name: and so the war went on, the outlawed remnant of the King's true men against the rebel lords and bandits.

"No," Niall said; and, besought again: "Leave me my peace." More, he prevailed on Caoimhin to stay awhile, a winter, at least; and then more days and more. This King-to-come, Niall argued, was a hope for younger men, a hope for another age— but not their own. They had won their rest. Their war and their cause were done.

So Caoimhin stayed, finding peace and enough to eat a far better life than the war Men fought outside.

But in spring came another visitor, not desperate as others had come to the steading, but blithely singing down the valley as if he had not a care in all the world.

Now Niall was troubled at once, sensing something of Eald about this young man, this harper who claimed to have come wandering by chance down the way that led from Donn; for Donn was a fortress set in hills as eerily reputed as that haunted woods across the Caerbourne to the south.

And in truth, that night the harper sang of the Cearbhallain, the hero, the King's champion—for this harper was Fionn

Fionnbharr, son of the old King's harper, the harper who had been slain by the King's murderers. Fionn had recognized Niall and Caoimhin from the beginning, and, confronting them privately, he told Niall how Niall's own cousin Evald, one of the traitors, had not only usurped Niall's hall of Caer Wiell, but also held the King's cousin in it and his wife by force. Now Fionn had hoped by telling this to provoke Niall to some feeling, to anger if nothing else. He was willing even to suffer blows from him if he could then follow him against Evald. He saw the King's champion as a sure means to the revenge he desired—for this Evald more than all the rest was his father's murderer.

"No," Niall said again, and tried to reason with the young harper, saying that to raise open warfare before the child-King was old enough to rule in his own right might draw the little strength they had and risk all future hope for Fionn Fionnbharr's revenge.

The harper was not persuaded. He left in the morning, bound on his errand.

But he had won Caoimhin, who set out to take up the war again.

So Niall was left behind; and in his self-doubt he asked a prophecy of the Gruagach.

"Should I have listened to Caoimhin," he asked, "and is there hope in serving this child-king?"

He was hoping of course for some surety of the future. If he knew how the battle would end, he could set out even to his death in the confidence that his sacrifice would mean something. He wanted an unshakeable guarantee, for he had lived too long to trust to simple hopes.

But the Gruagach, commanded to prophesy, gave him no reassurance at all. *Death,* he said first; and, pressed about the King-to-come: *Dark;* and a third time pressed, he passed into a trance and gave Niall his answer.

> *Dark the blight and dark the path and strong the chains that bind them,*
> *Fell the day that on them dawns, for doom comes swift behind them.*

This was hardly the response Niall was hoping for. Like most of the Gruagach's answers, it did not even seem to bear directly on his question. He made no sense of it, except to fear that all his choices were unlucky.

Of companions now only the boy Scaga remained steadfast.

* * *

The prophecy first began to work with Fionn Fionnbharr—for one night next spring, the harper came breaking into the haunted forest across the Caerbourne, exhausted, desperate, and carrying a very different harp from the one he had begun with.

The sound of that harp jangling on his shoulder waked Arafel a second time from her rest. She took less precaution than she should in investigating the disturbance of her woods, perhaps, but it was not all her fault, and some of it was fate. The harp was elvish-make, and the sound of it had power, even over her—or especially over her, she being what she was.

She accosted the terrified harper in the dark and drew him back with her to confront his pursuer, Evald of Caer Wiell. Evald wanted the harp and the harper; Arafel claimed both, the harp at least with some justice of ownership. But since she knew that Evald's claim on the harper was of some legitimacy, she agreed to bargain with him, treasure for treasure, though she warned Evald earnestly that things of Eald were always *in* Eald, and might therefore be unlucky for him.

Humiliated before his men and needing to save his pride, Evald chose the green stone Arafel wore about her neck, which she surrendered only after the harp and the harper were deep in the safety of her woods. And Evald, true to his nature, struck at her back as she left.

She evaded the blow nonetheless, having the power to step elsewhere. So the Men went defeated back to their hold across the river and she went to claim her harper.

She meant to take Fionn with her into her own realm then, but he refused, and she could not take him into Faery against his will. So she simply asked him to harp for her, and stayed in the mortal world to hear him, knowing that the evils which inhabited this Eald would make short work of him if she left him to his own devices. Besides, she still hoped to win him.

But the virtue of the stone she had traded was this in part: that it was full of dreams, and exchanged her dreams for Evald's. Her Eald and the mortal realm had their day and night opposed, times fitting together in a strange, extended fashion, so that she was abroad most by starlight in the mortal woods, when Men slept.

In that way, the harper's songs constantly invaded Evald's dreams, and Evald's bloody hunts and his waking conscience invaded hers—for this Evald, having killed his King and the

King's own harper, had hung the Harp of Kings in his stolen hall in defiance of law and honor; and now he feared its loss.

Fionn told her how he had planned his revenge. He had harped for Evald all the winter long, and in the spring he had stolen the Harp of Kings from that wall and mended it, singing a song which his father had sung, taunting Evald with it. So Evald hunted him to kill him and to have the Harp back, and to save his pride before his men.

But the Harp of Kings, Arafel told Fionn, was never meant for bitter songs and vengeance. There was magic in it. Since it was elvish and made in Eald, it had come straightway home when it was cast adrift in the world, first to Caer Wiell and then bringing Fionn into this woods and her to him by more than coincidence. This harp was heard in all three realms of Eald at once, the realm of Men being only the middle one. It waked things. She was only one of them.

In place of bitterness she tried to teach him elvish songs, recalling what she was—how all her people had been driven from the world by weariness and the encroachments of Men and iron. The elves had passed beyond the sea; but Arafel alone had stayed, guardian of this last forest, this last stronghold of the world that was.

Fionn was entranced by these visions, and almost she won him; but he could never free himself of his hatred. At times he slipped back into his old bitterness and played that deadly song.

Then Evald in his madness brought his men to hew the forest down. They began with axes at the edge of it nearest the Caerbourne, not daring to set all the woods ablaze because their own land bordered it. Trees began to fall which had stood from the foundation of the world.

And Arafel began to weaken. There was no more rest for her. Her dreams were full of terror, her days full of misery unrelieved except by the harper's songs. She had lost even the power to return to her own realm, and knew at last that if she did not give up harp and harper and send him to some place of safety beyond her woods, both she and he would come to terrible grief.

Then Fionn, when he saw what was happening to her, knew at what cost she had gained his songs.

He ran and left her, delivering himself to Evald, to trade everything back again, himself and the Harp of Kings for the stone that was Arafel's elvish soul.

Fionn received the stone into his own hand before he died. That broke the spell and Arafel raced to save him; but for Fionn it was already too late.

When she came among the Men this time it was without disguise, in all her anger. Any Man in his right mind would have fled, and most did; but Evald pursued her where she led.

So she dealt with Evald alone, in a dawn when the Wild Hunt broke across the sky and storm delayed the daylight.

Then she retrieved the stone, which ever afterward had harp-song in the heart of it; but Fionn Fionnbharr was past all help, and the Harp of Kings was splintered.

That evening Caoimhin came home to the steading, bringing Niall the news, how Evald was dead and the harper Fionn with him; how Caer Wiell no longer had a lord, and was ready for the taking, its men scattered and confused. More, Caoimhin had spent all winter gathering allies who were only waiting for the Cearbhallain to come forward and lead them.

Niall knew then that he had no choice. His peace was shattered; he could not refuse this. So he set out to fight again, and the boy Scaga followed him and Caoimhin, though much against their wishes.

He came by night on a hold in disarray, because Evald's men had wandered lost in the forest, and, arriving late, drank to calm their terrors. So Niall and his men invaded the hall and killed all the brigands Evald had gathered about him. In the tower Niall found Meara, Evald's captive wife, the former King's cousin; and at her knee, Evald's small son, named Evald too. Another man of his age might have killed the boy; but Niall accepted the King's cousin Meara for his lady and brought the boy Evald up as his heir when Meara gave him no other son.

Now young Evald had known only cruelty of his own father and only kindness of Niall—so he worshipped Niall Cearbhallain, growing into young manhood under the close guidance of Niall and Caoimhin and Scaga. But in the end this devotion of his doomed Niall to die, for Faery would have taken Niall back to its heart if Evald had not driven its emissary away from Niall's deathbed in what he thought was his foster-father's defense.

So a second Evald became lord of Caer Wiell, a good if sometimes hasty man; he wedded Meredydd, daughter of lord Dryw of the south, quiet, brave child of a fell, dark-eyed lord reputed as fey. Evald took Scaga for his chief advisor in those years, and always, though Evald never trusted Faery, by Scaga's counsel he maintained a tenuous peace with Eald—for the old forest lay only the river's width removed from Caer Wiell.

Evald and Meredydd had only one living child, a daughter

named Branwyn, on whom they doted, and when Branwyn was
very small, Arafel visited Caer Wiell.

It happened after this wise: that Arafel met Lord Death in her
woods and disputed with him on the virtues of humankind (with
whom Death had much to do). Then after so many human years
she recalled the harper and the hold and conceived a curiosity
about these visitors who had been so fatal for elvish kind.

So she chanced on Branwyn beneath Caer Wiell's walls when
Branwyn was a child, but it came to tragedy as Lord Death knew
it must. Arafel was far too long-lived and Branwyn's childhood
was all too brief; and they could only wound each other. During
one of Arafel's long absences, Branwyn went searching for her
into the woods, and lost her pony's life and very nearly her own
before Evald found her. After that Branwyn hated Eald, and had
no more to do with it.

But Branwyn's losses were not done, because not long after
this, King Laochailan, who had remained in hiding all his youth,
declared himself, so Evald went away to war for the King in the
stead of Niall Cearbhallain, and left Scaga in charge of Caer
Wiell. That war was long and bitter, and it filled years of
Branwyn's youth, separating her father and her mother most of
the time of her growing up.

At last the war took a fateful turn. The King had retaken Dun
na h-Eoin, his father's hall, in a great battle. But that victory had
turned the enemy toward Caer Wiell, for it was one stronghold
most remote from the King's lands, where the retreating rebels,
backed by the bandit holds of An Beag and Caer Damh, might
establish another foothold.

Now Evald and King Laochailan were not on the best of terms
in spite of the years of service Evald had given his lord. In fact
the King distrusted Evald precisely because he was the most
powerful of his own war leaders. This King, who had spent his
boyhood in hiding, in constant fear of his father's bloody fate,
had learned only distrust and connivance, and saw all men like
himself. He was so small-souled and imagined such contant
plottings about him he would have feared any successful warleader;
but worse, Evald was the son of one of his father's murderers;
and further, this Evald was, after all, his own cousin, having
some remote claim on the throne through Meara and the
Cearbhallain.

So the King denied Evald's request to lead his army home to
bolster up Caer Wiell, though it was already under siege by its
bandit neighbors. The King was not willing to see Evald get any

glory of what might be the final battle of the war; but more, he thought it good strategy to let this last battle ruin the land of this richest of his lords. For that reason he held Evald back. But because he also had no wish to have Caer Wiell in the hands of the enemy, he sent a young man with a message to reassure Caer Wiell and urge them go on fighting.

This messenger was Ciaran Cuilean, younger son of lord Ciaran of Donn. He made that dangerous ride through the remnant of the battle, but at Caerbourne Ford he lost his horse in an ambush of An Beag and fled wounded into the forest.

There he ran afoul not of An Beag's forces, but of Lord Death and the Wild Hunt, and lost a portion of his soul to the dark hounds. In his desperation he broke into the hallowed grove at the very heart of Eald, and stole an elvish sword to defend himelf, even holding Lord Death at bay, if briefly.

He would have fallen to the hounds all the same, but Arafel had seen it and summarily dismissed Lord Death as an intruder in her realm. So she took Ciaran's iron armor and his weapons from him, and brought him unconscious as he was into her own woods, where silver trees grew straight and tall, hung with jewels like the one she wore, with swords and armor all shining with light. When the wind blew in that grove the stones all sang with memories, that being the nature of them—all the precious treasure of the elves which they had left behind them to keep Arafel company in her vigil, these stones, their elvish souls, or memories, or a great deal, at least, of what the elves had been; and the armor which they had used in their own wars against the dark.

Arafel healed this Man, who waked thereafter in a great mistrust of all he saw, because there was no good rumor of elves among Men. Ciaran would have fled at once, but on the one hand he knew Death was waiting in the mortal world, and on the other Arafel was very fair and kind to him, and he perceived that she had saved him from one kind of harm; so he stayed at least to explain to her—how he had an urgent mission to Caer Wiell and how many lives and the fate of the Kingdom itself might rely on it.

So Arafel was deeply hurt a third time by Men. She had believed all her kind had gone, deserting her, but she realized now that some elvish blood must survive in this Man, this son of fey Caer Donn, and she had known it from the moment he had broken through into her Eald to steal an elvish sword. In respect of this kinship she had even told him her true name, which she had never told to any Man. And now he would go away. So not without darker motives she gave him a parting-gift—not the sword, but one of the stones, which had been her own cousin Liosliath's heart. Set about Ciaran's neck it would give him some protection against Lord Death. This much she told him. But that stone also had greater powers, and one of them was that law which said that things *of* Eald were always *in* Eald, wherever they fared. And this she did not tell him.

She set him safely across the Caerbourne, the river which the elves named Airgiod, and brought him through the battle directly to Caer Wiell.

Once inside the walls, Ciaran was quickly caught and brought to the hall, but he had Evald's ring to show them, and a message of hope to give them, of the victory at Dun na h-Eoin. So they accepted him as a friend, and took heart from what he told them.

In that hour also Ciaran first met Branwyn, and they began to fall in love.

But when Ciaran looked out from the walls and saw how the enemy had the hold besieged, how all the country round about was burned and ruined, then he began to doubt everything he had told them. It was well known that the elves might keep a Man a single night in their world and he would then wake to find a year or a hundrd years had passed. So Ciaran feared that days might have passed in Eald, or months, and the King might be lost or dead. Still he dared not admit where he had been, so he made up a story of how he had climbed the wall to get inside. Skaga believed him. The folk of Caer Wiell were kind to him. Then he feared that there must be some spell on him to make them trust him against all common sense—some elvish glamor betraying all of them for some dark purpose of Arafel's own.

That night Ciaran dreamed, terrible dreams which put him into the body and the mind of Liosliath, the elf who had owned the stone ages of the world ago, memories of elvish wars—Liosliath, who had despised all humankind. And when Ciaran took off the stone that night he dreamed of Death, so that he had no peace or rest at all.

The enemy rode near the hold in the morning, showing a severed head they claimed to be Evald's, and a tattered standard like Evald's own. Together with Branwyn and Skaga, Ciaran denied it could be true, maintaining that their rescue by the King could not be far off. But he was far from certain.

Attack followed, and Ciaran was anxious to take up weapons he understood against an enemy he could see—but the touch of iron armor was poisonous to him because of the stone, so it became clear to everyone, even Branwyn, that he was of elvish kind. By lady Meredydd's mercy he was only locked within his tower room and offered no worse harm, but now all Caer Wiell believed that he had lied out of some faery malice, and that they had no hope of rescue at all.

So that night, alone and unadvised, Ciaran tried to work the magic of the stone, to send a message to Arafel. By chance he sent himself entire, and fell into Death's realm; but Arafel rescued him at the third calling of her name, and brought him to her forest.

She was less pleased when she discovered why he had come, with what request. She refused him the help he sought; and in his desperation he used the command he had learned, to speak her name three times, that she should help Caer Wiell. In rage and distress she left him, and so defeated, he found his own way home to his tower room.

But Arafel arrived soon after him, in Caer Wiell itself, in front of everyone in hall, and she promised the help he had commanded even while the alarm was being sounded and the enemy was advancing on the walls. Hold firm, she said; they must give her time.

So Ciaran must wait for Arafel, and Branwyn, regaining her courage, waited beside him. All this while the stone told him the truth of what he had done—for Arafel had spoken of balances upset, of her own folk who could not lightly be disturbed . . . things no one in the room just now had understood, excepting himself; and perhaps Branwyn, who had feared Eald all her life.

Niall Cearbhallain might have understood, to whom the Gruagach had given his prophecy . . . for it was coming true.

Arafel returned, having gathered her armor and Liosliath's; and the elvish horses Fionnghuala and Aodhan. So before the whole company of Caer Wiell's defenders, Ciaran armed himself and rode out with Arafel against the enemy, astride a horse which had been Liosliath's, bearing the memories of an elflord against his heart, knowledge how to wield the weapons which Arafel named too dire to use on Men.

So they set out at the head of what riders Caer Wiell could muster. They were vastly outnumbered, and worse, by Arafel's riding to war, the dark forces had been loosed from their prisons beneath the hills.

Horror followed, on all planes of existence. Even Lord Death came begging them in the name of the gods to stop, for Arafel to withdraw from the field, but her aid had been commanded and retreat was impossible. Ciaran tried to release her, willing to perish and even for Caer Wiell to fall, to stop what had begun to happen; but it was too late: the enemy having taken the horrors underhill for allies, there could be no retreat without victory, for either side, and Caer Wiell was doomed already.

Then Lord Death gave them valuable news, that the King was held off in battle not far away; so Arafel seized on that chance and rode, leaving Ciaran behind.

He had no power to have held the field alone: but he saw one way. He gave himself up to the stone's memories; he *became* Liosliath, and the shadows knew their ancient enemy. Ciaran-Liosliath held the field in utter carnage, unable to help human friends, completely lost to the power which guided him.

He held until Arafel came bringing all the King's forces the shorter way through Eald, until Lord Death loosed the Wild Hunt and harried the fleeing souls through the heavens. He rode even as part of that, following after Skaga and others of the slain, but Arafel recalled him to her, and so to safety.

So the shadows had been driven away, and the King had won his Kingdom, and Caer Wiell had survived.

But Ciaran found men shying away from him in terror at what they had seen and what they still saw of him. Only Branwyn had the courage to stand by his side. His own father refused to speak to him and his brother Donnchadh walked away in rejection of him, both putting as much distance as they could between themselves and Eald, knowing full well that their heritage was tainted with the old powers and now seeing it revealed to their King and all the world, to the ruin of their ambition. So even the King was less than glad to receive Ciaran's homage, for he had been robbed of glory after all, and he had been handed his kingdom by a man more fearsome than Evald, whom he had tried to ruin, a man moreover linked with Branwyn, who was kin to him through Meara, through Evald whom he hated.

In the end Ciaran wed Branwyn and stayed with her at Caer Wiell, becoming Evald's heir. And on that wedding day he returned the stone, the armor, the elvish horse, all that he had had from Arafel. He had gained that strength, to let it go and to die. Death no longer frightened him. He knew the stone held far worse peril for him.

So Arafel watched him go from Eald, with Branwyn at his

side. And Lord Death granted a favor that day for the sake of an old comradeship—to stay his hand awhile.

"He will die abed, years hence," Lord Death said. "That, I give to him."

It was all that Arafel could gain.

ONE
The Fuathas

It was the old hiding game, and they laughed, did Meadhbh and Ceallach, while Muirne searched. They watched the skinny woman up close by the keep looking this way and that among the bushes and covered their mouths to keep from setting one another to laughing aloud. Then Ceallach threw a stone and made the bushes rattle far over to the right so that Muirne spun and looked in that direction.

"Come out," Muirne cried. "Come out this instant. Hear me?"

She was angry now. Meadhbh slid backward through the brush and tugged at Ceallach's sleeve.

Ceallach followed. "You hear me?" Muirne went on shouting while they slid and slithered away on the slope. "Don't play such games!"

But a path appeared in their way as they got up and scrambled crouching through the trees. It was a strange place to find a path, because no one came and went in the world except by the great dusty road, and no one went off this direction from Caer Wiell, toward the river and the vast and haunted woods—excepting sometimes their father, who went alone and without any armor at all, and taking no one with him, not even Beorc, who went everywhere else. The pair had asked why, of course. They asked everything, why birds flew and why the sun rose and where the wind came from. But no one told them any of these things, and no one told them why their father went walking down by the Caerbourne where no one else would dare to walk, no, not even Beorc, who was a huge red-haired man that no one would ever call afraid.

So a thrill went up their backs when they suddenly found that path so close to them all their lives and unsuspected. One keen quick thought brought their eyes to each other and a secret excitement brought their hands together, fingers locked in fingers, Ceallach tugging on his sister's hand when he had the lead. Then as he helped Meadhbh down over an old log, Meadhbh seized the first place and dragged him along. So they went, one and then the other, their eyes afever with the secrets of this path that seemed to welcome them. It was the way their father came. They were sure of that, and for that reason they had no fear of treading on it, never once thinking that he could lead them where he could not, if danger came on them, save them.

It was so sure in their minds that they exchanged only glances as they went, unraveling this path to its ending, one pulling the other, skipping over the old rocks, the bones of the ancient hill on which Caer Wiell was reared. They dodged through thickets which should have torn their skin yet magically refrained. It was a moment of magic. They were sure of that in the same fashion they were sure each what the other thought, as if some golden thread bound their minds so close there was no need of talking.

And never once did they think that where that path led might be farther than their young legs could run without stopping. They skipped and ran and fended the branches away, took wild chances with their leaping and dodging.

It was Meadhbh who slowed first, who first began to doubt the way that they were tending. She resisted Ceallach's tugging at her hand ever so slightly just as he had lighted on soft ground, so that he slipped and brought both of them reeling down an unexpected slope in the bracken. Meadhbh sat down at the bottom, plump among her woolen skirts, barking her skin on the tangle of roots and stones, and Ceallach slid past her right to the edge of the brambles.

"Ow!" said Ceallach. "What did you stop for?"

"Hush," Meadhbh said, shivering. "We've come near the river. Hear it?"

"We mustn't lose the path," Ceallach said. The brush seemed darker all about, and the water whispered like the breeze that sported in the conspiring leaves. "Come on, Meadhbh—it has to be just up there."

But Meadhbh bit her lip and tugged up her skirt to look at her shins, where her woolen hose were torn. The wounds stung. Everything was wrong suddenly. The woods were dark and the river was chuckling nearby, so that it was hard now not to think of the strict warnings they had had about the deep forest. "We had better go back," she said. "Muirne will come looking." She said it even hoping at the moment that Muirne would turn up suddenly and rescue them. She gave her hand to Ceallach to be helped up, ready to run as hard to be out of this place as she had run to get into it, although now her side and her shins were hurting and she was far from sure in which direction home lay.

"Ah," a moan came to them. *"Ah, ah, ah—"*

They froze like fawns, and turned wide eyes in the direction of the voice, which was mixed with the sound of the river.

"Ah me," it said. "Ah me, so lost."

"Listen," Ceallach said.

"I don't know whether it means it's lost or we are," Meadhbh said, and her teeth began to chatter as if with winter cold. Her shins stung, reminding her of misfortune. She and Ceallach held onto each other with a grip that hurt her hand. "I don't think we ought to answer it."

"O lost," it cried. "O me, o me, o where?"

"It's a girl," said Ceallach then, with a fresh breath of courage. "Come on, Meadhbh, it's only someone, after all." He stood up, tugging at her hand.

"O, o!" it wept. "O, I'm caught, o the hurt, the hurt. . . ."

The sounds of sobs came to them, loud as the river, a crying that was everywhere, and Meadhbh, who was pulling back to look for the path again, stopped pulling at Ceallach's leading— not that she thought better of it, but that the someone was crying as if a heart were breaking, and that sobbing tugged as surely at her heart as at Ceallach's. She stopped pulling back at all and followed Ceallach down past the brambles and down and down where the river ran.

"I don't like this," Meadhbh found the heart to say, when they came on that black water, and Ceallach seemed daunted too. The water was sinister and wide, and gnarled old trees hung over it with a stillness that prickled through the snuffling and the weeping. "Ceallach, let's be going home."

"Look," Ceallach said, and held onto her as she held to him, because of a sudden there was someone sitting on the black rocks, like someone wrapped up in weeds still glistening from the river water. That someone lifted a pale beautiful face and hair gold as pollen fell onto its shoulders among the weeds. This someone sat with legs curled sideways on the rock and arms holding the cloak of slickish weeds about her. Eyes dark as the riverwater looked at them both very solemnly. Then weed-covered arms lifted and flowed toward the water in one smooth motion as that someone dived, so subtly it was like the pouring of water into water.

"Oh," Meadhbh said, and pulled at her brother to make him run away.

But a face bobbed up in the water, flowerlike, with the pale hair flowing about in the river currents and the eyes staring at them and the mouth making a round of surprise and wonder.

"I am lost," the someone said. "Oh, please, I am lost, quite lost."

"Where are you trying to go to?" Meadhbh asked, curious in spite of herself and quite forgetting to run.

"Lost," the someone insisted. The bright head sank beneath the dark water and came up again with her hair sheeting away in the currents. "Who are you?"

"Flann," said Ceallach thinking quickly. "Floinn," said Meadhbh with a very uncomfortable feeling, because she had not been taught to lie, but names were not for giving away, and Flann and Floinn were safe at home, being two fat bay ponies and not at all in question. "Who are *you?*" It seemed completely mad to be talking to a creature floating in the river as if she were someone they had met in the field, as if she were someone dressed in honest clothes and not all in river weeds.

But the creature bobbed higher in the water as if she were standing up and brought her hands into sight, cupped as if she held some precious thing. "I shall give you a gift—see, pearls. Have you ever seen pearls or heard of them?"

"We have to go," said Ceallach.

"O, but you must never go!" The whole creature vanished again in a swirl of dark water and the waters boiled and broke at once in the appearance of a black horse's head, and neck and back, and the whole beast was surging up as a horse comes up from swimming, a horse that made all the horses of the hold look stock and dull, a horse so beautiful and sleek and black that it seemed that the night itself had come up out of the river. And they desired it, did Meadhbh and Ceallach, more than anything they had ever seen or imagined to desire. It was freedom, it was all the might of the river, it was a creature that flowed like waters and beckoned them with power. They saw themselves as queen and king, woman and man in an instant, with never waiting for tedious years to pass. They saw awe in the eyes of all about them and they never, never needed fear any man or beast anywhere or ever in the world.

It came closer, lowering its beautiful head. The water dripped off its mane and made its hide sleek and shining. It extended its foreleg and bowed itself, offering them its back, and Ceallach went first toward it with only the dimmest remembrance that he ought to be afraid, while Meadhbh came with her hands held out to it as she would come to her own pony, quite, quite forgetting the love she had for that poor, plain beast, because desire burned in her for what this one could give.

"*No,*" a voice said distinctly, "I should *not.*"

Ceallach stopped, and the black horse tossed its head. Meadhbh looked wildly about and her heart all but turned over, for a stranger stood at the edge of the thicket, cloaked in gray and deep in a kind of light and shadow that made it hard to see him. His hand seemed to rest on a sword hilt on the shadowed side, and his whole aspect was grim and dangerous. Of a sudden there was a splash where the horse had been, a scattering of cold water on them that made them cry out in fright.

And then whatever had possessed them to be here unafraid melted away from their hearts and left them terrified. The wood seemed dark and the figure dire and sinister. They held to each other in the nakedness of the riverbank, and Ceallach wound his fingers into Meadhbh's in the spell of a moment too terrible to move.

"Hardly wise," the stranger said. "Who gave you leave to be here?"

"This is our place," Meadhbh said to this intruder who was perhaps an outlaw and perhaps worse, perhaps some spy from An Beag or way up on the Bradheath; and she thought that she ought to have said nothing at all, but she was never skilled at keeping quiet. And nothing seemed right about this stranger, in the rapid shifting of this truth and that about the Caerbourne's dark banks. She could put no quality to the voice, whether it was young or old or what it sounded like, or make out clearly what the stranger looked like in the shadow which was not all that deep a shadow, except that some trick of the leaves and sun made it hard to see who stood there at all.

"Your place," the stranger echoed. "Most assuredly it is not." And the stranger brightened, just that, as if the light had stopped playing tricks or the sun had come out from behind a cloud. It was no man from An Beag, and in one way of looking at the stranger it was not a man at all, but a tall, slim lady in patchwork gray and green like a hunter's clothes, wearing a gray cloak over it all. She went striding right past them to the riverbank as if they had never mattered. *"Fuathas,"* the lady said in a voice that sent a shiver up their backs. It was oh, so soft a voice, but the water stirred, and a golden head came up very carefully, just the eyes showing above the water, eyes dark as the water was dark, and very wary.

So they knew then that they had seen two of the Sidhe—one of whom stood on the bank, there and not there, with a brightness that was different from the daylight.

"Come out," the Sidhe said.

"No." The golden head had risen so that the lips were above

the water, and now the creature looked frightened. "No, oh no, no, no."

"Out. At once. Shall I call your name? I shall teach it to these children and they will call you whenever they like."

"No," the creature wept. It slid to the shore and lay bowed in a miserable huddle of weed, only a knot of old riverweed which moved and bubbled.

"So you remember," said the Sidhe, "whose wood this is, and where you are. —Would you have its name?" she asked suddenly, and looked at Meadhbh so that all the forest seemed to have gone dim, and in Ceallach's breast his heart began to beat so heavily it seemed to fill the forest. "No," said the Sidhe then. "You wanted it once and you would want it again; and you would want it to be, and to do for you, and to do more and more until you saw everyone afraid of you. Is this what you should be?"

"No," said Meadhbh. She recalled the dream that was the water horse and the power of him, and suddenly she shuddered at the thought of her father and mother becoming very small and herself very great and tall. That was not the way the world was meant to be. She never wanted that. And: "No," Ceallach said, thinking of himself and Meadhbh powerful over everything and all alone, with no more games to play and only fear around them, and between them.

"Its name is Caolaidhe," said the Sidhe.

"*Ah!*" the creature wailed, "ah no, ah no, o mercy no!" She looked up at them, held up thin white hands as if she cupped the pearls. "O mercy, o mercy, o no, no, not to leave the river, never, no. I'll give you gifts, o such gifts!"

The thought of the pearls leapt into Meadhbh's mind. It was a good thought and unselfish surely, how the pearls would look about her mother's neck, how her mother would wonder at her having them to give. Surely to give them away would be the right thing to do. But the tall, gray-cloaked Sidhe was staring at her with a look so strange and piercing that no leaf could have moved in all the forest. She could only think that something was expected of her, something more than she had ever done and might ever do, a thing that was wise and at once as simple as understanding. "Let it go," Meadhbh said.

"Go back to the river and don't come out," Ceallach told it.

The creature cast a wild look about and bent and flowed away. "O kind," it cried as it slid into the water. "O good children, o kind—" The sound became bubbles, and the river flowed with its accustomed rush.

"My calling-name is Thistle," the Sidhe said gravely, as if the fuath had been no more than a passing breeze. "You might be trusted with my true one; I do think you might, young as you are. But I am no small matter, no, not like that one. You have done wisely at the last if not at the first."

"We have to go home now," said Meadhbh as staunchly as she could.

"I shall take you there."

"We can go ourselves," said Ceallach.

"Then I shall walk with you and see you safe."

"You mustn't."

"Ah," the Sidhe said gravely. "But I am your father's friend."

"Are you what he comes to see?"

"Perhaps I am."

"I had thought—" Ceallach said and let his voice fall away.

"Be still," said the Sidhe. "Name no names near the riverside. Caolaidhe is listening. Come. Come, now. There are worse things about this stream than the each-uisge."

She offered her hands, one to each, and as Meadhbh considered gravely, so did Ceallach, looking up at their tall rescuer.

"Now you are wary," said the Sidhe. "Good. But wary of the wrong one, and that is ill. Go as you please then."

"Come on," said Ceallach to Meadhbh, and took his sister's hand. They went climbing up away from the Sidhe, up the bank, fighting the undergrowth among the gray stones. Bracken grew here, but bracken gave way to rougher growth, and thorns scratched them and tore at their hair and clothes.

"I don't think this is the way," Meadhbh said after a while. "I think we should go more to the left."

Ceallach went, and it was better for a time, but it was not the path, and very soon they both stopped and looked about them, each holding the other's hand and feeling very tired and frightened and wishing desperately to be home again.

"We have to go on," said Ceallach.

"But which way?" asked Meadhbh. "I'm afraid I've lost us. The path is nowhere near here."

"I will show you," said a voice, and Thistle followed, shadowy and standing right amid a thorn thicket where no one could have walked.

"Is that herself?" asked Ceallach, "or only something like it? —Meadhbh, don't trust it."

"Wiser still," said Thistle, and walked out of the brambles and held out her hand again, clearer and sterner than before.

"But that way leads to An Beag and I doubt you would like that. Come, I say—Ceallach and Meadhbh, come now."

There was a wanting, a desire as strong as for the water horse, and first Ceallach and then Meadhbh started to go, but each held the other back in small hesitations that made one great one.

"So, well," said the Sidhe. "But I am called. I hear your father calling me. If he calls a third time I must go and leave you, and that would be dangerous. The woods are roused and he is in danger as deep as yours. Come, I say, come *now!*"

Meadhbh went. It was the part about her father in danger that won her; and Ceallach came running an instant later. "Ah!" Meadhbh cried in fright, for the Sidhe at once flung her gray cloak about them both and cut off the sun. Strong arms held them, and there was a scent of flowers and grass and a grayness which stole the sight like mist, passing then to dark. Meadhbh was falling asleep and knew she ought to be afraid, but she was not. Ceallach knew too and struggled, or thought that he did, but the sleep came on him: he heard the Sidhe whisper his name.

They slept, not wishing to, wrapped all in gray.

So Arafel carried them both as she came, and laid them gently on the bracken.

"No harm is on them," she said to their father. Her heart hurt her to see how the years had dealt with this Man. It hurt her most to see his fright, how he ran and fell to his knees next his children, and gathered them each in an arm, sleeping as they were, hugging them and holding them as if he had just had part of his heart torn from him and restored. Arafel sat down crosslegged where she stood so that she need not look down at him, and wistfully gazed on the three of them until Ciaran found his wits again. "They are sleeping," she assured him, for he might not understand that sleep. "It was easier to bring them so."

"Arafel," he said, holding his children against his heart, two red-and-golden heads nodded together beneath his fair beard. Tears ran on his face. The years had graven lines about his eyes. He was heavy with a man's full strength, and yet held his burden so gently his hands could not have bruised a flower.

So quickly the years fled. Each time she looked at him something of him had changed, and life seemed to have more and more power over him. "They have grown so," she said with a nod toward the children.

"Yes. They've grown." Pain touched his face, a patient kind

of pain, long-suffering. "I hoped this time—I had most hope of you, that when I truly needed you—I hoped you had them."

"I." Arafel laid a hand on the stone at her breast. It was like a wound, his look. "No. You wrong me, Man."

"Not that you would do them harm. Never that."

"Or misguide them. Or take them into Eald without your knowing."

"Where were they then? Lost? Only lost, after all?"

"O Man, *Man.*"

"I thought," he said, "perhaps there had gotten to be too much of the world about me for you to hear me any longer. That perhaps it was a place only they could go."

The pain was deep and everywhere, but there were no tears for it. He was at once too proud and too humble and it wounded her more than tears. "You do not understand," she said. "I've always heard you."

"And never came."

"The time—is not the same for me. There was a moment I could come, and I have left things now—O believe me, my dear friend, that you never walked in Eald unattended, going or coming."

"I had hoped for a word through the years," he said simply, and his brows knit together. "That, if nothing more." He wound his fingers gently in his children's red hair and looked down at them and up again earnestly. "But this is more. Far more. This is all I ask."

"There was a difference in this calling. I felt it. Ah, Ciaran, I ran, I ran. I cannot tell you all of it, not here. Never think that it was nothing to me that you came."

"They *were* in danger, then."

"They fared better in it than some would have. There's much of their father in them." She saw the fear and put out her hand to his. "A silly nix, a danger most to children. Keep them from the forest. And yourself—O my friend, no more of walks into the wood. I shall come to you, rather. Things are darker than they were and the way has changed."

He had always had more sight than most. Fear crept in where pain had been. "How, changed?"

"This is not the place to talk of it. Hist, Branwyn is calling."

"Branwyn." A thousand distracted cares drew at him, graving lines on his face. He hugged his children and tried to get to his feet, but Arafel was quicker, and laid her hand on his shoulder.

"Let me take the girl," Arafel said, "and come with me."

He yielded up his daughter and Arafel took the girl into her arms, within her cloak, while he took his son and rose.

It was the merest shifting through the shadow, the lightest journey—and very swift. The walls of Caer Wiell showed beyond the mist, and grew out of shadow into daylight.

"So they are safe and home," said Arafel, and already the children were beginning to rub at their eyes as at the passing of an ordinary sleep. She set Meadhbh on her feet on the ground and steadied her, and looked into her face a moment. "Are you quite well, then?"

Meadhbh blinked and nodded dazedly. And Ceallach waked thoroughly and hugged his father's neck as Meadhbh discovered her father and her home at once and hurled herself against him to throw her arms about him.

"They know me as Thistle," Arafel said, beginning to depart into the night of her own world. "And that is best."

"Come back," Ciaran cried after her.

She stayed, half in his sunlight.

"Come soon," he wished her.

"To Caer Wiell? Yes, if you wish that. I shall come tonight— Yes, I shall. It is time I did that. Look for me at moonrise."

The children blinked and then losing sight of her, tumbled words one over the other, of water horses and river nixes and paths and rescues. Arafel heard them, even so.

And went her own way.

"She sent it back," said Meadhbh to her father, "into the river then, and we were afraid of her—minding what you always said about strangers—" It stuck in her throat to tell him what choice she had been offered, for that was too deep and too dark and too much knowledge of her growing heart to show to anyone, most of all anyone she loved. Somehow she passed over all the rest of it, even knowing the Name of the creature; and so did Ceallach. She was not the same; she would never be the same again after knowing how to choose, and neither would Ceallach; and she discovered this as she faced her father, at once afraid and desperately sure what she was doing. She had begun to grow up and apart in a way she thought was right—but it was not something to speak of.

And Ciaran saw the secrets nesting in both his children, not being blind. "You have been with the Sidhe," he said, and felt the least and most desperate jealousy of those he loved most in all the world. "And some things are not for ordinary ears. There are those who would be frightened by hearing it, do you understand? Be wise and quiet on it." So he took them each by the hand and brought them toward the gates of Cær Wiell.

A horn began to sound from the walls, waking echoes across the hills. The lost was found, and now the searchers through the forest must come safely home. Following these echoes other horns began to sound through the forest and along the river as searchers heard and passed the signal on.

Women came running before ever they reached the gates, and quickest was Branwyn, who had been watching from the walls and seeking too with what small portion of Eald she held in her heart. She came running, her braids whipping loose, her skirts aflurry, her slippered feet hardly touching the stones. She caught her errant children in her arms and looked at their faces and up at Ciaran's and wept.

"They were with her," Branwyn said hotly. "I knew, I knew—"

"No. They were not with her," Ciaran said. "But she found them."

Branwyn's face went pale beneath its flush, all her knowings in disorder. She held Meadhbh's face and then Ceallach's between her hands and looked them in the eyes, kneeling there on the muddy stones beneath the gate—looked last and most desperately at Ciaran, hearing silences. Muirne came, wiping her nose and her eyes and begging everyone's forgiveness. "You must beg Muirne's pardon," Ciaran said sternly to his children. "You left *her*, as I hear it."

Meadhbh made a grave curtsy, difficult to manage within her mother's arm; and: "I beg pardon, Muirne," Ceallach said faintly.

Ciaran looked at all those round about, and still there was a hush on all the crowd except the children. "Our thanks," he said. "Nothing is amiss. The lost is found." He set a hand on his son's shoulder as Branwyn took Meadhbh in hand, and they passed through the gates of the hold he had held as lord the last ten years.

TWO

Caer Wiell

Branwyn wept, in the upper hall of Caer Wiell, her hands against her eyes as she sat huddled in her chair before the hearth. To her credit she wept alone, her children in their tower room with Muirne, her husband with his men down by the gate; for they were tears compounded of rage, of helplessness, of years and years of dread.

She hated Eald. It was a hate not born of anger, and yet having anger in it, for she had been betrayed. She had loved it once desperately, when she had been a child, and so she feared it for her children, with more than instinct. It and she were enemies, but quietly, gently—for all that she loved was tangled in Eald: her husband, her home, her children latest of all. She saw a vision of green leaves and dancing light, touching all she had, and this light was without substance: she could not strike it or hold it in the hand, but no shutters or gates could stop it. It slipped through chinks and the wind that came from the woods breathed enchantments more potent than her mortality.

Something had touched her children, something of Eald had held them today, and so she clenched her fists and remembered herself as if she hovered in the air above the girl on a fat Caerdale pony, and that child was herself and that which hovered was herself grown and trying to warn the girl—*go back, go back, never trust them.*

The vision always ended there, before the pony shied. It was more dreadful so, with every merry jogging step become horridly sinister, every stirring of the leaves a menace the child could not yet feel.

Go back, go back, go back.

It was strange, that she could never recall Arafel. In her mind she knew that there had been such a person, that this was the power that sat at the heart of the wood. She had spoken with her face to face, oh, many a time. But the face and the voice had left her mind, leaving only the memory of a memory, of something which had shaken her life and left a great gap about itself, making her doubt that it was ever true. She never admitted this to her husband, never spoke of it, but she knew that this was not so with him, that Eald was graven too deeply in his heart for him ever to forget. She hated Eald and embraced it, perceiving even in him, in Ciaran, in the father of her children, a green silence she could never breach, and thoughts she could never share, and a longing against which she worked all her mortal witchery— *Stay, o stay, never think of her, never listen to the wind, never remember—whatever it is I cannot hold in my mind.*

If she could shape this thing, she thought sometimes, she might gain power over it. Once she had walked into the heart of Eald, Ciaran's hand locked with hers, so that for a time she saw; but that memory too had fled like water through the sieve of her reason, and while she remembered that they had spoken with someone, that someone was lost to her. There had been a horse Ciaran had ridden; but she had not been able. In truth, she could not tell even looking at it whether it was a horse at all, whether something of surpassing beauty or surpassing horror, except that it was power, and it had carried her husband once to war, a thing of light and terror, and sometimes the memory of soft horselike breaths and sometimes the striking of a hoof, not horselike, but like the muttering of thunder in the distance.

She shivered, and gazed into the tiny fire they kept to warm this room in springtime. The memories faded, as faery things would, which was their camouflage in the world; faded from *her*, though once she had seen these things and touched the elvish horse and met Arafel face to face.

Stay away, she cried in her heart, *never come back, never trouble us*— for she knew that all the gifts she had and all her happiness came from that most untrustworthy source.

And faery gifts faded, like faery itself in the minds of its beholders, except for those of elvish blood.

She knew the rumors of her husband, that he was Sidhe and fey. He had never said so, but knew she had heard and did not gainsay. So the rumors were true, and that was indeed his heritage. She knew—knew things that troubled his deepest dreams, where Death pursued him and gained a part of him, only biding for the rest. And whether this had truly happened, somewhere in Eald, or whether it was only a portending dream, she was not sure, in that way that all her memories shifted like quicksand. But it was real enough that a night of storm could send Ciaran into dark despair, when they were private, after he had put aside the cheerfulness he wore for others.

On such nights he scarcely slept, and started awake at cracks of thunder, relieved only when the dawn brought back the day. And then he would smile and laugh as if there had never been a cloud; but she had learned to dread these times, and something in her grew taut and miserable when such nights began.

Away, she mourned. *Away, away.*

But that was not the bargain she had struck; and now and again in a far and shifting fashion like the recollection of a dream she remembered a face she could not hold longer than a breath, and a brightness that held something of green and something of the sun and moon at once. Children might stray after such baubles, after such bright promises. She had no children, did Arafel, none that Branwyn knew; and it was in Branwyn's heart that the elf might feel an envy and desire of children.

They told such tales of the Sidhe, that they could be so cruel, so thoughtlessly cruel.

Had not Arafel been so cruel with her, promising a small girl faery-sights, and luring her into the forest to the loss of her pony and almost of her life?

Come away, a voice still whispered in her dreams. *Let go and see things as they are.*

But it was only memory, a voice without distinction, like the face.

The things she cherished now were warm and solid like Caer Wiell, her husband's arms, her children's laughter. She had traded all of faery promises for these.

Come with me, the voice had said, *and see how the years pass, so soon withered like the violets; but there is no fading where I go. Take my hand, come with me, never hear them calling.*

"Branwyn."

She turned where she sat, startled by her husband's voice, so softly he had come up the stairs; but that was his way, this quiet. He offered his arms to her; she held out her own and he came and knelt down by her, holding her, patting her shoulders, making her look at him.

"Were you crying?" he asked, with the evidence of it on her lashes. "O Branwyn, love, my love, my heart, there's no need for crying now. They're safe, full of bread and honey, no worse than scratches and skinned knees—"

"What was it they found?"

"Something— She called it a silly nix, a thing—Oh, don't speak of it. It's nothing; it's gone, not to trouble us more."

"They will not go back to the river."

"They will not. They understand." He smoothed her hair, held her with great tenderness.

"It comes of this gadding about the fields, this—"

"You cannot grow flowers in the shade: they want the sun and wind, Branwyn."

She shivered, sat back from him, he kneeling and holding her clenched fists in his. For a long moment she fought for self-possession. "They cannot," she said, "grow like weeds. They cannot be deceiving Muirne and running off."

"No, they cannot. But they have the luck on them, they do, and that was on them today, and more than luck. —She will come tonight, Branwyn. *Here.*"

She needed a moment to understand.

"No," she said.

"How can it be no?" He was utterly dismayed. His face was stricken. "Branwyn—"

It was in the open then, his distress, her distrust; and then because she had never fought open war with her enemy: "Forgive me, I am distraught. I only want my house in peace, in peace—"

He gathered up her hand and carried it to his lips. She hardly felt the warmth. "Branwyn. You fear too much."

"What does she want?"

He had no ready answer. Some worry sat within his eyes, confirming her own dread. "Perhaps to warn us. Or to explain. Nothing more than that. Perhaps to be courteous. She is that. The Daoine Sidhe are much on courtesy. Branwyn, she is our friend. She has always been. Look you, what land since the war is blessed like ours, what fields as green as ours—"

"Or children," she said harshly, "so many and so fair? —I waited. I waited fifteen long years with every house in the land more blessed than ours. I held the serving maid's daughters and I ached after daughters of my own—and watched children I had held become brides before I held my own daughter and my son. O, if this was blessing, Ciaran, it was slow to come to us, and forgive me, forgive me if I am too fond—"

"And are they only yours?" he asked.

She had no answer. His look robbed her, so that she shivered.

"They were long years," he said, "but we cannot lay them on Meadhbh's and Ceallach's shoulders and crush the spirit from them. And they were good years, Branwyn."

"They were good years," she admitted, "but o, Ciaran, if we were so blessed—if there was luck on us—why not that simple luck that farmwives had and I did not? So I hold them close. And today—today I feared perhaps—"

"She is our friend. Branwyn, they are safe thanks to her."

She thought about that a time, and her heart grew a little broader, and her memory a little clearer, that once there had come a light into Caer Wiell, and in that light a shape, and a voice. Almost she saw her, a ragged figure in faded clothes, but she could not see the face.

"I would like to make her welcome," Ciaran said. "For so many debts. For friendship. Branwyn, this hall was *theirs* once and long ago. Its name was Caer Glas, and I do not know if there is another place in all the world like this, where she might be here and still in Eald. I would be dead; and so might we all—but for Arafel."

There is Donn, the thought leapt into her mind unbidden, *where you were born. That also was theirs once.* But she brushed that thought aside, as she did every unpleasant thing, keeping her own nest pure for those she loved. "We will set a table," she said, finding comfort in the proprieties of things, to tame the wild with bonds of courtesies, as if this were a charm to assure its civility. If she could once set it within her hall, she thought, and once fix it in her mind, if she could believe and once remember it, then she would feel safer; then she could get sureties of it, and learn to call its name.

Arafel she was, and *Feochadan,* which was Thistle; and other names besides. But the sound was not enough. She had to learn it with the heart, as Ciaran had, and she meant to do so, for the best of reasons, that Caer Wiell was her home, and she was born to it, of southron blood and of the line of kings and of an enemy Arafel had slain. The stones were hers, her home, the magic that she knew; and what entered here trod her ground. Here she might learn a thing, and remember this time, not letting it fade as it faded for others.

She still had power. It was herself her husband chose, to age in ordinary years, beside her; it was herself who held his children; and these were the things she dwelt on in her mind, that in Caer Wiell she was secure.

"There's my love," her husband said, and rising, touched his lips to her brow. "You'll see." He turned wistful and very grave. "At moonrise," he said.

It was long before Beorc rode in, for the searchers he had ridden farthest and deepest into the woods, and because of things he had seen or thought that he might have seen he would have no easy sleep for nights to come.

"Safe," he echoed when his lord himself had come down to

the gate to meet him. "Gods be thanked." And then he turned his face again toward seeing to his horse, for shame that he went so weak and his eyes stung, perhaps with sweat, but perhaps not. He drew his bow and quiver from the saddle and slung both over his shoulder before delivering his good bay gelding to the grooms who waited.

"Get him a cup of ale," Ciaran said. "Come to hall when you have had your ease. I want to speak with you."

"Aye," Beorc muttered, turning about again, nodding a courtesy to his departing lord. Others had come down—Domhnull one, his cousin on his mother's side; and Rhys ap Dryw, a lord's son himself, but youngest of seven sons; and others who had been among the searchers. A boy took Beorc's bow and quiver, another his muddy cloak. "Who found them?" he asked concerning the children. "Where found?"

There was strange silence among the men. "The lord himself," one said, but seemed to hold something back.

"Come," said Domhnull, taking his arm. "Come upstairs."

Beorc followed up the stairs to the wardroom, and there sank down on a bench, working himself free of his buckles, his armor and his sweat-drenched clothes. Domhnull and Rhys stayed with him, and a flurry of pages ran in and out with a succession of basins and towels and the promised stoup of ale.

"Oh, that's good," Beorc murmured, his hair and beard plastered with cooling water and his lips wet with the frothy ale. He drew a quieter breath and looked up at his comrades who leaned nearby, Rhys with one foot on the bench and his arms on his knee, Domhnull braced against the wall, hands tucked in his belt. They were not of a kind, those two—his young cousin's an uncommon fairness, hair brighter than new straw, eyes blue and clear as a babe's; and Rhys must have looked sullen from his cradle, a dark, lean man with a brooding stare: his mountains bred grim folk as they bred kites and hawks. "No harm to them?" Beorc asked again, for something in the answers he had gotten and not gotten nagged at him with the sense of something amiss. "Where were they, asleep under some hedgerow?"

"No one knows," said Rhys.

" 'Her,' my lady said," Domhnull answered. "And 'not with her,' my lord answered back."

"How far did you ride?" asked Rhys of Beorc. "Myself, as far as the old wood, and then up the road and back; and I did not like the feel."

"Farther," said Beorc, and frowned for memory of the dark

thickets, the haunted silences. "It was not An Beag I feared. Not in this."

"So thought I," Domhnull murmured. "And so I think it was. They simply strayed."

"They are fey," said Rhys. "How should they not be? And I did not like the feel."

"Hist," said Beorc, "say no such thing, ap Dryw. Say no such thing of them."

"No," said Rhys, "but 'tis true—Mark you, Skaga's-son, this is true. And those two will find their way to it, to the Sidhe, being whose get they are—O Man, do not you bridle at me; I am their mother's cousin and their own, and friend, and his, no less than you. Fey father, fey offspring; and I didn't like the feel of it today, not so far as I rode."

"I feared them lost for good," Beorc said hollowly, the cup between his knees. "When the recall sounded, I feared the worst. There was a day I would not have—It was all a childish prank, then."

"Our lord was close about it," said Domhnull frowning. "And I don't think he feared An Beag either. He—"

"*Hist!*" Rhys straightened suddenly, his hand on his knife, and strode to the stairway. "Up here! You!"

A head appeared down below where a shadow had flitted, round the corner of the landing of the stairs, a balding pate and hangdog look and a general slouching of the whole man round the corner.

"Coille!" Domhnull muttered in disgust. "Who else?"

"Out," Rhys ordered, "—skulk."

Coille held out a pail. "Bringing water up, lord Rhys, only bringing water, they told me to."

"*Out!*" Beorc shouted at him fit to wake echoes from the stairwell, and Coille fled, sloshing the steps as he went.

"Cursed gossip," Domhnull said.

"Bide here," said Rhys. "I'll put the fear in him."

"Stay," said Beorc. "Stay,"—for the southron was a fell man and wild. "Keep that knife of yours in sheath."

"Did I say I would mark him? Not I."

"No, but make much ado over his hearing and we'll not need Coille to gossip it. There's talk enough flying as it is."

"And will be," Rhys muttered. "Will be. That's the nature of you folk, to bandy everything about in market. You've no instinct for secrets, you valley-dwellers."

"There's nothing will make them love lord Ciaran less," said Domhnull. "Fey he may be, but tell them that in the steadings or gossip it in the barracks and they'll ask you fresher news." He laughed and settled the more easily, one foot on the window-ledge. "Myself, I confess to have walked in the woods now and again. Wishful thinking, mine. I'd give a great deal for the sight of one of the fair folk; and if there's harm in that, why, Beorc, your own mother and mine would put out saucers of milk at evening. And you who were in the war—"

"You are too innocent," Beorc said.

"You never will speak of it," Domhnull said, frowning now. He seldom pounced on this, but did so with greatest concentration in this moment. "It's nature to tell tales, isn't it? Like Coille, chattering everything he hears, sparrow-like. It's nature that when wars have been people talk about them, and make songs of them—like the old songs. Even the Aescford has its song, with the King dying, and the Cearbhallain—But no one sings songs now. Those that fought there are getting old, and we that weren't there can't make them, and even the harper won't sing any—because no one who was there will talk."

"The harper was there," Beorc recalled shortly.

"But you won't say. The Sidhe was there. Wasn't it so? Everyone who was out there must have seen—and no one says. I was in the forest today. Across the river. I felt nothing ill."

"Then you are numb and deaf and blind," said Beorc, "cousin."

"Perhaps I am." Domhnull looked at Rhys and sighed after things unseen. "But you see things."

"My grandsire had the Sight," the southron said wryly, "but alas, you valley-dwellers called him mad."

"Do they talk about the war there?" asked Domhnull. "Or are they all like Beorc, gone dumb?"

"No whit more," said Rhys with a sober stare, "and I was at the keeping of our borders, so I saw nothing. But things of the fair folk fade and take strange shapes, and there is luck on this land. Why question? If we were all Coilles we would have no peace of chatter."

"You make less sense than usual," Domhnull said. "And maybe where the young ones hid has faded, quite, and all of it was moonbeams. So they say the Sidhe rode inside Caer Wiell. Myself, I would only like to see one."

"Well, I have seen," said Beorc in a faint, difficult voice.

"What was it?" asked Domhnull.

"A light," Beorc said. "Like light." He shrugged and remembered his ale and drank it. "But that is why Caer Wiell sits so much to itself, young cousin, that others saw it too. And no one sings songs, because I for one wouldn't know how to make one; and maybe it's not a thing to gossip, because, well, there was nothing to liken it to, like sun, like moon, but not. It was more a feeling, was what it was. A man doesn't forget that. I know I won't. It wasn't the same today. It was darker-like. It wasn't good. —They're all right, are they? Did they seem—afraid?''

"They looked pert enough," said Rhys. "No, by the looks in their faces. There was no fear."

"I think you make too much of it," Domhnull said. "They strayed into the woods, is all; and maybe they did see something, but they hadn't any effect of it. I think you and this Sighted southron make too much of shadows."

"You see," said Beorc, "why no one who was on that field will speak of it? There is too much unbelief nowadays. You set out saucers, aye, your mother does, each and every night. I know. But what I saw would take no such offering, no."

"*What* did you see?" asked Domhnull, not for the first time that he had brought Beorc this close.

Beorc, not for the first time, shook his head and refused to say.

But there began to be a coming and going, late as it was, and Muirne rushing outside the walls by twilight, her arms laden with branches. (My lady will have fresh boughs, she said, making nothing of the fact that no guest was expected, nor had been since lord Dryw had called with his retinue a year and more ago.) And there was a stir in the kitchen, a coming and going of chatty pages who could no more keep secrets than they could walk on errands and not run. (For my lord's table, they said; and for those who searched, a fine good meal—which lifted hearts and expectations all through Caer Wiell, and set mouths to watering and stomachs to longing, for the smells went out from the kitchen of bread baked fresh, even at evening time, and there was honey called for and good butter, and cakes and no few of the best hams and sausages, and a side of venison that had served my lord's table went into roasts and pastries. And there were casks of ale and cider. Faces went blissful contemplating it.)

But amid all this Beorc took himself upstairs and Domhnull and Rhys with him, for Ciaran's word to them all was the same, that they should come up to speak to him in hall; and if there was little now in their minds but supper, and if they eyed the great table in hall with some longing, thinking of the greater tables set in the yard of the keep, they did not look that way with unseemly attention, but assembled there with great sobriety, well-scrubbed and combed and in their best, before their lord and lady in the hall, with the children abed or at least nowhere to be seen.

But there was nothing but anxiousness on Ciaran's face.

"My friends," he said, "my dear friends—there will be a guest tonight and you must serve in hall. No others would I trust. Would you do me this service?"

"Aye," said Beorc, but he knit his brows in puzzlement, and from anticipation settled his mind at once to business, setting his hands within his belt. It was quite mad, of course, but strange things had happened within these walls. It was not his to ask, though his mind was racing, whether some messenger was expected from the King, to deserve such a plethora of lights and fresh boughs and such a feast as that prepared both below and here above; or whether there was to be any guest at all. This might be some odd figure of speech, or pretense, or something Ciaran had made up for some purpose, perhaps—perhaps, Beorc thought, that he would have his small household to table together to celebrate the children's safe return, and ask his trusted men to serve them in lieu of pages, which would be strange, but no more reasonable thing could he think.

"*She* will come. The Sidhe," Ciaran said then. "Will you serve?"

"Aye," Beorc said after a moment's dismay. "My lord knows I would."

"And you others?"

"Aye," said Rhys, "without question."

"Shall we see one?" Domhnull asked, with all his heart. His eyes were blue and wide. "Here? Tonight? In hall?"

"Perhaps," said Ciaran, adding, "If she wills it you will see her. But if she will not, then not. You must not tell it—if you do."

"No, lord," Domhnull said, but his desire was in his eyes, wide as his heart was wide.

"Carry no iron," said Ciaran. "My guest will not bear that."

"No," said Beorc, "that we understand."

"She is not to fear," lady Branwyn said in a soft thin voice. "It is not that you should need it, or that we should not be safe."

"No," said Ciaran, "there is no question of that."

For Beorc's part he was not sure; and Rhys' look was the

usual, which was unreadable; but Domhnull's face was full of color, his eyes bright with hope, as if there were no ill thing in all the world, and this from a youth who had ridden borders since his sixteenth year.

Perhaps Ciaran saw it, for he looked longest at Domhnull, and a faint smile touched his face. "Don't count on it overmuch. She may not stay. But perhaps she will."

THREE
Arafel

She came—not without hesitation, for it was a harder journey than once. The mists had grown thicker between her Eald-that-was and the world of Men. She had delayed at the last, beneath the pale silvery trees, among the elvish treasures which glistened with soft brilliance under the wan, strange sun of her day; she had chosen certain things to take with her, and put on light elvish garments which she had worn for festival—oh, very long ago, when there were songs among the elves. She went tonight in trust, as she would not have gone for any Man but one, and so she came weaponless except for the lightest of daggers; and uncloaked, which was mere thoughtlessness: for they were friends.

So she arrived in the upper hall of Caer Wiell—was *there* upon the instant, striding out of the mists into a place she knew; and blinked at the glare and half-faded away again in alarm.

There were fires before her like a row of perilous flowers. Metal glinted. Her every instinct cried *away*. But there was Ciaran holding out his hand to her: there was Branwyn, less her friend, but not treacherous, who stared at her with wide and anxious eyes. And the fires were candle flames and torches; the metal was the glitter of silver plates and cups and the finery of her hosts. The place smelled of closeness and Men and fire and food and dying flowers and cut boughs. She stayed, dismayed as she was by the flames.

For it was honor they wished to do her, she saw that now. She was caught between horror and weariness and a great sorrow for them in their best that they put forward to welcome her. She had on the garments of peace for respect of an invitation: and as Men did things, they had turned this grim gray hall into a dripping of fat of slain animals, and burning fire, and slain trees, and dying branches—but silver plates, no iron which would harm her; and a blaze of light and warmth and all the best they had.

"Please," Ciaran said, and offered her first place at the table that was set. "Be welcome."

She stepped all the way within the room, a guest in Caer Wiell, in this small closed hall. She looked about her and at the place that was offered. "You have surprised me," she said truthfully, and looked toward the closed doors of the place. Torches burned all along the wall, candles lit the table, and fire blazed in the hearth. The dying boughs on the table sent up a great fragrance like silent anguish.

"We will serve," said Ciaran softly. "Or I have men I trust as close as brothers and they would do that service. They know about you. They're ready to do as much if I should call, no, more than willing. Anxious. But I wasn't sure you would bear with that."

"I have never guested with Men," Arafel said doubtfully, looking at him and at Branwyn; and then with her love of this Man, a strange mood fell on her, between despair and a remembrance of what had been, of the groves alight, of harping and of dancing.

"Might there be music?" she asked in diffidence; and, wistfully, from her heart's desire: "Might I see the children here too? And then we will talk. There is afterward for talking."

Branwyn's hand crept anxiously to Ciaran's, but Ciaran's eyes shone with pride. "Call them," he said to Branwyn. "Call them down." And himself hastening to the door: "Beorc," he called out. "Come ahead—and call Leannan upstairs, and Ruadhan, and Siodhachan too."

"Muirne," Branwyn called by the other stairs, "Muirne, bring Ceallach and Meadhbh and come down!"

Arafel stood still, feeling a certain dread at this multiplication of names. Once before she had faced the prospect of this hall and so many Men. But now was now, and if the place was strange and crude with glare and death, she schooled herself to trust, stood where they wished her to be and waited, to be amazed by them as they were amazed by her.

The stairs erupted with the patter of feet: Muirne, then, that was the name, a thin, pinched woman of no definite colors; and like sunrise and sunset the boy and girl beside her—who stopped at the bottom step and stared with open mouths—for Arafel had not come as she had appeared to them before, in gray and patchwork, but in silver and elvish jewels.

Then the Men came, and foremost in honor the harper, who came with his harp in his arms and kneeled before her: Leannan was his name—and she recalled another harper of Caer Wiell in looking into his weathered face. So *he* would have aged. The thought appalled her and filled her with sorrow.

"I have seen you once," the harper said, "lady, when you saved Caer Wiell. I remember. I was there. I only wish I could get it clear. I tried to make a song of it. . . .but it was never what I wanted."

His voice faded. He only stared, bewildering her, until gently Ciaran took his arm and moved him aside. She looked for those faces she knew. Meredydd and Evald were gone—no part of this gathering. Gone, she realized suddenly, of course gone, as Men went: Lord Death culled more than trees, and gently—she had never felt their passing. The faces about her were all different from what she had expected. On most of them she saw the marks of age.

"Beorc," Ciaran named a tall, red-haired Man, himself graying. "Scaga's son. And Domhnull his cousin. My right hand and my left, and I value them as much. Rhys ap Dryw. Ruadhan. Siodhachan." This last was an old, old Man, the oldest of them all.

"I rode," the aged Man said, his lips trembling with the effort of speech, "after my lord Ciaran on the field that day. When you came—" His voice wobbled away to silence and tears, something very like elvish warmth, so that she was touched in spite of herself. "Yes," she said full gently, not knowing this Man and wondering what face he had once worn. She grew desperate in these changes, among these Men. She looked toward the children who stood both in Branwyn's embrace, read there other change happening with fatal swiftness.

"Will you sit?" Ciaran asked of her, reminding her, and she sank carefully into the chair that was prepared for her, before silver plates, before the perilous fires.

"May we sit at table?" Ceallach asked anxiously, and receiving his father's nod, his face lighted and he hugged his sister and his mother, while there was some stir about, of benches brought, and extra plates, and places made, all with a clatter and a rising relief.

A few tentative harp notes sounded, sweet and pure, bringing silence and a settling quickly into places, silence even from the children. So the harper played, and played well for her, light songs and merry. And then was the meal. Muirne took the serving mostly on herself, being most careful of their guest, brought Arafel wine and pressed honeyed cakes and fruits on her when she refused other food.

Arafel was doubtful, but if there was something of Men about the offering, still it was sweet in her mouth, and the wine was good if smoky and strange to her tongue. Everyone ate, in a silence so deep the noise of a cup seemed loud, and Muirne's mouselike steps seemed like echoing footfalls. Even the children were grave and very silent, but their eyes drank in everything.

"We are not wont to be so quiet," Ciaran said desperately.

"May we talk then?" Ceallach cried in his high clear voice, which caught Arafel most by surprise. She laughed, which laughter found its echo first in Meadhbh and then in Domhnull.

"Yes," Ciaran said, "we may talk."

"Perhaps," said Arafel, "the harper will give us songs to make us light."

This pleased the harper, who took up his harp again, and soon had the children clapping their hands and all but bouncing in their seats; at last even the grimmest of them laughed, red-haired Beorc. The song minded old Siodhachan of a tale, which he told well and deftly, and there was more wine, at which Arafel, feeling strange diffidence among such brevity, told a small elvish tale, dismayed when it gained only silent stares. Then: "Oh!" breathed Muirne, and everyone breathed, and she saw that they were pleased and more than pleased, their eyes shining, the harper wiping tears.

"Tell another," said Meadhbh.

It had been a moment of peace, a precious time. The young voice tempted. But, "No," Arafel said softly, for she suddenly felt the hours, saw the candles low in their sconces, heard the fall of a log in the fireplace, saw one of the torches out, its flame-bearing head having showered its last cinders to the stones a while ago like stars. "No, now we must to your own affairs. Perhaps you will tell me—" She addressed herself to Ciaran "—how you have fared since last I came."

"Oh, well," said Ciaran. "The land never fails us. And my horses—my horses are surpassing fine."

"And peace. Have you that?"

There was a shifting among the Men. "The King has ordered peace," said Ciaran. "And I keep it as I can."

"Ah,' she said.

"Perhaps," said Ciaran, "the children should be abed."

"No," said Arafel; and Meadhbh and Ceallach, whose faces

had fallen at once, bounced in their seats and their faces glowed.
"Bear with me," said Arafel to Branwyn, and wandered in her
gaze to aged Siodhachan, to Muirne who had stopped in her
serving. Wisps of hair had fallen about Muirne's thin face and
her cheeks were flushed from her many trips this way and that
with plates and servings. She had never gotten to eat. Now she
had a pitcher of wine in hand and quite forgot it, heavy as it was.
And Ruadhan, who was supposed to watch the door, but whom
Arafel had called to table too, a Man who smiled much and
forgot to smile now; and Domhnull, a handsome fair-eyed Man
less than the others' years; and dark Rhys, of wise glances and
quiet; and Beorc Scaga's-son, a Man much like his father.
"Siodhachan's years are longest backward," Arafel said, "and
have their honor; and the years of Meadhbh and Ceallach are
longest forward, and extend this company into times and places
no one but I may see. So I speak to them as well as to the rest.
So counsel taken should be in their hearing, because I cannot say
when I will come back again."

Faces grew anxious all about the table, Ciaran's most of all
excepting the children's, but no one spoke.

"In all the years of Caer Wiell," she said further, "the
guesting has been of Men in Eald and not the Sidhe among Men.
But you wake old memories tonight. You remind me of times I
had almost forgotten. The blessing of the Sidhe is on you: your
step will lie light upon the leaves, your way will not easily
wander in the wood, your eyes will see truth when others fail,
and this for all your days. Eald will not fade for you. What you
see you will see truly. This gift I give. And one more I give to
Meadhbh and Ceallach—Come," she said when the children
hesitated to leave their places, and they excused themselves and
came to her seat at the head of the table, staring at her with eyes
as wide as fawns'.

"So," she said, and opened her hand, laying what might have
been a mote of light upon the table, but the light faded and there
were two leaves more silver than green. "For memory," she
said, "for memory that Eald is true. They come of the youngest
of my trees. Keep them near you and they will never fade. You
have never seen the trees as they are: I cannot bring you there. I
wish I might. But they are for hope when there is no hope, and
vision when there is no seeing. I have set a virtue on them of
finding. And for children lately lost, this seems a right gift."

They were confused and their eyes were wider still as they
took each a leaf.

"Mother," said Meadhbh, showing hers. And, "Lady,"

Ceallach said in a hushed voice, and looked down at his, and took it to his father to show.

"I have seen such trees," said Ciaran softly. Ceallach sat at his father's side and Ciaran put an arm about him, holding this dearest treasure time had given him very close as Branwyn held Meadhbh. Their friends and trusted folk were about them in this room, like a bulwark against the night, against shadows, against all the ills of the world. But knowledge sat in Ciaran's eyes, as if they saw the shadows beyond the walls. "You speak of going," he said. "And you have been about some business. Is it—something I might ask?"

"Do not." She passed her finger down the side of the cup before her, and looked up as Muirne, sensing want, moved to fill it. The gesture touched her strangely, the earnestness of brown human eyes which saw only need and offered what there was, if only wine. She bent a thought on Muirne, shed a grace which had not been there as the pitcher brushed the cup she held in her hand, and thought no more of it than the flowering of some blighted tree under her hand . . . indeed her thoughts traveled on and circled and came back again to the children—to Beorc, whose eyes met hers squarely as few Men's would. He was afraid: this she saw. And loyal and terrible in a way that stretched into a dark future. A shiver came over her, and she was not accustomed to such weaknesses. She looked past him to Domhnull, whose heart was clearest; and Rhys, who had a darkness in him, but so, indeed, had elves; last to Ciaran, finding strange still the sight of this bearded, older man with a son against his side.

"I will be direct," she said. "There is trouble near you. I cannot say the nature of it: plainly, I do not know. I warned you once of balances, and things are out of balance. Meadhbh and Ceallach have chanced against the merest straying visitor to your lands; do it no harm. It does not deserve it. And there are things truly baneful. This is not your affair. But a corner of Eald has gone into shadow, and Eald is both wider and darker than it was. There are things awake that slept. I have a watch to keep and I have kept it—aye, do you understand now, Lord-of-Men? So I have watched and will watch. You are my weakness and my strength, you, Caer Wiell, this little circle of firelight in the dusk. And that dusk is gathering. The night will come. Grant there may be a dawn."

A log crashed in the fireplace. The children flinched, and Branwyn cired out. The fire leapt up and shadows danced and died. The company shifted uncomfortably in their chairs.

"War?" asked Beorc in a hoarse, harsh voice. "Is it war you mean? Is it An Beag?"

"War." She laid a hand on the stone at her heart and for a moment it was hard to remain where she was. The place seemed insubstantial, a web of gray against the truth. And then it took shape again. "I have asked you once. Do you have peace?"

"With An Beag and Caer Damh?" Ciaran replied. "An uneasy peace, but the King rules."

She stretched out her hand toward the west, a vague reaching. "There is no brightness there."

"The King rules," Ciaran said. "He is lord in Dun na h-Eoin."

"And Caer Donn?"

"Is free."

"There is no brightness, I say, toward the west. Look to your borders."

"In Caer Donn my brother rules."

"I say what I have said. War is too simple a word."

"The King," said Branwyn suddenly, "ignores Caer Wiell. We are not favored. We are true to him, and few are, even of those who fought for him at our walls. And as for Caer Donn—"

"He is my brother," said Ciaran.

For a moment the shadow intruded, and Arafel shivered, blinking in the firelight. Again she touched the stone, and waked a harping these halls had known years ago. There was vengeance in it even yet. The Harp was broken, but the song went on. She stood up, and the company rose in confusion as Ciaran stood—as he held out a hand to her, wishing her to stay. She fought the drawing, the feeling of cold. There was a darker and darker melancholy on her and she fought it as she fought all the weapons of the shadow.

"Walk with me," she said to Ciaran, "as far as the hall outside."

He offered her his hand—confused, perhaps, for places were nothing to her, and had never been. But the shadow-ways were dangerous and she took the human way, passed the wooden door in Ciaran's company, alone.

"Close the door," she said when they had come into the hall before the stairs. "What I say now is only for you to hear. But what you say to them after, that is your choosing."

He did so, the lord of Caer Wiell, and faced her again. A solitary and dying torch burned and cast shadows everywhere about, made the lines of his face deeper than they were. He looked old and worn, so fearfully worn.

"What will you?" he asked.

"You have understood more than they. You know what is loosed. And I tell you that there is shadow on Airgiod's lower reaches; and over all the hills. Trees have come back out of it, but strange and dim and not comfortable. Not comfortable. Speak truth with me: speak your heart with me—have you felt no hint of trouble? Can you come and go in this land at your ease?"

"You know that I cannot."

"I know little enough of Men. Tell me truth—why can you not?"

"They remember me. They remember what I am. If I have luck they say it is faery-gift; if I have none they call it curse. Mostly they suspect—"

"—What?"

"Ambition. That, I think. Or power." He shivered and turned half away, and looked back again with the firelight moving on his bearded face. "How can they forget? How can the King sit at board with me and forget? And my brother—"

"Fears his neighbor?"

"Fears his own heritage. We pass no messages. There is only silence. Fear—aye. And distrust. I have had too great good fortune in Caer Wiell." He drew a breath and composed his face, shook his head, but the gnawing dread remained. "No, he would never do us harm. Donnchadh is a good man."

"But not wise."

"Is that so ill?"

"For one who sits at Caer Donn? Whose hold is named in Eald? Yes, it is ill, it is very ill. And a great many ills are abroad. I watch; I do not say I shall be enough. So I have come here. To ask your help."

"No." He shook his head. "Now I know what you mean to ask, and *no*."

"Keep it for me. Only keep it. And should the worst happen, should you know that there is no more defense—then you will judge what you should do. You are the only brightness, do you understand—the only. The small trouble in the Caerbourne—that is nothing, nothing against the other. Take it. I do not ask that you use it. Only that you have the choice. For your defense, for the defense of this place."

He said nothing for a moment, and she drew it from its keeping-place against her heart, the stone he had borne before, like that stone she still wore about her neck. It shone with a strange pallor beneath the torches, casting no shadows with its brightness, reflecting nothing of the fire. It rested so in her hand

and at last he put out his and took it, clenched his fist about it, and the hall seemed dark after.

"Do not walk in Eald," she said. "You must not come there. Call me if you have need, but never command; as you value your peace, do not command. Be wise, be wary."

"Arafel!— Shall I see you again—in my life—shall I see you?"

She had started to fade, to drift back to Eald. She stayed, and touched his broad scarred hand. "I have no surety," she said, but it was in her heart that this was indeed the last time. "There are hazards. Who can say? Fare well, cousin, half-elf, friend. In all things—"

The touch faded. Eald closed about her. For a moment she strove with it, reached out over all the hold, so that she seemed to embrace it, so that the strength that greened the trees was shed wide.

Scrub that had struggled in the cracks of the walls burst into sudden flower under a clouding sky.

A sickly child mended and sighed into restful sleep, smiling as she did.

The drowsing sentry clutched his spear, confused in a premature and fading dawn, or the belief that he had seen one.

Folk waked, and some wept, convinced of some wonderful dream they could not remember, or of some luck which had come on them, or simply that they were glad, and some sank deeper in sleep, feeling the world at ease.

One twisted thing resisted, and hid on the stairs where he had crept to listen; and the name of this one was Coille.

I must warn him, she thought, but fate was on her, and the thought with the power faded, like the moment's dawn at Caer Wiell. Eald took her back, a mesh woven of branch and limb, of the dark before the dawn in which even stars had less power. A tear had fallen on her cheek, and traced there a thin cold line.

"You take risks," a shadow whispered.

She turned her head in startled anger, dashed the tear from her cheek and stood straight, facing the darkness in the mist. "Godling, you have no leave to be here. *Keep from them.* I have warned you."

"You take risks, I say." The shadow became utterly black, a hole in the mist. A horse stamped in the fog. "I have fared along the edges. You have set something stirring. You set me to hunt the marches—but you will summon me here: no! name me no threats. I know them all. You have raised them all. But threats will not send *them* back. And it grows.''

She shrugged and turned away. ''You tell me nothing new. Try again.''

Steps trod beside her in the grayness, a soft and bodiless pacing. ''There is a place called Caer Donn. You would know it.''

She turned again, disturbed and caring not that he saw it, her Huntsman, her Warden of the marches. ''What of Caer Donn?''

''That its lord is close to the King. I have heard their counsels at Dun na h-Eoin. You should regard me. I come and go with kings. And beware Caer Donn, I say. Its history blinds you. You delude yourself. You take risks, I say, risks in which your allies have no profit and no patience.''

''My allies.'' She drew herself up and set her hand on the small hilt at her belt. ''You and your brothers have no interest in my defeat, that is the only sure thing. Let us say the truth. *What* have you heard at Dun na h-Eoin?''

''The counsels of kings. I have seen the lords of An Beag and Caer Damh sit with the King; I have seen Caer Donn and Caer Luel in the same company . . . and the veriest center of it is Caer Donn. Did you not know?''

''Perhaps I knew.''

For a moment the shadow was silent. Something dark and houndlike crept to his side and merged with him. ''You are cruel.''

''So they say of the Sidhe.''

''This Man, this Ciaran mac Ciaran—this brother of Donnchadh of Donn—''

''—is my affair.''

''You have tangled me in bargains. Your Man has loosed this on the world. It was his doing, from the beginning, and always you have protected him. Take Donnchadh to your heart: he is no less perilous.''

''Donnchadh is beyond my reach.''

''Yes. Beyond your reach. But not beyond the reach of other things. You are a fool, my lady of the trees. You are everlastingly a fool, and not alone, no longer alone. You have your enemies. And those seduced by them.''

''Leave me.''

''Oh my lady fool—were your own kind immune to jealousy? To ambition?''

She strode away. He followed, a flutter of darkness slipping through the mist.

"The King is weak and weakening; they poison him now with more than words. But I delay to take him. There will come the day I must. And what then—*who* then, but Donnchadh? Slay him, my lady: one thrust of an elvish sword—and the world is saved."

"No. Not saved. Leave me. I am weary of you."

"Of me, your messenger. Of the upstart you send to watch your borders—Oh lady fool, well if you had listened long before this. What a merry visitor has come to the Caerbourne! And I can name you others lurking here and there. Stop and listen! This Man of yours—let me have him. You cannot take Donnchadh; your reach is too short. But *I* could remedy matters. For fear of this Ciaran the King has taken evil counsel—For fear of what he saw on that field that day, of help you gave this Man of yours. Do you not know? There is no one in all the kingdom the King fears so much as Ciaran of Caer Wiell—no, certainly not those he ought to fear instead."

Lord Death had pricked her interest, however painfully. Again she stayed, and stopped in mortal Eald. "You know something you have to tell: you choke on it— Say it and be done!"

"I know this, while you have been interested in other things: that the King distrusted the old lord of Caer Wiell because of this Man, and others stepped in to widen the gap until there is no closing it. And worse with Donnchadh of Donn—ah, much worse. He has stirred up something. I know not what. You say you cannot touch him. But something of Eald has risen up there. It hovers about Caer Donn, skulking and vanishing and I can put no hand on it. Would that I could."

For a long moment she was silent, and the stone burned cold at her heart. "Would you had told me this at the beginning. This is no glad news."

"Come there. If Eald is there, there you can set foot. Deal with it. Let me have this troublesome lord of Caer Wiell. We may yet turn all this aside."

"No," she said, holding the stone within her hand. "*No.* I've no doubt your brothers urged it. But I take no counsel from you, Huntsman. None."

"Is it fear, then?" Death whispered. "Oh, you pretend to be wise—you pretend secrets. But say it: you are afraid—and you keep your life unchanged. For what? For what do you live? To watch, you said, to prevent what you yourself caused, and now you retreat and save yourself and your trees and this one favored Man—for how long, and to whose benefit but your own?"

"Spare me your venom. Tell your brothers this: that they will have felt a change in Eald and now you have told me why. Find me its name, Huntsman; find me its nature and its shape. And believe this—that my woods are wider than they were, in every direction, and I have not spent this time dreaming, no. Would that I had. Would that there were rest for me, or that I could find this thing. And keep your hand from Caer Wiell!''

''Elvish treachery!'' Lord Death wailed, and caught at her sleeve, but she was gone, faded into otherwhere. ''Hear me!'' he called. ''Arafel!''

But he had no power to use that name. He had no power over anything of the Sidhe, and in his anger he winded his horn and gathered the Hunt.

Wolves were prowling the hills again, they said in Caer Wiell; and a storm was moving in over the forest heights, sweeping in an uncommon direction for storms, toward the east.

But some in Caer Wiell guessed.

Arafel clasped her stone in both her hands and shut her eyes and drew on herself to find the way. It had grown that hard. When she came to the grove of silver trees, she drew an easier breath—but there were clouds across the elvish sun, and she fought them back again, until they stood over the farthest reaches of Airgiod, in shadow which constantly changed and shifted.

''Fionnghuala!'' She clapped her hands, and the horse came, shaking lightning from its mane. Arafel swung up and told it where she would go—and Fionnghuala shivered.

But the elf horse moved, if slowly. Aodhan was left behind, and whinnied after them, a forlorn sound and lonely in the shadow that began to be.

FOUR

The Heart of Ciaran Cuilean

Branwyn came for him, cracking the door carefully and spilling the bright light of the hall into the stairwell where he sat on the steps, arms on knees, head bowed, hands clasped about his ankles as a child might sit.

''My lord,'' she said tentatively. ''Ciaran, my love.''

Her voice was so gentle and strange he shivered at it, called back from the place where he had wandered, lost in mist. Branwyn's voice also seemed charged with power, of a different kind, and he must answer it, must come back when she knelt and called his name with such anxiousness. He had worried her and he must not. He felt her hands warm on his, lifting his hands to her lips. Her eyes bore into his, with the shadow falling across half her face, his shadow from the torch behind him. It was his own hall, the steps, the flickering light, and that blinding seam was the hall aspill with lamplight and the smells of banquetry and the plaintive voices of his children—("Has father gone somewhere? Is he all right? —Let me go, Beorc!" "Hush," someone said. "Be still, young sir.")

"Ciaran," Branwyn said, and gazed at him, at that place which hurt him so, there, just at his throat. She reached out and touched it, gathered the naked stone into her fingers, and he flinched at that, jolted by all the dread, all the love, all the horror at once. He might have cried out or she did; and then he was in her arms and his were locked about her as if he were drowning. There was a sound of footsteps, a cry from the hall, and light drowned them both as the door was flung wide, a looming darkness and gathering of shadows.

"Lord," said Beorc's deep voice, "my lady—" A higher voice a smaller shadow thrust forward. "Wait," Boerc said, but their children came to them, and Ciaran reached out one hand to Ceallach's, to Meadhbh, and felt their love like a draught of water where Branwyn's was wine, hers rich and theirs pure; felt the texture of their souls, which was too close even for father to know children, like gossamer, like wind with lilacs blooming.

"*Ciaran,*" Branwyn whispered. Thunder broke; but that was outside, above their walls. Almost he fainted, and felt her arms struggle to bear him a moment. Then he slipped his fingers between her hand and the stone he wore and thrust it safe within his collar, so that the room came clear again, so that he could make a pretense of command and look her in the eyes clearly enough, and look at Meadhbh and Ceallach. There seemed a light about them; but it was the light from the door. He drew a deep breath and gathered himself up to his feet leaning on Branwyn for an instant.

"I am well," he said. He looked beyond at the others who had gathered there. "I dreamed a moment. So Branwyn found me." He looked down at the children, set his arm about them, walked with them back to the hall, into the brighter light and the cloying smell of branches and the leavings of the feast. More faces waited for him—Leannan the harper, Siodhachan, Muirne, Ruadhan, faithful and concerned. He looked about at them. He reckoned that some small time had passed—that he had frightened them badly, not least of all his children, who were uncommonly still and clinging. And Branwyn—Branwyn— He felt her presence at his back, like something bleeding.

"Our guest has gone," he said. "She wished us well and spoke to me awhile, of such things—of such things that mean good will to us. Never fear otherwise from her. I sat a time to think on them. Only go to your beds. And keep the counsel of this room—even the youngest of us." He looked at the children, one and the other, into their eyes. "That means silence."

"Yes, sir," Ceallach said ever so softly. And, "Yes," said Meadhbh half whispering.

"Go with Muirne."

There was never a word further from them. They embraced him, one and the other, and he bent to their embrace, feeling their arms so very frail against his own, and their warmth so much greater than his own it might have been that of the living embracing the dead, but they never flinched. Muirne took them in charge and led them upstairs in silence.

"Go," he said to the others, but while Leannan gathered up his harp and Domhnull and Rhys their cloaks to obey him, Beorc stood still and staring.

"Go," Ciaran said again.

"My lady?" Beorc asked, prepared to defy him if Branwyn should judge otherwise; he saw as much. There was love in such disloyalty, and devotion. Rhys and then Domhnull came and paused at Beorc's side, seeing what was toward, and the others stopped in their departures.

"Go," said Branwyn softly. "Only—Beorc, will you sleep below, by the door tonight?"

"Aye," said Beorc.

"There is no need," Ciaran said, but he saw that Beorc did not intend to regard him, not this strange night. They made themselves his warders, his wife and his own chiefest man. He felt it like his children's embrace, powerless but warm. Beorc went, last to leave; and perhaps Beorc would not be the only one to watch. Domhnull too, he thought, and Rhys, they might take turns. Branwyn had many allies.

The door closed. Their steps retreated down the distance of the stairs. He stood still, not alone, for Branwyn remained.

"Have you subverted them all?" he asked in gentle whimsy,

and kissed her on the brow. "Go to bed, you too, only go and rest."

"Come with me."

"I am too uneasy." A chill passed over him like the wind from an open door. Outside the thunder muttered and rain sluiced off the roof. "An uncomfortable bedfellow. Will you sit by me, by the fire?"

She would. He drew the wide bench from the table and the ruin of the feast, set it before the sinking fire and made room for her by him, his arm about her. For a long time she asked nothing, but he knew everything that she would ask, and all that she would blame him for—for she knew that stone as no one in all Caer Wiell could know it. Dreams urged at him, and he fought the dreams—must fight them, with Branwyn so near. The mist threatened to take him, and he measured his strength against it, finding it for the present sufficient to fend the mist away.

"What she said," he began at last, in that silence Branwyn left for him, "was not all of comfort, Branwyn. But this—this *gift*—if I had had it today, do you see, Meadhbh and Ceallach would never have come so near to harm; and no harm could even come close to Caer Wiell but that I would know it—I must keep it. I have to bear this thing awhile." He could not bring himself to tell her all that he suspected and all that he doubted, that there was an end to his luck and to that of Caer Wiell, indeed, an end of many things. "I need not use it, I think, only keep it safe. I shall be wiser than to use it. But she may not come back again. And yet if she will help us, then this may be the way—a means to keep us safe."

"There is no safety in that thing!" Branwyn cried, and as if she had only waited the dropping of a shield she leaned on his arms and looked closely into his eyes. "Or let me carry it for you."

He was coward, he thought, for one brief moment hearing only the words that would free him and only then realizing that it was Branwyn, fragile Branwyn, who heard the forest singing in storms and had nightmares of being lost. "Love, no," he said.

"You would keep me from such safety?" she asked, deadly in her reason and defter than he with his mind all muddled. "What, will not share it?"

He stared at her helplessly, undone in all his arguments.

"Then it is not safety," she said.

"If my King had called," he said, "and told me to take the sword, then I would have gone and would you have held me? No."

"If the King had called," Branwyn said, "I would know it was a cozening lie."

Her treason shocked him. He had given her children and slept by her for twenty-two years. He had never heard such words from Branwyn so directly. They confused him now, coming as they did at the flank of his defenses.

"I was not speaking of the King," he said.

"Of her, then."

"And if she called," he pursued his reason, doggedly, distractedly, with the stone burning cold at his heart, "then also I would have no choice. There is war of a sort, Branwyn, and I am useless in it, except to hold to this. There is war." He saw banners and dragons in the fire, embers like falling walls, the silver sleet of arrows under the elvish sun. . . .

Liosliath!

His shiver surprised him. He felt her fingers at his neck, felt her loose the chain and lift it from him, and shivered a second time, rescuing the smooth teardrop stone from her fingers as it passed his head. He clenched it so, her fingers still caught in his, entangled in the chain.

"As a guest she was discourteous," Branwyn said in a short, small voice. "She gave our children gifts, and gave to you, and none for me—no gift for me at all."

He saw past the words, straight to the heart of the matter, to the fear in Branwyn's eyes. Perhaps it was the stone, in both their hands. But he saw, and Saw, and that Sight went on plaguing him, that he knew the difference between his blood and Branwyn's; and that Meadhbh and Ceallach were his own, for Arafel had given them gifts and in truth, brought none for Branwyn. There was nothing Arafel could have given to Branwyn. And Branwyn knew; and he did, with all his insight.

The last log fell, scattering sparks, and something crashed down in his heart then too, a lurching fall like that fall at the edge of sleep, like the chute in dreams, and the dream was the life they had had, their peace, their faith in age and death and passing beyond death together.

He would not age or die at all, not while he held the stone. And Branwyn knew that. Fade, he might, but never die. This was what Arafel had given back to him, a power he had carried once and returned to Eald because he had seen where it would lead him. He might have entered Eald, once for all, but Branwyn never could.

Already he felt the chill of it, which would leave him only elvish love, distant and cold; and make the human world seem crass and garish; which would show him horror and beauty and divide them forever.

"Branwyn," he said, like a talisman. "Branwyn, Branwyn." Names spoken three times had power. He longed for her love, her warmth to hold him. He did not want the dreams. "Be with me, Branwyn."

She took him in her arms. He let his head sink against her shoulder, his hand with the rescued stone fallen into his lap, a great tall man, for all the sons and daughters of Caer Donn were tall, as Branwyn's folk were not. A daughter of Men held one of elvish kind, a man the King himself feared, whose sword the Boglach and the Bradhaeth knew to their regret; and rocked him like a child.

So he slept a time, but only a little while, and woke and held her in his turn, her small fair head against his heart.

The fire died, and the candles guttered, until only the embers winked in the dark hearth, and the stone was peaceful for the hour.

He looked out over all the land in his vision, a swift unrolling of distances, and if he looked in one way it was mist and shadow; and if in another, only an ordinary dawn with the rain diminished to drizzle, dripping off the leaves. So the stone gave him power to do. There seemed less threatening than had seemed a few hours ago. He was conscious of Arafel, but dimly. Her days flowed differently than his, and this long night had been a moment to her, an indistinction of intent and motion and the feeling of the land, which fretted in its unease.

Liosliath, he wondered, trying to cross a gulf he had crossed once, but the stone was still now. He suspected that Arafel had willed it so, had set a kind of peace on it in giving it to him. That this gift was betrayal, he could not believe of her. She had no need for subterfuge with him: the debt was too deep and too absolute on his side. In this his trust was unquestioning.

Liosliath. But there was a sudden grayness between himself and the presence the stone had once held, as if all of Eald were cloaked in mist and the sea were cut off from him.

He slept again, with the chain tangled in his fingers, and his dreams were gray and dim.

But a darkness sat amid the mist, a piece of night perched on the stump of a dead tree by a sluggish river, for lord Death rested from his Hunt. His horse and hounds were nearby, a restlessness beyond the leaves.

"You need not be afraid," said Lord Death. "You have the stone, after all."

He was afraid, all the same. It was not their first meeting, not the first in which he had faced that shapeless dark inside the cowl and wished not to be facing it, for fear that he would see what was inside it. "She asked me to carry it," Ciaran said. "Do you know why?"

"I am not privy to her counsels. She shares them only with Men, it seems. But then—" The shadow moved in a semblance of a gesture. "Then you might invite me to your hall."

"Someday," he said, feeling the cold of a wind that blew from that third and dreadful Eald. "But not yet. I wish to ask you—what I ought to do. Surely you have some advice, my lord."

"Ah, not your lord. But I am lord of those you love."

"Have mercy. Were we not allies—and are we not allies still? You've hated me for cheating you once. But let me beg you. I know nothing else to do now, and I am not too proud, if it will make a difference. These of mine, my family, my friends—I need them. Everything I am asked I will do. But stay away from Caer Wiell."

There was a long silence. "You suspect me of kindness."

"Perhaps. Sometimes."

"Give me your hand. Do you dare that?"

The darkness extended the likeness of a hand to him. All his instinct rebelled, but he reached out deliberately, ignoring the cold, and felt the touch of fingers so dark the shape of them seemed cut out of the world, and the touch of them numbed, but not utterly. They brushed his forearm as if there were no cloth between, and a pain leapt through his body at that touching of an old wound half-healed. The hounds of the Hunt had made it years ago. He had left a part of himself in their jaws and they had devoured it, he suspected. This much of him Death already owned.

The touch passed on, and the robes enfolded him. Very tenderly Lord Death embraced him, and as if it were his brother or his King he returned the embrace, his arms about a body less body than burning cold. Perhaps Lord Death meant to mock him; but there had touched him such peace, and peace parted from him as Death drew back from him, leaving him chilled and prey again to the wind.

"You are bold," said Death, and the voice seemed gently wistful. "Few would dare that, even the most eager. It's your pride, is it not? If I asked that too, would you give your pride, to ransom Caer Wiell?''

Ciaran sank to his knees, one and then the other, out of practice, having been ten years a Kingless lord. He felt a flush of shame, and lifted his face. ''That too,'' he said.

But Death was gone, leaving only a swirling in the mist.

''Lord,'' he called after him, rising to his feet. He suspected Death of laughter at his expense; of cruelty passing his expectations. ''Lord Death!''

But a third time he dared not call, and he waked in Branwyn's arms, in the dark of his own room.

The children crept down in the morning, late, but not that they looked to have slept well, only desperately, exhausted. They came hurrying silently down into the hall with Muirne behind them, Meadhbh's bright hair flying loose and both their faces ruddy cheeked from a violent scrubbing, but pale all the same, large-eyed and anxious and very unlike his children, so unlike it chilled him.

So Branwyn left her breakfast and hugged them and wanted to do Meadhbh's hair herself, but they tore themselves from her and came to Ciaran's arms, touching him only carefully, as if he could be bruised by their small hands. *Laugh,* he wished them. *Oh smile at me and never look that way.* But they did not. In a single day they had learned to fear and to doubt and to know their father and their mother were not omnipotent to save them; more, they suspected helplessness. It was in their eyes, the touch of their hands.

But he gathered Meadhbh's small hands in his large ones and kissed them, and smiled at her, trying to restore her courage, if not her innocence. He set his hands on Ceallach's shoulder, feeling how slight the bones were, how frail his shoulders were for any weight.

''What,'' he said, lancing straight to the center of their fears, ''did you think I would vanish with the moon? There is nothing real about what happened; and there is—It was all very real. Do you understand? There are Men and there is Eald and they are most real when they are farthest apart, but when dreams come into hall and sit at table and leave a gift in your hand, it confuses things. Your mother understands. Perhaps Beorc does, though maybe not. —Do you, Muirne? No. Not truly. One should wake from dreams. But this one left substance. Do you both have your gifts?''

''Upstairs,'' said Ceallach. But Meadhbh, having pockets,

brought hers forth, unfolding her hand carefully as if she had trapped some moth. The leaf shone silver and incorrupt on her palm, which trembled.

"So," he said, "you must always do as she said and keep it by you."

"It feels strange."

"So does mine, you see." He brought the stone into view and prevented her hand with his own cupped over it, a slow and desperate move which left his heart pounding for dread, though he smiled gently at his daughter. "But one should not let another touch such things. Only keep it safe and secret. Did you dream last night?"

"There was a forest," said Ceallach after a moment.

"Was it a good place?"

"Mine seemed to be," said Meadhbh.

"So." He kissed her on the brow and folded her hand upon the leaf. An unpleasant thought came to him and he looked into her eyes. "But when you wander in your dreams, never let it go, this gift. Never let it go. Names called three times will bring a thing. Be careful what you call, that you can send it away again. Do you hear me? Do you understand? You must be able to send it away."

Their eyes were not so perplexed as he would have wished they were. They reached back into something they knew and agreed with him, silent understandings.

"My name you can always use," he said. "And I will come. I will be there. I promise it. Go have your breakfast. You can sit at table with us this morning, will you like that?"

They would. Their eyes were lighter. In a moment they looked like children, squirming into their seats. Ciaran looked past them to Branwyn, appealing for absolution, for all that had divided them; but she was seeing, mother-fashion, to Meadhbh's hair, to Ceallach's collar, and giving orders to Muirne, where they should be allowed to go this day and how Muirne should watch them.

"Mother," Ceallach said, downcast and shamed.

"Well, what would you?" Ciaran said. "I think you went far enough and saw enough for two young folk in a day. Let us have some little rest, your mother is due that, is she not? Is she not? And the next time I ride the west road you can come part of the way. Rhys will ride escort for you."

"When?" asked Meadhbh, twisting in her seat, her eyes childish again.

"Oh, in a day or so. If I find you have kept your mother happy."

"Meadhbh is my daughter," Branwyn muttered, "not your son, to be out with armored men."

It wounded. Meadhbh's face went blank and hurt at once. It was that sort of wound only friends and kin could deal, so strong he felt it in the stone. But Branwyn never saw, or if she knew, wrapped her common sense about her like a cloak, and poured cider to give to them, golden liquid spilling down into silver cups, smelling of apples and age. She was quite intent upon it. Of such tiny details was the hurt elaborated.

"I have promised," Ciaran said with finality.

Branwyn shrugged, hurting him as well, but this much he allowed. They deserved their wounds, he, his children, being what they were. He dealt none in return, except by being what he was. Neither did Meadhbh, being dutiful. In that moment he saw he had become their father in a protective way, for they had come out of him and only sojourned in Branwyn. He recalled Caer Donn, his own folk, his brother, parted from him—Donnchadh; and his father, dying without his being there, because of his exile. Only Caer Wiell would take such a man as himself to its heart, being itself close to Eald and accustomed to it over long centuries; only Caer Wiell could smile over such children as these two and give them stones to climb and walls to shelter them. He could not send his daughter off to marry, to be what she was in some strange hold, to wither or to smother what she was . . . if there were any one who would court her, the daughter of Ciaran Cuilean. Nor would any lord or King ever trust his son in alliance. The orderly, ordinary hopes collapsed about him, had never stood secure. He reached across the table and laid his hand near Meadhbh's.

Branwyn pretended ignorance of this, of all her injuries. But he loved her and knew that he was loved. When she was harmed, she struck and thought that she was right. When the world threatened to harm one of them, there was iron in Branwyn. He knew this and even Branwyn did not, who seemed to lean on him; but it was the other way around. It was so now, or the gulf would have taken him. She had been there, in the dark, when no one else knew how.

"Eat your breakfast," Branwyn said.

Beorc was looking askance at him when he went out along the wall into the daylight, on that narrow walk; but he was content to walk, to feel the sun's warmth on his back, to hear the sounds of voices in the yard, the laughter of children playing tag among the supports of the walk. He inhaled the smells of straw, of stables,

of leather and oil and woodsmoke and someone's baking, all the
scents of Caer Wiell and home. These things were good on this
morning, after the night, doubly and trebly precious. The colors,
the green and brown, the broad swell of lands he tended, the
sky, were all dazzlingly bright. The banner over the gate snapped
and cracked in the wind. The gray stone was spotted green and
white with lichens. Flowers spread themselves in yellow dust
like treasure on the hills. There was a delirium in such sights.
They had been there all his life, spread wide, stretched thin. He
cast back through his memory for the darkest mortal things, but
every dark thing in all the world had left some color in his mind,
like Dun na h-Eoin in the morning, with the mist lying near the
trees all pearled and strange in the first light; and the bristling of
spears that morning orderly as a woods on the move against
them, by twilight scattered like jackstraws among the dark,
humped bodies of the dead—lumps like sacks across the trampled ground, like the spillage from some cart, but a wreckage so
vast it covered all the plain as far as the eye could see—while
close at hand life glowed like pools of ruby wine in footprints
driven deep into the mire. And in twilight moths came to the
torches in small frantic sputterings, their wings trailing sparks in the
flames. Dun na h-Eoin was the midst of horrors, but these small
details were there among the rest; like the silence, the vast, vast
silence after so much clamor, the simple taste of air. The moths
came back, even on the last of their wings, for love of the golden
light. Even death had colors. He had been in worse places,
where there was no comfort, no refuge for eyes or mind. The
moths flew like prophecies, blind with their desires.

"My lord?" Beorc had come up behind him; or had been
there for some time. He turned to face this huge man with hair
like a burning fire, a violence at rest—broad shoulders, strong
back, hands capable of everything—and nothing, this morning;
they hung empty and offering, the honest face bemused. The
massive head held wit in a cup of bone; sense and love peered
out at him through a skull's eyes. Ciaran blinked and shuddered,
seeing it; or perhaps Beorc saw him that way.

"Lord?"

"I am well enough this morning." He drew a great breath and
looked toward the light, the fields, the hills. "The sun is bright,
is it not? A good day."

"Aye." Beorc moved up beside him, leaned his arms against
a crenel of the wall, likewise gazing outward. The sun glanced
off his golden bracelet, whitened scars which crossed and re-
crossed Beorc's strong hands, glistened among red-gold hairs on

his arms. The bearded face still frowned in its web of blowing hair. "Did you sleep, lord?"

"Somewhat. More than you, perhaps. No more watching at my door. Go to your own bed tonight."

Beorc looked at him, a sideways motion of the eyes.

"Your own bed," Ciaran said again.

Beorc nodded once, not moving otherwise.

"It was a strange company," Ciaran said, "last night. Did it trouble you—that?"

There was long silence, in which Beorc stared outward over the wall. "So I have seen one for the fair folk," Beorc said. "That was something."

"Not for the first time," Ciaran said.

"They say." A deeper frown settled on Beorc's face. "What I saw last night—I'm not sure. Like the war. The young men ask and those that were out there on the field will never say what they saw. Or we try, sometimes, and it never comes twice the same. Like men that meet bogles and the like in the dark—they tell the best they can and never agree, even in their own remembering." Beorc looked about at him. "It was like that, lord—last night. Like that."

"But you will remember. From time to time—nights are easiest. It comes back then."

"In the war—that faded."

"When Eald comes out in sunlight nothing seems reasonable. Except in the woods, in shadow."

"Whenever I have been there," Beorc said, "anything might happen."

"You followed her once."

Again was silence. "So you tell me that I did. Lord, how did my father die?"

"After all these years?"

Beorc shrugged uncomfortably. "I never doubted him; don't now. But you were there. I wasn't."

"He was at my back—I never saw just how it happened. But now and again I saw him in the battle. He was foremost, that day, of all that rode for Caer Wiell."

"But behind you."

"Where I rode—it would have been difficult to follow. More than difficult. But you know. You followed her."

"They say," Beorc said, and let his voice fade away. "We fought at the narrows of the river—the King led; and the battle spilled to Caer Wiell—twenty miles. We could never have ridden so far, spent as we were. But a kind of dark came down, or the morning never came. There was a light—or a banner; I took it for a banner. The lights they name that shine in the wood, and a lost man has to follow: he takes it for someone else walking in the dark, and follows, and it leads. It was something like that, but blazing in the dark—I thought it was the King—or his banner—or it might have been a rider; but it was a light, so clear in that murk, and not a man but saw it and went after it, with all the others, as if it was the only right thing in the dark, man and beast, but never sound of hooves—or sounds were far, and if anyone shouted, it was somewhere far away —Then the light broke, and battle was round us no different than before —But it was not where we had been, or we had fought our way there, over twenty miles.''

"She brought you through the shadow ways. Iron can never pass her realm—gods know what path she used.'' But he knew, was cold with thinking of that trespass, in Death's own domain, where neither Sidhe nor living Man belonged.

"There was light in front of us. That was all I saw.''

"Be glad.'' Ciaran felt the stone cold at his throat, like ice, like a weight too much to bear. The world was mist again. He heard a horse sneeze, heard the thump of hooves close at hand, then blinked and found himself atop the wall, in light, in human color, the stones rough and warm beneath his hands. "What was I? What did you see—of me that day?''

"Like light. Only there was shadow too, or like something wrong with my eyes, like a shadow on your face. But, lord, it was a feeling much as anything. There was this quiet, this awful quiet, like stopping in the woods, or in some dark place too old, where nothing moves or has moved—'' Gooseflesh stood on Beorc's arms. He was not wont to talk like this. He shivered in half a shrug and covered it with a laugh, turning with his elbow on the stone. The laugh died. "Lord, it was like that last night. Even through the wine.''

"Beorc, what do they say of me? Now. Across the countryside. Tell me the truth, even the worst of it. How do they see me, our farmers, our weavers, the men who guard my doors? What kind of lord am I?''

Beorc leaned there as if something had pinned him to the stone, as if that silence he had named had wrapped them both in too much intimacy. "Lord, I am your man. They know that. What would they say to me? But I have kin in the country, my mother's folk. Domhnull's too. And in the guardroom they curse you sometimes, the way men will curse hard duty, but, lord, they are your men. They say you have the Sight. They say in the

country that the land never fared so well, that there is some luck
on it since the war. In the country they set out pannikins of milk,
that they never used to do, so the old women say, but they say
now—to keep the fair folk on their side. That they fight for us."

"Pannikins of milk." Ciaran gave a frightened, bemused
laugh, walked a step away and looked back again. "Aye, I have
seen the like."

"There are the small things," Beorc said with a set of his lip
that was not to be argued with.

"In them, *I* have no trust." Ciaran laughed, for he had
dismayed Beorc. "Aye. In some things *I* do not believe."

"Believe you may, lord. My father knew the like."

"Then he was in danger of them. I trust none of the small fair
folk. There are such about. The each-uisge. The fuathas. Their
saucers may catch more than flies. They are dangerous, that
sort."

"All the same, lord, the fields have the luck on them. Burned
even to the trees, and no planting fails since, not a seed falls but
it grows, and apple trees shoot up like weeds. Trees bear before
their time, the rain misses the haying and falls at seedtime, all
these years. Where the blackest burning was, the cattle and the
horses were kneedeep in grass inside a year. Shall I say what
country folk say, lord? That you are too easy in judgment, but
always true; that there be no hiding a thing to your face, that one
look of you on them and a man thinks of all the wrong he might
ever have thought to do, so there were two neighbors up by high
Bainbourne settled among themselves rather than have it come to
court: the neighbors say for shame of all their doings for years.
So they say. They say a horse will not go lame crossing your
lands and a cow will drop twins; that the lightning turns in the
sky and hits An Beag, missing anything of yours . . . they say.
In short—aye, you are loved, lord. Have you never seen that?"

The light hazed in Ciaran's eyes; the colors blurred. Of a
sudden he found it more convenient to look out over the walls,
for the stone hurt him where it lay, a burning pang of things wild
and green and intricate.

"Lord?" said Beorc.

He wept. He did not know why, except that he was cold, as
lost as ever he was lost on the field before the gates. It was hard
to breathe, as if someone he loved were dying, that keen a grief.
"They make fantasies. The grass always grows."

"All the same," said Beorc. "It is the truth."

He shivered. It was panic. "I have Sidhe blood. Do they say
that?"

"Oh, yes. That too."

He folded his arms. "They expect too much. You are my right hand, Beorc. Does it not frighten you, to be the right hand of the Sidhe?"

"So was my father," Beorc said.

Ciaran looked at him.

"He told me tales," Beorc said further. "Did you not know? He served the Cearbhallain, and the luck was on him too, and the Sight. Ask Rhys. They tell tales in his hills."

"Watch after Meadhbh and Ceallach," Ciaran said hoarsely. "Mind, tell Rhys and Domhnull—to keep an eye to them, where they go. Always."

"This warning of the Sidhe—Lord, there's always trouble of some kind. Or is there more than usual?"

Ciaran forced a laugh. "Perhaps we have had the luck. But hereafter luck rests on what we do. Mind you talk to Rhys and Domhnull. Say—Say I rely on them in that." The laughter failed. He looked out over the land and for a moment the colors dimmed. A mist lay over the land, and strange forests rose about him. Toward the hills, the west, the north, everywhere he faced, there seemed a shadow, but to the south he could not see, nor to the east.

Liosliath! he cried in his heart. But now there were only echoes, and the pacing of a horse, the slow striking of hooves. And shadows lowered, flowing in small curlings about the hills, pouring between him and that presence.

"Rhys and Domhnull will not fail you," Beorc said, heedless of such things as coiled across his sight. "And I will watch them too."

"Do." He looked back at Beorc, flinching from what he had seen. He felt after Beorc's solid shoulder, found it, let slip his hand.

"Lord," Beorc murmured, courtesy. Ciaran went away. He had wanted something different than worship, had wanted friendship, brotherhood, something somewhere lost. But there were no more comrades, no one but Branwyn, and even there he suspected a gulf too wide to cross. He had served his King; he had a living brother: neither wanted the sight of him. He felt the grayness about him like a shroud.

So the elves had gone, the tall fair folk, the Daoine Sidhe. The melancholy came on them and they no longer suited the world, but faded, deed by deed. Death could not touch them. Like Liosliath, whose heart he wore.

It was his heritage. He was alone, except the few brightnesses of his life—like Branwyn; like Meadhbh and Ceallach; like what he had hoped was comradeship and feared was distrust—but it was all too great a weight of trust instead. He felt the stone as a burning at his throat; he was cursed to See while he carried it, and nothing he saw was hopeful.

The trees which had loomed black and barren out of the mist gave way to stranger geography, hills looming up out of shadow, themselves touched with the elvish moon. A stream ran here, still pure, and Fionnghuala leapt it with ease, running more smoothly now. Here were fences of stone and rail, neat pasturage and fields where never war had come. A farmhouse squatted against the farthest hill, under a tree broad and gnarled and strong; a cluster of barn and sheds stood near, with orchards beyond.

It was a human place, and not. It was refuge, where Arafel rode more quietly, like a wisp of wind along the reedy bank. Fionnghuala moved with the lightest pulse of thunder, like a storm muttering in the sky, but hushed, hushed, and ceasing, for Arafel whispered to her.

The elvish horse paused a moment, set one hoof into the clear running water, dipped her head and drank, for here she could drink, of waters which fed clear Airgiod. The wind whispered in the reeds. A heron watched in tall solemnity from a little distance away, seeming unastonished, but herons betrayed little. An owl called.

"Come," Arafel whispered, and Fionnghuala moved, delicately, softly. If sleepers had stirred in the farmhouse thinking a storm might be blowing up, they settled into their pillows again and thought that they had dreamed. Fionnghuala's steps glided soundlessly; she slipped like moonlight along the banks and finally along the fences, tossing her head somewhat, for this was strange to her, the fences, the hewn wood, the buildings in the very fringe of Eald.

There were horses here, who put their heads out of the barn as they came near and drank in the strangeness with eyes as dark as night and nostrils quivering, a piebald mare, a fat dark pony, plain and mortal-born. They watched, and ventured no farther from their barn. Wings stirred in the loft, then settled again.

"Gruagach," Arafel called softly.

There was, if only to her ears, a tiny movement within.

"Gruagach."

Stillness then.

"Will you make me angry, Gruagach?"

It was the third calling. He must come. A small, shaggy darkness crept out past the feet of the pony and the horse, a moving untidiness shot through with straw, a small brown man looking up at her with eyes darker than dark.

"I hear," he said, "I hear."

"So. I had thought you must. Has it slipped your notice, the trouble hereabouts? Are you so comfortable at night?"

It squatted, arms clenched about its chest, peering up at her as if it would tuck its head between its shoulders if it could. It shivered. "I have seen it, Duine Sidhe. I watch, oh, I do watch my Men to keep them safe; I make confusions in the hills. There was a nasty thing. I threatened it and it went running."

"So." It touched a sense of mirth in her, and not, for small and twisted that it was, the dark eyes sparked sullenness at her tone. She dropped lightly to the ground, still towering, and then, for she sensed its pride, bent down as it bent, until she looked at it eye to eye. "A secret thing have I to ask, Gruagach."

"*Ask,*" it repeated, flinching back ever so slightly, its shoulders tucked about its shaggy head. "Ask, she says. The Duine Sidhe belongs in the deep shadow, the far places. Oh leave my Men alone, elf. Leave them be."

"Is there no trust, small Sidhe?"

It flinched the more. "I love them. I will fight, I will."

"In truth you would," she said, resting her arms on her knees and gazing full on the round, dark eyes. "It is a warm place you have made. Even with the fences. Do you know I have guested with Men?"

The eyes grew rounder a moment, perplexed. It shook its head.

"In their hall," said Arafel.

This was too much to credit. The eyes blinked and the doubt grew. "An elf likes my fences."

"I did not say I liked them, Gruagach! I said I forgave them."

"Ah. Ah. *This* is the Daoine Sidhe."

She had drawn herself up somewhat. The Gruagach flinched back again, then frowned.

"There is bravery in you," she said. "Greater than your size. I have long thought so. So I have come to you. Will you listen?"

"The Duine Sidhe says what she likes and the Gruagach has to listen."

"There was a time—" she began, nettled despite herself, but made a further effort, her hands clasped upon her knees. "Gruagach, I beg."

The hair shifted backward, the lifting of unseen brows, showing bewildered eyes. The Gruagach clasped hands about its own knees, straighter now. "Please, elf, nothing against my Men."

"There are two children across the hills—such bright children, they are, uncommonly bright and good. Polite too. You would like them. And a land—not so fine as yours, but for Men's doing, very neat. I have seen them put out milk and cakes of evenings. They are mannered folk, even if the gifts go unnoticed. The children—you would know them if you saw them. You would never mistake them."

"But I have my land, Duine Sidhe, my farm, my Men to take care of—"

"It would take so little notice, only now and then. I do not say you should do the work of their fields; but shadows have come close there. If there were now and again your eye turned that way, or your care— They are very mannerly folk. They would appreciate the attention, I do think, small Sidhe. I have business to tend to. But the shadows do not trifle with you, I know that."

The Gruagach leaned forward. "What are they to you?"

"Something precious. Men that they are—precious to me. I ask, Gruagach. The Daoine Sidhe ask, and hope. I know it is no small thing."

"You made the hills to quake," the wight accused her. "You loosed them. Now you come asking help."

"I do."

It shivered then. Its eyes rolled up. It moaned. "The Grugach sees. Oh, I see, I see, I see, the dark thing."

"Is it near, Gruagach?"

A convulsion trembled through its limbs. A murmur began in it, that became words.

> *Dark, dark and dark it lies and lost is he who finds it;*
> *Cold it burns and heartless lives and never heart can bind it.*

Arafel shivered and rose, laying a hand on Fionnghuala's neck. "I read your riddle. I would I did not."

For a moment the Gruagach seemed lost to sense. Then it recovered itself, hugging itself, rocking to and fro. "Cold," it complained.

"Yes, cold. And my fault, among others. I own it. Will you grant my favor all the same, Gruagach?"

It stood, never tall, coming scantly to her waist, and having to look up at her, the more as she took Fionnghuala's mane and swung up astride. "The Gruagach will do what he can," it said. "I will try. I am very strong."

"Small cousin, I do not doubt it."

Its eyes went bright. "Cousin, am I?"

"Cousin," she said.

It laughed and capered by her as the elf horse began to move. But the thunder boomed now as the horse increased her stride, and the Gruagach had no such swiftness. Lightning flickered. The trees sighed with wind. The Gruagach fell behind, where soon a storm might break, light patter of rain and mutterings of thunder.

Arafel rode not fully in the shadow ways, not daring them. There was true shadow ahead, a darkness where no stars shone nor clouds rolled, an opacity and increasing cold not so far north.

They were old, these hills near Donn, older than Man. They were prisons, but their roots were shaken and what had been loosed had only gone back for shelter.

The greater things were slower to wake, for the greater binding was on them, but beyond this fair place the mists thickened, foreboding ill. It was not in her mind to ride against it blindly; but to find it out, how far it reached, and into what, and how arrayed. She might have stayed safe in Eald, for a time, but it would have come there when it chose.

She came for it. Heartless, the Gruagach had named it, in its half-crazed way, but that was a very true name for what she suspected of it, as true a name as any.

FIVE

The Sending

He slept, if fitfully, and Branwyn was by him, so that for most of the hours of the night he did not sleep at all, but lay with his hand closed about the stone, so that he was aware of it, but only dimly participant.

Dragons stirred in his vision, a glittering of lances, of elvish armor, ancient wars.

A face, elvish-fair, hovered near: elf-prince, the shadows

whispered, dreading this brightness. *Liosliath*, he addressed this apparition, but it was only dream. The years were many as forest leaves, as raindrops in the storm. The earth had passed its youth since this one had set foot on it . . . cousin to ageless Arafel.

But when he looked, truly looked with the stone, to see what lay about them, his vision went gray and strange, and he seemed lost among the trees which were not the trees he knew. He remembered the darkness which had coiled among the hills as he gazed outward, severing him from the sea, and still the disquiet crept through him, a sense of power that might do such a thing, silencing the stone.

Arafel's? he wondered. But the aspect of it had been dark, unlike her workings, and there was a dread about it different from the bright terror he knew of her. *Has she a dark aspect? Or had Liosliath? Or can anything dim such a stone?*

Arafel, what am I to do with it?

For your defense, she had said. *I do not ask that you use it. Only that you have the choice.*

Has it come? Or do I only see what has been behind our peace for years?

Do not walk in Eald, she had said, and he believed this, and avoided thinking of it in these gray, weak hours when the veil seemed very thin. *So I am not come to you.* And again: *Do I truly leave this place when I am there? Or do I dream?* The thought of Branwyn's fright if she should wake and find him fading kept him struggling against it no less than Arafel's command.

When light came he feigned to wake and smiled at his wife, gave her a morning kiss, with the birds singing beyond the slitted window and the gentle-hued light coming to them, for it was spring and they piled on blankets against the chill, but liked the freshness of the air and had the shutters off that they used in winter.

"They know nothing amiss," he said of the birds. "Listen to them this morning."

"Did you rest?" she asked, searching his face.

"Oh, aye." He was not wont to lie, but he did so smiling.

He smiled through breakfast—"Will we ride today?" asked Ceallach; and "Hush," said Branwyn sharply. "No, you will not. Let your father be."

Ceallach dropped the matter at once, so unlike his son; and Meadhbh tugged at her brother's sleeve and comported herself as if the question had not come up, very sober.

He grew desperate, even then, in the silence, but he roughed

Ceallach's hair and made nothing of it. "We shall see," he said. "Nothing is the matter, is it?"

"Oh no," said Meadhbh instantly, wide-eyed and all too quick.

"No," said Ceallach.

So they all had learned to lie. *That is not so*, he started to say, and smothered it, not to break the peace, only wishing that they would do something amiss, or fidget in their seats, or quarrel over the butter, or something like other mornings.

Instead he smiled, weary as he was, too weary and too little in command of his heart to contest with anyone dear to him. He was alarmed by his ready angers, put them deep and smothered them all and ate the breakfast which sat ill at his stomach, worried by the tiny frown which sat on Branwyn's brow as she chattered at the children about this and that duty, to which they kept answering meekly and unlike themselves. *O let me escape this*, he thought, with no thought toward the days of bearing this gift he had been given, or of their days to come. He was reduced to the moment, like some wounded thing. He set his cup down. "I have work to do," he said, and rose, and suddenly had all their eyes focused on his, even Muirne's, who was participant in the table, in this privacy. Her look was like the children's, her pale face all eyes, her hair combed taut about her face which had gone all smooth and strange to him. Was this Muirne, did even Muirne read him so well? And Branwyn and the children. . . . "I have work," he said.

Silence pursued him. He went out onto the stairs and made noise going down them, through the warding room with its armor hung like the empty shells of beetles, with its smell of oil and war and its iron closeness that quivered through his limbs like some noisome sickness.

He reached the open air, the walls, the sight of the sun, and lifted his face to it, eyes squeezed shut until he had purged the moment's touch of iron.

Liosliath! he called, not daring to call Arafel. But still there was nothing. The stone hung insensate at his heart, giving him only the things the wind and sun gave.

He took his breath and opened his eyes, and drew another and walked along the wall and down again by the stone stairs to the yard.

It was better in the light. He smiled at the pages, at the smith who was setting to his day's work, in his smithy over against the inner wall, with its tangles and knots of iron. This he avoided, making small deviations in the pattern of his day.

Youths gave him their silent respect as he wandered within his walls. They were farmers' sons, come at his asking: Ruadhan had their training at arms, which saw them drilling with sword and shield and bow. The skill with the bow was against beasts; that with sword and shield—against the sometimes bandits that strayed down from the Bradhaeth above Lioslinn and the forest to the east . . . for there were still bandits. It had been the Cearbhallain's way to guard the land; and Evald's after him; and it was his, that he kept no great number of men-at-arms lounging about the hold—less than a hundred, hardly outnumbering his craftsmen, and them mostly sons and brothers of freeholders, as much of Caer Wiell's land was given in freehold, save the fields and pasturage closest about the walls; but even from the farthest steadings the boys came eagerly to learn arms. It was Caer Wiell's way. The King looked askance on it. But the land was sown with swords, since the war; every farmer's cottage boasted some weapon gleaned from the fields; and bows were kept against wolves and such (though no wolves were seen). Caer Wiell had not gone to the winning of Dun na h-Eoin as some holds had, a-hedge with spears in untrained hands; but briskly, shielded, glittering with well-honed swords, a thousand blades sprung up from the land at Evald's summons, invisible the day before. This was Caer Wiell. An Beag sat in its hills like some bandit lair, fed by its serfs who had each some cruel lordling to support, each worse than the other. Caer Damh was much the same; so also they distrusted everything, particularly their own. Such lands bred nothing good, not those who ruled them, not even the occasional farmer lad who left his sheep and ran. Caer Wiell had taken in a few such, forlorn attempt at rescue, of folk who had grown up in knavery and expected nothing else. Most of them came to nothing. Some came to worse. Like Coille there, sulking at the scullery work, with no grace to recommend him. There was suspicion that Coille stole. Cook thought so. Coille knew nothing of arms; and that was, perhaps, as well. He was forever surly.

Send him off, was Beorc's advice. But Ciaran had not found any cogent reason for it, except Coille's unpopularity. Coille did his work. He had asked for land, but complained of danger in what Ciaran offered him, which was to go north and east, to clear land bordering the New Forest as others had done. So he did the work of the hold; and he sulked about that, cruel with the cattle and with every living thing, so that it was Coille got the work of killing chickens for the pot: he does that well, Cook had said, if nothing else. And there was no one in the hold but loathed him.

"Good morning, lord," said Coille, with a smile of the sort of all of Coille's smiles, and speaking up when the country lads were content to nod and pass. Coille was drawing water from the well in the shade of the scullery roof, and heaved a bucket up, wiped his brow, being very sure his work was seen. Ciaran paused, stared distractedly at the man, with the clatter of the scullery beyond, the kitchen, the maids already at their washing and water sluicing everywhere on the stones, before it got to the channel and headed downslope and under the walls. There was the granary, the pen beyond, though they kept most all the animals outside; there were the stables and the sheds of harness, and the Old Hall, that had been the first and oldest part of Caer Wiell, with part of the wall still standing, which was the wall of the scullery now, and had once enclosed the well; but the Old Hall they used for storage, mostly old harness and oddments of this and that; and the Old Granary, that was the barracks, lodging for his men-at-arms; and the older Barracks, that was below the Cearbhallain's tower, which came up by the gate— that was all lodgings now, for those who served the hold; and the Cearbhallain's tower, which added its mass to the gates and enclosed the wardroom stairs in its depths, that was Beorc's domain, where he maintained what little luxury he wanted. No wife, not in these years, no child, but a young widow off by Hlowebourne that he supported with gifts of more than small substance, and visited from time to time, but generally he courted Cook, a stout and dour-faced woman who managed the understairs as Beorc managed a troop of horse, with ringing orders and a precision of expectations.

"Coille," Cook shouted now, "Coille!"

The outlander moved, hunch-shouldered, carrying his bucket.

"Lord," said Ruadhan coming up beside—a cheerful man who looked always a little simple, but men mistook that to their misfortune. "There's some of the lads will hunt, by your leave."

Ciaran blinked and thrust his hands within his belt behind, with an inward flinching. Ruadhan stood there, having come up on him from the yard where the barracks stood, whence came the rhythmic thumps and noise of practice. "Is there need?" he asked.

"Naught but bones left. If my lord would go himself—"

"No. Not I. Rhys might go. He's chafed for exercise. Domhnull. Ask Domhnull."

"Aye, my lord." There was the lightest of frowns on Ruadhan's face. "Is something wrong, lord?"

"Nothing," he said. "Nothing." He walked away, up the stairs by the scullery, along the wall again into the storage, where a few unused rooms offered privacy, and sank down in a smallish windowed closet, finding a bench only half-loaded with dusty oddments of pottery. He set the pots in the floor and stretched himself out, tucked up on the bench, having found a safe place.

So he had done as a child, finding some nook of Caer Donn to make his own. He clenched the stone within his hand and brought it to his lips as he lay there, then sought the sleep the night had denied him, in this quiet darkness far from the iron and the noise outside. Here he need not fear, he thought. Here what befell when he slept was without witness, and if he should dream, he need not fear for Branwyn.

So he abandoned himself.

"Man," said Lord Death, settling closely in the room, on a stack of crockery which failed to break beneath his weight, "is this the lord of Caer Wiell, sleeping like a scullery lad above the kitchens?"

"Give me peace," he replied.

"Ah, that I cannot. I have lost that power over you."

"My friend," Ciaran said softly, never stirring from where he lay, his head against his arms, one toe resting against the floor, for the bench was narrow. "Why have you come here?"

There was no answer. The walls gave way to mist, and he was disquieted. This was what he had feared, the realm of dream, in which elvish trees grew like white pillars of some hall, in which the landscape was chill and gray. He drew back from it, recovering his little room again, alone, his body stretched on the unyielding bench, which was uncompromising in its discomfort.

The stone had troubled him before, when he had carried it in his youth. But iron had not seemed so painful then. He had passed the armory bearing it and not felt it half so keenly then. *It is the years,* he thought. His old wounds ached. He limped some winter mornings. *I could have slept on bare stone once, and never minded it.*

But his nerves were taut. He realized his fists were clenched and mindfully unclenched them. He thought that he might have a little peace if only he could take it off his neck. It tempted him, as once, his third battle, he had thought that he could run away; all that dawn he had waited for the ambush to break, hidden half-frozen in the autumn-red thicket as they fought in those years of the King's war, and it had occurred to him that he could stay there when the others burst forth, and that he need not go, because he had contracted a sudden, gripping fear, and felt sure that he would die. But his body had leapt when the horn sounded; and he had gone, after lying to himself all the while that he had had a choice. After that he knew that things seemed choices which were not, and that men lied to themselves sometimes for comfort in the small dark hours. So he could think now of putting off the stone, but he knew that his hand would refuse the act, because he had said that he would bear it, and he could not do otherwise.

Liosliath! he cried in his mind, and suddenly there returned to him that sound he had all but forgotten: the sea, waves lapping at the shore, gulls crying like lost children.

Does the stone remember? Or was more than that always my imagining; and was there ever a living voice?

She thought so, at least.

Silence came. For a while it was all gray, and he waked fitfully, aware at least that he had slept, caught himself short of falling off his precarious rest. His eyes drifted shut again, fluttered, for it seemed some sound had come to him, but it was only someone stirring about below, some clatter in the kitchens.

He sighed, and was home again. He lay asleep in the loft of Caer Donn, in that closeness he shared with Donnchadh, and any moment now his mother would be calling them both downstairs to breakfast, to that great table they all shared. His sister was alive again. He heard her voice; he thought he heard it, the way he had never been able to remember it, and if he could wake and go downstairs she would be there, his sister and his mother and his father who were dead but alive again in this new and precious dream.

Father, he would say, *you never let me explain;* and his father would sit by the fire in the great hall in the tall carved chair with the huge old wolfhound he had loved lolling at his knee and listen to him without really seeming to listen, which was his manner when he was thinking about something. *Listen to the boy,* his mother would say, taking his part as she always would. *He's your son.*

His father looked up and frowned, disturbing the tenor of the dream. Ciaran retreated from that moment, choosing another.

How did you come here? his mother asked him; but the horse that stood outside she could not see, nor could anyone see who did not know how: Aodhan was its name and it had carried him home as it had carried him to battle.

I can't stay long, he said, feeling keenly the stone about his neck, but he stood in the upper hall of Caer Donn where every detail was precious to his memory, wooden walls, where those of Caer Wiell were gray stone; and fine carving on the benches, for the folk of Donn had always been fine craftsmen and carvers. *O Mother, there was battle. The King has won. I've come home awhile.*

(But he had met his father and his brother afterward, and they had walked away, having seen what he was, and what he had become. The hills about Donn held old stones, for the elves called it Caer Righ, and there was elvish blood in them all, fey and different from men.)

And your father? his mother asked; *and your brother and your cousins?*

Well, he said. *Father and Donnchadh are very well. But Odhran died at Dun na h-Eoin and Riagan at Caer Ban; and Ronan and Hagan too—*

All dead?

Aye. Dead. He sat down in a chair he remembered. *Is there ale?*

She brought it for him; it had taken longer than this, with much stir about the hold, but in his dream it was instant, and she sat near him and asked him when they would come, his father and Donnchadh.

Soon, he said, *soon.* Cherishing the time that he had left. He would stay for supper. He would do that. He would stay all the days before he knew his father and his brother would come home and tell her that he was banished, fading only when he knew them passing the gates.

But he had not stayed the hour. The questions were unbearable, the reality of home insupportable when his mother persisted in her questions, when she grew angry and confused.

It happened now, and he fled outdoors, realizing only later that he had been mistaken, that he should never have come here.

He rode, and he was a boy again, with Donnchadh; they raced upon the heath and climbed irreverently on the ancient stones, their ponies tethered down the hillside.

It is a cursed place, said Donnchadh. He would become a lean, tall man, dark, for he was of their father's first wife; but as a boy he was gangling and his hair always fell so, into his eyes. *Do you dare?*

Of course he had dared. In those days he had no fear. They stood atop the world like kings, he and his brother, and looked from the hill to the mountains round about, shoulder to shoulder.

And stood eye to eye at Dun na h-Eoin, among the dead.

Take care, his brother said. And moths died in the torches outside the King's tent; and the dead lay in heaps.

Ciaran, take care.

The mist was back, among hills that he knew; and Caer Donn stood as it had always stood, high on its hill among the hills about, for its wealth was sheep, and the flocks grazed round about; but now the land was sere and brown like winter, and the treeless hills showed their bare bones of earth and ancient carved stones.

This was not the way it had been. He knew dismay, and entered into the hold, into the upper hall with the blinding swiftness of a dream, where the familiar chairs stood all unused, and only his brother slept before the fire as he had seen him sleep at a hundred campfires, his head at an angle, the fire leaping on his face.

Wake up, he said to Donnchadh.

But there was a sense of menace he had only felt in the wrong places of Eald, something in the stones.

They were boys again on the hill, and something wakened under their feet which resented their laughter and their youth.

It crept and circled in the dark places of the hold, and there was no kindred left. The servants had grown faithless. There was only his brother sleeping here alone, while menace gathered, and the shadow he had seen came nearer.

Donnchadh, wake up.

But the waking was his, and his hands clenched on the board of the bench, his balance for a moment deserting him.

Someone moved on the stairs outside. For a moment he thought himself truly in Donn, and blinked, his heart beating so hard it hurt. But he lay still, and the steps passed, with a clattering of the noise below.

He sat up and leaned his face into his hands, passed the hands over his head to the back of his neck.

More steps outside. The door crashed open. A shadowy man stood there glittering with iron.

"Lord? Lord Ciaran, is it you?"

"Rhys. Gods." For a blinded moment he had feared some attack and known better in the next heartbeat; it was his own hold, after all and only Rhys, whose lean figure and dark hair minded him strangely of his brother's in his dream. He stood up. "Has a man no peace?"

"Lord Ciaran, the hold's upside down with looking for you. Shall I—tell Beorc you're here?"

Ciaran laughed half of despair and took in all that Rhys had said. "Branwyn looking too?"

"She had asked; and one man thought you were here, and another thought there, and when the hunt returned and you were neither—Lord Ciaran, are you well?"

"Don't tell her where I slept," he said. "I didn't rest last night." He went toward the door, passed Rhys into the hall and shut the door after him, so that they were in dark unrelieved except for the slit window some steps up. "She was not alarmed."

"No, not except that she thought you with the hunt and wished you had not gone."

"So did *you* go?"

"No. Only Ruadhan."

"Was there luck?"

"Luck enough till they came back and questions started. Lord, you might have had my bed."

Ciaran said nothing, but surrendered himself to the daylight, rubbing at his eyes as he went down into the sunlight and trying not to look at the men who, one by one, realized he had been found and gathered solemnly to stare at him and Rhys walking across the yard.

Beorc came, meeting them halfway.

"There was no cause for this alarm," Ciaran said, and then, his eyes lighting on Branwyn atop the wall, who stood waiting for him: "Are you all my warders?"

That was short and undeserved. He went up the steps and gave his hand to Branwyn, already ashamed of what he had said, with no way to recall it.

"I was in the storage and fell asleep," he said to her, reckoning that the most of the truth was due and wishing he had said less below.

"Ah," she said, so easily it seemed casual, and wound her arm in his as they walked, taking him inside.

But someone carried tales, or Branwyn read more in his heart than he had thought, for that night there was a posset mixed at bedside.

"You must drink it," she said. "T'will make you sleep."

He was loath. This also was abandonment; he more trusted his own mind. And a dire thought came to him.

"If you took the stone from me," he said, "if you were to do such a thing, you might do me harm."

"I don't believe it."

A great weariness came on him, so great that tears came into his eyes. "But you must not do it, Branwyn. Give me the cup."

She offered it, and he drank: she had made it sweet with honey. Then he lay down to rest and she blew out the light, and came to bed beside him, listening long for the evenness of his breathing.

"Do you sleep?" she whispered, ever so softly.

It seemed then that he did, that the stone had no power to resist the cup that she had given.

But she lay long awake, as she had waked much of the night before, feigning that she slept, and anger gnawed at her, that he had cheated her, forestalling her as he had, with a word and his trust of her.

He had always had that way with her, that he was so simple and so knowing of her heart.

The elvish sun was near, but there was a murkiness which hung late, for here there shone no stars, and uncertain trees which were and were not by turns made the landscape harder and harder to recall, as if the land itself could not decide true from false, now from then. The nightwind that stirred the grass brought forth a hissing sound of dryness and the hillsides were patched with dust, and now and again with stone.

There was ill hereabouts, couched within the hills. Arafel sought it warily, with more caution than she was wont to use in this land that was her own.

There were Men. She saw the houses, but they were nothing like the cleanly houses and neat fields of Caer Wiell, but hovels of rough stone nestled on stony heights, unkept and many untenanted as if even Men had been disgusted with them. There were sheep now and again, and dogs, which little interested her.

She came to a brook in the strange last edge of dark, but Fionnghuala spurned it with a snort, and brought down a hoof like thunder in the night, that echoed among the hills. Something splashed and swam away. "Fuathas," she said, and heard the swimming stop. "I have no quarrel with you, fuathas," she whispered to the air. "Where are your brothers?"

"Duine Sidhe," the whisper came back from the black water, bubbling, "gone this way and that through the web of waters. Let us go. We do no harm."

"Your name is Hate."

There was soft laughter. "So do you go called the People of Peace by Men, and that name has no power on you. Hate are we; and Spite to Men, but that name will never bind us."

"Come out. I see your name. Shall I speak it to the wind and water, for anyone to hear?"

There was a stirring in the green leaves above the water, a

loud rude breath. A black horse stood there, and Fionnghuala shifted her weight and bared her teeth, laying back her ears.

"No," said Arafel. "Give us man-shape, pooka."

The horse faded and it was a dark-haired youth who stood there, clothed in shadow. He had a sullen face, and wrapped his arms about him as if he had taken a chill.

"The Duine Sidhe has come calling names," he said. "But give me my river back, Duine Sidhe." His heavy jaw made his frown the more intense; his thick black hair hung about his shoulders and all but covered his eyes which stared back at her like coals of fire in the shadow. "The wind is cold."

"The water is colder still, pooka. But truth I ask: what stirs hereabouts, and what is its name?"

"If I knew it I would bind it," the pooka said and shivered, for all his pride. "It knows mine, Duine Sidhe. O let me go. The sun is coming and I do not love the daylight."

"What is its kind, pooka?"

"It's kind is yours," the pooka said and shivered yet again. "Let me go now."

"No, pooka." She held it still, having had the answer she dreaded. "Where does it lodge?"

It pointed north, behind the hills, and its arm shook as with ague. It began to fade.

"Seaghda," she called its name.

The face grew clear again, distraught and woeful. "I have given what you asked, Duine Sidhe. But you were always cruel."

"Not I. I only ask you guide me. I do not command."

The youth threw his head and his burning eyes peered madly through the hair that settled. His nostrils flared, pale in the strangeness of the light. "I am bound here. So wise a Sidhe should know that."

"Ah," she said quietly, "where is your soul, o Seaghda?"

Now the eyes were wild, the dusky arms hugged more tightly.

"Show me," she said: "Seaghda, Seaghda, *Seaghda.*"

It vanished. The waters swirled, the reeds whispered in the dawning. It was back again, a dark-haired youth holding a small smooth pebble on his palm. The mad eyes stared.

She slid from Fionnghuala's back and came to him and took it in her hand, so small and plain a thing and unlike hers which hung like the summer moon about her neck, but very precious to him. If the eyes were not fire they might have wept or pleaded, but they had no such power.

It warmed within her hand. It took fire from her, becoming

and becoming, and so she gave it into his hand. "Be free," she said, "Seaghda. The binding is broken."

The shadow leaped up like a shout, a darkness, a wild flood of mane and eyes like embers. It whuffed wildness into the air and leaped the stream at a bound.

Fionnghuala bared her teeth and sidled close to Arafel.

"Come," Arafel whispered, taking Fionnghuala's mane. "It is Seaghda, a prince among its kind; and it will find the way for us."

The elf horse threw her head, shook it, rattling thunders from her neck, but lightly Arafel sprang to her back and she began to follow the darkness which paced ahead of them, in the delaying dawn.

The light began among the shifting maze, an uncertain gleam that lost itself among the trunks of trees which did not stand there in the mortal realm: she might have sped quicker as mortals went, but less sure, and come blind toward the hazard.

Now the pooka trotted, now walked a space, now moved again, shaking his mane: it was his doom that he could not speak, having no place but his mouth to keep his soul when he was in his true shape, and always fearful of losing it. But when the light had gotten to a murk that gave suspicion of color, when the sun was with them and they had come to the end of the trees, Seaghda stopped and took his other form, spitting his soul into his hand.

"There," he said doubtfully, pointing with his left hand beyond the wood, where strange carven stones rose up on the hillsides like a line of broken teeth.

"Dun Gol," she said, shaken in spite of herself, for that aspect should have passed from the world. She cast Seaghda a dire look. "Have *you* manifested this?"

"Not I," said the pooka. "I could not." He shivered in spite of the sun, or because of it. "But the waters are bitter that flow from this place, and taste of hate. Go back, go back now. Find your forests again. This one is not kind, and the stones are worse."

"It is a drow," she said. "That is what has waked."

"Do not say that here," Seaghda hissed, and his eyes glowed but dimly in the day. He hugged himself and shivered. "Enough, enough, let us be away."

She patted Fionnghuala's neck and felt the tremor. "She will stay with me, pooka. Go. I have freed you. Go where you like; I have no more need of you."

He was proud, but the terror in him was more. He turned

away and slipped his soul within his mouth: the black horse stood there an instant lifting its head toward the height of Dun Gol, nostrils quivering with dislike.

Then it fled, the slipping of a shadow into the murk.

Fionnghuala moved forward, softly now, treading lightly above the polluted soil.

Elves had perished here, on this side and on that of war. It had left the world, this hill, with its memories and its stones, so close to what Men named Caer Donn. Something had brought it back again, more, it was the place from which the strangeness came. This was why the trees returned, which had been lost to Eald: that this place remembered them.

And it remembered loss. It was Dun Gol, the hill of weeping, and it was reared above the armies which had met and perished here, to the ruin of the world.

SIX

Of Fences and Fugitives

Ciaran slept, past breakfast, and waked with the sun streaming in the windows and Branwyn's place vacant. He lay there a time, his hand finding the quiescent stone where it ought to be, his eyes shut on the day because the quiet was so good to him. But he gathered himself up at last and dressed and went out with a night's rest behind him and a brighter countenance to the days ahead.

He was quite deserted: the hold stirred about its day's business without him, but the maid went scurrying when she saw him in the hall, and Branwyn came in on the return, smelling of sunshine, with hope in her eyes and dust on her hands that she wiped upon her gown.

"Did you sleep soundly?" she asked, as if it were any morning of their lives, and kissed him by the mouth; he hugged her, finding the smell of her sunbathed hair the fairest thing about the morning he had met.

"Oh, aye, I did."

She drew back to look at him.

"My oath. I did." He smiled a weary small smile, not the

false one he could use. "You see, there is peace of it. I knew it would come." He gathered her back to his heart. "The Sight was too quick and keen for a time; perhaps that it had gone unused so long, and knew me—but it has settled now. It has quite settled. There's no more pain."

There were other things she might have said. He waited for them, but she judged the peace still fragile, perhaps, for she only found that she had gotten dust on him and brushed at it and straightened his collar as if he were a child to be cared for. "Meadhbh and Ceallach are out weeding the garden; I thought they should have the sun. Muirne is with them. I will have cook send your breakfast. Cein was here: the notch-eared ewe dropped her lamb this morning and the children went to see it. Beorc is somewhere about: the horses took down the north fence last night and got into the turnip field; but they have got most of them in by now."

He frowned. "I will go," he said.

"You will have your breakfast first."

He smiled and kissed her on the brow, on his way out breakfastless; he was vexed about the turnips, and halfway glad that there was something ordinary to set his hand to, that needed neither arms nor wit, except to reckon where the rowdier mares had gotten to, if they had not gone straight to bickering with the stallion in his stall: and if that had happened, there would be planks splintered and carpentry to do.

He had a gelding saddled from the stables and rode out from the gates, along the gardened north; and along that stout fence and hedgerow that kept the pasturage. He saw a rider on the horizon, close to the end of the row, and rode for him.

"All in but Whitenose," Beorc said. "I have lads combing the riverside."

"That mare was never a wanderer," Ciaran said. Of Slue he would have expected it, who was often leader of the trouble.

"Probably she became confused," Beorc judged, "having more conscience than the rest, and ran off."

"Where was the breach?"

Now Beorc frowned, pointing north. "Up by and trees yonder."

Ciaran frowned as well. Not by the new fields then, but facing open land. That was less like the mares. "Slue got the wanderlust again," he judged, "it being spring, and led the rest to mischief. Let us ride up there and see it."

So they went, the little way that remained, and there was nothing to be seen but some of the lads putting the fence to rights, stacking up the stones again and setting the rails. The ground was much trampled with the horses wandering this way and that.

Ciaran shook his head. There was no chance of tracking any single horse here. They rode back again, down along the road where it came near the river. "I think," he said, "that the watch might have seen them from the gate if any had wandered this way."

"I think that in the end we will find our Whitenose off by Gearr's steading," Beorc said, "if she went off north instead. Either the watch missed her in the dark or she went farther than the others. We might have a lad ride up that way. But the rough ground makes her hard to track."

Ciaran shut his eyes as they rode, a brief casting of his wishes: *if I am gifted with the Sight*, he thought, *cannot I find one straying mare?* But there was only mist as there had been; and suddenly a chill that made him draw in the gelding's reins sharply.

"Lord?" Beorc asked.

The horse had faced about under the pressure of his hand, backing still, it was curbed so hard: he felt its discomfort and yielded with a shiver. "*Donnchadh*," he said, for that darkness was back which he had felt the day before, when he had dreamed of his brother.

"My lord, is something there?"

Beorc's voice came to him through the mists, and trees faded which should not stand there, and the land he knew returned. He felt the sun again.

"Is it some ill?"

"Something ill," he said, and there was a presentiment on him still, so that the matter of the mare diminished in his mind and he recalled the dream that he had dreamed in the night, that was the hill near Caer Donn.

"I will get the men," said Beorc.

"No," he said suddenly, returning to himself, looking about at Beorc's ruddy face. "There is nothing to do for it. It does not concern the mare."

He turned his horse again. They rode and searched along the riverside, where the road ran, even leaving the road at times to come to the edge of the Caerbourne; and the boundaries of Eald whispered softly in the wind, and the water chuckled as it would among its reeds, mocking them with silences. He did not use the stone again. It was wrong to have used it so, in so small a matter; it was not given him for the finding of stray horses, but in trust, and he chided himself for his foolishness—as if it were some hammer or awl that he had borrowed, this thing that was precious to the Sidhe. Best, he thought, if he learned not even to think of it, if he numbed his heart so that it did not answer when the leaves whispered, so that he did not imagine liveliness in the waters or small things watching from the thickets.

The feeling was not good here. His horse and Beorc's fretted, and it seemed to him in that sense which came curling unbidden through the stone that no horse might love this place, that they wasted their time and their search, for Whitenose would never have come this way.

"Let us go back," he said finally. "Send over to Gearr's steading, see whether she might turn up there: that pony of his might speak to her."

"So I was thinking," said Beorc.

So they came back by early afternoon, and no sign of Whitenose, which put Ciaran in less cheer than he had been. It was a good mare, one of his finest, and he had had the breeding of her through two generations of Caer Wiell's fine horses.

"Maybe," said Domhnull, who had also been out searching and turned up at the stable as overheated and out of sorts as they, with Rhys, who looked no better, "maybe, lord, she strayed west."

Due westerly lay An Beag's lands, and that thought had grazed his mind, ready as any man of Caer Wiell was to blame ill on that neighbor. "I cannot think she would have so little grace," Ciaran muttered. "She was too well-mannered to think of An Beag. Rather she has gone off toward Gearr's, or somewhere about."

"There is the woods," said Rhys, who bore scratches on his face from searching amongst the trees, "and there she might come to mischance—but there is no natural cause for a horse to stray there."

Natural, Ciaran heard, and looked at Rhys's ever-grim face, and at suspicions. "If it was unnatural," he said, "and the small Sidhe had aught to do with it—well, grant she finds some farm when they are done."

The thought put him out of sorts even further, and he climbed the stairs. "It comes to me," he said to them as they went up, "that we might use the tower for the warding room, and that we might set the one we have to other use. Will you see to that?"

"Other use," Beorc echoed, somewhat out of breath.

"A table, a chair or two: a library; we should move the accounting here." The poison closed about him as they came from the wall to the room, among the dreadful iron; he bore it, shuddering as he reached the second stairs.

"Aye, lord," Beorc said, "but the accounts are small—"

"So, well, but do it, Beorc, see to it this afternoon. Set some of the boys to doing it. Move everything to the tower hall. Move what is there here." He reached the top of the stair, the relief of his own hall, where the table waited, with ale and the morning's bread and some of Cook's fine cheese. "Ah," he said, better pleased in the day, finding he had appetite, and that was good. "My lady has been kind. —Sit with me, you three."

"Is it father?" a young voice called from up the stairs inside, and Meadhbh came running down with Ceallach in her wake; so Branwyn came down the stairs, and he swept Meadhbh up in his arms and spun her so, a flurry of skirts.

"Did you find Whitenose?" Ceallach asked.

"No," he admitted, setting his daughter on her feet. "Likely she went off to some steading; but we will find her."

"If the elves have not got her," said Meadhbh.

"You do not call them elves," Ciaran said soberly, catching her with his eyes. "There is only one of *her* kind, and you cannot see her stealing our mare, can you?"

"Only one?" Meadhbh asked, her face gone very still. "Only *one?*"

"In all the world. The others of the Daoine Sidhe all went away, very long ago, so long ago no man can remember it. There is only one, and you must not speak ill of her."

"No," said Meadhbh, "but why did they go away?"

"Hush," said Branwyn. "Hush, no such questions. Let your father alone. Can't you see he's been at riding and might like to sit down? Don't be so graceless."

Meadhbh's face fell, her eyes so very earnest. *I am sorry,* they seemed to say, but not a whit for questions.

"Come," he said, moving the bench aside, "sit with us and share the bread."

Their young faces glowed, to be asked thus to sit with Beorc and Rhys and Domhnull and himself, small companions to a men's gathering. They scrambled to the benches, fresh and clean and scrubbed, while his company still reeked of horses, except for washing at the trough. But Branwyn took her place at table too, a waft of lilac and herbs, her fine hands laced before her.

"There was none lost but the one?" she asked.

"No, lady," said Beorc. Muirne had come, and took it on herself to be cutting the bread: she took the knife from Rhys and sliced the bread and cheese, while Domhnull poured the ale.

"A little for Meadhbh and Ceallach," Ciaran said. "Mind, a little. And no, we have set everything to rights we can, and the plants wanted thinning, I suppose. It was likeliest Slue that did it."

"From the far end," said Domhnull. "She has never gone that way before."

"We will have to stall that mare," Ciaran said. "I'll not be feeding her on turnips." It occurred to him strangely that he was given uncommon tolerance, that Branwyn said not a thing about the ale, that her eyes shone at him, that she was happy and that the children were. He gave a short pleased sigh, his mouth full of bread and cheese, his world at rights again, even if it turned out to be faery which had stolen the mare.

And then he thought of his dream, how they had sat at table like this in Donn, and for a moment he felt a deep distress from the stone.

"We have another lamb," said Ceallach. "It's a ewe lamb."

"A ewe," he said. "Well, good for that."

"And we pulled all the weeds," said Meadhbh, showing reddened hands.

"Hush," said Branwyn, "your father's men have no need for small chatter."

"Oh, well," said Ciaran, "but the weeds were well done, all the same." He smiled, and got a flicker of a smile from his daughter. "Better luck than ours, I should say." He ate his bread; his men wolfed it, having been hard at work since dawn. "Maybe we should test the fences all round."

"Aye," said Beorc. "I'll tell Cein to put some of his lads to it."

"I'll do that. You have your matter, with the warding room. —I've decided," he said to Branwyn, with a look that tried to tell her secrets, "to have the accounts moved there."

Today Branwyn would object to nothing. It had been the warding room all her life. "Well," she said quietly, and nothing more.

"Can we help?" asked Ceallach.

"Not in your fine clothes."

"We'll change again," said Ceallach.

"I think," said Branwyn, "you might find things to do that didn't get in the men's way. I'm sure I can find things other than that."

"Yes," said Meadhbh miserably, her hands folded before her.

"You might ask the scullery to send up some of the lads," Ciaran said. "There'll be cobwebs to clear."

"Yes," said Ceallach.

So the matter went, and there was scrubbing in the warding room, with a great deal of carrying of water and a smell of wet stone came up from it, and vinegar and burning pine, so that all Caer Wiell seemed dislodged.

And Branwyn went about ordering this and that with a preoccupied frown upon her brow and her hair flying loose from its braids in curling wisps from the abundance of water below.

Ciaran walked out along the wall, relieved, finding in the confusion of the day some solace, as if things had wanted to be turned upside down. He changed a thing which had been the same since the Cearbhallain, and he changed few things in his lordship, but this one was for his comfort.

They must bear with me, he thought, and realized that none of them had questioned him in his strange request, no, not even Beorc.

But they knew what iron was to faery. They knew. And silently they went about this change for his sake.

Only the rider came back from Gearr's steading and reported no sign of Whitenose there, though the farmer would be watching for her. The youth looked crestfallen and unhappy. "Well," said Ciaran, "but she may have gotten frightened and it may take her time to stray toward some farmstead; but any man who finds her would know where she came from." He felt a need to console the youth, who looked thoroughly downcast, for the lad was one who worked closely with the horses.

"She has never been one to run," the youth said, as if the mare's character were in question.

"Well, she may come home," he said, and sent the lad off, sorrier for the boy than for the mare: he had many horses, and little could touch him on this day, that he had mastered the ill which had settled on him and gained peace in the house again.

He watched the lad walk away, leading his weary horse toward the stables inside the gates, and then went upstairs, into warmth and light and the newly cleaned room that would hold no iron hereafter, but only accounts, still smelling of water and burned pine.

He went farther, up into the hall, where Branwyn waited, and had his supper in good peace, with the children, with Beorc and Rhys and Domhnull, Siodhachan and Ruadhan and Muirne and Ruadhan's Seamaire, and had Leannan to play them songs, so that it was more merriment than loss after so disarranged a day.

But Muirne who had gone down the stairs to the kitchens after a pitcher came back and never poured, but went direct to Branwyn, ignoring all courtesy of precedence. She leaned and whispered straightway in Branwyn's ear, and Ciaran saw Branwyn's eyes, the startled dart aside, the fixing on thin air.

"What is it?" Ciaran asked, and frowned at Muirne, so the harping died, ringing softly into silence.

"Coille," said Branwyn softly. "Coille has not been seen."

"How, *not seen?*" He ignored the quick and ugly thoughts, searched further afield. "How long not seen?"

"Please you, lord," said Muirne, whose voice was always soft and now hard to hear even in the silence, "Cook thought he had gone to laze about again, that he would say this morning he had been at the fence-mending; or this afternoon at the moving of the hall, and so some thought he was—but neither—where, at nothing, so they say down in the yard."

"Coille," said Beorc in a low and rumbling tone.

"Aye, Coille," Ciaran said. An anger came on him, so for a moment it was hard to breathe, then he thought of it. He clenched his fists upon the arms of his chair and felt the heat go into his face. "So this is my reward of charity—a good horse and gods know what else. I believed that hangdog scoundrel; I took him in. And straightway he goes home again to his masters at An Beag, with gods *know* what tale—Oh, this is beyond my tolerance."

"Lord," said Rhys, with all his dark fierceness, "send a few of us that way."

"Aye," said Beorc, "we'll have some An Beag cattle for it. And Coille's head for it, if we spy him."

"No," said Branwyn sharply, "*no*, there is no good in it."

"Branwyn," said Ciaran, "I will not abide this thing."

"Then do not abide it; but do not break the peace. You know how it sits with the King; and where your enemies are: give them no such help. Gods know they need none."

"I know where my enemies are. At the King's ear. And in my

hold, that I sheltered. Mind me of this, mind me of this, when I grow soft-hearted. They are laughing tonight in An Beag.''

"They will be pleased if you break the peace,'' Siodhachan said.

"We cannot bear this thing.'' He brought his hand down on the table. "We have farmers on the borders who will bear worse if we do nothing. If we let this thief, this scoundrel of An Beag get away with what he's done, then who is safe, anywhere?''

"No,'' said Branwyn. "Who is safe if the King's forces ride against us as peace-breakers?''

"Laochailan King would not have the courage,'' said Rhys, which treason brought a deeper silence in the room.

"Children,'' said Branwyn suddenly, "go to bed. Now.''

"Mother,'' whispered Meadhbh.

"Hush,'' said Ciaran without looking, and then looked all about the room, at all the anxious faces, at folk he trusted, men and women, all. "Friend's son,'' he said to Rhys, "friend to me—I wouldn't venture to say what the King would and would not do. But he has bad counsel. An Beag and Caer Damh have his ear, more than we. I don't say what the King might do; but what he would permit to others.—Well, Branwyn has the right of it: we have not been wise. The dale might rule the east, and he knows it—oh, he is wise in plots, is Laochailan. And what I say, I say to friends, to those I trust. We have one true ally: your father, Rhys, and how I have valued him through the years—that is beyond telling. But he has had the burden to stand by us more often than we have been able to stand by him.''

"Not so,'' said Rhys, "since he knows full well how this King would rule if not for fear of the dale.''

"Perhaps we've guarded each other's shoulder,'' Ciaran said. "But we have been warned of troubles.'' The stone lay cold on his breast, like a second, aching heart, and he forebore with difficulty to touch it. "It seems to me that someone other than An Beag might have sent this man among us. That the King himself might have wanted to know what passes here, and poor Whitenose might have a longer run ahead of her than we think.''

There was dread silence. "Then he would have a great tale to tell,'' said Beorc.

"Aye,'' said Ciaran, "well he might: how Caer Wiell's lord has gone mad, how he is feyer than they had thought; that magics are raised here that are gossipped in the halls—they are, are they not?''

"Aye,'' whispered Seamaire. "Too freely, everywhere in Caer Wiell's lands.''

"That man then can do us great harm. He has been witness to—gods know what he has seen, or how we may be reported."

"The Sidhe spoke of war," Beorc said.

"Of war of a kind," Ciaran said. "And I cannot sit idle and let us be meshed in it."

"You cannot be riding against An Beag," said Branwyn. "There is no gain in that."

"No. No gain. Especially if this Coille is not An Beag's at all. Far less than gain. But we must find us allies."

"Who, pray? Caer Damh? The Bradhaeth? The lords across the hills? Husband, we are not their friends. We could never be."

"There is Donn."

The company stirred as if some wind had blown, and Branwyn made an outcry.

"Donn! Donn is the heart of our troubles. Who speaks loudest against you to the King?"

"Who can be more bitter than a brother? But he is still my brother. It came to me," he said very softly, and glanced once at Meadhbh and Ceallach who sat crouched small at Leannan's knee, "it came to me that this silence was more of my making than his. I offended my father's hopes; I know why. And somehow when Donnchadh sat in his place, well, perhaps he had tales told him how it sat with me, and perhaps there was some bitterness in it."

"You sent three times to your father, and each time your messengers were sent away."

"The last was at his death. I had hoped, then. But to Donnchadh, after, I never sent, and perhaps Donnchadh would have answered me. He is in danger. I know that he is. The Sidhe said as much and I have felt it—" His hand went at last to the stone, unstoppable. "Here. I have felt traps meshed about us. We are none of us safe. And if things have gotten to such a pass that we have to fear spies and theft and treacheries—A shadow, the Sidhe said, a thing stretching out all round us; and I have seen something of it. You wonder that I don't sleep. The King is in danger. Danger surrounds us. And perhaps, if anything would forestall this—if I could gain my brother's ear and through him reach the King and stop this madness—"

"Donnchadh is your bitter enemy," said Branwyn.

"He is fey as I. And Sighted. It's in our blood, only like my father he has no peace with it. —He is my elder brother." He said this for Meadhbh and Ceallach, reluctant, for he had never spoken much about Donnchadh, but he felt it necessary now that they understand. "We met last in this room, when he had come to Caer Wiell; but he saw me—with the Sidhe's presence about me, and it was too much for him. I think he must not have slept well after that. He went away, he and my father, and I thought they would have fallen from the King's favor after that, but they spoke against me and grew closer to him for putting me aside. Perhaps the King thought there was some luck in them that would outweigh mine. Perhaps he still thinks so. But if I could speak with Donnchadh—"

"It's dangerous," said Branwyn, "and might do more harm than good."

"Ah, Branwyn, not dangerous; to my pride, perhaps. But I had a dream about my pride. One asked me could I give it up for Caer Wiell. And I think there was some foreboding in that dream."

"You are not thinking of going to him."

"That was in my mind."

"Lord, no," said Beorc. "Not yourself."

"What can messengers do, where messengers have failed? But perhaps it would heal the wound if I were to come myself."

"No," said Branwyn violently. "No, no, and no."

"I would go," said Domhnull. "Lord, if you think there's some use in this, send me."

Ciaran was silent, gazing at Branwyn, reading there adamancy.

"I would go myself," said Beorc. "Your brother knows me, at least by sight."

"That calls back the war years," said Ciaran, "and the King's councils, and maybe those are days best forgot."

"There is myself," said Domhnull again.

"I would go," said Rhys, "but I fear your brother and my folk are not close."

"I think it madness," said Branwyn, "and a danger to whatever man you send. Cousin, don't offer. He should not be encouraged in this."

"Lord, I offer," said Domhnull. His fair face flushed, young that he was and several times passed by. "If I name myself ~~Beorc's cousin and your man,~~ your brother will know it's no small thing that you send me; and as for the war, I never saw it, so he cannot fault me in that either."

"We will talk about this," Branwyn said. "My lord, if you please, we will talk about this thing."

Ciaran sat still a moment. Branwyn gazed straight at him.

"We will talk," he said, and glanced toward Domhnull. "Domhnull, I will think on this."

But as for his mind, it was already set, and he was already framing the message in his mind, what he would send and say after so many years.

SEVEN

Bainbourne

Their father rode ahead with Beorc and Domhnull and the other men of the escort, on great tall horses; and they rode next to last, ahead of the men who led the five remounts. They jogged along on their two ponies next their cousin Rhys, who seemed justifiably downcast about it all, in the troop of their house guard, all of whom they knew. They felt very important, did Meadhbh and Ceallach, in this faring out across the country. Meadhbh felt a freedom and fear at once, a fear which had settled into her like habit in recent days, since no one was going to tell her any of the secrets that drifted about Caer Wiell's halls, like the things her mother and her father said when they talked in private; or what her mother meant in those warnings she had heard in hall; but her father who often did things her mother's way (she is the wisest of us all, he had said of her one day to his men, when Meadhbh was there to hear; no snare will ever take my lady)—her father had left the hall that night with that look in his eye which meant he was not going to listen to anyone and their mother went about the next morning at breakfast finding fault with Muirne and with everything. Meadhbh accepted this sharpness in hushed patience, and Ceallach gave her a look which said he thought much the same, that it was their father their mother was worried about, that he was doing something dangerous even in sending to Donnchadh, and so it was easier to blame the breakfast.

It was that fear again, that no one talked about, whether it was fear of their cousin the King, or their uncle the lord of Donn, or faery, or something no one meant to name; it was always there now, like some great fish, Meadhbh thought, gliding here and there under black waters, and the surface gave back only the glance of light or branches, so that there was no way of knowing when the fish was somewhere upstream, or right under the surface staring back at them. No one wanted to talk about it, especially not to them; or to think about it, if there was a choice.

There was, for a while, the sunlight and the ride: she loved riding, with the creak Floinn's saddle made, and the motion, and the smell of horse and leather, and the earth and the land and even the sharp scent of oil and metal and leather and sweat and smoke that the men had, which reminded her—which would remind her every time she thought of it—of her father on winter evenings, when he brought himself and all his doings with his gear inside the hall with him, when the armory was too cold, and his corner vied with their mother's which smelled of herbs and the simples she made for folk who needed them in winter, hers all leaves and such and bowls, and his chair with all manner of oddments of horse gear and leather and oil-smelling rags. There was the slow scrape of the whetstone when he honed that great sword of his, the muddled scent of heat and oil and the fine riverstone going just so down the edge which had to be done just right, or spoil it. The blade had lines graven down the center of it which wove back and forth and turned into a running horse. It was precious and very fine and old, a sword which the Cearbhallain himself had cared for, and then Evald their grandfather and now their father had it in keeping; but he had seen them watching one evening and let first Ceallach and then herself ply the stone, steadying their fingers, being patient when their strokes went amiss and finally finishing it all himself—redoing what they had marred, Meadhbh had suspected; and her hands smelled of oil after, like his, which delighted her—*O Meadhbh*, her mother had said, who always smelled of herbs and roses, and scowled at her for the black marks on her clothes. But she always loved the smell, because it was his; and loved what he gave her, which was his cleverness of hand, his knowledge how to ride, and where foxes denned and hares might hide, and what were the names of trees and hills and lands beyond horizons.

But now their father rode armorless among men who were armored head to foot, carrying shields upon their backs and many of them carrying the long spears which they never used for hunting. He had left the great sword at home, had banished it from hall with the things of the warding room as if it were nothing. They did not ask why. But they had marked that he had put off even his dagger in hall. He had only the stone with him, always that. They did not speak of it, she and Ceallach, even to each other. She was in sum uncertain whether this gift was at the heart of the trouble or whether the trouble had come and the stone upheld him in it; it was far, far different from their own small gifts, she knew.

And tucked away in her mind was the suspicion of her own guilt and Ceallach's, that if they had not disobeyed and run off to the river in the first place, none of this would have happened, the Sidhe would not have come and their house would not have changed, and that was a weight of guilt too heavy even to think about, let alone to speak of. No punishment would mend this. No one would so much as accuse her. It was like when the Sidhe had looked into her soul and asked her what she would do with another living creature.

So at best she tried not to do another such rash thing as she had done, or even to let herself be a child any longer. She felt robbed by this: she wanted to grow her own way; but suddenly all she wanted seemed very small, and all this war she had begun to fight of being herself and disobeying when *she* wanted something, seemed something mean and selfish, because no one in the world was getting what he wanted, not even their father, who was lord of Caer Wiell. They had seen him lean his head into his hands when he thought that he was alone, as if he had had all that he could bear, and that brought back that awful sight of him on the dark stairway, when he had fallen, fainting in their mother's arms, which figured in their nightmares. They wanted it not ever to have happened; they wanted things as they had been, but they could not be. Even their father could fall, and they had seen it, and so separately they understood that growing up was not as they had thought, always having their own way. Meadhbh suspected suddenly that it was something like what the Sidhe had asked, that meant *not* having it—or at least not being tricked by thinking one was owed it, even if it was the thing one wanted most in all the world—like home and parents.

People should always be with him now, Meadhbh would have said to her mother if she had had the courage, because her mother would have been there in a trice if ever their mother thought their father needed her help, and gods defend anything that stood between. And her mother might have lost most of this particular struggle, but not all of it, because it was Domhnull who was going to Donn at the end of this ride, and not their father himself; because Beorc had stood firmly with their mother on this, and Beorc and their father had gotten to words fiercer than usual between them.

"We will set him on his way," her father had decided then, of Domhnull; and so that was how it was; and: "You promised we should go when you rode the west road," Meadhbh had reminded him at breakfast, with devious and loving motives.

"No," their mother had said, at once and sternly.

But. "As far as the crossroads," their father answered. "Yes, I did promise. It's a small ride. They'll turn back there, and Rhys will be with them."

"This is no ride for Meadhbh," her mother had tried then. But her father had only looked at her in that way he had had, half sad and half determined. So her mother yielded them both up with nothing more said on either side and the ponies were saddled along with the horses.

Their mother had not come down to the gate as she sometimes would, but to Domhnull she sent a special gift, food all done up in a napkin that Muirne brought down to him, meat and bread and not the common fare that the men took. Domhnull was frankly embarrassed by it, the more that no one else was so favored, not even their father, who went out just with common stores; so Domhnull had tried to give a share to others, but their father laughed and would none of it, nor would any of the rest of them.

So they were on their way; and Meadhbh let her heart rise then, what with the jingling of armor and the horses jogging along at a fine fair gait. After all the fear and the arguing, they rode out into the morning with sharp weapons and high spirits and the men joking and making light of all that ailed them. These were the best men Caer Wiell had, the best in all the land, and every enemy was afraid of them. If their father should ever somehow need someone's help, Beorc seemed likeliest, the strongest man they knew; and Rhys, the fiercest and hardest and in many things the cleverest; and Domhnull who had taken all the danger on himself, and the men who would go with him, Boc and Caith and the others.

She touched the tiny pouch she wore at her neck, the same as Ceallach wore, that Muirne had shown her how to make for them, for the leaves of the elvish tree never left them now. They did not die, those leaves, nor fade, nor lose their fragrance. And they kept them close, since that morning, as their father had said, waking or sleeping having the gifts with them. Whether they were luck or not they were not sure, but they wore them as their father wore the stone, as faithfully, not understanding why, and hoping for luck from them, like safe homecomings and not losing things they loved.

If she could be like Beorc, or Rhys or Domhnull, she thought, and strong and brave to stand beside their father. (To her father's stature she did not aspire—he was too complex—but if she could be like Beorc. . . .)

Meadhbh watched him, the tall red-haired man who rode at a slouch and looked in many points disreputable beside their father and Domhnull; but men jumped when Beorc ordered. She practiced that slouch herself a moment, deciding then it wanted broader shoulders. She hated what she saw for herself, being slight and keeping to hall, smelling of lilac and of herbs like her mother and waiting, always waiting to learn what the world had done—or what it wanted—or telling her daughter hush, whenever someone mentioned faery, because her daughter would run away if she did not, doing foolish things and thinking hopeless thoughts of Sidhe and losing herself in the woods and bringing trouble, the way she had already brought it. If she could *do* something to make it good, if she could slip away and ride with Domhnull to An Beag—*I am Meadhbh,* she would say to her uncle, in his hall, with Domhnull in his armor standing by her, *and my father sent me to talk with you.* It would have been sensible, she thought, that she should go, being young and having no quarrel with her uncle, but of course no one had thought of that and even her father would have laughed at such an offer. She imagined bandits from An Beag descending on them out of the trees beside the road, and herself and Ceallach proving themselves—but they had no weapons, not even a dagger. The wish collapsed. Her brother's Flann and her fat Floinn shuffled along at pony-pace while the tall horses took longer strides, not working half so hard. They were childish figures, that was all; and the plump bay ponies were all their measure. And soon they would reach the safe limits of their riding, and their father would send them back, children who had had their outing.

Domhnull would go on: they all would, but themselves and Rhys, as far as the north road, and their father would ride back again later, having seen Domhnull well set upon his way. And perhaps, she thought, their father felt the same as they, wishing he was going on, but no one would let him—"Because," Beorc had said when they quarreled, "You bear *that* about your neck, and if your brother has no liking for the Sidhe, what when you come bearing *that* with you? You think that would win his love? And what when you drift off, as you do with me?"

"I should not," their father had said. "With you, it's trust, that I do it."

"So, well." Beorc had looked embarrassed, his ruddy face flushing twice its ordinary red. "But all the same it's madness.

You know it is. And if you will not part from that thing, and you say you will not, then don't go to Donnchadh.''

"What you say is sense," their father had said then; so whoever it was who had won with him, whether their mother or Beorc, he would not go, and perhaps he would have thought of these reasons himself at last, but it was Beorc brought it home to him.

Our uncle would not like us either, Meadhbh thought. *How can a man have the Sidhe in him and hate them? Perhaps if the Sidhe could only come to Donnchadh—she could win our uncle.*

And again: *I could call her name,* she thought. But something turned in her heart, forbidding it. *I am no small matter,* the Sidhe had said of herself compared to the fuath, *no, not like that one.* Their father could surely call the Sidhe if anyone could, and did not, for his own reasons.

So at length they came to the crest of that hill below which the road divided, one branch going toward the dark wooded side of the Caerbourne; and that way was unkept and unridden, because it led west to An Beag. The other branch, well-traveled, went northerly, through their own lands, the way farmers took, and their own patrols.

Here their father stopped them all, so that it was clear this was the parting-place. He beckoned to them; they rode forward, not jogging, but with that deliberation taller riders on greater horses used. "Well," he said to them, "this is as far as you go."

"Yes, sir," said Ceallach very quietly.

"Yes," said Meadhbh as soberly, looking up at him.

"Come, come." He drew his tall horse close to Ceallach and leaned from the saddle to hug him, passed close by Meadhbh as well and leaned down to kiss her brow. For a moment he lingered, frowning. "Be good," he said.

"Yes, sir," Ceallach said. Meadhbh only stared. They had broken off the trail here before when their father went on his journeys, and always complained when they had to do it, and had more to say to each other. This had an ill-omened feel, this brevity. Of a sudden she kicked Floinn up close to her father's horse and offered a two-armed hug. He hugged her back, leaning down. Then: "Back by tomorrow eve," he said, and gathered up the rest of them and rode away, leaving them with Rhys to guard them.

There was a knot in her throat. Her pony tried to follow the horses and she reined back.

"Come on," said Rhys after a moment. "Come on."

She looked at Ceallach, who also looked afraid, and turned Floinn's head for home.

The familiar fields unfolded, brown and green. The once-traveled road lay dusty and safe, ever so safe, and Rhys had never ceased to frown. He was dark, their cousin once removed, with brooding, heavy-lidded eyes, and frowns came natural to him, natural as the weapons about him. He was smallest of the men about their father, and hardly seemed likely for a lord's son, but he was. And patiently impatient of them, of which they were acutely aware in his long silence, his sullen carriage, his gaze which wandered everywhere—to the riverside, to the fields, anywhere but to two children who had become his unwanted burden.

It only added to her misery. Tears threatened Meadhbh, an irritating swelling in her throat. She kept her eyes open and let the wind dry them. She did not say anything. She did not feel equal to Rhys' wit, not weary as she was; neither, it seemed, did Ceallach.

"Uncommon quiet," Rhys muttered at last.

"Yes, sir," Meadhbh said in half a voice, and they went a further several hills in silence.

"Gods," Rhys said suddenly, "quit moping. The hazard is Domhnull's, no other's. Your father will turn back, long before the border. He has said."

"Yes, sir," Ceallach said.

It was a while more in silence. Rhys scowled for a while, and looked only worried then. "Aye," Rhys said, "aye, I know."

"You could leave us here," Ceallach said, more brightly, "and we could get back home ourselves. We would. Then you could catch up with father and be with him."

"Your father's orders," said Rhys.

"Yes, sir."

After a while longer riding they had come to the ford again at the Bainbourne, which ran down to meet the river, a shallow spot surrounded in reeds, well trampled mud on either side where they had crossed not so long ago. Rhys drew rein and let his horse drink before they crossed, at a spot less mired, and the ponies had their fill too, then behind Rhys' tall disdainful horse, plodded across the stream, up to their fat bellies before they had come out again, all muddy-hoofed and sorry-looking. "It's hot," Rhys complained, looking at the sun. He had stopped on the level bank where there was grass, and there stepped down from the saddle. "Rest a few moments," he said with a look at the ponies.

They had not brought food for themselves, and Rhys was not the sort who would think of stopping to eat the way their father might. But he looked to his girths and theirs and then wandered off his silent way to the grassy margin of the brook, where he squatted down and drank upstream from the crossing, dousing his face and neck with both his hands, for it must be warm in all that padded leather and metal.

Since Rhys took his ease Meadhbh and Ceallach slid down off their ponies and let them crop the grass, bits and all, since Rhys let his gelding do it. Rhys still crouched there, his hands upon his knees, staring off across the stream as if he were lost in his own thoughts and paying them no mind, so Meadhbh went down to the stream a little up from him where a tree hung over the water and the shade was cool, and Ceallach followed her. It was a place they knew, from the first time their father let them ride out with him; and they had played at being on campaign like the heroes Leannan sang of, and had mock battles among the reeds, with sticks for swords, which made their father laugh, he and his escort; or they had shared food from a basket on the streamside. They had taken cover under this old tree once when a shower caught them, their father and they and Beorc all snugged up under a tent of cloaks listening to Beorc telling them how it had been to live in tents, the years of the King's campaign. Reeds grew on the sandy shallows opposite, which had been mysterious hedges of hostile fields; and tiny flying things still swarmed there and made patterns on the dark and gentle currents.

"I think Rhys is going to rest a while," Ceallach said, squatting down on the bank and gesturing with a glance, where Rhys had lain down in the sunlight, letting the horse and ponies graze.

It was not like Rhys, to be so easy: he was all scowls and moods by habit, and while they liked him well enough they did not expect patience of him, or easiness, or anything but business. When Rhys laughed it had a hard sound, and his laughter was at hidden things and things men laughed at with each other. But perhaps he was weary after being up too late; or perhaps in his silent way he was meaning to be kind, not knowing much of what they wanted, but reckoning not to push them hard on their return. Meadhbh heaved a sigh and sat down on the bank herself, liking the coolness of the shade, the water, the nodding reeds and humming bees. Ceallach took leaves and launched them one by one, faery barks asail on the smooth miniature flood, as they had done before at this place, the first time their father had let them ride with him, when Flann and Floinn had seemed as tall as mountains. Ceallach was not playing now, but thinking. So was she. She plucked a leaf and launched it beside one of his, not playing either, watched it race Ceallach's down the dark swirls, past towering forests of reeds. They had grown too old. There was only memory in it. Her eyes followed the boat, but her mind was on her father, on Domhnull, wishing her uncle in Donn might prove better than they suspected.

"Rhys is in the sun," Ceallach said finally with a second look that way. "I think he's gone to sleep."

It disturbed her too, that Rhys had been sweating so, and lay down in the sun in all his armor, which was not the kind of sense she expected of Rhys ap Dryw. She wrinkled her nose, reckoning indeed Rhys might have been at too much ale last night, but it simply was not like him, and he had not seemed so tired on the way, simply out of sorts and wishing, she thought, that he were going on with the rest of the men and were not left to guard his two young cousins.

The strangeness of it worried at her. She got up and went toward him very quietly, with the sun beating down on her back. "Meadhbh," Ceallach objected, a faint whisper; he had gotten up to follow her, leaving his faery-boats, but she paid no heed to that. Often if Beorc were sleeping he would wake at the least sound and come out of it suddenly: never play pranks, her father had said once sternly—a man who had slept where Beorc had slept was dangerous waked that way, like many who had spent years at war. She remembered Beorc and others of the men, dozing with sometime slitted eyes, looking up foxlike from time to time and napping in the sun, never quite abandoned. Her father napped like that. But Rhys was sleeping with his limbs loose, face-up to the sun and with his eyes shut, his lips parted like a child's. "Rhys," she said aloud, from a safe distance. "Rhys?" She went closer then and squatted down by him ready to spring away if he should wake angry. "Rhys." Her heart was beating hard. She put her hand on his ribs and shook at him. "Rhys, wake up."

Ceallach had come up on his other side. He dropped to his haunches and shook at Rhys hard. Rhys' body was loose, like something broken.

"Is he dying?" Ceallach asked. "Meadhbh, can people die like this?"

She did not know. Rhys' breath still came. There was no other sign. He was a capable man, was Rhys ap Dryw. He lay there with his weapons and his armor, more defenseless than they were. Of a sudden she felt a creeping sickness of her own, a deep malaise which lay at the pit of her throat, where the leaf rested. Ceallach lifted his hand in the same moment to his own throat. His eyes were frightened and wide.

"Caolaidhe," he breathed.

But it was quite, quite another thing which stood there beside the water, in the shadow of the tree where they had sat. That was deep shadow to them, who were in brilliant sunlight; it was hard to see because of that, but it had no proper shape, and when it moved gave out a rustling like grass. It shuffled forward into the light and squatted there, small and brown and shaggy.

"Rhys," Meadhbh cried, shaking at him, and Ceallach snatched Rhys' dagger.

"Brave," the shaggy creature said. "But iron bites, bites you."

"Stay away," said Ceallach.

It came no closer. It sat with its arms about its knees and regarded them with old and shadowed eyes from under its fringe of hair. "Bites."

Ceallach's hand was shaking. He braced it with his other clenched about his wrist, and sweat stood on his face. The dagger tumbled. Meadhbh caught it up and the cold of it burned her fingers. Neither could she hold it. The pain ran through her bones. Run, she thought; and thought of Rhys helpless with this creature; thought also of the elf who had stepped through thickets effortlessly to pursue them.

"Thistle," she called to the empty air. "Thistle—"

"No, no," the brown man said holding up his hands. "She would not be pleased. She sent me. You must not call. I came to see the children, the children I would like."

She had stopped, falling half under the spell of the small piping voice. She heard the hum of bees, the sighing of the rushes, and struggled to disbelieve.

"Rhys," said Ceallach. "What have you done to Rhys?"

"Sleep," the brown man said. "No harm, never harm from the Gruagach. See, I give my name."

"We will not give ours," said Meadhbh.

"Ah. But I know a name that you own: children of the Cearbhallain. I feel it in your hearts." The brown man hopped up very quickly and somehow (it deceived the eye) hopped to the rump of Floinn, who lifted her head from her grazing.

"She's my pony," Meadhbh said with all the fierceness she could muster. "Let her be."

"Nice pony." The Gruagach scampered into the saddle, crouching like some ungainly bird, and leaned close to whisper something in Floinn's back-turned ear. Meadhbh sprang up and snatched a stone from the bank. She held it in threat, and Ceallach took another.

"Let my pony be. And wake Rhys up."

"Rhys. Rhys." It hugged itself, savoring the name they had given it. "Be more careful where you give names. You might give away his heart, but the Gruagach has no need of it."

Shame flooded her cheeks for the mistake they had made. "Then let us all go," Meadhbh said. "Let him wake up again."

"I have seen you," it said. It hopped down again. "Fine sensible ponies, brave and good. They like you, but mostly they like their comforts, which is what ponies love best. And they are clever. Many ponies are. But your way is darker than theirs, o darker. I know now why she sent me."

"Thistle?"

"You have bright eyes. They see—o, they do see. The Gruagach knows you. He sees why. Be wise, o be wise, good children. Trust no iron. Be kind but be not foolish. The Gruagach sees, o yes, the green shadow on you. You are old, old as stones and your roots are deep: new growth on a hewn tree."

"You make no sense," said Ceallach. "Let him wake up. Let Rhys be. He never did you harm."

The Gruagach hugged itself and spun on one foot. "Go home, he must go home; the south must come to aid. Go home, go home, walk wisely through the shade. The four-footed friends will serve you while they can. The wind is coming and on it something rides—o I see, the Gruagach sees. Go away! Go away! The Gruagach has these children and the Man you cannot have!"

It was gone, it was straightforwardly gone, with only the sunlight in its place, and the ponies and Rhys' tall horse never starting from it. The bees kept up their humming, undaunted. The wind was gentle in the rushes.

And Rhys stirred in his sleep and waked with Ceallach and Meadhbh beside him. His eyes were peaceful at the first and then took alarm and shame at once.

"We were worried," Meadhbh explained as Rhys sat up on his hands. "You would not wake up."

Rhys had a desperate look, and ran a hand through his black hair. He looked at them, at the sky, at the streamside and the hills, seeming profoundly embarrassed.

"I have never done such a thing," Rhys said. He started to his feet, missed his dagger and found it on the ground. Again he looked about him and at them. "Did you sleep too?"

"No," said Meadhbh, sure that it had not been a dream, and that it was not for telling, though she wished to. She felt sorry for the man, who was almost a lord of sorts and very proud, and truly never one to be so careless in a charge. He would confess it to their father, she was sure. And their father would see through it all and worry for what had happened.

"You frightened us," Ceallach said.

Rhys said nothing to that, but walked to where the horse and ponies grazed, and they followed, not without looks at each other—not conspirators' glances, but troubled ones. They joined hands as they walked after Rhys. Meadhbh understood nothing of what the brown man had said; she doubted it made more sense to Ceallach—except that it was to them the brown man had come, and to them he had spoken, and said he came from Thistle, whatever her real name was.

Dark on their path: that he had promised. And something on the wind. But the sky was clear and blue and there was no hint of it. She did not take comfort of that: blue skies were quickly changed, and this one seemed very fragile, and the sunlight like reflection, even at noon. There had been something about roots and leaves; she made no sense of that, either. But it spoke of some kind of change in them, of iron—and neither she nor Ceallach could hold the dagger. Her hand still ached from trying.

Things of Eald and iron would not agree together. That was why their father had ridden out armorless and weaponless; and even now the pain went shivering through her mind, the iron pain, when the stone their father carried had such force or such danger in it he shielded it from her fingers, when he had fallen on the stairs after taking it and she had seen him in pain.

She had felt something like. She knew. And he went on carrying that stone, which was far more than any slender silver leaf. Her mother made him possets to drink so that he could rest. And at times there was still pain. Now she knew where it came from.

She hugged Floinn's shaggy neck and took up the reins and climbed into the saddle as Rhys mounted his tall black horse. Ceallach climbed up on Flann. The ponies started home without any touch of reins or heels, and the black horse went with them as if it were still a dream.

EIGHT

The Way to Donn

The wind blew warm on Ciaran's face and the horses moved in easy rhythm, a sleepy kind of progress up a road still well within Caer Wiell's lands, but the hills of An Beag's domains were at their left, across a rolling shagginess of hedges. There were freeholds hereabouts, where staunch dale families had settled on border land and held it. Caer Wiell aided such folk, who were Caer Wiell's bulwark; and if the company had turned aside to left or right they would have found welcome and a cup of ale gladly given to each, ale and not unlikely a supper offered, had they come at sundown. They prospered, these freeholds, and so the road proclaimed, barely fit for carts, but still traveled often enough that no grass grew in it, a fair fine road as roads went on the marches.

They wended up from the turning of it and met the Bainbourne again where it wandered, a reedy stream crossed here and there by fords and trampled by sheep, of which they saw several flocks in the distance; or by pigs, where Alhhard's steading set its back against the water, a rough cluster of buildings next old and twisted willows, and rough fences made of willow logs and stones the Bainbourne scoured. The place prospered. The boy who kept the pigs called out to the company as they came, and stood on the fence across Bainbourne to wave; others appeared, men and women, and dogs and children who pelted across the stream in a great splashing of water to run beside the horses.

"It be the lord," the children cried, jogging along beside the column, and there would be gossip from steading to steading by the fortnight; but Ciaran smiled to see them, and the horses tolerated the dogs and darting bodies. "Lord," the eldest shouted, a boy whose stride was longest and near that of a man, running along by his horse, outdistancing all the others. "Will you not come across to us? There be ale and cider."

"Thank your father," Ciaran said, "and wish all the house well from me. I cannot stay this time. Gods, Eada, your legs are longer, are they not?"

"Aye, lord." The boy panted along with all his kin outdistanced, and the last of the dogs about him. "That they be. And I know the bow, lord."

"Do you? But your father would have taught you."

"I have fifteen summers, lord."

The lad was falling behind now. He shouted the last. "So, well." Ciaran turned somewhat in the saddle. "When you have sixteen, then come to Caer Wiell a season."

The boy trotted to a halt among his dogs, waving his hand and grinning. The whole company waved back at the steading, and so the willows took it back again.

The horses protested, having caught a whiff of shed and shelter, and it took curb and heel to keep their minds to the road instead.

But the company moved with purpose, if safe among their own folk, in lands that knew them, and no man of the escort muttered or said anything of regret for the ale.

"The stars and sky tonight for all of us," Ciaran said. He looked beyond Beorc where Domhnull rode—silent, Domhnull, which he was not wont to be. *He is a boy*, thought Ciaran, Domhnull looked very young in that moment, affecting not to hear them—so young, so young Ciaran dared not half so much freedom as Beorc used with him; so young his pride was green and tender. *I was wrong ever to have agreed to this.* He thought of the boy Eada, running by the horses, eagerness for battle shining in young eyes which had seen no sight grimmer than autumn butchering, and he shuddered.

Moths and torches. The glory blinds them. O Domhnull, I never should have heard you.

"It is a long road," Ciaran said then quietly as they rode. "And there are places in it—Domhnull, the more I think on this—Listen," he said, having the youth's attention, marking the quickness of his eyes to imagined slight or praise. "The way by Lioslinn—I rode this when I was a boy and never since. But mind it lies near both Damh and Bradhaeth."

"I do mind it."

"It winds, between the hills once you have come up from the lake. There are rocks above you." For a space he tried to tell it, every stone and turn that he remembered, where they had hunted once, far afield from Donn, he and his brother and his cousins. Domhnull listened, frowning in his earnestness to remember all he could, and Ciaran felt again a narrowing despair. "I should remember," he said once, "if I saw it."

"I shall manage," said Domhnull and made light of it if only for his pleasing. "Lord, the sun will guide me; and I shall look for the spring. And for the rest, we will go quickly and stir up nothing; or outride it."

It did not comfort him, the more they rode within the sight of the hills where the way bent westerly. He rode silently and the men with him were quiet now for the most part, having fallen silent while he spoke and taking the contagion of stillness from him.

The mood had come on him gradually, and lay darker and darker, from the bright morning when they had left the keep, Meadhbh and Ceallach trotting along with them . . . *because it is safe*, he had said to Branwyn last; *because there is no cause that they should not ride in the fair center of our own lands, with Rhys to watch them. And to watch Caer Wiell while I am gone. No farther than the Crossroads. Is so much to be made of this?*

Now it seemed mad to have done, and a light sweat lay on his limbs, for all that the sun was sinking. *They must be safe by now*, he thought. *Rhys must be sitting in hold, they at the fire with Branwyn, Muirne too, and Leannan, and Rhys doubtless having a drink with Ruadhan.* . . . He built the ordinary things, a fragile structure, stone by familiar stone within his mind, while the sky turned golden and perilous about them and they came near to parting.

I wanted it so, he thought, recalling the peace of the morning. *I wished to believe it, the way I want to believe Domhnull will meet no hazard.*

But he will not. And they have not. He persuaded himself again, gathered up his courage in both his hands and tried to be cheerful. He smiled against the silences, rode with his hand attentive to the reins.

"Lord?" asked Domhnull.

"I was thinking how I am a prisoner, young friend, and how this great cousin of yours and I would be at swords-point if I were to go beyond Lioslinn. And yet—"

"Lord," said Beorc, "no."

"What, my guardian, not try you?"

"Lord," said Beorc, "I beg you."

"You are worried, old wolf." Ciaran heaved a sigh. "There would be no peace for me at home if I were to do that."

"I should be on my way," said Domhnull, glancing toward the distant hills where the sun was setting. "For my part, lord, I had as lief know you had the shorter ride on the morrow, and if you were home sooner than you had promised, you would make your lady wife the happier for it."

A while longer Ciaran rode in silence.

"Lord," said Domhnull. '

"Aye," he said. "So you are right." He reined his horse aside off the road, as they had stopped to rest many a time this day, not to tire the horses beyond quick recovery. But this time Domhnull and the four who would go with him unsaddled the horses they had ridden and set the gear on the five remounts, which thought ill of the matter.

"So you must take care," Ciaran said, still afoot when Domhnull and the others sat ahorse.

"Lord, I shall."

"You carry that token I gave you."

"Lord, I have not forgot it." A small smile played about Domhnull's mouth, a twinkle in his eye, so Ciaran smiled, reminded that somewhere, somehow this man had happened, instead of the boy he kept remembering, and that the man was strong and had his wits about him.

"Aye," he said, "speed you well, Domhnull."

So he had to send him, with little ado, making little of the uneasiness that troubled him; and so Beorc sent his cousin off and friends of the escort parted.

So beyond Caer Damh and by the shores of Lioslinn Domhnull would bear westward, a long ride yet to go before they should rest; and Ciaran looked after the dwindling figures, his hand staying his horse by the cheekstrap of its bridle.

Mist lay about them. The others could not see it, but there was mist, all the same, and trees rose about them straight as pillars when he looked with that Sight he had. The trees lay between on that plane and he lost sight of Domhnull, of the way they rode, which did not exist here. There was only tangle, and cold mist, and comfortless forest. He stood staring into it, quieting his horse which stood with him; but the men with him seemed like shadows less substantial than the trees.

"Lord," said Beorc, and thrust something loose and heavy into his hands, a skin of wine. "Here."

He drank. The wine seemed rough and strange.

"We might rest at Alhhard's steading," said Beorc. "There's that ale, remember."

"No," he said. He offered no reasons. Beorc asked none, willing to humor him in his whims, so long as they did not involve following after Domhnull. He thrust the vision away, brought the sky back golden.

He could not see in this place. The stone could bring him no help against it. He doubted, suddenly, everything he had done, but it had seemed wise till now . . . to defend Caer Wiell.

He thought of Donnchadh his brother, of Lioslinn in the sunlight, when they had climbed the hill above it; or again at Dun na h-Eoin, in the twilight; and then he realized with a strange shock of passing time that this was not the man he sent to. It would not be the boy, nor yet the man at Dun na h-Eoin, dark-bearded and slim, as he was not what he had been then. *He will have gone gray,* Ciaran thought with a shock, setting his foot into the stirrup and rising into the saddle. He had never reckoned with the years. *He is older than I and darker; so the years will sit harder on him. He will have gone to leanness: he was always thin.* He tried to build this man in his mind, cast away the image for the one he remembered, brother, companion. Longing came over him then, to be where Domhnull rode. The fair-haired boy he had been would have leapt to horse and ridden, defying all the hazards. He had ridden for the King once, and in that wildness he had gone, and parted from his brother.

So I would come back to him, he thought, remembering better times. He would leap from his horse by the gates. *See, I have come home.*

But it was the lord of Caer Wiell and the lord of Caer Donn now, and the gestures between them must agree with that, full of wariness and the weight of years and anger.

I have concern for you, he had wished Domhnull to say to Donnchadh in his name, but he could not even send that simple thing. *I ask peace,* he had said instead, humbly, caring nothing for his pride, *in these times. This silence profits neither of us.*

There was more, if Donnchadh should be disposed to listen.

Lioslinn lay black by starlight, reflecting nothing, not even shimmers on its surface. It stretched far and shallow, and for sound here there were only the creak of frogs and the soughing of the wind in the reeds.

"I have seen it fairer," said Boc, who was oldest of the escort.

"More bog than lake," said Domhnull, "by the reek of it." He had set eyes on it, but only from a distance, and now riding close beside its midnight shore with the stench of decay going up from it dispelled any illusion he had still cherished of it as mirror of the hills. It lay beside them like a pit, darker than the reeds, and the chiefest concern in his mind was that some misstep of his horse might put him into a reaching arm of it, some hole unseen in the dark. The night was moonless, and the dark sky had seemed friendly until now, shielding them from Caer Damh as they passed it on the road.

They rested the horses as they could, and kept silent for the most part, leaving the conversation to the frogs and nightbirds. Voices seemed to carry all too clearly, and the night was listening.

They were good men lord Ciaran had sent with him, Domhnull knew; indeed, they daunted him with their knowing what ought to be done before he said it; or knowing before he knew it, for they were older than he, and Boc many years so. *Sent to watch me,* he thought, having less and less confidence that he led them at all; but they would never say as much. Only what little he had to tell them he said in brief and noted every breath of theirs, every shift of stance that seemed to say to him: *yes, boy, yes, we were wondering when you would say so,* or perhaps: *well, boy, but we would not advise it.*

He had faced this journey with more confidence in the morning, by daylight, parting Caer Wiell and far from Lioslinn's boggy, reeking shore. He had, he thought, taken a great deal on himself. He had seen that much in Beorc's eyes when they parted, a cool kind of reckoning he had gotten in the drillyard.

Well, lad, Beorc had told him more than once, *get to it. Do something or do nothing, and if you're truly one of the world's fools, then the world is sure to learn it.*

The frogs went silent at their splashing. Something started away with a splash of its own, and the horses did not like it. Somehow, by some persistence of his horse or that the others kept reining back, he would end up in the lead again though he reckoned that Boc knew this ground better—he must, for Boc had been here and he never had; but at last he took the foremost position for his own and held it, seeking with his eyes and senses and thinking perhaps that they should not try to ride this ground at all, but walk ahead of their horses.

It was old, this place. Legend said so, but more, he felt it in his bones, that the lake was no wholesome place. He thought of water-horses, of selkies and such like: if there ever was a place where a fuath might lurk it was Lioslinn, among the reeds and moss. There might be shellycoats and bogles, to come rattling out of the bog with reaching fingers.

A thing hissed at them and dove with a heavy splash. His horse went sideways, and trod afterward as if it were poised to spring; he curbed it, his heart clenched and trying to beat again.

"Gods know," said Boc, "what that was."

"Come," Domhnull said. A cold was down his back. His

teeth wanted to chatter. "Stay together. This place is too boggish to have one of the horses bolting."

"I have them," said Brom, half a whisper from behind.

"To think," said Boc, "they named this a road once."

"The lake has risen," said Domhnull, "or I've led us amiss." His eyes strained into the dark, where the hills rose up in a blackness deeper than that beside them. "That must be our way yonder."

"Gods grant," muttered Boc.

The nearness tempted him, to urge the horses to speed. He resisted, plodding their slow and patient way, and now and again there were other splashes and the sound of something swimming.

No one spoke. The hooves sucked and slid in mud. The horses snorted, closer and closer to that cloven wall of rock that loomed before them. The ground grew more solid, the steps more firm, and once, indistinct in the dark, a cairn of stones bulked beside the way.

"We are out of it," said Boc.

"I would not be glad to camp here," Domhnull said, feeling his horse laboring with exhaustion. "Best, I think, to change horses and be out of here entirely."

"Aye," said Boc, full earnestly.

They did so, and Domhnull passed round the wine he had from Branwyn: "This should go first," he said, and felt their spirits lighten for it before they took to the saddle again, riding into the narrows.

"Lord," said Beorc, and Ciaran looked up at him in the dark, from his seat beside the spring. The others lay asleep, or feigning it, even the youth on watch.

"I sent the lad to sleep," Ciaran said. "Go to sleep yourself; I will wake Boda when I feel the need."

"I promised—"

"—Branwyn. Aye. To hover by me." He frowned, for Beorc squatted down before him, solid as a boulder. "I need no nurse, old wolf."

"Then go to sleep, my lord."

"You harry me, Beorc. If—" A shudder took him, which he tried to prevent. The land rose about him gray with daylit mist, with ill woven in it. "The sun has risen."

"Lord?" Beorc settled there, arms locked, patient of any madness.

"The sun in Eald, Beorc. When things have most power. But

it is cold. Cold. This land has come back; she said it. It was lost
to Eald and somehow it has come back again.''

"How—come back?''

"Would that I knew how.'' He felt the chill again and touched
the stone within his collar. He shut his eyes, seeking with that
second sight, through all the maze that pent his vision. The stone
seemed like ice in his hand. "I am cut off on all sides. It
frightens me, Beorc. *She* was afraid. Trees, she said, as if one of
the Sidhe could be alarmed at trees. But these are ghosts. And I
cannot see past them. Neither could she, I think.''

"Lord, let it alone.''

"And sleep?''

"Let me rouse the men. We will set out now, and get you
home again.''

"I have sent Domhnull out there. I do not think I should have
done it. The longer I am out here the less I find this place
comfortable.''

"He's a clever lad, and Boc is with him; and Caith besides.
And Caer Damh has lost its yen for mischief, look you, not a stir
from them all winter.''

"They have been quiet,'' he agreed. "But, Beorc, the woods
go *around* An Beag as they do us. I am not so sure of Damh.
And I can no longer find the sea.''

"What woods?'' Beorc asked patiently, questioning a madman.
"What sea?''

"Give me your hand, Beorc.''

Beorc settled to his knees and gave it, and so Ciaran drew it to
the stone.

O gods, Beorc said, or tried to say; and there was all of
Beorc's self with him, far too close, and the trees were about
them both. The earth began to sink beneath them.

No, Ciaran said, and took the stone in his own hand, trembling.
The open land was about them again. The nightwind blew gently
on his sweating face, and Beorc still knelt before him. It had
been close, that third Eald which was Death's own. The wind
from it still whispered.

"O gods,'' Beorc said, "how do you bear it?''

"Did you see the trees, old wolf, how they grow here?''

"I saw something. Like shadows. I'm not sure what shape
they had.''

"You have iron about you,'' said Ciaran. "I should not have
done that. Beorc, I should not have sent him. There is something
amiss I took no account of. This is not the Eald I knew. It blinds
me. I think it would blind her. And I have less and less trust of it

now that I'm out here near it.'' He looked into Beorc's face, finding fear where fear was not accustomed to be, and doubt, where doubt had never been. It occurred to him that he might lose this man, that he might already have lost him, his loyalty, his love, whatever it was that a man gave who had served him as Beorc had. The man that Beorc followed had never faltered, never erred, not to this degree, not with the lives of all else he loved. Small wonder Beorc hearkened now to Branwyn, born to this land as she was, heir of the Cearbhallain, as she was. Like Rhys. Like all he had inherited. He came as interloper, and led them all amiss. ''I don't know what to do, Beorc. I don't *know*.''

''Lord, who does, in this? You have done the best thing. And if it were wrong, then Domhnull will make the best of it if it can be made: you sent those who can bend what can be bent.''

''Blind.''

''With the Sidhe's blessing on him. Do you not recall it? On all of us who serve you.''

''Can you remember, then? Do you remember?''

''Not with clear sight, maybe, but I remember *something*. That I have seen the Sidhe. I remember—someone at the table; and there was silver, and she was dressed in white and gray—''

''No gray. She had no cloak about her.''

''Or something like. But she spoke to me. I remember. *My weakness and my strength*, she said. And about dark and morning. I remember that.''

''There was a time,'' he said, ''that the stone let me see. I have seen dragons, Beorc. Once. I have seen the Sidhe ride to war. They are memories, or something like, pent in the stone, but I can't find them now. Only the mist and the ghosts, and I have led us deeper into them, and sent Domhnull and Boc even farther. But the King . . . the King, if he stood with us and not against, if I could win my brother back to reason—'' He shook his head. ''O gods, this mist surrounds him. Maybe I was to do nothing. But they forget, the Sidhe; or they have their own concerns and Men are small and brief among them. Maybe if Men are to be helped—that is for me to do.''

''Lord, let us get you back to the hold. Tonight.''

''No,'' he said, just that. *No*. ''Let me be.''

Beorc nodded slowly, gathered himself up and retreated to his blanket, spread on the ground beneath the oak, where the earth was bare. The others slept. The horses were still. The wind stirred, in this world. The others were bound in leaden stillness.

Ciaran sat, and leaned his eyes upon his hand, for they stung with weariness, though there was no sleep in them. The mist gathered about him again when he looked outward with his heart.

Then a small lumpish thing hopped out of it and perched before him in elvish day. For a moment his heart froze in fear, but there was no ill in this creature.

"Man," it said, hugging its arms about its knees, "Man, o Man, this is a lost place. *Fair,* she said, a fair land, but Eald is strange here."

"What are you, wight?"

It sniffed and wrinkled its nose. "Wight, *wight* he names me. O why do you sit, Man? Things are amiss, amiss here. I have met the children and seen them home to the Cearbhallain's walls; and the dark man with them."

"What have you to do with them?" he asked. His heart was pounding. "What cause had you to meet them?"

A lank shaggy hand touched a shaggy throat. "Eald is about them. *She* sent me. O there is much amiss, Man."

"With them?"

"They are safer than you, far safer. O Man, Man, Man, there is dark, dark about your path. The Gruagach has seen it. Dark and bright together."

"She has sent you."

"To guard the children. She said there were saucers of milk for me. And the Gruagach has had them. He has seen your people, fine, polite folk they are, but o Man, there is trouble near them."

"Where?"

A shaggy arm reached out, long fingers waggled.

"The Gruagach. Is that yourself?"

It bobbed, still crouching, and its eyes glinted in their darkness. It seemed to shiver. Whites showed as its eyes rolled. Its voice grew thin.

"Dark, dark and dark it lies—
O Man, there is ill, ill, ill."

It was gone. Vanished. He sat on the cold earth and a chill had come on him.

He leapt to his feet. "Beorc!" he shouted. "Wake!"

Men reached for weapons, scrambling to stand, sleep-mazed and frightened.

"Ride back," he said, "Tuathal, get to horse; ride back to Alhhard's steading and send the boy to Caer Wiell: they have a pony, bid him go, and tell my lady we have need of half the men up here. The rest must stay with her. The rest of you, we are going north a ways.''

"Lord," said Beorc, "you must not."

"Come with me," he said, and Beorc hesitated half a breath, then went after him. He had not doubted it, as he did not doubt now which way he was going, and that he was beyond advice.

They followed, muttering questions and doubts among themselves, but Tuathal was off as soon as he could fling a saddle on his horse, and for the rest of them it was northward.

Amiss, he kept thinking as they rode, and perhaps his face was grim, for Beorc fell in beside him asking nothing at all until they were well on the road again.

"Lord," Beorc objected, "we are nine men, and Domhnull too far ahead of us to recall him."

He said nothing to this. There was nothing to say, but perhaps Beorc had hoped there was an answer.

"You are not armored," Beorc said. "And against some things no Sidhe luck is proof."

There was iron. It made his bones ache, even such as the men about him wore. He argued nothing in return, only rode, and Beorc fell silent.

So they came beyond Caer Damh, in that strange fell hour when the sun was only promise; and far away on either side the land seemed wild and empty. The light had caught Lioslinn, which spread itself before them, a glimmering only, to show that it was water; but the day would make it mirrorlike, turning sky and earth upside down. The pass showed beyond, cloven between the hills. The horses shuddered under them for weariness.

Ciaran drew rein, seeking outward with the stone, but the mist was thick, making all his sight gray.

Then he felt the stirring of the land, the poison of iron. It was ambush.

"Men are there," he said.

"What men?" Beorc asked, implicit in his faith. "Can you tell that?"

"No. But about the lake: Caer Damh, perhaps, or the Bradhaeth folk." He shivered, and possessed himself again, in cold clear sight, with the dawning on the water. "Here we stay, Beorc."

"Nine men."

"Well," he said, "Tuathal will find us."

Beorc looked on him, ill-pleased by humor, then gave it the short reaction it deserved and gazed off toward the pass. "Gods grant Domhnull got through."

"So," said Ciaran, and stood in his stirrup, stepping down

from the saddle. His horse was lathered. He patted its neck, and it stood three-footed. "Well, if things have gone wrong, we are soon to learn it. I think he has gotten through; I might feel it else. But when he comes back again this way—I think that we should be here."

"I should be here," said Beorc, sliding heavily from his horse, a weight of man and metal. "You—"

"I can see somewhat, and know them coming. What man of you else can do that?"

"One Bradhaeth arrow. That is all it needs, lord, and then how do I face your lady?"

"Ah," he said softly. "Well, but you will save me. You have done it before, old wolf. I have trust in you."

"Gods help us," Beorc muttered.

NINE
Bearing Word

The sun began going down and Branwyn waited, in the hall, by the fireside; and Rhys hung about the hall, which was not his wont, but his brow had been dark since yesterday.

"I did not like this," Rhys had said when he had brought Meadhbh and Ceallach home. "I like it less now."

So he stayed and fretted, her cousin, and shared their dinner with them. "My lord will come when he will come," Branwyn had said, having made up her mind to it, resolved not to fret herself with expectations, for it was no small ride that Ciaran made. She knew it, having ridden here and there with him in their first years, as far as she ever had ridden in her life, which was to the sight of the Bradhaeth. She had reckoned already that there was no profit in standing all anxious on the walls, nor even in keeping supper waiting. When it came the hour she had her supper with Meadhbh and Ceallach and Muirne, and Rhys as well, and Leannan, who played now softly as she spun, the fine wool making a thread in her fingers, so, so, so, by firelight; and Meadhbh doing likewise, and Muirne; and Ceallach at nothing in particular.

"You were at making something," Branwyn said to him, for

Ceallach often carved with his knife, and now his eyes seemed
sad and his hands unnaturally idle. "Where have you put it?"

"I forgot," said Ceallach softly, with that same desperate
look, and a small suspicion of ill crept into Branwyn's heart, the
sense of something wrong with her son as Meadhbh's downcast
obedience was unlike her, her uncommon attentiveness to the
spinning she hated. Branwyn drew her lips to a taut line and kept
the wool running, this way and that with the turning spindle. She
wanted to ask, and did not—*Iron,* she thought wildly, *iron, iron,
iron in that little knife. Ciaran could not bear it, and now my son
and daughter.*

Rhys stirred abruptly and walked out, again to the wall, she
reckoned, and never her fingers faltered. Something was amiss
that Rhys knew and she could not ask it, not with Meadhbh and
Ciaran to listen, and in no wise would they want to go to bed
tonight until they had seen their father.

"Was it good, your riding yesterday?" She was light in her
asking, as if she had never in the world objected to their going.
Two bright heads nodded, catching glints of firelight, and there
was not a glance from their eyes. "Well," she said, lips pursed,
the spindle turning ceaselessly, "well, your father has his ways
about him. I recall when we were younger we would ride out,
when your grandmother was still alive, you can remember her?
And you would stay with her and Muirne. And we would ride and
ride, once as far as the border, your father and I. And do you
know, he would chat with every farmer. Come along, I would
say—sometimes we had cause to hurry. But they could always
hold him, with ale to try or some complaint to give— Many a
time he would go tramping off across some soggy orchard
soiling his boots to see how the fruit set on, or off to see some
steading's new plowed field up by the border."

"He would not delay now," Meadhbh said looking up, and
her eyes were fierce. "He would be thinking of Domhnull."

There was such temper in her daughter. It dismayed her, how
so small words offended. Branwyn was quiet after, only keeping
to her spinning, taking her offering back. It was the Donn blood
in her son and daughter, that made them wild, and sometimes, as
now, that wildness wounded. One of them was enough, her
husband breaking out in stubbornness, brushing aside all her
counsel. She worked, flung all her attention at the thread. Her
children wanted nothing of her comfort. Her son sat disconsolate,
her daughter—*O Meadhbh, Meadhbh, Meadhbh! if I could hold
you*— But they were too old for holding. Nothing she said to her
daughter was ever right. And Ciaran would not uphold her.

His daughter. He was his son. Could I not have my daughter? Am I always to be wrong with her? Round and round, the spindle. A bright-haired girl a-horseback, riding in the meadow, red her hair and black the horse, like fire and deepest shadow.

The thread broke in her hands. She shook her head and bit her lip and mended it, mending the vision, the fat bay pony Meadhbh loved. *No,* she thought, afraid of the sight she had seen, Meadhbh and not Meadhbh, and not the bay white-stockinged pony. She saw leaves in her mind, and water and greenness, the child walking into the forest. *His children,* she thought, *both his.* She wanted to talk to them, to chatter idly, to talk of something to fill the silence, but Leannan played that song he had made, sweet and minding her of that night in hall, after which all Leannan's songs had changed, and his old eyes had taken to looking into distances while he played.

A Sidhe song, she thought, the wool flowing smoothly again, and the harpsong moved like water. A memory rose up in her, of that night before this fire, and the smell of the boughs she had brought and the candles; but for all her gifts the Sidhe had ignored her and touched all the rest. *Feochadan. Thistle. So I called her. And now the children name her so. But it is Arafel. I know her name. I might call her. Where is my husband? I would say. Why does my son have such a look and my daughter spurn me?*

She looked at Meadhbh and tried a smile, finding her daughter looking up. Meadhbh smiled back but it was hollow. "That looks very fine," Branwyn said. How often had she found fault? Too often?

Her daughter frowned and bent her head to the hated work again, then glanced up. "I hear a horse," she said.

The harpsound died upon the air.

"Meadhbh," said Branwyn, but Ceallach was already running to the stairs, and Meadhbh was on his heels, trailing yarn and wool together.

"Lady," said Muirne, who need not have said a thing: there were hooffalls, but of one horse, and the sound of the lesser gate. One rider.

Branwyn said nothing, but kept at her spinning. Muirne rescued the yarn that Meadhbh had trampled and sat down again in her place, started the spindle turning again.

"I will go out and see," said Leannan.

Branwyn nodded, never stopping the work of her fingers as if it worked a charm against calamity. *I must not run, not I, Caer Wiell's lady. It will be some small thing, some one of the boys strayed late and far at hunting. O gods, but one rider, but only one—It is some message, something amiss; he is not coming; he would not come alone, not he, not Ciaran; last to retreat, my husband, if there were trouble.*

There were voices, calling this way and that. Muirne's hands and work fell into her lap. Branwyn never stopped, not though light steps sounded on the stair, Leannan's, returning.

"My lady," said the harper, "it's some lad come with a message. He's coming up."

"Well," she said, and let her work into the basket, "well—"

But more than one was coming up the stairs now: Rhys, and Ruadhan and a sweating farmer-lad with tousled dark hair; and Meadhbh and Ceallach hurrying after.

"Here is the lady," said Rhys. "Your message, lad."

"Lady." the boy was short of breath, seemed prone to stammer, an agony of waiting. "Lady, the lord he be going up by Lioslinn last night, his man he bid me tell you. Rode back last night, this man—Tuathal were his name. He said the lord had sent him, and word were I should ride here, but our old pony, lady, she were hard put to run much, and I did try, lady, but I could come no faster—"

"Was there more than that?"

"Aye, this Tuathal said the lord said half the men must come to Lioslinn and quick as may be. He said, he said, lady, the rest must stay by you."

"What token?" said Rhys. "Did Tuathal give a token?"

"No, lord, he said he had nothing, that the lord had sent him so quick—I be Eada, Alhhard's son, up by high Bainbourne; and they passed in the day, they did, and I saw this Tuathal with the lord, and after, in the mid of the night he come—lord, my father and grandfather and my brother be gone to him, and my sister run overland to fetch them from Haraleah and all—there be men there—best bowmen in all the border."

"Well done," said Branwyn. "Well done in that—Ruadhan—"

"Half the men," Ruadhan said, "as quickly as they can arm, by your leave, lady."

"Go," she said, "go. Muirne: get this lad somewhat for his stomach."

"Lady," said Eada, "I'd ride back again, where my folk be—"

"Where you choose," she said. She looked at Meadhbh and Ceallach, at their pale faces. "Doubtless some matter with Caer Damh," she said, for them, wishing to believe it. "And he has wished to keep the way open for Domhnull's riding back again."

Ruadhan had left, taking the boy Eada with him; Rhys should have gone, but stayed, looking at her with that black-eyed stare of his.

"Branwyn, cousin, I am going south. Tonight."

"This is some small thing," she said, "some matter with Damh, and they have dwindled—"

"This is a small thing," said Rhys, "but it is on me I should go south, now, tonight. I should have gone long since; now I know it." He came and offered his hands; she took them, looked up at him.

"I can spare you ten of the men with me; none that are bound with Ruadhan."

"I shall go faster alone." His hands slipped from hers. Meadhbh and Ceallach stood aside for him as he strode for the door. He went out down the stairs into the dark, and Meadhbh and Ceallach stared after him, hands linked one with the other, so solemn, so unnaturally solemn—

"Meadhbh," said Branwyn. "Ceallach. The men will see to it."

They turned. They stared at her with the stillness of thoughts she did not fathom. Not amazed, not bewildered. Anxious.

She held out her arms to them, wanting them. They came, and she folded them in her arms, and they rested there against her skirts. She told them no lies. One could not lie to them. It was the Sight; she guessed it. She might have asked them questions, but feared the answers.

"Rhys is going home to Dryw," she whispered; but they would know that. "To your great-uncle Dryw in the mountains in the south; there are all our cousins, and if there is trouble your father will come riding back in a moment; and we will shelter behind our walls if it comes to that, but it will not. Once our kinsmen come from the south, then there will be a reckoning, whatever the matter is. And perhaps Domhnull will persuade your other uncle from Donn, perhaps he will listen: your father at least is trying. But however it is, we will be safe here."

He has no armor, she was thinking. *O gods, at Lioslinn, in the passes up by Damh and him unshielded.*

"The road goes through the forest," said Ceallach, of the way that Rhys took. "And over the Caerbourne."

"Hush," she said, "hush, Rhys knows that road, and will he not be safe there? The Sidhe would never harm him."

They said nothing, nothing at all to that, but no one was comforted.

Soon the noise of the horsemen sounded departing the yard,

and the greater gate groaned open. Branwyn kissed her son and daughter each and looked at Muirne. "Go find Siodhachan. And Hugi. Tell them I set Siodhachan over the hold and bid Hugi take nine men with him, scatter and rouse the farms from Gearr's northward and west and east—but quietly, quietly, no watchfires must be lit, nothing to rouse An Beag. Tell them—no, bid them both come to me, and I will tell them. Haste, Muirne."

Muirne sped.

"What shall we do?" asked Ceallach.

"Go down," she said, "Ceallach, tell Cein and Cobhan and the boys to bring in the horses at far pasture; Meadhbh—Yes, go with him. But neither of you without the walls: hear me."

"Yes," said Meadhbh, and dropped a kiss upon her cheek; Ceallach pressed her hands and ran, and Meadhbh scurried after.

He will say it was all unneeded, she thought. *I shall have alarmed the countryside. Perhaps An Beag will hear it and o gods, bear word of it to the King and do us hurt for it. Caer Wiell, they will say, is warlike. And Rhys, gods, Rhys will have roused Dryw, a moving of their forces northward. The King will know it beyond any doubt. And how then will we fare?*

She almost wavered. But her messengers were gone, Rhys away from the gates, the riders sped for the marches. She clenched her hands and waited.

The hold loomed shapeless on its hill in the darkness, a mass which thrust up only one of its corners against the backdrop of starlight. The rest was hid against the higher hills about it; but it massed large, like some crouching giant above its stream-cut valley.

Perhaps, Domhnull thought, they should have stopped before this and not pressed on, but they had begun to come under sight of cottages set high on the flanks of the hills as they entered twilight—no great expanse of tillage, not like Caer Wiell, but pasturage throughout the hills; and dogs, most likely, and wart folk who might view strangers with suspicion. It seemed best to him to keep moving, quietly, and not to chance the country.

"No lights," said Boc. "Gods, how dark that pile is."

"I think it is the face we see," Domhnull said. "Its walls and not the keep itself." Rough, lord Ciaran had called his native hold; mostly shepherds, flocks scattered in every fold of the hills round about; a keep which had grown up as chance and invention built it, a wall here, a shed there, a hall of rough stone and timbers—it had never had to stand siege, Ciaran had said, except by wind and weather.

They rode closer, the lonely clop of the horses' hooves echoing off the cliff.

"Are we not reported?" Brom wondered, rearmost, who led the other horses. "Surely the shepherds saw us coming."

"Gods know," Domhnull said, and unslung his shield from his back where he had carried it. So did the others then, a rattle of wood and metal. With that thumping on his left arm he felt at least some cover about him, for they rode near brush and jagged stone as the road followed the streamcourse. It was a place apt for ambush. His weary horse picked up its head, skittish at the sound of the shield, snorted in the darkness. He touched his heels to it and it moved a little faster on the dark trail, past trees and up again, with the walls and gates rising now above them.

"Caer Donn," Domhnull called out, "ho the watch, Caer Donn!"

"Who is it?" a voice drifted back to them. "What purpose?"

He was relieved at that hailing, reined in his horse with his men about him. "I am Domhnull Gaelbhan mac Gaelbhan, Beorc Scaga's-son's cousin, of my lord of Caer Wiell the messenger, and four men my escort. Open your gate for us."

There was long delay. Domhnull sat his horse and kept his shield on his arm while his eyes scanned the rim of the wall. His heart was beating as hard as it had at the worst of their journey, dreading words this time, not arrows: go away, go back unheard, our lord will not admit you. No man behind him spoke, Boc, Caith, Dubhlaoch; and Brom who led the horses. Hooves shifted, clattered, restless: the horses saw a gate, thought of hay and straw and shelter, unwitting of all politics.

"You will come in by the lesser gate," the voice hailed them from the wall, "your shields at your backs, Domhnull mac Gaelbhan."

It was no more than reasonable, at this hour, with the dark behind them. "Do what they ask," Domhnull said, and slung his own shield to his back, tapped his horse in the ribs and rode forward as the lesser gate eased open outward, showing torchlight beyond it.

He passed beneath the arch, among boys who came to take his horse, no different than at Caer Wiell. He stepped from the saddle, looked about him, not missing the men who stood above the gate: archers, if they were needed. Caith came through, and Boc and Dubhlaoch, Brom last of all, with the string of horses. The gate slammed shut. The yard passed into the confusion ordinary with lads and half a score of horses.

"My lord will see you," a man came to say, a graying,

square-faced man wearing a gold chain that glinted in the torchlight, wealthier than the look of this place.

Everywhere was timber. Not a hold for war, lord Ciaran had said: it was far too much of wood, a mass of wood and stone before them, like some shepherd's cottage turned fortress, as if some giant had tumbled a hundred such cottages together: here was a wall, there a corner, a second story of wood and stone overhanging, and some of the roof timbers jutting out from all of it. Steps went up to the doors, thundering and creaking under their heavy tread, and so they came into a smoky, timbered hall, a great long table in the midst of it, a fireplace burning, torches lit, so that light chased the shadows; and a great carved chair where a man sat with others standing by him.

Donnchadh, Domhnull thought, finding uncomfortable this place, this sitting in chairs like some minor king, when his own lord would have come down to the yard to meet a guest, or at least stood up to meet him.

"Domhnull mac Gaelbhan," said Donnchadh—there was no brother—likeness, none. This man was lean and gray as a wolf, where Ciaran was fair and golden. Half-brothers, they were. "My brother has some word for me, does he?"

"Lord, he sent a ring to you." Domhnull slid it from his hand—easily it slipped, when Ciaran had worn it on his smallest finger. He offered it, and gave it when Donnchadh held out his palm.

"Yes," said Donnchadh, "I gave it him."

"My lord sent it for a token." He looked into Donnchadh's eyes and for a moment lost all its thread of thought, everything unraveling—*I cannot,* he thought, *I cannot do this.*

"And wishes?"

"Peace," he said. "Peace and other things . . . He said—" His wits rallied; he gathered his forces, embarrassed. "Lord, his word was that he wished peace. That foremost. He says that silence profits neither. He spoke with me—" *O gods, this is not easy. This man hates him.* "I am close to him. I know his heart. He thinks often of Donn, has thought, through the years, and wants to see you. Go to him, he said to me, and answer his questions, whatever he might want to ask—and bring back news again, and perhaps—"

"Perhaps?"

Shame flooded his face with heat. The word tangled on his tongue, echoed in this hostile hall. "Forgiveness."

Long silence afterward. Donnchadh stared at him, looked

down at the ring, looked up again and his eyes were less fierce. "That is strange to hear from my brother."

"His word, lord."

"I have waited many years," said Donnchadh. His lips clamped taut. He looked down and slipped the ring to his own hand. "Well," he said then, "well, Domhnull of Caer Wiell. I know your cousin."

"Yes," he said, "lord." That little seemed safest.

"News. Is it news my brother wants? Well. You have had a long road and a dangerous, and I am bound to listen. I have long thought he might have sent to me; and tomorrow you will tell me what is in his mind. In the meanwhile—in the meanwhile, there is rest and food, whatever you have need of." He beckoned to the man who stood nearest at his shoulder. "Geannan, see you to it."

"Lord," said Domhnull, "thank you."

"Tomorrow we shall talk at some length," said Donnchadh, "and I shall have thought, and you will. Go with Geannan."

Domhnull made his respects and his escort with him, and followed after the slight man in rich clothing who led them from the hall.

My lord, he thought, *would call for food and drink in hall, would be frank and open-handed.* He dismissed such carping thoughts. It was another hall, another custom, a sterner lord. He felt young before this man, young and simple, and felt the eyes of Boc and the others on his shoulders, expecting him to uphold Caer Wiell's honor, while bowing and giving courtesies in this place, before this wolf-eyed lord who sat high in the councils of the King in Dun na h-Eoin.

Pages came, meeting them in the hallway beyond the great hall. "I shall show you where you will lodge," said Geannan, "and the lads will see your men well fed and comfortable."

"I will go with my men," Domhnull said, but Geannan soberly caught his arm and drew him on.

"We would not have you say in Caer Wiell that we lodged you meanly, sir Domhnull; you will not report my lord in that way. Come, come, no mean lodging for your men; plenty of ale and perhaps cook will find some of that lamb we had for dinner. For yourself, perhaps some wine, and I know some of that lamb is left, and perhaps a slice or two of that good ham we had. I shall entreat the cook myself, and hot water, yes, and a fine feather bed, I'll warrant will be far better than the saddle. Did you ride straight on, then?"

"We had come into your lands. We thought it best to come and give an account of ourselves straightway."

"Wise, yes; the shepherds have the dogs out by night throughout the hills. There's little stirs but what they set to it. Ho, page, where are you going? Go straight ahead with that light: open up the west chamber."

Sir Domhnull he had become. This man Donnchadh had sent beside him spoke him fairly, delivered him to a room of wooden walls and fine appointments, sent the page scurrying with orders for fire, water, servants. Donnchadh from close-handed began then to seem generous beyond all expectation. He was dazed by this, and yet afraid.

Where am I in this great place? he wondered. *And where are Boc and the rest of us in this rambling warren?* He shivered, and looked anxiously in Geannan's direction as the man left him with promises of food and wine to follow, with a flurry of servants seeing to the fire, the fine soft bed, the warming of water for his washing. He was afraid. He did not know why this was so, only that it was in the air, the walls, a silence in which the soft sounds the servants made were all too loud. He remembered the shores of Lioslinn, the silences of the passes, the uncanny stillness of the rocks.

I have done a foolish thing, he thought, wishing he and his escort had never been parted; and then he shook off the feeling as too much caution. *I start at shadows,* he decided, suspecting the lord of Donn of some vague and tangled irony, to house him like a lord, exaggerated courtesy. *I should have been sharp with him,* he thought, wishing he were older or wiser in statecraft, or somehow more subtle in the ways of lords other than his own; or at least that he knew how to treat such courtesies as they offered.

The shadows were deep by the river, where the road ran, and the water whispered louder than the leaves. Rhys went warily in this place, marking how desolate it had become, how in want of tending—the King's road that linked all Caerdale with the plain, and all unused by honest folk, or by Caer Wiell in these years. He rode with all his weapons, with his saddlebags full of Cook's gifts, and now with his shield upon his arm, for he came to that point which ran between the river and An Beag.

Now, now, he asked speed of his horse, knowing silence would not serve him. It was less than likely that An Beag would watch the road, that any of those bandits would be devoted enough to duty to sit out on the riverbank in ambush in the rare hope of a man of Caer Wiell to murder—but anything was possible with trouble abroad in the land.

Brush loomed close on either side. Grass had grown in the roadway, and here and there a bush had taken hold, or brambles flung their spite out where they might rake the horse. The black gelding disliked this nighttime running, this uncertain ground: he used the spurs he seldom gave it and kept it going, reckless of such hazards.

It spent its strength, began to labor under his armed weight when they had come well toward the hills. He let it slow its pace at last, still beside the river, and now tending to Caerbourne Ford, the place he liked least of all.

The trees took him then in their embrace of willow fronds, trailing like a curtain darker than the starlit skies, caressing, cutting him and the beast off from sight—whisper of leaves and water. The horse danced and shied suddenly, finding something to alarm it. He touched it with the spurs, fended the willow leaves with his shield.

Now came Eald. He felt it, the haunted quality of the shore before him.

Now lend me luck, he wished, remembering that one had shed a blessing on him. He kept her memory in his eyes, in the dark before him—*o Sidhe, you promised.*

He found the ford, itself more perilous in the dark, in length of time untried: the river might have carved new ways, made pits to trap horse and rider, brought down uncertain sands instead of solid bottom. He slid down and led the horse for prudence, waist deep in the Caerbourne's sluggish water.

The horse plunged. A thing slid past his thighs, large and live and horrid. He kept the reins and stumbled on, struggling in the water, and now the whisper of the river had the sound of laughter. The shore wavered before him. A second time the touch came at his legs, his waist, soft hands reached upward, clinging to his armor.

He flung himself toward the shallow water, fell to his knees and made the horse stumble by the pull on the reins, then regained his feet and hastened through the reeds, on soft and yielding mud, past dead and breaking branches.

He set his foot in the stirrup, heavy with his weight of metal, with the horse shifting this way and that and starting to move at once. It threw its head as he hit the saddle, and leapt forward, catching panic; he reined it hard, for branches whipped at them: they went blind and at hazard.

He held it; it walked, shivering. He shivered likewise, soaked to the skin and remembering what had touched him.

Each-uisge, Ciaran had said. Water horse. River nix. A thing to frighten children. He feared as he had never feared in battle, in this path that he had taken, and ever and again he heard the sound of hooves, like a horse running where no horse could run, like the thunder of a gallop that grew loud and soft by turns, now on this side of the path and now on that, where the way to his own lands bordered Eald.

"Grant you mercy," he whispered to it. "We were quiet neighbors."

He did not give way to panic, not even when eyes like coals stared at him from out the thicket. It might do him harm, he knew it; but it went beside him, and his horse shuddered and shivered and snorted at its presence, that moved on hooves.

"Pooka," he said, "you do not frighten me. I have leave to pass here, and you cannot stop me."

The eyes never came again. The beat of hooves stayed with him.

TEN

Caer Donn

The morning came quietly in Caer Donn, a hush so deep and wide Domhnull waked slowly, eyes searching the place a moment, finding wooden walls and not the stone of his own room in Caer Wiell about him nor the swaying of a horse under him, but the steadiness of a bed softer than his at home, the breaking of full sun through the slitted window.

Daylight, he thought, ashamed, recalling that he had finally, far, far toward the dawning settled into sleep; and waked at first light and found his limbs still heavy, the place so quiet he was sure he had waked even before the servants were stirring. *A moment more,* he had thought then and shut his eyes, cherishing the warm spot he had made on the feather mattress, beneath the covers, and he had slept again, after all his restlessness, his night of listening to sounds where no sounds were, of nightmares of riding endlessly through the narrow passes so that the bed seemed to move under him, or again, his imaginings that there was no safety, that he had become lost in the windings of this place and that it had closed its gates on him to swallow him down.

If they wished, he had thought in the loneliness of the night, *I might vanish from the earth, I and all those with me.*

What men did you send? lord Donnchadh might say to his lord. *None ever reached me.*

Or Donnchadh might say nothing at all, since Donnchadh had said nothing in lo these many years. Silence could drink them up, and walls entomb them.

These are fancies, he had thought at last, with the light come to the window. *Now they will know by my eyes I have not slept, and what a figure I shall cut with them this morning.* So his eyes had closed. So they wanted to close now, as if all the due of days before had fallen on him.

But a certain disquiet began to grow in him. The halls were still quiet. There ought to have been some stirring about by now. He might have been mistaken in the hour the first time he had wakened.

See, my lord, the servants might be saying, *he is still abed for all these hours.* And Donnchadh wondering to himself at his guest's discourtesy.

His wits had come back to him; his limbs must follow. He flung the covers off, met the chill highlands air and braved it, more and more awake. He looked out the narrow window, with its view of daylit mountains, for here the keep met the wall and the window faced the land round about, the Brown Hills, stony and harsh and forever untilled.

It was far unlike Caer Wiell, with its girdle of fields and forest, of pasture where yellow flowers bloomed. The Brown Hills were well named, desolate and fit for sheep. Even the air was different, having no perfume of growing things from this windward side. The little stream in the cleft at the foot of the cliffs sent no sound up the walls; there was no rush of water and wind that was always with Caer Wiell. The hills were full of stones and harsh with brush and no flowers seemed to bloom here in this season.

He shivered, turned from the window and sought his clothes, the finer ones he had brought in hope of gentle welcome.

And so prepared, leaving the armor and all but his dagger that was fit for meat, he went to the door and opened it.

A page slept on a bench nearby, a thin lad, pinch-faced, who lifted his head at the noise and leapt up. ''Lord,'' he said.

"I have slept too long," said Domhnull. "And not a lord, no. But where is your lord this morning, and will he see me?"

"Oh, he be hunting. A wolf have got some sheep hereabouts, and my lord and the men be gone to find him."

"Ah," he said, chagrined. "Well, may I go to hall and wait there?"

"It will be long waiting."

"And breakfast."

"Oh, aye, breakfast, surely, breakfast."

"The men with me—where are they this morning?"

"O, my lord he breakfasted them in hall and took them with him. They thought they should not wake you. Stay here, my lord says to me, and see to his comforts."

Domhnull frowned, and the least niggling fear came on him, that Boc should have gone off without his leave. Perhaps they hoped thus to win Donn's favor and make amends for his shameful lateness, or perhaps Donnchadh had insisted, or a thousand other tumbling thoughts, not least of which was the suspicion that men who had known the war like Boc and Caith and Dubhlaoch might go their own way. "Well," he said, "well, I shall have the breakfast down in hall."

"This way, lord."

The boy led; he followed, down halls that thumped and echoed, with wooden floors, wooden stairs and walls, the antlers of deer hung here and there and whimsically adorned with candles unlit now that the sun came in the windowslits.

It was not the way they had come last night, in this warren. He remembered other stairs, no such decoration; but they came into a small warm hall where a cheerful fire burned in the hearth.

"This is not the hall," Domhnull said.

"Oh, it be the lesser hall, this," said the page, "and here my lord will come when he will come. It be far more comfortable than the other with its drafts and echoes. Sit here, lord, and I will see to breakfast."

"I am no lord," Domhnull said again, distracted in looking at the place. A table waited. There was a single chair and benches about it. *No lady. Donnchadh has never married.* The thought struck him strange, that he had heard somewhat of Donnchadh all his life, but never that he married, nor got children. He was rich and high in the King's favor—and for certain seasons of the year Donnchadh went down from his hills to the plain across the passes, and to the King's seat at Dun na h-Eoin, with entourage and banners and all such things, while lord Ciaran sat in Caer

Wiell and never made the journey, save once or twice and that years gone, with bitter issue.

He had expected, somehow, more wealth and less of the rustic about Donnchadh. *It is very like some steading*, he thought, looking about him as he sat down at table. *Or some shepherd's cottage, if monstrous large.* It might have been a warm place, a cheerful hold. But here were no children, no running feet, no games nor childish laughter—no children of the lord or any of his folk. Perhaps they had kept them out of the way of untrusted guests; perhaps there were such besides the harried pages.

And women—surely women lived here. But there was no lady such as Branwyn, to have been in hall last night: that was the reason the hold had so strange an aspect, such a grimness, that no children disturbed the lord's dignity with games or broke the silences; a man could become like that surrounded entirely by men—*I should marry*, he thought distractedly, *get children, half a dozen at the least, have a wife to my comfort*— for until yesterday he had hoped only for some brave word that others might say of him, a litte glory in his life. He had seen only Caer Wiell, and had ambition to see Dun na h-Eoin and the King, to ride to some war or other; and now that he had come into this place so different from his own, his longing was all toward home again, recalling how beautiful the fields were, how green the forest, how fine these things had always been and he had never seen them; how rich his lord was, and he had never known it—not in gold, not in such ways as Donn, but in many others.

Perhaps tonight, he thought, will be harping, and folk will begin to laugh, deciding us no enemy.

What will he ask? What shall I say to him? Gods, Boc, and why have you done this? It was not well done, to leave me sleeping.

His breakfast came—no maid came to serve him, but only the servants, a succession of dour men bearing bread and cheese and meat in greater quantity than any breakfast he had had in Caer Wiell.

Perhaps, he thought, *their guests were gluttons, or accustomed to choose and have their whims satisfied.*

"I shall ride out," he said, "and see whether I can overtake your lord. Have my horse saddled."

There was silence for a moment. "Lord," said one, "we will tell the seneschal and he will come to you."

So he waited, and so the seneschal came, that man who had met them at the gates, he with the gold chain, a graying beard, eyes very dark and narrow.

"I did not have your name last night," said Domhnull. "Forgive me."

"It is Breandan."

"I would ride out," Domhnull said, "and join this hunt."

"So the servants told me."

"I shall need a guide."

"Our lord gave no such order."

"So," he said, and all at once his heart was beating harder, his wits racing this way and that.

"For your safety."

He gave a laugh, casy and merry. "Well, but I rode that way by night, and worse."

"I could not permit it."

The laugh died. He stared at this Breandan. "Then I take it on myself. Must I find the stable?"

"I could not permit it."

Do I then break with this pretense? Ask them where be Boc and Caith and the others? He walked a pace or two away, disliking the gray level stare upon him. *O gods.* "And how long will this be, before your lord comes home? How long must I wait here? I didn't plan to stay overlong, sir Breandan. That was not my order."

"Not so very long," said Breandan.

"I shall go back to my room, then."

"As to that I have no instructions. I pray you wait here."

"Is it so?" He walked to the fireplace and looked back at Breandan. *And my weapons may not now be there. No, I can be sure they are not.* "Where are my men, sir Breandan?"

"I will inquire," said Breandan and walked toward the door.

"I had heard—" Domhnull raised his voice, "—that they were hunting with your lord."

"Why, that may be. I will inquire, sir Domhnull."

Somewhere below a door shut, hollow in the wooden halls. "That may be my lord."

"I did not hear the gates."

"Why, this is a rambling place, hall upon hall. All sorts of sounds come and go, playing tricks with the ears. Come now. I am certain that is he. Bide patient."

"And my men, sir?" He stood quite calmly for all that his heart was racing. "Do you think they might be with him?"

There were footfalls on the nearby stairs, a great number of men by the sound of them; and Breandan stood there smiling with perfect falsity.

So Donnchadh came, cloakless, in light boots, not a thing one would wear in hunting; and men came with him, all armed, all armored, and filled the back of the hall.

"Where are my men?" Domhnull asked, following with his eyes this brother of his lord, this thin unsmiling man who went and took the chair at the head of the table, and drew it aside, and sat down in it at the front of the hall, as a lord sat who disposed of cases.

"What?" Donnchadh asked him. "What talk of men? I thought we were to speak of trust. Of peace. Of forgiveness."

"How was the hunting, lord? Did you take the wolf?"

"Ah. The wolf. It did not fare well, sir Domhnull."

"Where are my men, lord?"

"You have one refrain, it seems."

"Until I have an answer."

"Young fool. You will give the answers, alone here as you are."

"Alone. Is that my answer?"

"Fey you are. I have felt it since you came. There was a night, Domhnull mac Gaelbhan, that doors were shut in Caer Wiell; and strange things passed there, the sound of harping, all in private—they say that bargains were struck there."

"What, they? Have you made them say such things, to agree with all your fancy?"

"Bargains such as my brother struck before. Such as on the field at Caer Wiell. We know what that portended, and mark you, he was born least and youngest of all our house, and now has hold and lands and a name far and wide as defying the King. Evald of Caer Wiell took him in, and that was his undoing."

"This is all fantastical."

"Oh, but truth, all the same, sir Domhnull. Evald was a strong man, to die still hale and with a good many years before him."

"My lord loved this man. Evald was more kin to him than any of his house."

"But Evald died untimely, did he not?"

"All men die, lord. And none of us know the time of it."

"And there was this meeting, this gathering behind doors; and bargains struck and plans laid, how there should others die, opportunely. No lord has richer lands, more wealth of cattle and horses—the King's own cousin for his wife. Oh, aye, all men die, lad. Luck, for one, may leave them. He has bargained with the Sidhe to gain all that he has gained. I know it. There is nothing natural in his lands. And now he aims higher—oh, I don't doubt he looks to win me now. The King is failing . . . I doubt will last the summer. And now behind these doors in Caer Wiell, bargains are struck. You were in that room. You know what words were passed, and with what, and with what issue.''

''The Sidhe warned him of hazards.''

''I do not doubt, warned him of me. Come to me, he says now, come and be my brother, help me overthrow the King—''

''He has served his King better than the King has served him. Were even two of the lords of my lord's mind, then Laochailan King would be better served than he is. The Sidhe warned of danger; of some shadow hanging over us; and so my lord sent to you—''

''That I should take him to my heart.''

''He has loved you. Twice he sent to your father. Now to you.''

''This hall was lighter once, filled with my kin. Their bones are at Caer Wiell.''

''They chose to be there, following the King. As you did. As Evald. As my lord. And without him—''

''And his allies of the Sidhe.''

''He won your battle for you; and if cousins of his died, do you think he didn't mourn them? So did others die there. So cousins of mine, and my uncle. So no one of Caer Wiell but lost someone on that field. You are not unique, lord of Donn.''

''And so he prospered. He and his allies. And now he sends to me, hoping to gain even more than he has. I will know what was said there that night.''

''Nothing of concern in this hall. Much of reason. Of friendship.''

''With the Sidhe.''

''Lord, if what they say is so, there is Sidhe blood in him—on your *father's* side, lord. I do not know why you hate him.''

A vein beat in Donnchadh's temple. His nostrils were white about the edges. ''One of us knows another. I have the Sight, yes. What bargain has he made?''

''There was no bargain.''

''And what is this thing he carries?—Oh, I do know, lad. I know many things.''

''But the truth. Did you get that from your watchers? He sent us here honestly. He purposed nothing but your good.''

''This meeting—this—visitation—''

''This meeting. You are too fearful, lord. There was no— bargain.'' *Back again to this*, he thought. *So we are out of words*. He half turned, to measure those between him and the door; and one face caught his eye among the five that guarded the way out, a small and scowling man who seeing him, smiled his ugly best.

"So," Domhnull said, feeling the sands slipping farther beneath him, "Coille. We wondered where you had gotten to." And louder, not taking his eyes from Coille: "Lord, did you know you shelter thieves? Or do you breed them?"

Hands went to swords, steel rising to the light. "Alive," came the word from behind him. "Take him alive."

"*Coille!*" he shouted and flung himself, dagger coming so deftly into his hand—Rhys had taught him: and into Coille's belly. He never stopped to account of it, ducked low, snatching Coille's fallen sword and ran, staggered by the blow that struck his back, by hands that tore at him. He spun against the hallway wall, swung a two-handed sweep across bodies oncoming from the door. He ran. He felt a wound, his back, his side—some edge had struck him. The whole keep thundered to running steps, to shouts of rage: pursuit was close behind him, below him, coming up the stairs he wanted.

He went for light instead—for the slitted window that gave day into the dingy hallway: he was high in the keep, he knew it, but that death was quick and better. He leapt for it as they rushed about him. Hands grappled at his clothes. The hills, the daylight blinded him to the height. He thrust off from the sill and took it, a long, twisting fall with the clean wind rushing past him.

Branches took him, snapped, speared at him in rapid course like weapons.

He caught at them, tried to hold; and after, another space of air, another hurtling, past rock where there had been branches, one impact and another before his sight was darkened.

Dogs were in his hearing, that fell sound echoing among the rocks, with the sound of voices. "T'was on the cliffside; he never got to bottom."

"Go round," someone shouted, "go round, up on the hillside. If he is not below he has fallen to that brushy shelf."

"T'is a long climb, that."

"Go, get the dogs to it, fool, and quickly."

His limbs drew up like a child's, like a child's kept moving restlessly, and that movement relieved one pain and brought another torment of sharp gouges at his body, brush beneath his hands, then smooth and heated stone, and the taste of blood, an ache so deep it had shaken to the roots of his teeth and the center of his bowels. *Bones are broken*, he thought, hearing the dogs, and scrambled all the same, having his sight back, a jumbled

view of bristly foliage, of light on stone, of leaf-patterned shadow.
He felt no pain clearly. It was all one ache, and he got his knee
up, the one that was not battered and strengthless, and staggered
to his feet on the cliffside. Depths swayed into his vision,
sunbright and deadly as he stood holding to the gnarled limb:
they beckoned, sunlit jagged stones, without dread in them, but
he veered away, took a step, another, for the hills and sky were
in his sight, and he went to them.

Dogs are there, he thought. He could not remember how he
had come there, or where he was; then did remember that there
were two sets of voices, that men hunted him, that somehow he
had come to die here. He recalled wooden hallways which had
suddenly become this nightmare, and he had hit his head, and
fallen. There had been branches: still he felt the sting of them,
and those that had rammed into his body; he bled, wiped his face
and brought his hand away liberally reddened.

Donn, he thought then, a sudden settling of vision; these
strange hills which had made no sense to him were the hills of
Donn. He felt the mass of the keep looming over him, himself
toiling along a ledge full in their vision. The edge was there,
another hurtling fall awaiting: his courage failed him. There were
the trees, there was hope, if only for the moment, and that
moment was all of life now. There was a man who meant to
come up that hillslope, round its shoulder, so up to the cliffside;
and that was one man, only one man of all those who served
Donnchadh to hunt him through the hills.

He reached the hillside, the grass and brush, where old stones
thrust up black fingers, doom among the wildflowers, the first
small touch of color in this brown, dead land. He was naked on
that hill, beyond the concealment of the trees, limping now with
great stabs of pain up his battered leg and sides. Dogs barked
and yelped. They were coming, his enemy; and now his sight
was failing. The sky was dimmed to night, the place seemed
stark and horrid, and small things chittered among the stones,
wry and twisted shadows.

"This way," someone said. "O Man, keep coming. Hold out
your hand to me."

He saw now a glimmering like a star amid the dark, and it
grew as he went to it, a light, a warmth, a hope he went to for
haven. His wounds ached with cold. His hand reached across the
gulf and fingers touched his, took his, held them as he began to
sink. A grayness wrapped him about, a cloak and enfolding
arms. He was on his knees, rested his head against a shoulder,

felt a hand upon his head as if he were a child come home.
"There, be still, I have you."

There was the scent of leaves, of greenness, of rose and lilac,
reminding him of Branwyn. For a moment he was content, but
thunder muttered, and wind swirled about with voices. He lifted
his face, met hers. The wind was in her hair, her eyes—her eyes
were Sidhe and dreadful.

"O Man, what do you here among these stones? This is no
place for you."

"Donnchadh, the lord of Donn—my lord sent me, Duine
Sidhe, to make peace, and Donnchadh has done murder on us. I
fell, I cast myself—o Sidhe!" He heard a thing crying down the
winds, and struggled to his feet on the sudden, staring blind into
the dark where stones rose like pillars lit by fitful lightning.
"Sidhe, they must not take me."

"Hush, they will not." Arafel stood beside him.

"There is something out there," he cried, for something
lurched and bobbed among the pillars, lost in dark.

"That will not harm you. O Man, you should never have
come here. Did I not say there was no hope in the west? Did I
not warn you? Go back, tell your lord—tell your lord—that there
is neither hope nor help in others. Here least of all. Donnchadh
deserves his pity."

"Pity? A man who has done murder on guests?"

She was a whiteness in his sight, as if some inner light shone
through her; and then dimmer, the whiteness blotched with black
about the breast and hands; dimmer still, and it was his blood
upon her. "For Donnchadh. For Caer Damh, An Beag and
Bradhaeth. Pity, yes. They are only Men, and snared in evil they
tried to master. It lies beneath, about them. I gave you a gift to
see such dangers, but you could not heed it: this place is
overpowering, and it drew you here, *here*—" The thunder broke,
and the wind battered at them in a circling, so that her cloak flew
and her hair streamed on the winds, a scattering of light as if she
bled; and the cold knifed into him, probing the depth of all his
wounds. "That is from an older Eald," she cried against the
whirlwind. "It blows from Dun Gol, from age and ill and
malice—You fade, Man; you must not! Take my hand!"

He sought with his. Her cloak whipped about him, and she
found his hand and led him. He struggled on his aching leg, felt
the wind even so, that shook them.

"*Arafel!*" a voice wailed, high and thin. "Arafel! Yield him
up!"

"It is coming. O cling to me, Man. There is no iron about you, and you can hold here if you will. Do not let it shake you."

They came among trees, strange gray trees that groaned and gave hoarse voices to the storm. There was another light before them, nigh to the ground, like the fitful gleam of lightnings, and beside them as they went a small wizened thing scampered, hopping and leaping, using hands as much as feet.

"O," it wailed in a faint, piping voice, "o Duine Sidhe, ride, ride, ride. It is too great here, far too great. You must not contest it."

"Get him to horse," she said. "Gruagach, I bid you."

She was one from him. He stumbled, full of agony, and arms took him up, arms warm and strong, bearing him like a child, as if his weight were nothing, with a scent of straw, of sun, of earth, a leaping that confused his sight and drove pain through all his wounds.

It hurled him up then, at the side of a startled pony, and he tried to hold to its mane, tried to drag his knees across: the wizened creature scrambled up before him, held his arm and pulled him.

"Come, come, come," it chided, "dark it bides, dark and lonely; o Man, o Man, the Gruagach must help her, the Duine Sidhe. O hurry, Man! This pony will not lose you."

"Help her," he wished it, but it was gone. The pony began to move, the trees flowing past: it ran, and he could not feel the running, as if it were not ground it crossed but air, a stocky, shaggy pony.

It came. The winds howled. Arafel held her ground and as it came she drew her sword, slender and silver, star-bright against the night. "Fionnghuala," she called, and behind her in the wind came the sound of thunder.

Then the winds fell, and the night grew very still, there among the ancient stones, which made an aisle: a barrow-walk, to the hill's dark heart.

And darkness stood there, which became a slim tall elf.

"Arafel," he said.

"Duilliath."

He smiled. Cloaked in black he was, and light that came to his garments died there. She held the sword before her and even its silver dimmed: this was his place, his power.

"Free," he said, "and of this place the master. Master of all this land. I have brought back—"

"Ghosts. Naught but ghosts, Duilliath. And sorrow. Let be. Go back. Sleep again."

He dimmed, and then became something more of substance. A sword like hers was in his hand, but blue stained all down its length—a thing of venom and tarnish. "O Arafel," he said, and settled on a stone, sword-hand on his knee, and gave her a gentle smile. "The bonds on me are broken, quite—and shall I tamely sink back to sleep? Oh no." The sword lifted, pointed at her heart, and the wind stirred among the grasses, a breath of cold. "We are too old in malice."

"Drow," she said. "I find pity for you."

"Pity. I have no such. I lost it."

"Is it a heart you want? There are many left; I keep them. Name the one you wish, and I will give it."

"Even yours?"

She laid her hand on that stone at her breast, feeling cold within it. "Is it what you ask? Yes. I will yield it."

"How clever." His lips smiled. His eyes did not. "And were I to take it, then you might bind me with it—so you hope. So you have bound that Man—oh, yes, I know, you've lent such a stone, but all useless to your minion. My workings overpower it. Soon they will overpower him. You are too liberal with such gifts."

"I had hoped you had more courage. What, doubtful which of us is stronger?"

"I am not a fool, to hand you such advantage." He rose, and held the sword before him. "The land is mine, Arafel. Its King is mine; its lords are mine—even that one yonder. Donnchadh. He hates us. And seeks powers of me to match his brother's—is that not humanity? He is in my hand. As Caer Wiell is in yours, but not forever. Ah, cousin, how well you kept things—Eald shrunk to so pathetic few trees, and no Sidhe stirring from it. Where are the rest, Aoibheil? Liosliath our cousin—gone too? You cast the world away. You might have ruled it. Fools!"

"You made one Dun Gol. Will you heap more dead there? More elvish bones? Duilliath, I remember what you were. I mourn what you cast away."

"Is that Man's blood on you?" The sword lifted. "Mortality. It makes breaches in your armor. But I shall let you go. Retreat, Arafel." The point advanced. "Or yield. Surrender I shall allow you. That would pay for my long waiting. We are many—oh, very many, we are thousands upon thousands. And yielding would be wiser."

"No," she said, lifting her sword, for he came nearer. "Take counsel from you, Duilliath? It never served you well. Why should I trust it?''

The wind hit, bitter cold. He leapt and thrust at her, and narrowly she parried. His face shone before her, pale beyond the lacery of blades, the leap and dazzle of light and elvish quickness. The winds fought for him. The numbness grew within her. Lightnings lit the hill and leapt among the stones, making his face a dark-eyed mask, his blade a blue-edged flicker. His armor turned the point; hers, human-tainted, must fail her; and constantly she gave back and back, her fingers gone numb, her defenses waning in the bitter wind. The blue-stained blade crossed her guard, its poisoned edge kissed her hand in passing.

She thrust at him in that approach, slashed his face and marred him. He shrieked and vanished from sight among the stones. The pit of the ancient mound yawned before her, whither he had gone. From it came the wind and the murmuring of many voices, malice beckoning. ''Come,'' they said, ''come down to us.''

''Duine Sidhe,'' a small voice wailed behind her. ''O Duine Sidhe, don't listen. The Gruagach cannot reach you down in the dark with him. Do not follow.''

Thunder grew around her, and the light that was Fionnghuala. A small dark shape sat astride the elf horse that had come to her. It clung to the mane. It reached out a hand.

She took it, sprang with her fading strength for safety, and Fionnghuala bore them both away, the thunder of her hooves echoing off the valley; but that sound was dimming.

''Do not fall, Duine Sidhe,'' the small voice begged her, and strong arms wrapped about her. ''O do not fall. They would all be on us.''

''Get me away,'' she whispered past the thunder. ''O cousin, I am poisoned. Get me home, to Eald, my Eald across the river. It wakes, it wakes, and now I cannot stop it.''

The shadows deepened in the hall, and servants moved soft-footed. *Lost,* the men reported. *Lord, we cannot find him.*

''Then *search,*'' Donnchadh had said, so lights winked back and forth like fireflies through the brush and the dogs coursed this way and that, but then the rain had started.

Now he kept close within his hall, and drank red wine to calm the fears that gnawed him. *Lost, lost, lost.* The boy had had something about him, something of the Sidhe, and his men swore that he had fallen, that they had seen him hit the rocks. But he had vanished.

Man, the whisper came, just at twilight, with the rain adrip from the eaves, apatter on the wooden roof; and the Dark Man was there, in the shadows of the corner as he was wont to come, so that Donnchadh reckoned him a part of dreams, or some manifestation of the age of Caer Donn, from the ancient stones. His brother had the Sidhe; but he had ghosts, dark ones that flitted, that knew nothing of the perilous green shade, that whispered to him at night and brought cold where they passed like honest hauntings.

Man, he has slipped you, quite.

The presence came closer. It seemed to bleed, and the blood to steam upon the air, in thin streams down its pale cheek, like warm water on snow and ice.

What shall I do? he asked his counselor. *What advice have you to give? Who marred you?*

The Dark Man leaned near, two hands on the arms of his chair, confronting him so that his icy breath struck him in the face and the wine dregs spilled from his tilted cup. *Arafel is her name, the name of this power that aids your brother. She has taken this your brother's minion to safety, and now what tales do you suppose that one will bear to him? Fool, Donnchadh, fool ever to have breached your gates. You would not heed me.*

Donnchadh glowered, shifting in his chair. The eyes were close to his and dark and dire. He tried to face them.

My brother. I know my brother's allies, what they are. This power you promised me—where is it? Where is this Sidhe-touched boy? Man, the apparition said, leaning close and smiled, beautiful and dire at once, *Man, what do you imagine me to be?*

Donnchadh thought of this, and it was hard to think of, the way it was hard to hold this face in his mind, even when it was looking into his own. *Ciaran,* he thought, recalling a fairness in his past, and sunlight on the hills, his mind shifting the way the face before him shifted, before there were the Sidhe, before he had known what his brother was, or what it was to rule. They had laughed in those days.

I am Sidhe, said the ghost, very softly, in a voice so indistinct it might have been any voice, but fair and shifting like light on dark water. *Does this fright you, Donnchadh?*

Ciaran! he appealed to that safe past, that time far away from this. But the sunlit hills slipped from him, bringing back the mist. *O Ciaran, was it this way with you?*

Does it fright you, Donnchadh?

The pale, the beautiful face filled his sight. There was the scent of damp aged stone, of old wood, of wind in the night. There was a touch at his heart, more subtle than these, and it was fear and desire of power. "Begone," he whispered—a whisper was all he could muster—and the mist was all about him. "Leave me, ghost."

Would you command me? You would need my name.

Ghost, that is what you are.

My name is Duilliath. Banish me if you will. But do you think your brother will do as much with the Sidhe ally he has taken? Oh, you have always known what I am. I have whispered it in your dreams. I have said it over and over and tonight you have to hear it. Banish me, Donnchadh. And be alone. You have killed your brother's men. Come, speak my name; banish me if you like, now you have done murder. Why, I might side with him—or with some other lord of the land of Men, to make him King. Laochailan is fading. Your brother has his own ambitions. So does every lordling in the land. Will you banish me, Man, and wait for the armies to come against your wooden walls?"

The sweat was cold on his face, in the morbid wind. There was such an ill ease in him, such a gnawing uncertainty creeping through him as he had grown all too familiar. He feared. There was fear in the very stones underfoot. He felt stirrings all about him. The Sidhe owned Caer Donn; he had always known as much. The Sidhe like Men knew malice, knew connivance, made plots among themselves. This one sided with Donn, belonging here.

Will you bid me go? it asked. The beautiful eyes were windows into the mist, the touch at his heart quite deft and sure. There was no resisting it.

No, he admitted. He did not want to admit this, but it was so, that he had no counselor but his ghost, whose advice had always been true. He knew the world; he had fought a bitter war; he had fought a different sort of war after, his house disgraced, his parents failing in health, his kinsmen all dead in the war or turning on one another. His counselor's advice had won the King, after all; gained him power while the lords of the land conspired and connived with a King who knew only plots and murderings.

Listen now, said the ghostly Sidhe, his Dark Man, the voice which had whispered through his thoughts for years so subtly he thought the thoughts his own. *You must gather your forces, quickly, before your brother can prevent you. You must not stand siege here. Caer Donn was never made for it; and if you are pent within these hills he will reach to Dun na h-Eoin and cut you off from the King. Move now, this night, while you have the chance.*

And do what?

Murder came to his mind, so soft and deadly a whisper it was not a word, but a vision, the King lying lifeless on his bier, the armies with their lances shining in the sun, advancing on the Dale.

Prevent him, said the voice. *Prevent him.*

ELEVEN
Retreat

They were still there, the skulkers in the brush, and sometimes arrows flew: men of Damh and perhaps the wild men of the Bradhaeth with them, lurking round the margins of the lake, in reeds and willows. And in every hiding place of the hills sat the countrymen of Caer Wiell, farmers skilled with bow and spear, and sword if it came to that, grandfathers and striplings not a few, for the word was out and the archers came, not alone here, but all along the marches, bands of kinsmen and not a few bow-skilled daughters ready for any outbreaking along the border.

"Go south," Ciaran had said then to the folk of Alhhard's steading, who had come first and feathered a good many of the lurkers about Lioslinn. "You and all your neighbors, go up and down the Bainbourne, and keep a watch, in case An Beag should grow restless."

So Alhhard's sons went and Ciaran watched them go, not without misgivings. "An Beag will carry tales," Ciaran said glumly, "and the King will hear how I make war and stir up the whole countryside. If there is some attack of An Beag they will say it was I who moved on them."

"Go back to Caer Wiell," said Beorc. "There is no more need for you to be here. Less talk if you are back where you belong, and what passes up here is my doing."

Ciaran gave that no answer. He was weary of Beorc's asking, and walked away, sheltered by the hill. He wore armor of a sort, that country folk had gotten him, of laced leather; and there was talk. There could hardly be otherwise, how their lord was faery-touched and could not bear sword or iron, how he bore an elvish stone next his heart and flinched from Damh's iron-tipped arrows.

He saw their looks as he passed them in his wandering along the
lines, and felt the silence they paid him as if they had seen some
direr sight than a tired, graying man in motley leather. By day he
had stopped and joked with them as he had talked sometimes
over fences in his riding through the land, but there were always
whispers in his wake: he knew it. Now he passed along the ridge
without a word except sometimes to greet a man familiar to him,
like Cuinn of his household troops or Graeg of Graeg's steading.
But mostly there were whispers. Likeliest, he thought, the folk
of Caer Wiell had done a good deal of free talking to their
cousins and brothers of the steadings; and there was no stopping
the tale-bearing.

He wearied of it, beyond all bearing, felt solitude heaped upon
his shoulders, and even Beorc resisting him, Beorc, who spoke
less and less of Domhnull and took wilder and fiercer chances,
flinging himself toward any point of hazard he suspected his lord
might take instead. An anger burned in Beorc; he felt it in the
stone, a dark thing that looped and twisted all round their long
comradeship, through blame and guilt and a rage that smothered
itself like banked fire.

*You never should have sent him, lord. He went to keep you
from it. And you were blind.* But Beorc would never say it.

He went back to that post he had kept in the evening before, a
stony knoll that gave view of the lake and hills. Here they had
held when the riders from Caer Wiell had reached them—reached
them in the midst of battle, and taught their attackers somewhat
of respect. That had been one of the good moments of their
holding here—but less good for Boda who would not be riding
home to his wife; and for other lives they lost. The sky threatened;
a feeling of ill had grown in the air since morning, and now the
darkness that lay over the northwest was deeper and direr, shot
with lightning, though it seemed only a cloud to mortal sight, a
bit of weather to the west. . . . "Get firewood under cover," he
had heard his captains order. "That'll be on us by nightfall."

There was no sunset; the west was bound in murk too thick for
sun to color it; and if that sight was grim, the surface of Lioslinn
took on a leaden gleam that made it even less wholesome than
before, a well of mire and dread, rimmed in shadowy reeds.
Wrong, it cried to any with eyes to see it. Elvish sights should be
fair, of green trees and silver; and this was not. This was
corrupted. The hills rose like iron walls beside it, and trees were
fallen, burned, laid waste.

"I do not like this," Beorc had said a day ago, when they

waited attack. "This place weighs on me as nowhere I have ever been."

That from Beorc, who was not one to start at shadows. And the house troops, newly arrived, went about with haunted looks, glancing much toward the lake and toward the west, but that was no more than the countrymen had been doing before them.

"Lord," said Beorc now from behind him; but he had heard the tread in his wake all the while he had come this way, and known Beorc was following, his relentless shadow. Beorc reached him and crouched nearby on another stone, his guard, his warder, not to be shaken from his heels.

"It is worse," Ciaran said at last, for with his Sight he saw no difference now in day or night toward the west.

"I would you were away," said Beorc.

He had no more to say to that than before, and for a long time Beorc was silent.

"I feel it," Beorc said at last, "this storm. Others do. I'm sure of it."

"Was it not her gift," Ciaran murmured, "to see such things?" He thought of Domhnull, as he reckoned Beorc was thinking— the boy, loyal to him, going ahead in spite of all his Seeing.

Then it seemed to him that he heard hoofbeats in the dark, and the stone began to burn against his breast.

Beorc had spoken. He could not get it clear. He rose. "Be still," he said. "O my friend, get your distance from me—"

It was coming from the pass, he thought. All the world seemed stretched and distorted, like iron under fire and hammer. He saw fires in the murk, and twisted trees and a darkness coiled and monstrous within the lake, stirring in its sleep.

The hoofbeats grew louder, and hounds bayed, voices mingled with the wind.

"Lord Death," he whispered, and struggling to see the Man beside him: "Beorc, Beorc, run, get away from here."

Iron shuddered in the air, the rasping of blade from sheath, and poisoned the wind. "Not I," said Beorc, there by him, if dimly through the pervading murk. "Lord, *what is it?*"

"The hounds, hear you?" The baying filled heaven and earth, and the brush and grass whispered about them like a gathering of many voices. There were clouds, and dark shapes coursing among them. His arm, once torn, turned cold and painful as the stone upon his breast. Fleeting things shredded on the wind, and voices shrieked in it like voices of lost children, of wounded animals, of dying men and the clangor of battle.

A moving shape appeared in the distance, like a shape cut out

of night, and that shape became two riders, one tending northward and one coming straight toward them, smaller than the
other and less dire—it seemed no more than a pony, running
silently amid the wind and the lightning, its shaggy coat and
mane aprick with points of light as if marsh-fire had settled
there, and light glowed on the bright, bowed head of the rider
slumped across his shoulders.

"Domhnull," Ciaran murmured, and louder: "Domhnull,
Domhnull!" —with his hand upon the stone and running now,
half in faery, to reach the pony. The hounds of lord Death
coursed about it, a tide of darkness: the pony threw its head and
shied, and for a moment there was mist about them, and whirling
shapes wind-carried.

"My lord!" Beorc cried, and reached him, as the winds
turned watery, sluicing them with rain. The world had shadowed,
the clouds had gone to greenish murk shot through with lightning
and rumbling with thunderclaps that shook the ground. "Lord,
stay—the men of Damh—"

He shook off Beorc's hand, running and wiping the water
from his eyes, sodden with it, searched among the gorse and
brambles and found a body lying, bright hair darkened with rain
and twilight, in soaked clothing better suited to some hall; and
that torn and stained with blood the water sought to purge.
"Domhnull," Ciaran said, sinking to his knees. "O Domhnull."

Beorc likewise knelt and turned Domhnull over, his face to
the rain, white and stark in the lightning; but breath stirred and
one hand moved as if he would fend the flashes off him.

"Domhnull," Beorc said above the rush of water. The lightning flashed again. Pale flesh shone through the shreds of his
garments, and Beorc rested his hand on Domhnull's side, on pale
new scars. "A month or more healed—o gods, what could have
done this?"

"The Sidhe," Ciaran murmured, shivering in the rain. "He
has been with the Sidhe." He took Domhnull's cold face between his hands and wished upon the stone. "Domhnull,
Domhnull, *Domhnull*, hear me."

The eyes opened, bruised and vague, blinking in the rain.
"Lord," he murmured, "cousin, I fell—the dogs, the dogs—"

"Hush, be still. You fell from the pony. But the dogs are
gone."

"Lord," said Beorc, "let us get him behind our lines."

"They are dead," Domhnull murmured, "the others,"—but
Ciaran took this without question, and worked with Beorc to
gather him up between them, his chilled arms locked with theirs.

Domhnull tried to walk, limping as he did, and kept talking as he went, of treachery and dark and shadow, of murder and the lord of Donn, but this Ciaran had already begun to know—long since, that all his hopes were fallen, and he had sent good men to their deaths.

"At least I have you back," he said to Domhnull when they had lain him in warm dry blankets in such shelter as they had. "You must rest now." But he had seen the scars, the dreadful marks on him in the lightning.

"Go home," Beorc said gripping his arm, making him listen. "You would see them return, you said. Now you have got back all. There are no more. What more is there to do—what hope here?"

"None. None here. I shall go home." Ciaran stared into the dark with the rain trickling down his neck. "I shall withdraw all the forces but what can keep the Bradhaeth in its place. And Damh. We shall more watch than fight. My brother has answered me, I understand that well enough." Breath was short in him. He caught another, that pained him like the stone, and his eyes burned in the rain. "I shall go home."

A moment's silence. Then Beorc left him.

He shivered, flinching at the thunder. The rain in the puddles gave back the lightning where horses had churned the ground and rain smoothed it again in pock-marked sheets. *Arafel, was I wise? I think that I was not. O gods, answer me. Arafel!*

Domhnull slept, sometimes, clinging to the neck of the pony they had gotten for him, a farmer's elderly beast with a placid, rolling gait. Sometimes he dreamed that it strode the winds or trod on mist, swift-footed and magical, but in the intervals of his waking he found an ordinary pony and plain dalelands mire squelching about its muddy hooves, so that he grew confused, whether the other had ever been, or whether the horror that had happened to him had ever happened at all.

But now and again Ciaran rode by him, and then he would speak disjointedly the things that he recalled, knowing that he was making a muddle of them and trying to pull them into order—of Caer Donn, of Donnchadh, of Boc and the others.

"Did Donnchadh do this to you?" Ciaran asked, and there was anger in his voice. And at last: "Domhnull, give me your hand, give it me."

He gave it or yielded it, one, across the gap between them; and then a kind of strength flowed into him, surcease of misery. They had gone somewhere together, he and his lord, and it was gray and full of mist. He was sitting—somehwere, on the grass, it seemed; and his lord was sitting by him on some higher place gazing down at him—but a Ciaran strangely changed, whose brow was smooth, whose fairness burned like the sun in this shadow, whose eyes compelled the truth as he questioned him, this, this, and this, and he answered as he must.

He is like a king, thought Domhnull, surprised to think it. *And if the land had had him for King and not Laochailan, then none of this grief would have happened.*

He remembered other things, the Sidhe, the darkness: he told it, remembering now.

"Stay," his lord told him, and rose up from where he sat and tried to go further into the mist. It seemed he sought something, but the mist was everywhere concealing it.

"Lord," Domhnull cried, getting up from where he sat, fearing to be left behind. He tried to follow after him, but he had not the strength, and small twisted things writhed out of the mist to draw him down into the depths with them.

Of a sudden his cheek was against the pony's rough neck, his wounds paining him with a dull ache, and when he struggled to sit his lord was riding safely knee to knee beside him.

"You will fall," Ciaran said quietly. "Don't try to sit up."

He paid no heed to this, riding for a time with his hands on the pony's withers. Beorc came to his other side.

"He has come back to us," Beorc said.

"Aye," said Ciaran. "Domhnull—don't fret yourself. We are bound for home now, well inside our lands. Rest."

There were armed men about them, more troops than they had begun with; but he let that confusion pass. He felt of his wounds and found scars instead, and bone well knit, if aching. The wounds had stopped bleeding and hurting while the Sidhe had held him in her arms. He had come home, revenant among the living. He had gathered things instead of his youth—wariness and toughness. But he had been outside the safe world and came back meshed in Eald so thoroughly he drew shreds of it with him into daylight, to haunt his waking. He had the memory when he shut his eyes of that hurtling fall past rocks and branches, that long, long tumbling in the air and the shock of landing that was no bodily pain, but a shattering slippage between life and dream.

Arafel, the voice had called her name. He recalled her bleeding light and strength into the gale like a candle that must soon fail. *Arafel. The Gruagach, and the Horseman.*

The wind blew cold on his face, on the tracks of tears. Something bumped his knee persistently and someone drew a cloak about him and touched his shoulder after. A face lingered in his vision, hair and beard like blowing fire.

"Beorc. I fare well enough."

"That you do, cousin. But let me take you up. Old Blaze can carry double."

"Boc is dead," Domhnull said. "Caith and Dublaoch and Brom—all dead; I hope that they are dead. There is an evil in that place—" Panic beckoned. He refused it, speaking calmly, his eyes fixed on the pony's ears and the riders in front of him. "I let them part us. I never should have done that."

"No more of it," said Ciaran, close by him on the other side. "Boc at least was a wily old wolf and so were Caith and Dubhlaoch, and Brom was a borderer; don't suffer so for their sakes. They were not children to need your guidance; and living past a battle where friends were lost is no shame, gods help us else. They had many battles, themselves left friends behind, at Dun na h-Eoin, Caer Lun, Aescbourne, and Caer Wiell."

"A plague on leaving friends."

"Oh aye, but that is life and death, my friend." And with that came so bleak a look on Ciaran's face that his own grief seemed dim and cold. They rode side by side, he with Beorc and Ciaran; and in time the dimness came on his eyes again. Hands steadied him; he went forward gently, lay his head against the pony's neck, lost but homeward tending.

Fionnghuala went slowly now, among the silver trees, and so the Gruagach slipped from her back, leaving Arafel to ride while he walked before the mare.

Here was home, and peace, but the elf horse trod on leaves, fallen leaves upon the grass, where seldom a leaf had fallen, under the elvish moon. Ruin had touched here too, if more softly.

There was a stream. Men called it the Caerbourne; in Death's realm it had a name. But here it was Airgiod the Silver, and its waters were clear and healing. Fionnghuala waded it and the Gruagach went across like an otter, shaking the water afterward from his shabby pelt as the elf horse tended on her way with her quiet, drooping rider. But the Gruagach delayed, cupped up water in his ample palms and hurried after, his wrinkled face all anxious and earnest.

"Here, Duine Sidhe, here, o drink, the good bright water, will not the Duine Sidhe?"

Fionnghuala stopped very gently. Arafel leaned from her back and bent to the brown, uplifted hands and drank, then rested so, her arm about Fionnghuala's white neck, her eyes gazing into the earthen brown of the Gruagach's.

"Go," she said. "Have you not your farm, Gruagach? Have you not your Men? You have stayed long from them. Who will weed their gardens, little cousin, small brave Sidhe? Weeds will grow there, and brambles. Be free and go tend them."

"You must not die," wailed the Gruagach. "You must not leave us."

"See the leaves. Go. You cannot help me more. And your land will need you. I do not know the issue, but of that one thing I am most sure. This is Eald's heart, and if I am not safe here I am nowhere safe. Go. Go home, the third time I command you."

"Duine Sidhe!" it cried, but Fionnghuala began to move again, gently, leaving it behind.

So Arafel rode deeper into the wood, where trees rose like silver pillars, and the leaves shone with light. A gentle chiming sounded here, in concert with the breezes that wafted sweetness. She passed into the heart of this grove, where rose that grassy mound spangled with flowers, and shading it was the greatest of the trees: Cinniuint was its name. Upon it hung thousands of such jewels as that moongreen stone about her neck; and elvish swords and arms such as her folk had carried once in their wars, hung here and upon Cinniuint's fellows, so that all the air in the grove seemed alive with light and sang with memories as the winds would stir the stones.

Here she found strength at least to slip from Fionnghuala's back, and she sank down full length on the grass, where the coolness of the earth touched the fever in her. For a time she rested so, from time to time feeling Fionnghuala's breath upon her.

"Go," she bade the elf horse. "Go back to Aodhan."

There was a clap of thunder, a breath of wind. So she lay alone, upon the mound in the moonlight, and for a long time she was still in her pain.

Then a leaf settled to the earth before her open eyes, and others. She lifted her head, seeing a rain of leaves, the trees all dimmed.

Horror touched her, a shivering of weakness. She gathered herself up and laid her hand upon a bough of Cinniuint, so that his light brightened and greened somewhat, but that healing cost her dear. An ancient, irreplaceable tree perished then from her Eald, at its far margins, faded into mist and into Duilliath's domain forever.

From Cinniuint to others she passed, and to the youngest, precious to her. Miadhail was his name, the only tree to be born in Eald in long ages; and he was slim and new, scarcely of her own stature. Here too were fallen leaves, silver and shining in the moonlight. To him most of all she gave strength; and touched the leaves and the stones of Cinniuint, calling forth memory— but all the stones recalled was war, the dread age of conflicts past, and despair that followed.

"Miochair," she named her lost comrades, "Gliadrachan." From those two stones came no help, but sorrow. She named others, yearning. "You have left me," she cried at last, "and where have you gone across the sea? Is there hope there?"

There was silence, only silence, except the wind striking stone on stone, a hollow chiming.

"Liosliath," she whispered; but the lord of Caer Wiell had that stone, and those memories were lost to her, dearest of all. All about that name slipped away into the mist, leaving only the sorrow, the memory of the gulls she could no longer hear.

Fear was on her. Poison ate at what strength she had. Once the deepest despair fallen on her had been that sound of waves which sometimes whispered from the stones, the promise of the sea: *Dreary*, they said, *is all the world that Men have touched. The Sea is wide: who knows what we shall find?*

But now the darkness lay between, and there was no hope of such retreat. The trees went one by one into Duilliath's Eald, and ghosts rose up to haunt her.

Duilliath, the leaves whispered, shivering. *The spring is past, our summer passing; there is only autumn and then the winter. Liosliath is lost, lost, lost.*

War was all about them now. The Bradhaeth stirred; there was the ring of steel in An Beag and in the south, where one she had touched had come to his own; there was ill in Dun na h-Eoin, and worse to follow.

She sank down, shut her eyes, her arms folded about her, shivering. She had no more refuge but this, and somewhere the Gruagach scampered and hid, for evil had gotten to the edges of the Caerbourne, and swam within its waters, not the water-horse, but some more baneful thing.

Fear touched her; it was the poison in her veins. And when the elvish sun had risen she cried aloud to see the trees, for there was the touch of golden autumn about their silver green.

Fool, lord Death had called her. Men had spun this thing, an outlaw in her forest, a harper, a throneless king she had never seen; An Beag, Caer Damh; and latest of portents came Ciaran

Cuilean, son of Eald and Men, who had called her name three times and bound her to his aid.

The most innocent had done her greatest harm. It was the way, between elves and Men, that they were fatal to each other. And now the leaves fell, edged with gold, and the wind from Dun Gol came skirling among them.

A resolution settled on her. She lifted her head. "Aodhan," she called. "Aodhan." And without the third calling of his name Aodhan came racing down the winds, with Fionnghuala close beside him. His ears were pricked, his fireshot nostrils drank the breeze for all that it could tell him, his coat gave back the elvish sun in light; for a moment he had joy in all his bearing, then sinking sorrow.

"No," Arafel said softly, touched to the heart, for each time that he was summoned there was so clearly one thought in Aodhan's heart, one hope. Of all the great horses who had served the Sidhe, all had gone beyond the winds but these two, Fionnghuala because she served and Aodhan because he waited, hoping still for one special voice, one remembered touch, that had been Liosliath's, last of elves but herself. "He is not here, Aodhan. Go. Seek for him as far as the sea if you must. Be wise, be wary; call to him there and maybe he will hear."

It was scant hope, when all others failed, when the stones went silent, that Aodhan could link her to the sea. But Aodhan flung up his head and was gone upon the instant, the both of them sped in a clap of thunder. Then the thunder came back again in little mutterings, for Fionnghuala had stayed, stamping and pacing and shaking tiny lightnings from her mane. The elf horse gazed at her in seeming sorrow, walked closer and nosed at her where she had sunk down upon the grass, giving her soft breath upon her offered hand.

"No," Arafel said softly, "not for me the sea, dear friend, not now. You do not understand, do you? I would you would follow Aodhan. It is almost without hope, his going; but let him try; and when the darkness comes, then run free, run far, be wiser than Aodhan."

Fionnghuala nosed her cheek gently, breathed in her ear and went away, head dropping, disdaining the tender grass. A few leaves drifted down, sliding off her white back, and she vanished within the silver wood like a ghost of a horse.

Then Arafel drew her sword and strove with trembling hands to clean it of the tarnish of the blood that was on it, while constantly the wound on her hand burned, healed but not healing, painful as iron. Constantly she must give what strength she recovered to keep her Eald from fading. The sun itself seemed dim—chimerical as elvish suns might be, yet this day seemed dim and strange, and now and again tendrils of cloud drifted across its face when it was high. She did not trouble to banish them; she had not the strength now to spare. But when the sun had passed toward the west a premature darkness took it, and elvish night came early.

Then she shivered and wrapped her gray cloak about her, for the wind out of the north was cold, and the clouds took more and more of the sky to themselves, cutting off the stars.

Something snorted, horselike, and hooves trod the earth. She leapt up, startled by a darkness greater than the night, and twin gleams of red within it; but it took a twofooted shape then, betraying itself.

"Pooka! When had you leave to come here? You are too bold by half."

"The Daoine Sidhe were never hospitable." Seaghda tossed his head and blew a snort hardly less horselike. "Men have entered Eald. Do you not feel them?"

She folded her arms the tighter about herself. The world seemed shrunken and cold. "Go away," she said.

"You are dimmed," the pooka said. "Something has befallen you, Duine Sidhe." His nostrils flared; his eyes were wild, his hair blowing in the wind. "You would go further, in spite of all my warnings; and now the shadow comes, it is loose upon us. The Daoine Sidhe have betrayed us as they did once before— faithless, faithless."

"Not all." Her voice trembled. "I tell you so. Flee for some safer river, pooka, safer than the Caerbourne. And be not forward with me. This is no place for you. Nor any place of safety."

"Where will safety be? Where is refuge? Or do you know one? They wake, Duine Sidhe, they wake. And you are fading. See—" He held out the simple brown stone that was his soul, cupped in his dusky hands. "I have not forgot. Run with me. I am strong to carry you. I shall never tire. No master have I ever served, but favors I remember."

Anger fell from her. She smiled somewhat, despite all the pain and dread, so simple he was, so earnest in his offering. "O pooka, I wish it were so easy. No. I cannot. I was rash, and bitterly I paid for it. I shall try to mend it."

His shoulders fell; his hands dropped. A third time he snorted, seeming to laugh. "A Duine Sidhe is wrong."

"O cousin, all of us have been wrong at one time or another; perhaps the Daoine Sidhe more often than most."

"There was a Man," the pooka said after a moment, perplexedly, and tossed his head as if to mark the way, "dark like me, Sidhe-blessed. He walked in Eald and I did not frighten this one."

"Ah," she said, "yes. I know him."

"Others I might have harmed." His head lifted. His red eyes glowed like coals in the murk. He took the stone into his mouth and the black horse whirled and fled, mad as all its kind, and wild.

She gazed after him, seeing only darkness about Eald, Duilliath's advance. The pooka would, she thought, fare well in the coming storm. Mirth and lawlessness were in his blood, and he was short of memory. No drow could ever tame him.

The night wrapped the more deeply about Eald. Small creatures, the fey, strange deer, hares, a timid hedgehog, foxes and a moon-eyed owl—these had crept to the grove and now returned, the latter with a flapping of wings. Here was a little safety in the dark, in the glimmer of the trees.

But the leaves flew, dying, on the wind, and the stones jangled discordant, dimmed and all but lightless.

"Listen to me," a voice breathed through that wind, like hoarse, resounding brass, "failed you are, but the task was hopeless. Come to me, come to me, and I shall give you Caer Righ again, the trees, the smell of them on the air. Come, Aoibheil."

She shivered. "Begone!" she cried. "Go to sleep, seducer! My kin you won, but never me, never shall, old worm, deceiver—go back! Go back!"

In the depths of Lioslinn was laughter.

She banished it, gathered her strength, wove silence about the heart of Eald, a web of light and quiet. The stones shone again. She forgot the voice. But her heart had weakened. She lay still then, on the mound, amid a drift of golden leaves, and slept in the dreams of vanished Sidhe.

A dragon rose in them; he whispered, and Sidhe cast away what made them Sidhe—*Duilliath,* she mourned, remembering. *My cousin.*

"Come," it said. "Enough of Men. It is too tame a thing, that the Sidhe should pass like this, unresisting. You have power. Use it to save the land, to keep the world what it is. What has pity won you? Think of pride and anger."

"You wish to live, old worm," she whispered back, still dreaming.

"Do not you?"

It was the poison in her, the pain that flowed like ice. It filled her dreams. Vengeance, it whispered.

But even in her dream she wove the web, and the wind died into silence.

TWELVE

Of Home and Hope

Nothing was the way it used to be, Meadhbh and Ceallach reckoned that. The men went armed back and forth out of the hold, and their father talked seriously to farmers who had come from the farthest steadings afoot or on hard-ridden ponies. They eavesdropped where they could, hearing news of skirmishes that made small cold discomforts in their stomachs, names like Lioslinn and the Bradhaeth, and a fight over by Raven Hill where Caer Wiell's farmers had thrown stones at An Beag riders. Rhys had not come back; perhaps he would never come back, but no one seemed about to say so.

And there was Domhnull, not the same as he had been, but worn and pale and looking sometimes as if the world had gotten too heavy for him. At first they had thought that he might die: his mother had come in from her steading up by Gearr's to tend him. He had lain days abed and fevered, with her by him, and Muirne hovering over him no less. Now at least he was up and walking, but like someone far older. He was a hero, of course; everyone in Caer Wiell knew it, and whispered how every bone in his body had been broken but the Sidhe had healed him.

"But will he not get well, then?" Ceallach asked their father, one day that Domhnull was nowhere in their hearing, and they stood out on the wall near the gates. "Could not the Sidhe have done a little better while she was about it?"

"No," said their father sharply, and then more gently, looking down at them: "If there had been time, she would have. So I don't think there was." He ruffled Ceallach's hair, which the wind was doing too, blowing at all of them and making Meadhbh's skirts fly so she had to hold them knotted in her fist. Their father had that look of his that kept things from them. "He is still mending, Domhnull is. Mostly he would be himself again if he could, and not know what he learned up there at Caer Donn—do you understand that, Meadhbh and Ceallach?"

"Yes," said Meadhbh, and Ceallach nodded soberly.

"Do you?" their father said, staring at them strangely sharp. "Then get him ahorse again."

"We?"

"Not in the wood or down the road; not beyond sight of the walls. Say that I gave you leave to ride and ordered him to watch you."

Meadhbh looked toward the high hall, thinking of their mother, not wanting to ask whether their mother knew about this riding, because she wanted it. Ceallach had her hand and tugged it; so they went racing back to find Domhnull and get their ponies and a horse.

That was the best day of any day since their father had come home, even riding a sedate pace along the hedges close about Caer Wiell; for Domhnull's eyes grew bright again and he talked of the crops and the new foals and calves, and laughed to see the lambs playing in the meadow. Then they felt like laughing too, feeling that they had done something good and that the world was right again, at long last and overdue: that they had been wrong to doubt it.

But when Domhnull had come to the farthest point they might ride, at the end of the fence, he drew his tall horse to a halt and sat staring out north and west. The border lay that way. Caer Donn did. He only sat and sat, his horse cropping the grass, while the silence grew long and painful.

Ceallach urged Flann a little closer and looked up at Domhnull. "When we were lost," Ceallach said carefully, "there was a water horse; but Thistle sent it away."

"Thistle."

"We're too young, she said, to know her real name. When you have a name you can do magic on it. But I think it would be a mistake to try with her. The river horse—she gave us its name."

Domhnull was looking at them now, both of them. He was a man and grown, having gotten lines on his face and a new scar on his brow (too quick a scar), but he was looking at them eye to eye and heart to heart, as if he wanted to talk and had something boiling up inside him.

"I saw her," Domhnull said; but the greater thing stayed unsaid.

Meadhbh took that pouch which hung about her neck and offered it, although it was like giving her pony to someone else to ride, or letting someone rummage among her treasures. "It's my gift," she said. "You could carry it awhile. For memory, Thistle said. For hope, when there isn't any."

"Hope of what?" he said. He scared her, so harsh his voice was. But she doggedly refused to be put off, and covered her confusion by taking her gift out of its pouch so he might see it, a silver leaf held carefully between her fingers because of the wind. She held it to her nose, then offered it again.

"See. Smell. It's still new, after all this time. It makes me think how the woods smell when it rains."

He took it; and then he slowly rode away from them, beyond the point where they were to follow. He stopped and only sat there in the center of the pasture with his back to them.

She decided then what it was, and she reckoned that Ceallach understood, because he said not a thing either, but simply sat his pony waiting.

"I think we should ride back a ways," Meadhbh said finally, "and then maybe Domhnull will feel like coming home."

"He might not, you know," Ceallach said.

She thought of Donn then, of Domhnull riding that way alone. But she turned Floinn's head for home all the same, and Ceallach's Flann turned without his doing anything. "He has my gift with him," she said, though parting with it made her anxious, "and they have a magic on them, don't they? A virtue of finding. So he has to bring it back. Doesn't he?"

Ceallach simply shook his head, still looking worried, whether over the gift or for Domhnull or for both at once.

But in time they did hear him behind them, and turned to look when he came near, not riding fast, but fast enough for his long-legged horse to catch them.

"So, well," he said scowling. "You ought not to be off by yourselves, didn't your father say that? Come on."

Their ponies took the pace of his long-legged horse, and they went briskly for a time—*he would joke if he were men, or quarrel if we were his friends,* Meadhbh thought, *so he has to find some fault with us, that being all there is to do.*

"Look," she said, finding welcome distraction, "the foal is lying down."

"Tired," said Domhnull after a moment, "and the sun is warm." He offered back her gift then. "It does smell sweet."

He pleased her by that last, that he thought her sensible enough to give a courtesy to, as if she were growing up all of a sudden. Then she spoiled it all by blushing. She felt the heat in her face and had to pretend to have all her mind on putting her gift away and hanging it about her neck.

She thought that she had made him feel better, all the same. He looked eased, could smile again—perhaps it was the Sidhe gift: she looked at Domhnull in a way she had never looked at any boy her age, and felt desolate and hopeless. He was a man already. Women from the smith's daughter to the scullery maids sighed after him; even Muirne, whose devotion they had had all their own—even Muirne had taken to doing small things for him; and somewhen she had gotten—happier, or younger, or at least different, for all that she was older than he was. So Meadhbh felt twice robbed; and once more—that it was the first thought in her life she was worried Ceallach might learn and laugh at her.

Then with a sigh she recovered all her sense and gave Domhnull up two breaths after she had first loved him, deciding to look him straight in the eye and to be his staunch friend, the way he was her father's; and Beorc was; and Rhys—o Rhys!—and to go on riding out with him on summer days, as long as such days lasted.

Caer Wiell will not be here, she thought suddenly, having seen it the sudden way dreams unrolled at night between two blinks of the eye; and the leaf ached at her throat. She saw the land burned, changed, and smoke going up from blackened fields.

"Ceallach—"

He had got it too, the same awful dream. She saw it in the sudden pallor of his face, his glance toward her.

"What is it?" Domhnull asked, not the way someone might ask children, but anxiously.

"I had a dream just then," she said. "It seemed Caer Wiell was gone."

"There was a hill," said Ceallach while the horses plodded on, relentless, toward the walls. "It had bones under it."

"I never saw that," Meadhbh said.

"Caer Donn," said Domhnull, all hoarse. "It was Caer Donn you saw." He gathered the reins which he had let go slack. "Come." He put them to a quicker pace as if that could make them safe, to get them behind gates and walls.

"They had no business to be riding out in the first place," their mother said, over by the fire where she had gone to stand.

Meadhbh looked at her distractedly, as if she had gone mad. With all that they had come panting up to the hall to say, that was what their mother settled on, with their father sitting still in his thoughts and Domhnull sweating and pale from their climb up the stairs. "The Bradhaeth loose and Caer Damh stirred up and they riding out as if there no trouble at all."

"I saw Caer Wiell burned," Meadhbh cried.

"Hush!" said their father. "Come here. How was it burned?"

Meadhbh shook her head and came to her knees by her father's chair. Ceallach hung on his other side.

"Perhaps," said Domhnull, "when she lent me her gift to hold, she confused things in it. Maybe it was some other place."

"And Caer Donn?" asked Ceallach. "I saw Donn, did I not?"

"Maybe," said Domhnull, "you caught it from me, something I had seen or imagined."

"Doubtless so," their mother declared and came back again, sweeping past Muirne who hovered near the fire with large, frightened eyes. "I've held the stone. It was like that. One remembers things."

Their mother wanted it to be so. Meadhbh looked at her, understanding now and wishing for once the same thing her mother wished, that what she had seen could turn out to be something past, something of Domhnull's rememberings and nothing yet to come.

"Meadhbh," her father said, "give me your hand, and you, Ceallach."

She did that, and for a moment thought he only meant to tell them something; but then he shut his eyes, and the world turned gray and full of mist.

"Ciaran!" their mother called.

The hold was burned and the land was waste, with smoke over all the hills, that spread to the forest; and there was a hill of bones, and a shallow lake with something coiled at the depth of it, and deep places under the hills that had cracked open like eggs, empty in their darkness.

"No!" It was their father's voice. He let go of their hands, a fierce shove, and for a moment Meadhbh was lost and breathless in the mist.

But it was her mother's arms she felt, smelled the lilacs and herbs of her skirts against her face, and her mother was shouting at her father.

"It's going to be true," Meadhbh said, "it's all going to be true."

"They are *children*," their mother cried.

"Yes," their father said. Meadhbh blinked him clear, and there were tears on his face. That won her silence. She wanted not to look at him but there was no other place she could, not now. Her father reached out quite calmly and ruffled her hair as he had not done since she was very small, and tousled Ceallach's after. "Domhnull."

"Lord," Domhnull answered quietly.

"The Sight can mislead. Sometimes it is not quite what it seems. But all the same, with the Bradhaeth roused, with all our enemies combined—and Rhys not here—well, I have no kinsman, Domhnull; and where I go, Beorc is like to go. My lady's kin—something untoward has delayed them, or Rhys would be back by now. Be in a kinsman's stead to her and Meadhbh and Ceallach—if need should be, stand by them."

"On my life, lord," Domhnull whispered. Meadhbh felt her mother's arms tighten about her as she rose. Her mother smoothed the hair her father had ruffled. *Let me go*, she wished, wanting to shout it, and turned instead and hugged her mother, thinking that someone ought to.

"Caer Wiell will never fall," her mother said without a doubt in her voice. "This nonsense comes of meddling with the Sidhe gifts, that's what it is. Or listening at doors where they shouldn't."

No one said anything. Their father only sat still and gazed at all of them with that look he had when he was far away, and then he got up from his chair.

"Domhnull, go rest. Muirne, see he gets a pot of cool ale—I daresay it would come welcome. Maybe a bit for Meadhbh and Ceallach too if they would like."

"A very little," said their mother, measuring with pinched fingers and frowning at Muirne. She combed Meadhbh's hair then with her fingers and held her face steady, looking in her eyes. "You are too old to be riding about the country, do you hear? You will not be doing such things again."

It would have galled Meadhbh even if she thought it would come to no more than the other threats, but now it had the sound of doom, louder than any intent in the words. *Not again, not again, not again.* She pretended she had not heard; saying anything to it might seal it like the magic of true names. "May I go?" she asked instead.

"Go. Comb your hair." Her mother was distracted. The hair was something she said without thinking. Meadhbh went with Muirne, beside Ceallach, and Domhnull came after, but Meadhbh cast a backward glance where her mother and her father were, her mother standing with her arms hugged about herself, her father standing staring off toward nothing at all and with a grimness about his mouth that tokened words to come.

Not be doing such things again, Meadhbh thought, and her hands were cold. It was not the riding, but the country that would change, no more sun, no more green fields, no more of foals playing and them laughing with Domhnull outside Caer Wiell. She held to her gift and tried the while she went down the stairs after Muirne, to foretell where she would ride and to what, but even Floinn was lost to her, and there was darkness, everywhere darkness and mist and only the stone of present Caer Wiell under her fingers to remind her where and when she was.

Ceallach, she thought, *o Ceallach*.

"I shall be gone awhile," Ciaran said quietly to Branwyn. "Don't fret for it."

"Ciaran."

"Hush. I know." He pressed a kiss on her brow and held her a moment. "Forgive me."

"What did they see?"

"Desolation. Give them comfort. They have need of it."

Her hands caught at him and clenched. "Ciaran, Ciaran, if Rhys would come—He *will* come. He's too clever for anyone to have stopped him—"

"Things may happen; he may have had to give up his horse and go afoot after all, if the road was watched, and that would have taken a great deal more time."

"If anything were amiss, if what they saw—Ciaran, we were destroyed before and burned and here we are. If we had had the Sight before the King came to Caer Wiell, we would have lost all our hope. Those were dark days. But they were not the end of us."

"Tell *them* so. They need hope."

"*I* need hope. Ciaran, do not you leave me!" Do not you go anywhere, not unless you leave that thing behind and take your sword, hear me? What can the men think, that you go empty-handed and moon-eyed with that stone—Forgive me, listen to me now. What good has it ever done? None. Love, love, you should have had all the men about you up at Lioslinn, o gods, and gone up there armed in the first place and taught that brother of yours how to treat his guests."

"So would your father have done?"

"So would I do if I could wield a sword."

He took the reproach he had not looked for and stared at her a moment, then let fall his hands and turned toward the door, patient because there was nothing else to be.

"Ciaran." Heartbreak was in Branwyn's voice. He stopped and looked back with hope of her.

"So would I do," he said quietly, "if *I* could wield a sword."

"Put off the stone. Will you kill us all, and the children too?"

He brought a hand to the stone and felt it cold as it had been cold for days, like ice against his heart. He had nothing to say, nothing that would not give Branwyn more to fear than already she had; anger was better than anguish.

"Answer me."

"No, Branwyn."

"O gods!"

His cloak was on the peg. He gathered it up. "I shall not be going far. No riding off."

"Take me with you."

He shook his head. "No."

"Into Eald. Into Eald, is it?"

He put the cloak on, pretending he had not heard. "It may be cold."

"O gods, Ciaran, don't go."

He managed a little smile, not an easy one. "Back by supper," he said, as if he were only going out to the fences.

And then he stepped away, not a little parting, but a great one, so that he caught at the stone and held it clenched in his hand, lost for a moment in the chill gray mist.

"*Arafel!*" he cried, "*Arafel!*" but he did not call the third time, not daring that. He listened a long time, hoping for any small sound, searching with his heart for any trace or hope of her. "I am here," he shouted into the gray mist, in the green of the forest with the moisture dripping off the bracken and glistening on black bark. "You said I should not call your name—but that you would always know what I was doing. You said that I shouldn't walk here—but the world isn't as safe as it was either. And I do need you."

There was silence, profound silence, in which no wind stirred, nor leaf moved.

"What am I supposed to do?" he cried, forcing his voice amid such stillness. "If there is any help at all you can give—or even give me some advice. Sending Domhnull up there—I know that was a mistake. I'm afraid I have made all too many mistakes. I could go to the King at Dun na h-Eoin—but that would leave Caer Wiell with too little strength for safety, or send me out with too little on the road. What should I do, stay here and do nothing? Was that what you wanted? What was I supposed to do?''

Still there was silence. He walked forward, carefully, remembering the way, believing it in spite of the mist and the black and ghostly trees; but then he thought of what he was doing, like a man looking down when he ought not, and then doubt began to grow at his shoulder, and shadows began to deepen on this side and on the other, and things to gibber and rattle in them. He doubted the power of the Sidhe which supported his own—doubted she existed, doubted all the wisdom that she had given him and all the way he knew.

"Help me," he cried in the thickening mist. "Help me if you can! I need you! Help!"

He heard hoofbeats then far away and from the west of the world; and something familiar touched his heart. A wind blew over him, lessening the mist, a wind from the sea. He heard the cries of gulls and shivered in a melancholy that leached away all life and love and purpose.

Then he heard the hoofbeats closer, and the stone remembered a whiteness, swiftness, fierceness.

Aodhan, leaped into his mind like some answer to a question long forgotten, implicit in the thunder and the storm.

"*Aodhan!*" The horse was his, had always been, if ever he had thought to call him, if he had ever thought of journeying those ways through Eald where Aodhan might go.

"*Aodhan!*" he cried. "O Aodhan!"

The wind blew stronger from the sea, and there came a flickering of memory from the stone.

Man . . . it whispered, full of anguish. *Man, is it you? What have they done?*

"Liosliath! Help me—"

I cannot come. The shadow—Man, the shadow—

The wind fell suddenly as if someone had shut an open door. Then it rose from another quarter, miasmic, heavy, wafting from some place of water and corruption.

"Liosliath! I am still here! Liosliath!"

But there was only mist, and the voice faded in his mind as faery things would, leaving him robbed and bewildered, whether anyone had spoken at all; or whether he had imagined the salt wind or the sound of hooves.

Something chuckled at his despair, and brush stirred by him. He had slipped somehow. He did not know this place. The mist wove through it in threads, so that one moment he had a clear view of trees and more mist beyond, and then he passed into that mist and lost all bearings, all certainties. He was looking for Airgiod, but the stream he found instead was fouled, choked with leaves and stagnant. A reek went up from it that assailed the soul.

Then his heart failed him, for strange pale eyes stared up at him from beneath that murky water, and blinked when leaves drifted down, silver tarnished black. The eyes rose closer to the surface, glowing like some double reflection of the moon.

He backed away, met the corpse of a tree whose branches clawed at him like fingers. He felt past it, retreated step by step.

"Man," a voice said.

He stopped, looked toward that darkness darker than the skies. "Lord Death," he said, his heart beating as if he had been running. His arm ached with his old wound. "Where is she, do you know? Or where have I gotten to?"

"She is fled," Death said, and his voice came thin and strained. "Man, I had thought to follow *you*."

"To her?" Wariness came on him. "To her, is that your meaning?"

"She sent me out, Man, to learn a name; but she would not stay for it." The darkness drifted near, loomed, shutting out the little light that sifted through the branches, and the air was bitter cold. "If you can reach her, do. I have more messages for her."

"She met something at Caer Donn. But you would know that. You were there."

"She met something, yes. Use that stone of yours and call her."

"I tried. The stone gives me nothing but the sea. Trees are where they should not be . . . and Airgiod, if that marsh yonder is Airgiod—"

"The sea," Lord Death whispered. "And Eald deserted. Man, Man, if *that* urge has fallen on her, we are all lost. Call her. Call her name. You have that power. You proved it once before."

"I can't."

"You *will* not." The shadow swept closer. A hand gripped his arm with strength like bone. "Man, listen to me. The drow are roused. Do you know that name? Whatever this stone of yours may be to a Sidhe, they are without. They have lost it, cast it away—a drow is what a Sidhe becomes, when he has lost whatever that stone is."

A cold settled into his marrow, and the stone stung his heart like a lump of ice. He remembered then a tree shining like the moon, like a thousand moons, agleam with jewels and elvish work. "No," he said, "not always." Warmth came then, reassurance, and he shrugged off Lord Death's hand as if it were spiderweb. The stone grew warmer. "I am sure of that. It is what a Sidhe does to the stone himself, of his own will; that makes the difference. I *remember*, Lord Death." The strength in the stone grew poignant as tears, as a shout going through the forest, then faded, leaving the cold. He turned about, sought that retreating touch with all his heart, as if that door had opened again and let out warmth and kindness and all the things this place had long forgotten. But Death laid his hand on his shoulder and came before him again, cutting off all his vision.

"Fool and servant of a fool! Use the power you have. If there are weapons, take them up. You will need them all. No, do not turn from me. This is all your doing, the loosing of this plague. A thousand or so human lives you bought with it, and your own. Caer Wiell might have fallen, yes, would have fallen that day; but suppose—no, hear me, never turn your back to me—suppose you had not roused all Eald to help you and Caer Wiell had fallen. The King was on his way; he would have come there sooner or later, if you had only sold your lives for enough of An Beag's. He would have come on an enemy in their looting, disorderly, in a hold with gates broken. Then Laochailan King would *be* king in his own right, by his own hand and never reigned in fear—fear of you, halfling, married to his kin. But no, you refused to die there; saved your life and a paltry thousand more and waked all of this evil and cost every life you saved. You doomed the *world*, Man, and all that might ever be, to save your life!"

Ciaran tore himself away, but brambles snagged his cloak, his clothes, his hands, and Death was still before him.

"You waked power, Man, and would not use it—destroyed the peace, destroyed the King, destroyed your mother with grief and your father and your brother with fear of you and it. You were lord of Donn if you had reached out your hand. You could have taken that sheepcot and compelled your father and your brother instead of moping about waiting for them to send to you. You could have gone to Dun na h-Eoin and faced Laochailan: who could have prevented you if you had had the stone then and used it? Your king feared you. The whisperers at his side would have scattered like deer. You would have had him in your hand for good or ill, and then was time for compassion. You could have made him great, shaped him however you would have him, made him a name to remember, gained him a kingdom greater than any king before him. Fear of you broke what little there was of him and made him clay for moulding; but you would not. You cast him away, cast it all away. You stayed at home, breeding your horses and raising cabbages. This small realm of yours, have you not made it fair? But at what cost?''

"The kingdom has had peace of me.''

"Are you virtuous? But you could have murdered father, brother, King, host, and done far more good in the world after all this murder than you have done with your peace. You could have piled corpse on corpse and burned holds and tortured and plundered and done more good than this.''

"Then where were you? Why did you stay your hand from me?'' The taste of ashes and tears was in his mouth. The thorns held him impaled. "There were years I had nothing. I was so slight a matter. I expected you—in the forest, in fighting with An Beag, somewhere on the stairs—Where were you, that you could not do so slight a thing, if all the world hung on it?''

There was silence. The shadow drew back and seemed to shrink. "You are not the only fools there be. I bound myself by a promise in your case, old comrade. She asked. And I promised.''

"And my brother? Was *he* beyond you too? Or the King? Any of us would have sufficed, would we not?''

"But on them I had no claim. And *she* would not. I begged her!—I! slay this Donnchadh. One stroke and the world is saved. She would not. The Sidhe are fey and mad. This abdication of yours—it must run in the blood.'' Lord Death drifted closer. "Listen. A night ago your brother quitted Caer Donn, bound for Dun na h-Eoin where the King lies dying—a long dying, believe me. It amazes them that one Man could survive so much and so deadly poisons. But they are out of patience with such methods. Do you not understand, Man? Laochailan has been no King. They divided him from you, from the one who might have saved him, and murdered the lord of Ban, who was the best of them. And not they. Donnchadh. From the beginning, your father and Donnchadh.''

He shook his head vehemently. "My father—no. I will believe it of my brother, but my father, no, no man was truer to his King.''

"Your father was halfling like yourself, and the curse was wakened at Donn. You wakened it. It was waiting for him when he came home, lurking in the stones, the earth, the foundations of Caer Donn. I will tell you the name of it; I will whisper it: *Duilliath.* And doubtless the drow came whispering to him: *half-Sidhe, half-Sidhe, kinsman, where is your younger son? More powerful than his King, more than his father—what would stay him from coming here? Power must fight power, and there is power in this place. Dig deep, search it out, master it.* —But it mastered Donn. Of course it could. It whispered, it grew— without scruples. Your King already feared you; and when they came whispering in their turn, kinsmen against kinsman, why, conspiracy was a thing Laochailan King could well believe, when he would not have believed in virtue. *Power against power*, they said. *Magic to oppose the Sidhe that sits in Caer Wiell. How else can we survive?* You wed your King's cousin, begot an heir while your King has failed. Evald died to your advantage—*Now he has Caer Wiell*, they whispered, *and was not Evald's death untimely young?*"

"O gods."

"Oh, but you are beyond gods, halfling. I cannot hear your prayers. You have the stone. Your brother is on the road. You might be there, suddenly, beside him. Against Sidhe I have no power, and his life is guarded now, I know so. It was him. The drow will have Donnchadh on the throne in a fortnight; and armies at his command. If you have power, use it! Call *her* name, not mine."

He doubted. Doubt crushed him. He shook his head. "No. Call her into this place—no. I will try something else—to go to her." He held the stone still in his hand, and it remained cold and lifeless. "And if I find her I shall give her your message."

"Do so, then," said Death. The darkness drew aside. "If that is all that I can win, do so. And be wise. The border is not the greatest danger. I have sent a dream to Beorc Scaga's-son: his father. *Come home*, I have bidden him. *Your lord has need of you.* And mark my words, you will."

"Keep your hands from my folk! They are not yours to be sending here and there."

"They are mine when I call them—when their hour is come. One of them I found wandering and escorted to your hands. Was I thanked for that?" The voice faded on the wind that rattled dry branches and stank of stagnant water. "No. But our interests are liker than you know. Farewell and fare better, Man, than you have fared before."

He shivered. Somehow he had gotten to his own woods again, less dire than the place he had quitted, and the sun shone through tangled limbs and summer leaves. He was not held. The brambles did not grow here and it was Caerbourne that flowed at his feet.

Then with a jolt of his heart he knew where he was, a place

where he and Lord Death had met before: it was Caerbourne Ford near Raven Hill. He had strayed half a day from home.

At least he knew his way from here, a path Rhys must have taken, a path which once he had run with the hounds of the Hunt at his heels. A spur of it led from here to the heart of all Eald, to that grove where he had first met the Sidhe, beneath that tree which grew rooted in his woods and hers at once.

That was the place she would be, he told himself; there lay hope if hope there was, if he dared come there now, with Arafel unwilling. But things were changed. It was his own safety she had thought of. Now he was concerned for hers, for all that depended on her. He made haste going down the bank, fevered haste, trusting this Caerbourne far more than the stream he had just quitted, though his shoulders itched between with the memory of arrows and An Beag so near to this crossing-place.

Danger. He felt it suddenly near him as he waded the dark stream, a shivering in air and water, a poison in the winds. He struggled the harder, panting, sought the far bank and gained it, soaked and heavy in that climbing and already reaching elsewhere with his mind.

An Beag, he thought. *Watchers at the ford*. He fled into Eald as if it were a dream, recalling another day that he had met evil in this place. *The grove*, he thought, but he could not find the way. The mist thickened. Brambles caught at him. Iron shivered through his substance like poison, so that he staggered, almost losing Eald.

A darkness loomed up before him in chill and fetid wind. It rattled and gibbered and mud clung to his feet, holding him like nightmare. Other things leapt and clawed at his boots, strove to reach his hands, and the cold was terrible. He lurched aside in defeat, tried another way, but dead wood crumbled beneath his weight, and another of the greater horrors lay that way. The air was presentient with ill and malice, so that it stung his chest and sped his heart. It came toward him. More and more the lesser ones had power: one sat on a dead branch and plummeted suddenly upside down, laughing and clinging with hands and feet, its face still rightwise up.

He plunged on, thrusting it and its branch away, but something drifted before him now, black and unwholesome, with long white hair, and dodge as he would, he was overtaking it.

It turned suddenly and looked at him with a white elvish face. *Arafel*, he thought in sudden relief, because they were so like; but this face was cold and not what it had seemed a moment ago.

It reached out its hand, more terrible in its beauty than all the rest in their ugliness.

"Duilliath," he guessed.

It laughed. "You are wrong, Man, and powerless to name me." It came closer. "Yield up the stone. You are hopeless else."

"No."

"Lost, then." Other creatures had come, and iron shivered in the air. "Ciaran, Ciaran, Ciaran—*back to your beginnings*!"

It hurled him. The black limbs spun, the earth came up at him and he struck it, brown wet earth, slick leaves, clinging to his hands.

He heard dogs. He leapt up, in the sunlight, in the dappling of the leaves of Caerbourne Ford; he heard horses and movement and the cleaving of the air, the shivering passage of iron from the bowmen beyond the trees.

Arrows struck him in quick succession. His heart burst in dazing pain. He fell a second time, shattering the shafts and numb after the first hurt—rising then because his limbs still moved: he saw the An Beag bandits, saw bows bent again to add more arrows to those that pierced him.

He ran. He turned and plunged into mist, where the pain began in earnest, robbing him of breath.

"*Ciaran*," Liosliath cried, fair and far and desperate. "*Cling to the stone—o run, run, run!*"

The wind came then, tearing at the mist, and he heard thunder, the howling of the gale that yet smelled of sea and wrack. A glimmering shone like a star amid the murk, and grew, steadily oncoming, while the thunder swelled.

"*Aodhan!*" he cried, remembering. He had called three times. The elf horse had come, from the ends of the earth it might be: Aodhan had come.

Thunder came down on him, and wind battered him as Aodhan came near, a shining pallor in the dark, a shoulder offered to his need. He caught the mane amid which lightnings flickered, harmless to him; strength burned from the stone toward his hands, needing nothing of his heart, and he flung himself astride, or somehow he had gotten to Aodhan's back. The elf horse began to run above the ground, carrying him with shockless steps and racing not through distances but faster and deeper into Eald.

"O Aodhan," he whispered, "take me to her, take me there now."

The elf horse snorted, shifted in his stride, almost losing him from his back, and whinnied in dismay, shifting this way and that. They ran; a wall of bright mist loomed before them, poured about them. Ciaran cried aloud, so fierce the pain of iron that split his heart, cried a second time in dismay to find them in retreat.

"Again," he cried, "Aodhan, take me through!"

The elf horse turned and tried the chill mist again, laboring. The cold pain shot through him, but he clung to the mane and held, feeling the horse fighting and veering beneath him. Trial after trial the elf horse made, shying back to lunge forward again, and now small things chittered and leapt at them in growing shadow; he cried aloud, and Aodhan whinnied and veered aside.

There was a darkness then, and Aodhan was running to the baying of hounds, away from the barrier, for the pain had ebbed. Thunder muttered. There were other hooves, and leaping shapes of dogs, and swift-flying shadows.

A rider drew even with them, moving with them, on a horse like night, in which there was the pale glimmering of bone where Aodhan's lightning flickered; the rider was Lord Death.

"No," Ciaran whispered. "Let me go on trying. Let me try, Lord Death."

"Turn then," the answer came; and he called out to Aodhan, to no avail. The elf horse ran on, a swift striding that lost not a pace. He sank on Aodhan's neck in defeat, unable to do more, clinging as the sunny road stretched suddenly beneath them.

Death stayed with him, a shadow in the day. They had left Eald and ran now on the river road, that which led home. The elf horse had failed as he had, ran now with a stretching and gathering of sinew, a flutter of mane, a blur of sunlit dust.

THIRTEEN

The Bain Sidhe

Domhnull made the steps, leaning on his stick, for his legs would still betray him, and went out along the wall, seeking somewhat of refuge, some little solitude where no one else could come at him with questions—Ask my lady this, it was, and ask my lady that, and pray, sir, what of the grainstores? —and the riders be home, sir Domhnull, nothing found, no hope, no luck and less of substance.

He leaned his arms upon the wall, his stick resting by him, and bowed his head, for it ached; but he thought again how that would seem and lifted it, looking outward on a sight that today seemed worse than yesterday—for sun shone on Caer Wiell's lands, on green pasture and growing fields and the gentle swells of it west and north and even on the trees about the river. But beyond that circle of sunlight the sky was darkened with walls of cloud, towering fortresses of cloud that had begun as wisps and mare's-tails.

It did not advance as storms did, on wind and claps of thunder. It built new outposts, a mare's-tail first, a gray, dull wisp, and then an outwelling of the stormcloud near it, all silent, proceeding no more swiftly than any growth of clouds on a summer's day. A man had to watch, not look, and then he would see it, this wall-building all about them. They had hardly noticed it beginning, first as a line of cloud in the far northwest, and then in the west, spreading over the forest to the south as the clouds built; and then one night it reached out an arm toward the north again, darkening the dawn with strands of murk that became another wall.

Daily, folk had begun to remark on it, and to cast anxious glances from the fields and the crests of the walls. Night and day it grew, until the first strands of it appeared in the north, completing the ring about them, and the cloud over the forest advanced until the line of sunlight could be seen plain on the treetops at noon, so that now shadow lay visibly along the tops of the trees that overhung the Caerbourne and off across the hills; and overhead now, above the gray walls of the keep a cloudy rampart towered, up and up into bright sun and blue sky, its gray surface knobbed and gnarled and changing and somehow not moving, as if it had pressed against some barrier that made this well of sunlight. Domhnull did not look at it, no more than a glance, but there was no escaping the sight of it outward, where its arm swept round across the hills, and the marching line of shadow had now come all the way over the hills, so that that horizon too was dull and dark.

The circle had narrowed again in the night, from the north. No one talked about it. Only there was a traffic to the walls or out the gates, each looking for himself, from lady Branwyn to Cook in her apron, floured from morning baking—to himself, latest, not wanting to look at all, but drawn here. It was the sunlight he looked at, the impossibly brilliant sunlight shining off the fairness of the land, barricade against the shadow, which had now assumed a perfect roundness on its nearer edge, marking the size of the circle that yet would be.

Gods help us, Domhnull thought, but it was not gods he thought of, but rather Arafel. He still hoped. The sunlight was reason for hope even if it was narrowing, even if their lord was the seventh day missing.

"He has gone away," lady Branwyn had said, with such a look in her blue eyes that he dare not question it. *Gone*. Domhnull knew where lord Ciaran had gone, and watched the cloudwall veil that forest day by day.

But the circle remained about them, and the folk of Caer Wiell went about their business, knowing quite as well as he, he reckoned, that their lord had not ridden to this place where he had gone—since his horse was still in stable and no men had been called to go with him. Gossip would happen, but there was a strange calm about this gossip, a matter of factness like the confidence with which his own mother had set out bowls of milk for visitors in the night. This cloud was a sign, it was clearly a sign, and not a good one; but a steady hammering went up from Smith's forge, and smoke and sparks: and riders went to and fro on the road keeping up contact with the borders, while wagons groaned their way in from the steadings, and the storehouse filled day by day, preparing for siege.

So now a wagon came, lumbering from distance to nearness, and when it had come near enough, Domhnull came down and stood leaning on his stick while the wagon came through the gates. A farmwife drove it; a girl was on the seat beside her.

"Where from?" he asked, hoping for news from the borders.

"Raghallach's Steading," the farmwife said. "The boys be all at the border, and that cloud—yon's ugly, an't it?"

Domhnull cast an involuntary glance upward, shrugged, leaning on his stick and grinned. "Sun's fair, goodwife."

For a moment the stout face looked bothered, grayed hair sticking with the sweat, lips clamped. Then a spark came to dark eyes and a grin showed gapped teeth. She clapped the girl on the shoulder, smoothed her tangled hair and nodded. "Oh, aye, 'tis."

"Stay in hold," Domhnull said, "if you like."

"Brought the stores, I did, all's to spare. Left my mark on t'door so's my folk won't worry. It's my granddarter, see—" She looked down at the small face, and up again. "There be trouble about the steading. I be a fair shot wi' my man's old bow, but them things comes at nightfall, run off the cow, they did, and got the sheep, e'en Sobhrach's lamb, poor thing.''

"Nothing here," said Domhnull, "to trouble you—Cein," he said, the man being among others who had come up. "Take them through.''

So he let them pass and turned away, thinking most on his own kin and glad that his mother had already come in and stayed. Beorc was on the border still. He found himself, but for Branwyn and Siodhachan, chiefest in the hold now, a thing he had never looked for. He had become Sir Domhnull and respected; but it seemed to him that all it meant was standing still and not doing the things he would do: like riding with the searchers, like going where he knew how to look, like seeing for himself and not relying on messages days old.

Thunder muttered. He glanced up at the clouds and saw no darkened source of thunder. About him in the hold no others seemed to have heard it. Folk were going about their business. That strange deafness disturbed him, the more as the thunder grew and no one noticed. He strode for the walls, his limp pronounced, his stick forgotten in his hand. Behind in the yard was the squeal of the oxcart wheels on pavings. Children played. A rooster crowed, long and loud, fit to break the morning.

Then thunder clapped, deafening, and horses whinnied and cattle lowed. There was a pause in voices, a sudden exclamation.

Lightning blazed in Domhnull's path, just within the gates, a thunder-rumbling, the shape of horse and rider burning like the sun and dimming then.

"Lord," Domhnull whispered. It *was* himself.

"Domhnull. Help." It was the ghost of a voice, and the shape reached out to him. He went, flinging his stick aside, offering his hands, and Ciaran came down to him, sliding into his arms. For a moment there was no weight, and then there was, as the white horse of the Sidhe retreated. He could not bear it and sank to the pavings on his knees, shielding his lord's head and shoulders at least. Ciaran's face was waxen-pale, his flesh seeming to glow inside with light beyond what fell on it, and the bones standing out. Arrows had pierced him, three in the chest and ribs, broken stubs of shafts that moved with his breathing, and yet there was no bleeding.

"Gods," Domhnull said, feeling tears dammed up in him. "O gods." He trembled. He brushed dirt from Ciaran's cheek and the closed lids flickered. He stared about him, stunned, realizing he could not lift him, that he knelt in a ring of people in the gateway. "For the gods' sake do something. Help him. *Arafel!*''

"No," Ciaran whispered. His eyes opened and there was a murmur from the folk. He moved. It was incredible that any man could breathe, his body so pierced, but breaths continued. His hand sought the pavement and pressed to raise himself. The stone glowed upon his breast, like a moon by daylight. "Don't call, don't use that name."

"Lord," Domhnull said, and then another arrived running, Branwyn racing breathless through the crowd. She stopped. One might have expected a cry, a wail—something. She only came quietly and knelt and took her lord's hand and brought it to her lips, bloody that it was.

"I have had dreams," she said. "The children saw you coming home—o Ciaran, Ciaran!"

"He is sleeping," Domhnull said when he came out to the children, there waiting in the hall; he had rather face enemies than this, these young faces, these hearts hanging on every turn of word for hope or something hidden from them. They stood there like two waxen images, with vast bruised eyes, and so, so lost, not knowing how much folk lied at such times, or how much a man might want to tell two children, or what horror might have been up there, while the door was closed. They waited. He opened his arms to them both. They came and he hugged them tight, like comrades, like something more than the children they were treated, and felt his senses aswim with panic and with loss. Perhaps it was the talismans they wore. For a moment he could not get his own breath, and felt somewhere lost, in mist, as if they stood in some space without boundaries or safety, naked to evil and to good. "O gods," he murmured, "but he will heal. I did. And she loves him more."

They looked up at him then, two pairs of eyes staring into him; but it was only the hall about them, solid stone, and the light came from torches in this unwindowed room.

"Iron," said Ceallach, half-whispered, "Domhnull, they shot him with iron."

" 'Tis gone now. We drew it." The image was vivid in him, the waxen skin, Siodhachan's knives, but only a little loss of blood—He saw the young faces, their pale, pale faces, as if they were drained of tears as their father was of blood. They could not know such things, must not be privy to them, with the cloudwall building over them, their father so unnaturally pale and still beyond the door.

"Can we see him now?" Meadhbh asked.

They were not to do so. Their mother had forbidden it. But

Branwyn had not seen their faces, heard their voices, so calm and reasoned they broke his heart. "Yes," he said, "but from the door. You would not want to wake him. Listen to me. From such great hurts—well, sleep is best."

He took them then to the door which Muirne was leaving. He took it from her hand, and cracked it wider, so that they could see where Ciaran lay abed, Branwyn kneeling at his side. His face was calm.

So was Branwyn's now. She gazed at him and them and motioned to them, laying a finger to her lips to sign them quiet, and noiselessly they came to their father's bedside.

Forgive me, Domhnull sent with his eyes, but Branwyn hugged her children, Meadhbh and then Ceallach, wiped with her thumb the tears that spilled silently down composed, pale faces. So silently she urged them to go after they had seen their father. Domhnull held out his hand again, not without a look at his lord lying there so still.

Ciaran's eyes had opened. "Hush," said Branwyn, "go back to sleep."

The faintest of smiles touched his face, the smile of a man looking on what he loved, and then it faded and his eyes closed. Sweat broke out upon his brow, and his face had again that waxen light, his brows and nostrils and the edges of his mouth so drawn that it seemed another man, the lines of age smoothed by pain into an illusion of youth and fierceness.

Like a King, Domhnull recalled the vision. *Or the Sidhe*.

"Father," Meadhbh whispered. "*Father*—"

"Go," Branwyn said distractedly, her arm about the pillow on which Ciaran's head rested. "Let him sleep."

Meadhbh fled. Ceallach hesitated a moment, his face anguished, and Domhnull took his hand and led him.

They wept afterward, like children. Muirne came and brought them sweet cakes and a bit of ale and this at last tempted them; Domhnull won smiles from them, the sort without laughter or happiness, but brave, their father's kind of smile when he had looked on them. There was the smell of rain in the air, reminding them of clouds, even in this room, and sometimes thunder muttered.

"That's the white horse outside," said Meadhbh, her eyes wide, her hand upon the talisman at her throat. A chill ran over Domhnull's skin, and comfort at once, that there was still something of the Sidhe near them.

"Perhaps," he said, "its owner is not far."

"It is lost," said Ceallach in that same distant tone, as if he were listening to something else at the same time. "It grieves for someone. O Domhnull—something is wrong down by the river."

"Hush," he said, "hush. Be still. Come back and drink your ale. Get them more, Muirne. I think they could well stand it."

"No," said Meadhbh.

A strange sound was growing on the air, so that Domhnull stirred, thinking of thunder, of the clouds, of the creature that he had seen—but it was a different, earthy sound, of hooves, of echoes off the wall that had nothing to do with thunder.

"There are riders coming," Muirne whispered. "Domhnull, do you hear?"

"Aye," he said, and thrust himself to his feet in haste, in dread, for they were coming hard and they were almost at the gates. "Where is the watch, that we get no word? Gods help us." He started down the stairs. He had followers, Muirne, Meadhbh and Ceallach, but he did not delay to stop them.

So they came out onto the walls where others had gathered, as the gates groaned open and the riders thundered into the yard on lathered horses, riders whose colors and whose metal brightness had been obscured with dust until even their faces were masks. They were Caer Wiell folk; and no dust could hide the foremost, for his size and fiery hair and beard.

"Beorc," Domhnull breathed, and headed down the last stairs to meet his cousin.

There was yet another visitor in the room, perched on his bedside. Ciaran saw him without opening his eyes, saw him best that way, a lump of darkness sitting there staring at him, but Branwyn had not seen him: her golden head was bowed, the light coming to her so that it picked out the silver amid her braids, dancing on the stones of the wall, but never, never touching the darkness. The pain was deep in him, a gnawing pain of iron where the poison had spread. He felt an ache as if he had gotten a hailstone for a heart, pain of wounds, of loss, of seeing Branwyn sitting there so lost and helpless. He could not move. The world seemed too still for that, or too fragile. *I shall slip away*, he thought; *I shall never see her again, and the children, and my fields and all the rest, the table set for dinner, Meadhbh laughing, Branwyn in the sunlight, none of these things. It will tear like spiderweb, this world.*

"Take off the stone," Lord Death said. "You have that much strength."

"Is that what you have come for?"

Death stirred, came closer, leaning over him while Branwyn

drowsed. "For you—yes, my friend. Give up the stone. Turn it loose and give me your hand—o Man, there is little hope enough; but at least you will be spared the worse things." There seemed others beyond him, mother, cousins, friends; a tall brooding figure hung back from the rest, and that was his father, still frowning.

"Ciaran," his father said, "I was wrong."

"I have seen your son and daughter," his mother said. "They are very fair. Will you not bring them? And Branwyn too?"

"My daughter," said another, shadow-wrapped, with a golden-haired woman by his side.

There were others, shadows, crowned with gold. One face was brighter. It was Laochailan's, and tears ran on his gaunt face. "Ciaran, Ciaran of Donn," his King said. "They have murdered me."

"Lord," said others, a shadow-host, folk of his hold. Blood and dust marked them. Arrows pierced them, men he had left at the border, farmer-folk who had rallied there. "They never cease to come. What shall we do?"

"There is no luck in Donn," his father said. "Nor hope now."

"Murdered," said his King.

"*No!*" He opened his eyes then, caught a breath that pained him. Branwyn caught his hand.

"Beorc is here. Beorc has come back safe from the border."

He said nothing to this. He was not surprised at this passage of familiar faces, not then nor later when Beorc came with Domhnull to stand beside his bed.

"He is sleeping again," Branwyn said. "Domhnull says that he will mend. He will."

He smiled to hear that, wishing to believe that and not the dreams.

"Come back," said Lord Death, but the sound of waves was in his ears, and a white horse came running toward him in the dark.

Man, said another voice, *cling to the stone. There is no other hope. There is none in all the world. You must help me.*

"It hurts," he said.

Ciaran, that voice cried, at the margin of the world, *for the world's sake, hold on!*

The white horse waited. Thunder rumbled from its hooves.

A black one waited too. Death was there, with other riders. "There is battle coming," said Lord Death, "in which you cannot share. How long will you lie there suffering? They suffer too, who love you. Free them. There is no more hope. But you at least might be safe in my hands. I shall gather as many of them as I can. Old friends, kinsmen, family. Be free of this world. There will be other heroes. Make way. Make room. Call one you trust and pass on the stone. Domhnull might bear it.''

He felt after the stone and held it clenched tightly in his hand, ignoring the voice. The pain came in little waves, like the rocking of the sea, and greater ones, like the blowing of the wind. He held fast, feeling at times the coolness of sweat on his face when the world's wind would stir through the window. Now and again someone touched him and wiped his brow, now and again raised his head to give him drink; at times he looked and Branwyn was there, and he slipped his other hand in hers.

Thunder cracked.

"Is it raining?" he asked.

"No," she said, "not yet."

He drifted back again, having gathered up the scattered threads. "Liosliath," he said, "Liosliath, Liosliath." It was a misty way, out among the trees. The white horse ghosted among them, and lifted his head toward the sea. "Hear me," he said, "Liosliath. I have lost her. She has gone somewhere into the wood, and something has gotten loose in the world. I dare not call its name, but I think you would know it."

There was no clear answer, but a touch at the stone, a flooding of strength into it.

"Come," a voice said then, a whisper hollow as the sea. "Hear the gulls?"

"Beware," said another voice, "to hear only true voices. Some will doom you. A mistake will doom the world . . . and some seem very fair."

"I hear something singing," he said, and fair it seemed, wailing on the wind.

He was asleep again, his face so drawn and thin: Branwyn never let the candles die, seldom quit his side, though Muirne came and gave her drink and others came, like Beorc, big man that he was, so soft-footed in his tread, to look in and then depart again.

Now Beorc knelt, bending to one knee, to take her hand in his huge one, to press her fingers.

"Lady," he whispered, "go to hall awhile, go to bed, and let me watch—Do you think some harm could come to him with me beside him? Nothing in this world or the other would I let pass.

You have children, lady. They need you. They need you to sleep a bit and eat a bit, and wash your face and smile.''

She understood. She gazed at him from that distance of long patience, having wept all she meant to weep while her lord was living, but Beorc's loyalty touched her to the quick. "They're not my children," she said, "but his. Do you think I dare have them near him, Sighted as they are? They saw him fall; they saw him coming home. What more should they see, Beorc? I'm blind to such things. I can only watch him, not—not suffer the other things. And my children know. They know where I have to be.''

"They are children," said Beorc, "and see their own hurts too well.''

"Do they?" She thought back on breakfast tables, on childish tears, on baby faces, and first steps, and skinned knees; and the forest when they were lost; and the gateway, when they were found. But she gazed on Ciaran's sleeping face and that had more power than all these things. "No.''

A singing had grown again, some old tree wailing in the wind, some thing of nature, for the wind was strong outside tonight and thunder muttered. For a while that was the only sound. The wind came into the chamber, and Branwyn tugged the covers higher.

"No," she said, when Beorc got up and went to the shutters. "He refuses to have them closed.''

He stopped, his mouth set, his eyes troubled. "Curse that thing.''

"It's some old tree down by the river; a limb must have broken." She smoothed Ciaran's hair, used her kerchief to wipe his brow. "Hush, hush, go on sleeping.''

"Tree," Beorc said. "Lady, do you not hear it?''

She looked at him with a sudden stricture of the heart. "I hear the wind," she said. "Give me none of your imaginings.''

"It must be." His shoulders fell. His eyes settled beyond her, on Ciaran, with vast sorrow. She knew the tale. She had heard it, outside the door, the border in disarray, steadings burned. The last refugees were coming. They did not say such things within this room, in Ciaran's hearing. Here the talk was all of peace, of calm, of home and will you take a little soup, love? but he would not. And the borders were afire, the clouds above them narrowing day by day. There were creakings and groanings they could not disguise. *What is that?* he would say. *Oh, supplies brought in,* she would answer: he seemed easy to deceive, forgetting that she had said that before; and meanwhile the yard filled, and tents were set, and Caer Wiell prepared for siege.

THE TREE OF SWORDS AND JEWELS

"Not the wind," Ciaran whispered, and his eyes had opened somewhat. "Love, don't you hear it?"

"Out on it," Branwyn said lightly. "Listening after all." She smiled then for him, and dabbed his brow. "Look you, should we not close the shutters?"

"Is that Beorc? Gods, who's in command up there? Ruadhan?"

"Lord." Beorc came anxiously and held his hand. "It's well enough."

"Well." Ciaran's eyes drifted shut again. "Old wolf, to lie to me. I know. I can see, better than either of you. And hear." The voice came faintly, at great effort. "I can't stay longer. I have a ride to make. Aodhan is waiting. Branwyn, Branwyn—"

"O gods, Ciaran." She put her arms about his neck, held him so, her head against his. "I will not let you, *No*."

The sights afflicted her if she let them, a place of mist, where dark shapes twined amid ghostly trees, where a white figure washed bloody rags in Caerbourne's waters, wailing as she worked. She banished the visions, keeping her eyes open, fixing them on the familiar solid stones; and Beorc, Beorc was there. She heard the wailing clearer now, a hungry thing and nearer.

So Rhys came riding in, all unexpected. There were cheers from the walls where anxious folk had gathered to see what this dustcloud meant in the waning of the sun—waning, not setting, for the sun died daily into murk, choked by the cloudy ramparts in the west. In this greenish twilight the folk of the south came riding with their black and silver banners, three companies bristling with spears.

"Dryw's folk!" the cry went out—"Rhys is coming!" from place to place along the walls, from those who had vantages to those who did not.

"Open the gates," Domhnull cried, for once the great gates were shut, someone in authority had to open them; and he sent a page running to bear word to the hall, to Beorc and to the lady, who might whisper it in their lord's hearing and so give him cheer.

And: "Rhys," he said, embracing the smallish man who dismounted and met him on the stairs, the while the folk still cheered. "Rhys." Domhnull limped. His face was scarred. There was haunting in Rhys' dark eyes and a gauntness about the cheekbones, new lines about the mouth. They held each other at arm's length and tried to read each other, but Domhnull simply hugged the southron a second time with all he had to tell dammed up in his throat, and looked at him again. Others had come up to the foot of the steps, smallish men, two of them, much like Rhys in their dark cloth and darkened metal. "My brothers," Rhys said, "Owein and Madawc ap Dryw."

"Our lord cannot be here to greet you," Domhnull said, "or he would. But welcome to his hall, in his name and in his lady's your cousin. Gods reward you for this, all. Ale and supper for your men—we are not scanted of that." He spied a captain on the wall; he shouted orders. "Come," he said then to Rhys and his brothers. "Come upstairs. I would ask you which you would, rest or news, but this much first: lord Ciaran is hurt—" The truth stuck in his throat. "My lady is there. Come see her."

"Sore hurt?"

He nodded, lips clamped on words he would not say. "Will you come there first? My lady will not leave him."

"Aye," Rhys said. His tired face took on a resolution for still worse than he had seen.

Branwyn wept, quietly, at their coming to the room; and hugged them one and all, Rhys and Owein and Madawc, though talk went in whispers: "He will mend," she said as she had insisted a hundred times. "He sleeps a great deal, and that is to the good. I will tell him you've come. He'll want to see you."

But Ciaran lay very still, his breathing hardly stirring the coverlet, so pale that his flesh and the moonstone on his breast seemed little different. "Yes," Rhys whispered back. "Tell him we have come."

And afterward in hall Rhys hugged his youngest cousins and sat down to ale and meat, he and his brothers, trail-worn and haggard, while the dark fell outside and the wailing began again from the riverside.

"You had no easy ride coming here," Domhnull said. They were all at hand, Beorc, Muirne, Meadhbh and Ceallach by the fire they laid of evenings; Leannan with his harp encased and songless; Siodhachan whose wrinkled face was a map of years and present sorrows.

"No," said Rhys, "it was not. But An Beag has men to bury, by the ford."

"Well done," Beorc said. His eyes burned. His huge hands knotted up in fists.

"There were other things," said Rhys. He did not look up, but the thought was there, the ring of cloud, the darkness through which they had ridden. "There were men we could not bury. Gods help them." His mouth was drawn at the corners. He took a drink of wine and Domhnull looking on him caught a glance of his eyes when the cup had lowered. A chill came on Domhnull then, a keen ache in all his wounds, kinship with all those who had fared outside of daylight, in fell places and old.

"What happened here?" Rhys asked.

"Misjudgment," Domhnull said. His muscles all were hard, and ached on mended bones. "How did you get through?"

There was darkness enough in Owein's and Madawc's eyes, of proud men not used to fear; but Rhys' was more. "With small things in the bushes and arrows in the dark; and two horses gnawed to bone and men we never found. Nor could delay for." Rhys shivered, and leaned on his knees, the cup clenched between his knees; a fury was on his face. "Mist. A lot of that. An unnatural lot of that. We hoped for better here. Some of my folk went home: Gwernach and his folk—I sent them for my father's defence. We saw the sunlight; we had hoped beyond Caerbourne Ford. Easier An Beag arrows than the forest road by night; but something went with us—whether a fair thing or foul I know not, but at the last it led us fair. There have been such things. I saw a pooka once."

"And followed it?" Domhnull asked.

"O, friend, it followed me. That was on my way. This was smaller, a noise in the leaves—it loved the trees too well to leave them, and hung about the streams. And we none of us liked it, but there was no parting from it. And we saw it scampering through the brush, small and quick it was, and always ahead of us til the ford, till the cursed singer—" He fell silent. There was the wind outside, and always, the singing. "We have heard that wailing at night. Two nights upon the road."

"It can sing all it likes," said Muirne. "It's not coming in, that thing."

"It's Sidhe," said Meadhbh, a small voice. She sat by her brother, by the fire. "It wants our father."

"Be still," said Muirne, "hush, Meadhbh, don't speak of it."

There was silence then. There were a great many things not fit for speaking tonight. Domhnull's heart went out to the children. He moved close by them and sat down on the hearthside, his arms about them both.

"You'll want your beds," said Beorc to Rhys and the others. "I'll have bedding brought."

Rhys looked about him, at the hall where bedding was scattered in corners, pillows tucked in chairs, that told its own tale of how they rested. "I'll wash," he said. "I'll watch here."

Beorc nodded, gazing steadily at him. " 'Tis hard to think of riding, Rhys, but those men of yours would be a welcome sight northward: Ruadhan is hard pressed on the border. Gods know I should be up there, but—''

"We will take the beds," said Madawc in a voice like Rhys', quiet. "Owein and I will take our men north. That is why we came. Or west. Or where you like."

Beorc clamped his lips together, still staring, moist-eyed. "Gods reward it, Madawc."

"Gods send us enemies," said Owein darkly. "Our folk have need of them after such a ride, with things no arrow troubles. We have arrows saved for the Bradhaeth, or Damh, and gladly for An Beag."

"We are Dryw's sons," said Rhys. "And there is blood between us and these northrons. Much of it."

Beorc rose up and led them down the stairs. Domhnull sat watching, but his heart was not eased. He held Meadhbh and Ceallach against him, frail-seeming, watching much, they were. He felt them shiver. Oftentimes they gazed off into nothing at all, or watched the fire, or drowsed and picked at the food Muirne kept offering them. *They are in danger*, he thought, perceiving war of a different kind than spears. He held them tightly.

Be kinsman to them, Ciaran had said. He thought of his own mother, busy among her neighbors down below with this and that matter, the baking of bread, the ordering of shelters, meddling even in Caer Wiell's kitchens on the strength of her connections—nothing daunted her. She always had an answer; and these waifs, the children of a lord and a lady too wrapped in grief, he wished he could bring them to her; but he could not. They would not be comforted. *Go to bed*, Muirne had told them, had sternly ordered; but Meadhbh had sat down, plump upon the hearth three nights ago, and Ceallach had folded his arms and lifted his chin with a look that was Ciaran's own, which few had seen but his men when things were at their worst; and Meadhbh had one of his looks too, that quieter one, which measured distances and battlefields. So there had been pallets laid down, and both of them like weeds did as they liked, when they liked, where they liked; only sometimes they turned anguished looks toward the stairs when there was some sound, not often asking with more than silence; or their shoulders would droop or their heads fall, when, as now, they were willing to be held, to lay their heads against him, being not all grown. In his mind he railed on Branwyn, to desert them; and in his heart he knew why, as Ciaran had known—that they were strangers to Branwyn and grew more so. He bent his head, overburdened with knowings, brushed Meadhbh's brow with a kiss for comfort, as if she were his sister. She never stirred, nor did Ceallach. A stone of the fireplace bore into his back, but he did not move.

Rhys came back upstairs quietly and settled to sleep, the quick hard sleep of a man long without, in the dimmed hall; others settled; the fire burned down to embers and Muirne drowsed in her chair, her head on pillows.

And still the voice wailed, outside.

Go away, he wished it fiercely. *Bain Sidhe, go away: he cannot die, our lord. Give up and go away.*

Meadhbh lifted her head suddenly, violent and lost; Ceallach stirred. "Hush," Domhnull said, "it's just the same noise."

"*My father!*" Ceallach cried, thrusting him away.

And from the hall: "*Beorc!*" Branwyn cried. "*Beorc—o help me!*"

"He's abed again," Beorc said, closing the door at his back, facing them in the hall; stood for a moment as if he were set to keep that door, but then his shoulders fell and he looked more shaken than Domhnull had ever seen him. "He is weaker," Beorc said. "He is growing weaker now."

The children stood there. Muirne set her hands on Meadhbh's shoulders. Domhnull locked his arms about Ceallach's as if that could protect them.

"Curse that thing," Rhys said suddenly. "Curse it. It's that howling, it's no luck to the house, that thing."

"It is Sidhe," said Siodhachan from his corner by the fire. The old man's lips trembled. "And there is no fighting it. Speak no curses. Speak no curses, ap Dryw."

"Bain Sidhe," said Leannan. "It wants a life. It could have mine. Gods know it could. I would give it." And the harper wept, wiping at his eyes. "O gods."

"Or mine," said Ceallach. "It could have mine instead."

"By the gods, no!" Beorc cried. His face twisted. "Talk of appeasing that thing—by the gods, no giving that cursed thing any life of ours. It'll have to take me first, by the gods it will." His eyes were wild as battle. It was contagion. Rhys was on his feet, his dark face flushed, his hands clenched.

"We won past it once," Rhys said. "It's at the river. Do you dare, Scaga's-son?"

"For the gods' sake," Muirne cried. "No."

"And you, mac Gaelbhan?"

Domhnull shivered. It was mad. To attack a Sidhe—it was a thing hopeless from the start. But its price for leaving was a life.

He dropped his hands from Ceallach's shoulders. "Tracking a Sidhe—aye, let's be at it. At that I have some advantage."

"No," Muirne whispered, "no, o gods, no."

Beorc headed for the door to the downstairs; Rhys went; Domhnull did, mortally afraid. But Beorc got his cloak from beside the stairs and Rhys borrowed one, and they headed down the stairs. "Wait," Domhnull said snatching his, less agile. The madness grew in him, after so long waiting, so much fear. He hastened on the stairs, using his hand to steady him, gathered his sword where they left such things nowadays, at the bottom on their pegs, far from their lord and his hall. They did not run; they went with purpose, opened the door outward to the wall and went out where lightning flickered and wind battered at them.

They bore iron. It was sure at least the Sidhe had no love for it. Domhnull belted on his sword and came after Beorc and Rhys. "Open the lesser gate," Beorc bade the watch as they went down the steps, and such was his voice that the man did it, and let out the three of them afoot, hunters of the Sidhe who wailed death into the winds—afoot, for it could not now be far and no horses could be trusted.

"By the river," Domhnull said. A sense had settled into him for days now, that he knew where it laired. He shivered in the wind, in the dark; and drew his sword, keeping up with the others with difficulty. He remembered the stones about Caer Donn, and wind and mist. It seemed he could hear the hoofbeats of a horse, racing this way and that in distress, like something pent and desperate.

The shore was far, far, and there were dangers on the way, a maze, barriers forbidding and dark.

"I am still here," said Death. "Still here if you want me."

"My friend," said Ciaran. His heart ached. "Give me up."

Death settled on the windowledge. His sword was in his hands, and the hands were darkness, but bone was in them too. His hooded head was bowed. His face was still concealed. Outside, the wailing grew shrill, and hoofbeats circled, circled, wilder and wilder, like the beating of a heart.

"Give me up," Ciaran breathed, and pain rode the breath. "Go away. And take the Bain Sidhe with you."

"Over the Sidhe I have no power. Least of all that one. It gives me gifts. It goes before me. I do not rule it. It will have its due. And your friends have gone to hunt it."

"O gods, gods, stop it! Prevent them!"

"I have only one power over Men. Which shall I choose, lord Ciaran?"

"Ciaran," Branwyn said. The visions shattered, became pain, became the room, hard to keep. Her hand enclosed the stone. For a moment he felt her grief, her love. She slipped her fingers beneath the chain.

"No," he said, "no, Branwyn. Let it be. If you take that I shall die."

She wept. Her hand trembled. He felt her desolation in the thing she had resolved to do.

"No," he said, loving her for that. "O no."

She took her hand away. She held his. She looked into his eyes, hers all astream with tears, but she composed her face and smiled a desperately false smile. "Well, awake?" she said. She began to talk, softly, to weave a spell of words; and he knew what she purposed, that she would keep him while she could, but that when there was no hope left she would cast the stone away, to steal him back from Eald.

"You mustn't," he said.

"She loves you," Death said. "She means to do this. And so I have to be here, until the Sidhe is sated."

Branwyn washed his brow, whispered on, of Meadhbh and Ceallach; Rhys had come—he blinked, wondering when he had ever gone, or where; she talked of siege, fiercely, telling him things he could not remember even while he was hearing them.

"The King is dead," he said. "Had I said that?"

She carried his hand to her lips. "Hold on," she said. "Would you ever give up Caer Wiell? Hold fast. Hold on while you can. You have to defend the hold. Stay here, beside me."

That much he understood, that little thing she asked, who had right to ask so much. He hovered there bewildered, remembering their youth, such as they had had together, in the long ago.

Then:

"Man." It was Liosliath. He knew the voice. It had been part of himself once. He heard it speaking to him. A white thing rose up between, wailing and bloody-handed.

"Hold on," cried Branwyn.

"No," Meadhbh said, thrusting off Muirne's hands. She ran, raced to the corner where Ceallach had fled, themselves against Muirne, Leannan, everyone who guarded them; she clutched Ceallach's hands in hers, cast a wild look on familiar faces, anxious faces. "We know where it is. Let us go and tell them. It wants him, that thing." The sound was everywhere the wind blew now, everywhere, in blood and bone and stone and timber of the hold.

"Let us go!" cried Ceallach.

And then they went, so suddenly, into such a blast of cold it took the breath, a passage into the place of mist and trees.

"Where are we?" Meadhbh said, shivering. "Ceallach, where are we?"

"*There*," he said in a voice fainter than the wind and the singer. "O Meadhbh—I think we're *there*, on the riverside."

"Find the men, O Ceallach, we have to find them."

"We're lost, Meadhbh!"

"Not we." She clenched her hand about the gift she wore. "We can't be! We can't be lost, remember? It's the men who've lost themselves." She heard the river mingled with the singer and the trees the wind was tossing. She trod now on wet grass. There was moonlight from above, lightning from the cloudwall, a curious and dreadful luminescence. She gathered up a stone. Ceallach took another, silently.

They saw it then, a small white thing that perched among the trees—so small a thing, like a withered woman all gauze and rags, washing, washing something in the stream.

"Ciaran," Branwyn said. "Ciaran."

Lord Death only sat there, head bowed, the sword within his hands.

"Branwyn," Ciaran said. His eyes were shut or open: he could not tell. The visions crowded close. The singing grew. A horse whinnied desperately. "Listen to me, Branwyn."

"Woe," the Singer wailed, "woe and worse to come. Woe and desolation—"

"Get it," Meadhbh sobbed. She drew back her arm, cast a futile stone.

"*No*," piped a reedy voice. "*O no, do not touch it, never touch it, throw no stones.*"

They started at that crashing through the brush, at the small and hairy thing that peered up at them.

"You," said Meadhbh.

The Gruagach hugged itself, it rolled its eyes, it shivered in the lightning. "Let be, go back, go back, you do no good."

"No!" She took another stone and cast it at the singer; Ceallach's hurtled after, splashing in the water, two sets of rings in the lightning where the Sidhe had been.

"*Woe*," wailed down the winds.

"Get it," Ceallach cried, gathering another stone; the Bain Sidhe drifted on the water beneath the wind-whipped trees, clutching bloody rags against its whiteness. He cast.

"Ceallach," Meadhbh cried, for it had grown again by half. It grew straighter, brighter, striding on the river.

"There it is," someone cried, and: "*Gods!*"

It wailed. It towered above the trees, a shape more and more terrible and swift.

"It grows!" Meadhbh cried. "O no—no—no—."

"*Beorc!*" Ceallach shouted, and started to run, but brambles held them, tore their hands and faces, and threads of white went everywhere in the brush, the wailing grew and grew, everywhere about them.

"Stop it!" Meadhbh cried, struggling in the thorns. "Thistle, help! Thistle, Thistle—stop it, help!" But nothing came. The tendrils wrapped them round, cold as ice and ghostly. *A name,* she wished, *o gods, a Name, anyone.* "*Gruagach!*" But it was small and weak. "Caolaidhe, Caolaidhe!" she cried. "*Caolaidhe!* Come help us!"

The white tendrils drew back from them. The wailing went away down the river, to the other side. The water surged, a large body coming up.

It was there, the river horse, black and shining wet. It waited for them. It threw its head. Its eyes shone like gold lamps in darkness.

"Get it," Ceallach said. "Follow it—keep that thing far from here."

It threw its head; it whuffed the winds and trumpeted its challenge.

"Branwyn," Ciaran whispered. He thought he did. He heard the hoofbeats coming. She bent close and kissed him. He could hardly feel the touch. The world was dimmed.

"Gods help me," he said.

"We have lost you," said Lord Death.

"Meadhbh!" It was Beorc's voice, cracking in the wind, obscured in thunder.

"Go," she cried. "*Never let it near him!*" The each-uisge sped, a flowing of water toward water, that scattered them with drops. She flinched from it and turned, grasping at Ceallach's shoulder. The men came, Beorc and Rhys and Domhnull, Domhnull last and Rhys swiftest to reach them, running down the hill.

"O," a small voice piped from among the rocks, "too late, too late, o run, shelter, o haste, haste, haste! He is gone, gone, sped!"

Meadhbh ran with Ceallach, each dragging the other, into Rhys' arms, and Beorc's; and Domhnull coming last.

"We drove it off," Ceallach wept. "We sent it away. O Beorc—it mustn't have him."

"Too late," the small voice wailed, *"late, late, late."*

Hoofbeats confounded themselves with thunder. The hillside burst in fire, a shock of lightning; a tree blazed up and scattered fire and fragments into the river.

Then the rain, pelting down on them, drenching them to the skin. Meadhbh held her gift and thought of home, now, at once, but the men bore iron, poisoning the air, and the lightning played over them, flickering through the rain.

"Run," Domhnull cried, seizing at them, his fair face drowned and stark in the flashes. "Run, get under cover."

Rhys dragged her up the long hill to the walls; she ran, ran, ran, after Beorc and Ceallach, till her side split and her senses swam, and the gate opened for them and closed after.

They came up the stairs, drenched and shivering; the men cast away their swords with hollow clashes, and got them up into the hall.

Their mother stood there. So they knew. Meadhbh stopped, too numb to think, except that they had lost. Someone pulled her to his embrace, touched her cheek, but she had no tears, had nothing.

"He—left," their mother said, in a still voice they had never heard her use, a whisper, like the rain upon the roof, all hollow and toneless. "Meadhbh, Ceallach, he just left, in that way he could. He couldn't die, you know. The stone wouldn't let him. Sidhe fade. It was like that, that all of a sudden I couldn't feel his hand, but I could see it. *Aodhan*, he said. That was a horse that was his once." She came to them, held out her arms. Meadhbh came and hugged her, wet as she was, and Ceallach came into her arms. She smoothed their hair; her hands trembled. "Did you see him?"

"No," Meadhbh said. Thunder cracked about the hold, shaking the stones. She remembered the cloud. Her mother was being very quiet, a restraint that was worse than thunderclaps; and there was this footing about the truth, of leavings and goings. *Too late*, the Gruagach had said. She lifted her head from her mother's shoulder and looked her in the eyes, hard and straight. "You mean he went away—like us? Like that?"

"Like that." Her mother's lips moved, forcing breath into the words. "He said good-bye. There's a place Sidhe go. He talked about the sea. He didn't die. He can't, now. Ever." For the first time her lips trembled into tears. She hugged them again, shook their heads back and looked at them. "Can't you cry?" their mother asked.

Meadhbh shivered. Her clothes were cold; it got into her bones, except where the Sidhe gift rested about her neck. She patted her mother's cheek, feeling it soft and warm and remembering the smell of lilacs and oil and metal.

They had lost him after all. They had not watched him well enough. She felt herself at fault; and touched the gift about her throat, remembering what it meant: but all Eald faltered, crashed in ruin overhead, around, about them. Her throat ached.

"My lady." It was Leannan's voice, from over by the corner, a-tremble and very soft. "Forgive me, lady— He's gone. Siodhachan's gone."

The old man looked asleep, nodding in his corner by the fire. His face was peaceful.

"O gods," Rhys whispered, and his voice broke. "The old man outran us."

FOURTEEN
Fugitives

They had a burial to do in the morning. It was not the burying Siodhachan would have wished, being quiet, in the black-clouded dawn, with no cups of ale or tale-telling through the night; they were in too much haste and the matter of their lord weighed too heavily on them. They built the old man a strong cairn of Caer Wiell's gray stone and vowed him a greater one in better days. Leannan for his part meant to make a song for him; but there was no singing it until things were worse or better. So the harper only sat awhile by the cairn after everyone had gone, bowed with his head on his arms; and came in finally, drank a cup and washed his face, and wandered among the tents and shelters, among the hapless who had come for refuge.

"Sing a song," the steader children asked, of the friend who had always cheered them; for the night had been dreadful and the day ahead looked ugly.

"Hush," said their elders sternly. "He is the lord's own harper; and he is sad today. Show respect."

So silence went about him.

But rumors flourished, in the harper's downcast silence; in the grim rebuilding of the cloudwall after last night's storm; in the whispering of one nightwatch to another and them to others of the men . . . for the Bain Sidhe was silent today: *She wailed for the old man,* folk said. *Now the lord will live.*

But down in the kitchens: *No more orders come from hall to scullery. Something is amiss up there.*

And again: *His men went out last night. And came back with his children, but they never passed the gates before that. The Sidhe magicked them.*

The lord is dead: it's himself in that cairn, and the old man's just gone to hiding.

"Lord Ciaran left last night," said Beorc to the men he gathered, with Rhys and Madawc and Owein, his own folk and the southrons. He said it loudly, so there would be no doubt and no mangling of the news. He shouted it out; and country folk gathered beyond the knot of men at arms and southrons. "*He is not dead,* hear? And where he went and how is his business; but he took his leave of my lady before he left and had a good reason for going. The rest of it is not for our bandying about in the yard. Get to business. Mind your tongues and reckon the lord knows what he's about. Meanwhile we have the Bradhaeth to deal with; the lord's order—*look to it!*"

Domhnull watched the people. He saw the stricken looks, the bewilderment on faces that had seen too much of disarray in their lives. But no one disputed what Beorc said: no one met that scowl of his or argued with that voice. Folk listened; and Beorc told them what wanted doing and how quickly.

When Beorc let them go again, Domhnull climbed the stairs, past Rhys, who stood on the bottom step; and Madawc and Owein near him. He had no part in what was toward now—in the defense of the north. The orders now were for others. He went up into hall to watch over Meadhbh and Ceallach, that being what his lord had last charged him to do, and it seemed to have been left to him even now that their southron kinsmen were at hand.

Muirne was there, infallibly, Muirne—sitting on the bench and spinning by the light of the one torch they kept burning, beside the pallets where the children slept at hearthside. The room was in order again; blankets had been taken away—doubtless Muirne had seen to it, the way she saw to everything.

He settled on the hearthside bench in the warmth that remained of the fire, taking comfort in Muirne's presence, watching the deft work of her fingers that coaxed thread out of wool, a work he had watched hour upon hour of his long convalescence. This was Muirne's Sidhe—gift, he had thought then, to spin, spin, spin peace out of chaos, comfort out of hurt. He had been ashamed once, when he had come out of the muddled days and nights of his sickness, that anyone should have seen him as he was. But Muirne never flinched, more, she had looked up from her spinning from time to time with a glance he might have laughed at once, seeing it from Muirne, shy and girlish and wishing, years older as she was. His mother had been there in his fever, when it was worst; but Muirne had been there when the memories came, and beguiled his moods with questions—of the land, of places he knew; he discovered she had never been beyond sight of Caer Wiell's walls, though she had seen war and siege beneath them. She knew little of the world. She had always had the spinning, the children, the duties of the hold, for lady Meredydd, for Branwyn, as isolate in her world of women as some soldier in his world of men—shy, suddenly, to be in such different company but treasuring the moments in their trade of what they had to trade—*Can friends be so opposite?* he began to think. *O if she were younger—*

She went on spinning. He watched her fingers, the firelight on her face. So, so tenderly she had soothed brows in this room and in that through all these dreadful days, and whispered that she was there, close by, between them and whatever they feared—as if she were protection. But she was, he thought, if love and steadfastness meant anything in the world.

The hall seemed strangely silent now, empty of the orders and instructions that had always flowed from it. My lady slept, exhausted; my lord—gods knew. And out in the courtyard, Beorc prepared revenge, a gust of red-haired violence, ordering weapons and supplies and wagons and whatever horses they could gather.

And above them all, the clouds—for he had looked at the sky this morning—the cloudwall was taking shape again, after the wreckage of the night. Rampart-building moved apace in heaven, so that the forest was all dark and dawn winked out as the sun rose into the wall of cloud. The daylit space narrowed; and there were ominous mare's-tails to northward, many of them, advance from that border Ruadhan was holding.

A chill had fallen on him when he had seen that, not a sharp fear, but one that mingled with all the others of the day, so that the shouts Beorc gave to the wagoners, the noise in the yard, the whisperings and the movements and the colors, all seemed perilously thin, like some last outpouring of vitality.

Before death, he thought. *Before the world goes dark.* He finally named what he had feared out there in the yard, that Caer Wiell's strength was ebbing, that everything they were preparing was wrong, while the clouds narrowed like advancing armies. Lord Ciaran was gone. *Not dead,* he insisted to himself but he remembered Ciaran tumbling from his horse, the black arrows, the waxen flesh that sustained itself only by the stone—To go back into Eald, to enter it foredone as he was, to seek the elvish horse and fare outward on the last of his fading strength. . . .

O ride quickly, he wished his lord, *go where they go, find peace, whatever this fading is.* When he shut his eyes he saw the hill outside Caer Donn, a black and terrible wind that blew the Sidhe's white fire in tatters.

He shuddered, a quick convulsion of his limbs. The air seemed thick and foul.

Something touched him; but it was only Muirne when he blinked, laying her hand on his shoulder.

"Hush, it's all right."

"They can't do it," he murmured, having a sudden clear vision of the yard, the wagons readying, Beorc amid it all, going north to the defense of the steadings. "They mustn't. The north is already falling. O gods—"

"Domhnull!" Muirne whispered. She was on her knees, clenching his hands in hers. He felt her grip at last when she shook at him. He was still cold, and what had been in his mind slipped from him like a passing dream.

"Forgive," he said, confused, forgetting it all like some fading glimpse of faery.

"Hush, you mustn't vex yourself. You were sleeping sitting up just then. You were dreaming. Go down to your own bed and rest. It's time you did."

He remembered then, distantly and coldly, how futile everything had seemed to him. He had had such nightmares often since Donn. He feared he might have cried out just then in his sleep, and heat touched his face. He glanced aside, where the children slept undisturbed on their pallets. He felt aches in his shoulders, in all his bones. "If Eald should fall," he said, a scattered thought as all his thoughts were scattered now, like doves before some hawk, "maybe I would go to moonbeams and cobweb. Or be what I was, where I was, on the rocks below Caer Donn.''

''Hush.'' Muirne's fingers stopped his lips. Her eyes were anguished.

He caught the hand, touched it a second time with his lips and held it. She remained distraught, seeming so weary, so very weary. Her eyes were full of tears and fright. ''Muirne,'' he said, ''if there are heroes in Caer Wiell, you are one. Did you know that?''

''Why?'' she asked, as confused by this as by the other.

''Because you are.'' He let go her hand, for her cheeks burned red. Perhaps she suspected idle flatteries, herself unarmed and unarmored against the only man she knew. He sensed so. He rose, aching from the stones, awkward. There were few he let see him in pain, but Muirne knew, and so he indulged himself, too weary to hide it. A restlessness gnawed at him. The fears that had made sense a moment ago were vague, and he had the urge to see the clouds again, to do something toward the hold's defense, even to stand idle and watch those who were going to it. *I still might go myself,* he thought in the scattering of his thoughts. *With a horse under me I might be well enough. The shield-arm . . . I can bind it.*

Then he recalled the children, and in that same instant he felt relief that he had an excuse not to be faring north, for he sensed something wrong.

''Domhnull?'' Muirne asked. ''Whatever is the matter?''

He blinked, gathering his mind back from that gray place where was such loneliness, so little formed and certain; where something flitted lost in the winds.

''*Meadhbh!*'' he shouted. ''*Ceallach!*''

''Domhnull——'' Muirne cried; but he had gone to them, gathered them in his arms all limp as they were, holding them as tightly as he could, on his knees beside the hearth.

''Wake,'' he whispered to them, in that place where they had gone. ''Come back. Meadhbh. Ceallach. Your mother needs you, do you hear?''

So they came back to him, obedient.

''Domhnull,'' Meadhbh said, and he laid his face against her chill one. ''We're here,'' Ceallach murmured, and began to wake, stirring in his arms.

''O gods,'' Muirne said.

''Watch them, my lord said.'' Domhnull's heart was beating against his ribs. ''*Watch them.* He had this danger in his mind all along. And I thought of leaving them. O wake up, wake up, hear? I know where you are and that's no road for you. Come. Come back now.''

"It was dark," Meadhbh said. "The light was blowing away. Domhnull!"

"Wake their mother," Domhnull said fiercely. "Muirne, wake her, go!"

Muirne sped, flying on the stairs.

Then Ceallach shuddered in his arms and drew a great breath, and both of them were there.

He let them go when he was sure. Meadhbh rubbed her eyes. They sat looking at him with a sadness dawning on them, that it was only Domhnull holding them, he thought, and not the one they loved.

"If I could have gone in his place," Domhnull told them, "o gods, I would have."

Meadhbh wept, sitting there amid her blankets, tears rolling down her face. She wiped at them. She ran her hands back over her sleep—tangled hair. Ceallach sat as if lightning-struck. Domhnull gathered them both again, rocking them, though his bad leg ached on the stone.

"Morning's come," he said, "and the world is what it is, and you have to stay in it."

They said nothing, nothing at all.

"Your father said I must watch you," he said, "and so I will."

Steps came hurrying from the door. So their mother arrived with Muirne, herself all dishevelled, in a plain white gown, with her fair hair flying about her shoulders.

Then Domhnull worked himself painfully to his feet, leaning on the stones of the fireplace and on Muirne's offered arm. He saw the children go to Branwyn's embrace, saw tears shed, which ought to be—but then he watched Branwyn fuss at Muirne for their hair, and at them for sleeping here instead of upstairs in their beds. She rubbed at Ceallach's face with the tail of her sleeve and in all delivered as much roughness as of love.

She does not know what happened to them, or what danger they are in, he thought with a chill to his heart. *And knows she doesn't*. Branwyn had waked from sleep, only sleep, a sleep heavy or light, but nothing more, never more. *She is only clay*, he thought, *as he was half of air—and knows it*. Mortality was on Branwyn. Her shoulders stooped. There were lines about her eyes this morning. She turned from fretting over her children and looked at him.

"Where is Beorc?" she asked.

"With your cousins. Making ready the men that will go north."

She stared a moment. "No," she said.

"Lady?"

"No, they will not go."

"Lady, little good they will do the land here, in Caer Wiell." He felt heat go to his face. His tongue tied, that he had forgotten to whom he spoke. He stared into her eyes, which were blue and pale and passionless. "The border," he finished, trying to mend things. "The northern steadings. They can't stay waiting." But she was of Caer Wiell, bred and born here. She knew the needs of its defense. That too he remembered.

"They will not go," she said. Her mouth set, making lines at the corners. She folded her children against her like a wall. "Tell Beorc so."

"I will tell him." He cast a desperate look at Muirne, then bowed his head and went in haste, knowing how Beorc would hear it.

She was adamant, when Beorc came thumping back upstairs with him to argue, when Rhys and his brothers arrived on his heels and Rhys shouted at her—which spoke how desperate Rhys had become, how desperate all the men. Horses, saddled, fretted in the yard; wagons already loaded, stood with their teams outside the gates, their drivers waiting. Folk murmured from wall to wall of Caer Wiell, once again confused, frightened what with the ominous sky above them and the shifting orders of those that led them.

"Good gods," Rhys cried, "you cannot take on like this. Grief is one thing, madam, but this immolation of your people is profitless. You have a border crumbling at this hour, horses readied, men standing in their armor, rumors running rife in the yard."

"The King is dead," she said. She sat calmly, in her plain blue gown, dressed and coiffed now, her hair severe in its braids, her face very pale. She might have been an image graven out of ivory. "Do you understand?"

"Laochailan dead." Rhys paced the floor, when the rest of them would have wished to, fretting as they were. Rhys stopped, held out his hands in entreaty. "Well, that would be no great surprise, cousin, but how do you suppose to know that?"

"My husband said it," she answered in that firm still voice. "Before he left. Send riders out, over all our lands. As far as the borders. Bring our people in and bring Ruadhan home with all our men."

"Lady cousin," Rhys said gently, "lord Ciaran was fevered."

She rose, unfolded upward from her chair, and for a moment small as she was, they were daunted. "Cousin—do you understand me? My cousin Laochailan is dead. He hated us. But he is dead. They murdered him, smothered him in his bed, since their poisons failed. The King is dead."

Domhnull's eyes wandered to the corner, where a slight, red-haired boy sat watching by his sister, and a chill went down his spine. *O gods,* he thought, which he had not thought, for until yestereve there had been Ciaran, and the chance of alliances and maneuverings; and that Laochailan would declare some heir. But nothing was the same this morning. *Ceallach. Gods, gods, this boy is King.*

So others fell silent. The perhaps-King stared back at them in distress, his hand locked in his sister's.

Then: "Cousin," Rhys said, "if it were true—we may have little time. If it were true—there might come trouble up the dale, and quickly. All the more reason to take care of that matter to the north and be ready to face trouble from the west when it comes."

"No," Branwyn said.

"Cousin, give orders in the hold. Not in matters of arms."

"I tell you no."

"This is grief," said Beorc. "Lady, you know me, that I am your man as I was his. And I say the same. Leave this matter of the borders to men who know them."

"The King is dead." Her voice rose, losing both calm and dignity. "And we need all our forces here. And my husband is not dead, Beorc. He has gone away, but he is not dead. You are still his man, and don't forget that."

Beorc bowed his head and lifted it sorrowfully. It was clear what his opinion was. "Lady, wherever he is— But this matter of the border—Lady, it can't wait."

"Beorc, he looked at me. It was the last thing—the last thing he said. He looked at me as clearly as I look at you: 'Branwyn,' he said, 'look to Dryw. Go there if you have to. Go soon.' "

"Impossible," said Rhys somberly. "Would to the gods you could; but that is no sunny ride, cousin, not now. Almost *we* failed it. Safest to secure that one border northward and then close the westward pass."

"They will come through the hills like ants," Branwyn said.

"Lady cousin, that they may; but that will put them in our hands: Owein and Madawc and I—do you think any lowlanders can best our folk in the hills? Let them try. We will hold here."

"Domhnull." Her gaze turned on him, her hands outheld. "Donnchadh—it is Donnchadh who killed the King. Do you understand me?"

A chill went over Domhnull, a memory in once shattered bones, fear driven deep there, and doubt. "Beorc," he said, "Beorc—that one has allies—O gods, Rhys, the Brown Hills and the north—there is too much moving on us now. I saw it—It isn't the armies. Not the worst of it. She may be right."

So they looked at him too with pity and something worse. Beorc had his hands in his belt; at last he ducked his head and lifted it with a frown, looking at Branwyn. "Domhnull will stay here," he said, "to order the defense. You are my lady, but my lord is gone; and until he's here again, I do what he told me last, and I mind me that I never had his leave to be coming back here in the first place. Rhys, Owein, Madawc—"

The color has risen to Branwyn's cheeks. "I have told you," she said. "But you refuse to hear." Her lips trembled. Her eyes were filled with tears. "So go. Do as you will, Beorc. Domhnull at least will stay."

Domhnull stood still, feeling the heat in his face, looking still toward Branwyn while Beorc and Rhys and his brothers left, a martial clattering on the stairs behind; and his eyes went dim and blurred and painful.

"Well?" Branwyn asked sharply. Muirne stood there, witness to this. The children sat in their corner, in the corner of his sight.

"I will go out, by your leave," Domhnull murmured painfully, "and see my cousin off."

Branwyn nodded and turned her shoulder to him, finding something to do in the clutter of herbs and jars in the corner that was hers.

The gates stood open. The wagons already groaned their way out onto the road. "Take care," Domhnull said, standing close beside the way, looking up at Beorc as he rode past; and Beorc reined aside from the others.

"Domhnull." For a moment Beorc sat looking down, a line between his brows; and then he heaved himself down from the saddle and offered an embrace, tentative and shamed-seeming.

Domhnull took what was offered, looked Beorc in the eyes, at arm's length. "Take care," he said doggedly. There was a fear in him like sickness. He saw the riders pour past, almost all Caer Wiell's strength. He was conscious of the sky above them. *Donnchadh*, rang in his mind with the rattle of the armor. *Donnchadh, Donnchadh.* "Do it quickly and come home."

The fear showed. It woke pity in Beorc's eyes, who was not accustomed to failings. "Cousin—" he said, and bit his lip on what he would have said. "See to matters here. We'll be back as quickly as we can."

The ache of Beorc's fingers lingered on his shoulder. He stood there staring from the gate as Beorc galloped off to the fore and the column of riders bent northward. His heart had gone cold, for all the brave color of the banners of Caer Wiell and the black of the sons of Dryw, the thunder of horses, the clash of armor of riders hard upon their way toward the north, toward the gathering mare's-tails of new rampart building. There were folk about him, above him on the walls, watching from all manner of vantages, and only a few had cheered, a silence unlike Caer Wiell.

"Son."

His mother stood close, by the stairs. He turned to look at her and her face changed at his look to something quieter—a tall woman, his mother, her hair shot through with gray and her eyes full of living. "Come," she said wisely, as she had coaxed him in younger years, of bruised knees and falls and prizes missed and loves spurned, in the years before he thought himself a man and ran off to Caer Wiell. "Come, I've somewhat to spare this morning. Come breakfast with me."

It was not the food he sought. His lady wanted him in hall; he had duties and no time to spend, but Beorc's look still stung, and he had duties here in the yard as well as anywhere else, if Branwyn and Muirne had the children well in hand. Someone had to be seen out here, someone to still the rumors.

So he let himself be seen; folk stared at him and murmured. Of the breakfast he took only a cup of cider and a bit of bread, while his mother talked of everything but wars. He sat on a sack of goods by the scullery door and the traffic came and went, of impudent goats and running children, of women going this way and that with water and food and stores. Most in Caer Wiell now were women; and the young and halt and old. So he listened while she talked of neighbors' lives and scullery gossip, and children played tag in the sunlight (but there was shadow beyond the wall) and squealed and screamed until the noise was like to drive him mad in one moment and seemed precious in the next. She asked no news of hall; no, she had no wish to go there. She had her friends and neighbors, and insisted on telling him of them, small, simple things, so he knew it was like Muirne's bravery, innocent and wise. And others lingered near them, pretending tasks and errands, listening ears and watching eyes of women all thinking of their sons, of husbands, brothers, cousins— and himself one maimed man, one marred and somewhat broken and now, with a handful of men left to him, commanding in Caer Wiell.

So he lifted his head and looked at his mother and marked how she was beautiful in his eyes, how other women deferred to her. It was the way she was, full of good sense. His father had loved her for reasons he only then saw, having only then come to manhood, this morning it seemed, in Caer Wiell.

He felt a great calm then amid his fear, finding himself knowing more of the world than he was wont. He knew where he belonged, and where his oath to his lord was pledged. "I have to get back to hall," he said deliberately. "There are plans—" Several score breaths bated. He knew. "—My lord left clear instructions to carry out; there are things to do." His mother sat quietly, her wise fair eyes intent on him, well knowing what he did. "Say that." He pressed her hand where it rested on her knee and looked straight into her eyes. "If others ask. Our lord is not lost. I've been where he fares now. And *I* came back. He's gone for healing. As I did. Say that too."

He rose. His mother did. He had become a liar. He had no shame in that at all. He kissed her on the brow and turned his cheek for her. So he walked away, not limping, though his bones ached.

He crossed the yard, took the stairs under hundreds of silent eyes. He felt them on his back. He heard the tide break behind him as he gained the wall, a flood of women's voices. He did not look back even so, but walked on up the inner stairs and up again through the accounting-room to the hall.

"Well?" said Branwyn, pausing in her combing of Meadhbh's hair.

"Nothing, lady. They've gone, that's all. A while ago. I've been down in the yard. Taking breakfast."

Branwyn tightened her lips, and Meadhbh braced herself and suffered, her head bowed as she stood. Her red hair shone and sparked in wisps beneath the strokes of the comb.

And after a moment: "And where would Leannan be?"

"Somewhere about. Since the burying."

"So. Well." More strokes of the comb. "Now hear my morning's orders. Bring in every horse we have, mares and foals too. Find every cart Beorc has left us, and every weapon. We shall be going south tomorrow. Every soul in Caer Wiell."

"Lady—" His certainties ebbed from him, regrouped behind

his reason. "You want a man to ride after Beorc, then. To force him and Rhys."

Two motions went on, Branwyn's combing; and Ceallach, who was at the grinding of Branwyn's herbs. There was the talisman about the boy's neck, that swung with the fierce effort of his arm. There was a madness in all this, that ordinary things went on, that Branwyn insisted on them. The air was full of rosemary and grief.

"If they would listen," Branwyn said, "they would have. Are you faithful, Domhnull?"

"Lady, those men are faithful to you. They only see a danger—"

"So do I."

"I will ride after them, persuade them—if I stood with you, to do this, then they might listen, and fortify Caer Wiell."

The combing stopped. She patted Meadhbh's shoulders, dismissed her. Meadhbh only stood and stared. Branwyn looked straight at him.

"You do not well hear me. And Beorc would hold you to prevent me," she said, "because he sees a danger. No. Send last to them. Before that, bring the last few steaders in. Send riders."

"The folk will be afraid, down in the yard."

"Say what you like. Send Cein's boys: they have close mouths. Find Leannan. And Cobhan. This hold will be ready. Tell that where you like. Take every weapon, everything that can be mended and every hand that can hold one. Most of all keep them busy. Will you do these things?"

"Aye, lady." He looked at Muirne and at the children both, at Branwyn, last and longest. "What is in your mind to do? Lady, you were not there when Rhys told us what he had seen on that southern road. Things that took men and horses. The forest is deadly."

"The Sidhe will protect us. For my children's sake, they will save us all."

There was fey madness in Branwyn's eyes. There was fear there too. Both were contagious.

"Lady—for the sake of those out there—who would suffer in siege, but most would live—with a half dozen men I might take you south to lord Dryw. If you are sure the risk is worth it. But to set out on a road like that with the old folk and the infants still in arms—gods, my lady, that's a forest trail we're speaking of, no way for carts and wagons. We haven't enough horses for all of them to ride."

"Domhnull—the King that sits in Dun na h-Eoin is *Donnchadh*. You of all people should know his manners."

"Aye," he said after a moment. *O Beorc, come home, come quickly, reason with our lady.* "But if Donnchadh comes into the dale he would waste no time on Caer Wiell if we were not in it."

"You think in numbers Caer Wiell could raise. You never saw the armies Dun na h-Eoin might lead. Well, *I* have seen them. Do you think they couldn't divide that force and come at Caer Wiell too, to let Damh and Bradhaeth and An Beag loose inside these walls? No." She drew her daughter back into her arms. Ceallach had come to stand beside her. Lines seemed graven in her face after these last, horrid days. "My husband's word, Domhnull. Do you believe it?"

"I saw Caer Wiell burned," Meadhbh said, so faintly he could hardly see her lips move. "I dreamed it last night, Domhnull. I think that it is true."

The world seemed cold and frail about him. He stared at both; at the boy-King who came to join them, red-haired, his sleeves rolled up, hands dusted with herbs and country simples.

"I will do what I can," Domhnull said to Branwyn. It seemed impossible to him that his lord was not there, that they were left with such choices. The Sidhe to protect them, his lady believed. But he lived with the ache in his bones, the memory of the hill and the fading of the light.

The Sidhe has lost, that is what, he thought, on the stairs leading down from the hall. He limped, using his hands to steady him, he, the guardian of Caer Wiell. About him constantly he seemed to see the stones, the lightning, the Sidhe tattered in the black winds.

Sidhe faded. Ciaran had gone, Sidhe-like; but even in that place was no refuge—or he would have let the children seek it. Branwyn was blind, hoping to pass the forest, hoping because she had no other hope.

But Meadhbh had visions.

Your brother is gone, the Dark Man whispered. Lost.

Donnchadh started and looked about him, in the solitude of the gloomy hall in Dun na h-Eoin. Armies were about it: his; the lords had gathered like carrion birds at the King's failing; and among them had come one eagle.

"What—*dead?*" he whispered aloud; but the voice came creeping inward, cold as ice.

Last night, the voice said, soft as spidersilk. *The Bain Sidhe has sung it. Ciaran of Caer Wiell, of Donn, Branwyn's husband—he is gone.*

Donnchadh sat down on the plain wooden throne, that being where there was to sit. He felt it like a blow, a hammer-strike to the heart. He felt like weeping; and felt relief at once. *Dead—of the wounds An Beag gave him?*

Dead— The voice grew softer still. *Ah, well, but nearly. At least as dead as Sidhe can die.*

This was a dagger-thrust. He looked up at the shadows, but there was no one to see. *A man is dead or not, ghost.*

Oh, but a Man is—dead or not. But there was less and less of Man in him—cousin. Now he has no boundaries. He might be here, this moment—or stand beside your bed of nights. He might easily come this way. He would still defend his hold, his son— with every means at his command, and those means are many.

A chill came on Donnchadh. It grew, as if warmth were leaving him forever. It was true: there was his brother's son, heir through Meara, Evald, Branwyn; and all those armies knew it. It wanted so little to produce one rebel, one of those lords to rouse others in the name of a boy who could be brought up as they pleased, if he fell into their ambitious hands.

That is the first danger, he thought; and it *was* his thought, perhaps; or it was the Dark Man's, who had come so close now there was no distinguishing one from the other. *The boy. Ceallach. Laochailan's heir; and my brother's; and Dryw's kinsman. In Caer Wiell, near the Sidhe.*

"It is quite mad," Leannan said. His pale blue eyes were mazed with ale when Domhnull found him outside the scullery, with ale and too much of losing folk he loved; and with doings of the Sidhe and a sky that seemed worse and worse. But: "Say no word of it," Domhnull said. "Only give me help—to keep the folk quiet. Go among them. Find out how many there are here; and how many of those could not ride—somehow. Or be carried."

"Aye," the harper said, who had a skill at remembering things, and at numbers.

"Southward," Cein said when Domhnull went to him at the stables. "O gods. With wagons?" But: "Better Sidhe luck than Donnchadh's mercy," Domhnull said. "I can swear to that. Don't say anything here. Send your boys for the steaders. I want them back by sundown. And tell them to be discreet in it."

And last to Cobhan, who was grooming Ciaran's Iolaire, stubbornly, faithfully as every morning: "Every horse, Cobhan.

Every one. We leave none of my lord's horses to An Beag bandits. Bring them in. And oxen for the wagons.''

"Aye," said Cobhan, tight-lipped and thinking. He called a boy to him and gave instructions, never pausing in his work.

So the matter proceeded. There was further gossip: *The enemy is near. The border is giving way. So these preparations.*

Domhnull did not gainsay that rumor. It served him. He went here and there with a worried frown and cared little now who saw it.

"Is it so?" his mother asked. "Is the north in danger?"

So there was another soul he decided to trust. "It may. Mother, it's southward we are going. And soon. For good reasons. It's not to be told, not yet. But if Beorc is driven back—we will move quickly; for our lives, we must move, to shelter with lord Dryw until this thing is over. You know the steader woman, who's to rely on. Name them to me, the ones to move the others.''

She set her lips, frowned a bit, and named them.

There was smithery in the yard, the hammering of iron, the mending of a wheel. Leannan moved here and there like a fish through troubled waters, visiting shelters, playing small songs to keep minds elsewhere, asking after this old man's health, that old woman's, the weeks a baby had. Cein and Cobhan brought in the horses, a great protesting of mares and nervous foals; of old geldings too long out to pasture and showing their tempers; of oxen, lastly, moving their great bulk past shelters and collapsing one tent by the Old Hall, to wails and protests of the old woman in it.

Domhnull went from place to place, keeping pages and steader lads busy sharpening old weapons and the old warriors at more meticulous tasks restoring old horse gear out of storage. He took care to be seen often; he gave, if not detailed orders, at least approval of what experienced folk would do; and wider and wider he spread his trust where he dared, taking oath of this one and that one to keep quiet.

Even silence begat rumors. *There is too much quiet,* folk began to say. *There are those that know things.* He heard other whisperings and murmurings which he could not make out; and these made him uneasy. Whenever he chanced up to the wall he could not forbear looking northward himself, wishing for some sight of riders, just enough to be Beorc and Rhys coming home, with Ruadhan beside them: but what he dreaded was a larger band—the whole of Caer Damh and the Bradhaeth turning up on that horizon. And always there was that unnatural ring of sunlight, against their walls now on east and south: *we must pass under it if we go south—into that shadow.*

When such chill thoughts came on him he would think, unthinking: *Lord Ciaran would know what we ought to do—*

Then with a reeling of his mind he would remember why they were doing all of this at all, that lord Ciaran was not in hall, nor likely to be again: that there was no chance of things being what they had been, no days stretching before them of summer and harvest and winter and spring, no more, no more, forever.

O gods, he would think then, and there would come a leaden pain about his heart and a panic desire to go up to hall if only to look and be sure no further calamity had fallen. *They do not know how to watch them*, he thought of Meadhbh and Ceallach, remembering that they were fey, and willful, and desperate. *I would know. I might. O gods. Muirne; my lady—keep them from wandering.*

But he had tasks enough at hand. The counting of the horses came to him; Leannan brought him the tally of the people. "Cipher me the thing," he begged Leannan, helpless in the profusion of numbers; and so they squatted together by the steps and made an obstacle of themselves while Leannan traced figures in the dust and told him the tale of it.

"The fittest men have to have the good horses," Domhnull said. "To ride at the fore. They cannot carry double; we must not tire those horses or those men—for our defense."

"So," said Leannan. "But what will we do with the twenty-odd left walking?"

He had no answer. So Leannan left him, saying nothing more. He ran his hands over his aching head, sitting as he was on the step; and remembered then that there were always eyes on him, and gathered himself to his feet.

A shadow fell, abrupt twilight. Thunder rumbled. He looked up at the cloudwall, towering up and up above them. A dark thread had torn from it and streamed across the heavens, headed northward. Another mare's-tail, in sky that had been pure. A chill went up his back.

"Domhnull."

The voice was high and clear and urgent, from the steps above him. He looked up at Meadhbh and Ceallach.

"Go inside," he said. A dread was on him because of the clouds. He felt the whole of Caer Wiell defenseless, naked to storm and lightning. "Get back inside!"

The thunder cracked. They flinched together and looked up. He took the steps, reckless of the pain, and suddenly saw another sight but Caer Wiell stone—saw the border hills all shadowed, tangled figures locked in battle, men in route and dying in the black hail of arrows. *Lost,* he thought, between two steps; and like a thunderclap remembered that he had dreamed this once before, in early morning. *The north is fallen. Ruadhan!*

"Domhnull—" Small hands gripped his, thin arms embraced him at the stair's crest. He swept the pair up with him, carried them both, aching with the pain and stumbling. An icy wind rose; it battered at them, carried dust, smelling of rain. He thrust them inside the doorway where there was some shelter, and looked back again. ·

"They're going north," said Ceallach. "The clouds are going north."

They were: the gray mare's-tails streamed off the cloud-wall above them, all tending in the same direction like strands of black wool all drawn by some invisible hand.

"Like weaving," said Meadhbh. "Look!—there are more coming from the north below them."

The lightning cracked. Wails of dismay came from the yard, the screams of children. "Get inside," he shouted at them. He went out onto the wall and yelled at the men who were running down the steps to safety, to the folk who were hurrying in the yard. "Get everyone within walls! Go to the Old Hall: go to the barracks! The doors are open!"

Wind whirled up sand from where it gathered by the stairs. Leannan came out of nowhere, clutching his harp like a babe before him, rushing up the steps. The awning of the scullery ripped loose; a stack of pots overturned and went racketing about in the wind. A stray horse bolted through the yard, shying from the pots and running children.

"*Domhnull!*" It was Muirne's voice behind him. He stood staring outward. The sun was going. Shadow covered them. The winds howled. If he let himself he could see dark and flickerings of lightning, like that night at Donn.

"Domhnull!" A hand seized his arm. It was Leannan who pulled him back inside shelter. The door slammed: Muirne dropped the bar. Meadhbh and Ceallach hugged him as if they feared he too would fade; he hugged them blindly to him and went up the stairs inside with them, while thunder shook the stones.

Branwyn waited there, sitting by the fire.

"It's happened," Domhnull said. The children were mute beside him, too prophetic, shivering. He held to them. "Lady Branwyn, the border's fallen."

She was unamazed. She stared at him. Her eyes were dry. She

was stone, ice, immobility. "So Beorc will come home now," she said. "If he can free himself. Rhys with him."

"No," said Leannan. "Likeliest they will be at Hlowebourne by now. And if Ruadhan retreats Beorc will stand there, Ruadhan's shield."

"He mustn't," said Meadhbh. Her teeth were chattering. Domhnull clenched his arm about her. "It's coming. Something dark—*dark on your path*, he said; he told me."

"Hush," said Ceallach, "Meadhbh, don't."

She grew cold a moment. Domhnull felt it, as if some winter wind had chilled her skin, even beneath his hand. "Meadhbh," he said. "Stay, stay *here*."

Eald quaked. The silver trees shed gold in the darkness, a cascade on the hill, an ebbing of their light even with the first glimmering of dawn.

There was silence for the moment. Then the wind began, driving more leaves before it, and the day hesitated, whether it could dawn at all.

The night's cold lingered. Arafel sat still within the grove, head bowed against her knees, her sword embracing them in her hands. The moonstone's light was dimmed, murked with shadows, and she could not bear to look at it.

Darknesses crept close among the trees, regaining courage in the fading of her spell. They whispered there.

Then she lifted her head and clenched her hand on the sword hilt, and the silver light gleamed.

"Where is the horse?" one mocked her. "Do you know that, Duine Sidhe? Has it run away like the Man? Or has something caught it?"

"There were two," said the other, whose eyes were lamps in shadow, "but she has lost them both."

Her heart grew cold. She rose with the sword held before her. "What mean you—run away? Be plain, wight."

They edged back into darkness. Others were there, tall Sidhe, slim and pale of face. They were armed and armored, and the rising day shone through them.

"Begone!" she cried. "Dun Gol hold you! *Begone from Eald!*"

They vanished. They were prudent still. Her wound ached. The sword sank point against the earth, impaling golden, once-silver leaves. The leaves still fell, spiraling about her, gentle and desolate; and a longing was on her—how fair they had seemed, even as they were, how fair and how proud and how much what the Sidhe had been.

"Fionnghuala," she whispered. And aloud: *"Fionnghuala."*

Rain began to fall, cold as death, hazing the struggling day, making the leaves one sodden carpet and sending shivers to her bones. It heralded change, like the falling of the leaves. Even Miadhail, the youngest of trees, had green only in his uppermost leaves; a dozen at least fell to the onslaught of the wind.

"Fionnghuala."

There was a breath near her. The elf horse stood drenched in rain, her bright head lifted, nostrils wide.

"So you *are* here," Arafel said, and shivered at the doubt that had been so easily sown in her heart; like the rain, like the death of trees, it was the waning of her strength. And Fionnghuala hesitated, as if that doubt had come between them.

She went to the horse, offered her hand. Soft breath came against it in return, trust and faith. The night was past; elvish day had come, even a murky one and dim. And time—mortal time— how much of it had fled?

Ciaran—Ciaran—*Ciaran!*

Run away, the voices had whispered. She felt something, but it had changed, vastly changed. She felt another presence when she strove to reach through the mist, the prisoning, black trees.

"Aodhan," she murmured. The stone pained her, went cold. "What of Aodhan—Fionnghuala?" She stroked the damp neck, felt the shiver, brisk and impatient. A fey dark eye regarded her, full of dread and madness. *Come*, it said. *Come. There are things yet to try.*

She sheathed the sword, seized the mane and swung up, and Fionnghuala began to move, in a muttering of thunder, shifting through *here* and *now* with increasing swiftness. In the long night she had lost much. The day promised to be brief and dim—but it was her day, all the same, when the drow must wane.

Ciaran, she thought, and shivered at what the stone brought her, a lost and lonely grayness, far from any sun. *"Aodhan!"* she called, and the names wound together inseparable in their fate.

She rode even into mortal Eald. But here there was no sign or touch of them. "Lord Death!" she called.

But even he was gone.

One touch of Eald remained in this world. *For memory*, she had said once, *for memory that Eald is true.*

And again: *I have set a virtue on them of finding.*

*   *   *

Thunder rumbled in the night. Meadhbh wished to be brave, but she shivered, even wrapped as she was in warmth, in the hall and the glow of fire and the presence of those she loved.

Fire, she thought. She imagined the small safe hearthfire licking out at the floor, running the stones, down the stairs, cutting them off from safety. Her gift prickled at her throat like nettles and when she shut her eyes there was the mist. Her brother wandered there; and they were afraid, both of them, of something nameless.

Their father would have warned them back; but he was not with him; and they did not know this place.

"Meadhbh." That was Domhnull. A callused hand took hers and held it, ever so gently. "Ceallach."

So they were back in hall, within gray stone walls. Muirne and Domhnull were by them. Their mother slept in her chair, and Leannan nodded, while the rain came down against the roof above them. It was like that night, the last night, the rain, the dreadful rain, their father lying abed.

"Leannan," Muirne said. "Play. Play, will you?"

The harper lifted his head, weary that he was, settled his harp on which he had been leaning, sent his fingers wandering over the strings, and the lightest music came, the gentlest, saddest beneath the rain-sounds.

It is a Sidhe song, Meadhbh thought; and so long as the harper's fingers moved it made a magic in the hall.

But when the song was done the silence seemed the grayer and the thicker for it.

Sometimes she heard horses; heard sounds she had only heard in the practice yard, the hiss and strike of arrows: but harsh cries followed. She heard the clash of metal, smelled iron like poison in the air. She rested her face in her hands, and could not escape it.

She slept true sleep but little. Domhnull held her and Ceallach, each in an arm; and so she had a little rest, her head against his heart, with Muirne close beside her.

The light failed, no longer than a mortal day now: the nights grew longer and this one would be longest of all. The sun was rising in the mortal world. Armies moved. On Airgiod's banks darkness returned.

But Fionnghuala strode in and out of this world and the other, searching.

And in Caerbourne's waters she found it, a quiet creature, hiding, baleful in its shadows.

"Come out," Arafel said, in mortal dawn; it fled to Eald, a quick shifting; but Fionnghuala was quicker. It shifted back again: and now it shivered, white and shriveled in the rocks where it had hidden.

"Despair is your name," Arafel said. *"Andochas."* Her sword whispered from its sheath and the water shivered. "You have trespassed, hear me."

It shrank farther. Two pale eyes shone like moons beneath the water.

"Where is he, fuath?"

The moons rose. The white face broke the surface. The air shivered to its wailing. "I warn, I only warn, Duine Sidhe."

"Baneful, spiteful creature!" Lord Death is patient! I am not, not today—Andochas. Tell me!"

"He fled, fled, fled. Another life went out." The Bain Sidhe shifted into elvish night; but Fionnghuala did not lose her.

"Where?" Arafel asked.

"Dark to me, dark his path. Death lost him." The Bain Sidhe shrank farther, became a pale strange fish, that dived deep into Death's dark realm, leaving only a ripple on Caerbourne's surface. And into that place Fionnghuala would not venture unbidden.

"Men," a far voice whispered. *"Men have failed you, Arafel, Aoibheil, whose name is Joy. Aoibheil, Aogail—joy and death . . . o Arafel, Arafel, Arafel. . . ."*

"No," she said ever so softly. "No. You do not have him. *Here, Duilliath—come here to me here, Duilliath, my cousin."*

Her whisper sped, winding through mists and among the ghostly branches of that other Eald. She clenched the moongreen stone she wore and willed a harping from it, an elvish sound, of a harp now broken. It had power in it. It was heard in all three realms of Eald. It was heard forever; if that harp had been whole she might have changed that song, but it was not and that was beyond her power. It bound and drew, having magic in it; it had Men in it, for a Man had made it.

It reached to the halls of Caer Wiell, where that harp had hung; it reached to Dun na h-Eoin, where Kings had had it; it reached even to the plain before the gates of the King, where in the dawning Donnchadh rode on a black, powerful horse. The eyes of that horse were green and sometimes it seemed other than what it ought. And Donnchadh seemed other to his men than he had been the day before—or perhaps they had never seen him so fired with purpose: he was lean and fair and strange and sat straight as a younger man; no one looked him in the eyes, no more than they looked at the horse more directly than they must.

The standards moved. The points of countless spears glittered wanly in the greenish, stormy dawn; these were the contingents of the plain. There were archers: and these were the Boglach folks and their lords. They had gathered to Laochailan's deathbed, to seize what could be seized; to have power; but power had seized them instead, and they had no doubt now who of them was most perilous.

"Hail," the shout went up against the murky sky, "hail, Donnchadh King!" The hills rang with it like the sighing of the sea.

"*King*," the voice whispered which had become Donnchadh's own. "*O sweet self, I shall make you more than this. What you dreamed of is dross beside my dreams, long and long inside Dun Gol. King is only the beginning of it. Caer Wiell was ours once, like Caer Donn; but those were not the names. I shall teach you to call them. Of all Mankind only you will be left, my self, my very soul. You wanted Eald thrust aside; I shall cast it down, and make the world again what it was. And you will see, self, what wonders there are to see—of jewels like the sun and moon, of elegance and pleasure, of things so rare no Man has seen them. We shall scour the world and own it.*"

He had no fear now, of his brother, of armies, of any shadow. Least of all of the Sidhe. He gazed about him and Men flinched. He moved to the fore, the black horse at a canter.

That harpsound reached one other, far lost in gray and cold. Aodhan had slowed his pace, wandered in the woods, in the maze of darksome branches. But that sound came like light through the murk the world had become, like springtime through the winter, like a friend's hand offered among a world of enemies.

For a moment he knew the way. He made himself remember. There was very little of him left. He looked at his hand that clung to Aodhan's bright mane, and he could hardly see it.

"Come," he said to Aodhan. "This is the way."

The elf horse began to move again, running uncertainly, shaking the lightning from his mane.

FIFTEEN

Of Fire and Sword

The rain had stopped. Branwyn sat listening to the silence in the hall. About her, her children slept, and Muirne, Leannan, Domhnull—all, all finding a moment's peace at the end of night. She sat staring at nothing, feeling tears dammed up in her throat. She had laid all her plans; and now they lay in ruins, the roads a quagmire, Caerbourne rushing high for days, an obstacle for her poor folk, less for a determined army, none at all when An Beag should rise to cut them off from the ford. She had had dreams in the night, and they were all of ruin. She imagined other desperate things, of sending Domhnull and Cein and Cobhan with Meadhbh and Ceallach, to cross the flood alone near Caer Wiell somehow, and to go afoot through the heart of Eald, seeking Dryw, seeking—whatever refuge there was for a King the world rejected.

Perhaps her life had been all a mad hope. She had believed too little in luck at the beginning and believed in it too much at the end—but she had hoped all the same, not even understanding Eald, with the last hope in all her world.

"Arafel," she whispered to the silence. "Arafel. Arafel. Do you hear me—Feochadan, Thistle, whatever name you use nowadays? Ciaran, do you hear, can you hear?"

But in the one she did not trust, and in the other she could not hope, no matter how she tried.

Then came the sound of a running horse, lonely in the thick-walled silences, up against the walls. From the watch there was no hail or challenge. The hoofbeats continued.

Ciaran, she thought. She dared not breathe, for fear the hope would perish.

No, one of the horses was loose, that was all; some horse strayed before the walls.

Or Arafel had come.

She rose, shedding her laprobe; she walked barefoot to the door, then heard the door open down below, a soft padding on the stairs—but nothing mortal could have come inside so quickly, ignoring gates and watchers. She held back, her heart hammering with dread.

"Domhnull," she said, never taking her eyes from the door. "Domhnull, wake—"

There was no stirring from behind her. The door opened. A head thrust through at knee level, of a small hairy thing whose eyes glittered in the torchlight. "Domhnull!" she cried.

It came inside, hugged itself and leaned against the door. "They sleep, sleep, o the fair children; the Gruagach knows them, knows this Man, comes for them—for you."

"Keep away!" There was no weapon here, not so much as a dagger; they had moved out every piece of iron for Ciaran's sake, for her children's, who could not bear it. She edged toward the wall, thinking of the torch.

"Never fear," the small creature said, "o no, no, no, friend am I; such nice, kind children—so polite the people, saucers of milk they leave me, fine cakes, brown ale—but the Gruagach has his home, and he cannot linger. Come with me, come with me, fine cakes, brown ale, where sun is kind forever."

Her hand fell. She saw the green shadow, the jogging pony, the blonde girl in search of faery. *Come with me, take my hand, never hear them calling*— Her eyes blurred. "Is there still time?" she asked. "Is there place—for all of us?"

"All," the small wight said, and bounced up to his full height. "All the good, kind people; no iron must they carry. Haste, haste, haste."

He was gone, out the door and the door shut so quickly that the eye could not believe anything had stood there. Branwyn shivered and looked back at the hearthside where her children stirred, and Muirne; Domhnull wakened then, and Leannan in his corner.

"Get up," she said, "all of you. Get your warmest cloaks; Domhnull, go rouse the yard, everyone."

"Lady," Domhnull said, his face bewildered; but he gathered himself up.

"No iron," she said. "Not even in the bridles, no cooking-pans, no knives, nor brooches, no least thing."

"Lady—"

She drew herself up, wrapping the shreds of her pride about her—perilous, she thought; might pride shut the gates of faery? So she was afraid to claim what she had claimed before, that she was privy to faery's secrets. "I think now we have help," she said quietly, "and o, I fear we'll lose it." Beyond Domhnull her children gazed at her with solemn eyes. "Get your cloaks. We'll go down to the gate. Hurry, Domhnull; Leannan—help him."

Leannan took his harp; Domhnull paused for nothing but his cloak, and the door closed behind them.

"Wash, dress," she said to Meadhbh and Ceallach. "And then we go down."

For once she held secrets and Meadhbh and Ceallach did not. But they hurried.

She went to the empty bedroom, washed, dressed, while Muirne tended the children. She took Ciaran's next-best cloak oiled wool, warmer than her heaviest. *It may be cold*, he had said once, setting out on such a journey.

Now she thought of Beorc and Rhys and Ruadhan, of the men up at the border, and for a moment the glamor faltered. *O gods, what will become of them when they find Caer Wiell deserted? What if our enemies should take it against them? O gods, where are we going? Where am I taking these folk?*

But then she thought of Ciaran, of the way he had gone, and what they faced from the west, and no chance seemed too desperate. The vision recast itself, the small girl on the pony, the desire she had had once. She had seen the green silence; this beckoned differently, made her think of sun and meadows, not moon and sun together, not the dreadfulness of that guest who had come to their hall. This was warmth and laughter. And whereever it would go, *he* might have gone before them.

She hastened; she gathered up Meadhbh and Ceallach in the hall each by a hand and they went down the stairs together with Muirne close behind them bringing a bundle of clothes— "In the case," she said, "someone should need warm cloaks. 'Tis a waste to leave them."

The dawn broke as best it could over Hlowebourne, a dim redness before the clouds should take back the sun. The reeds were black, like so many spears; the bank loomed, and Beorc was glad when they put that rise behind them. All the land seemed full of ambushes now.

Of Ruadhan they had seen no sign; of the Bradhaeth folk nothing; the road was mire and even Hlowebourne denied its name and fought them.

But now something came toward them in the murk, a band of riders: they heard them in the distance. They were already carrying their shields uncased on their arms: now they took their swords from sheath and those with lances spurred their horses forward to meet whatever came.

The riders poured over the hillcrest into their midst, shadows in grim red light with neither face nor feature; but the foremost horse had a broad crooked blaze and two white feet—"Hold, hold!" Beorc cried when he saw it, and spears went up and horses shied under the rein as friend met friend in the feeble dawn. "Where's Ruadhan?" he asked Swallow's rider. "Blian, where are you going?"

The young man's face was haggard; he bled from the temple; his armor was battered and it seemed his wits were too. "Beorc—" He held his frantic horse. "They bid us go, fall back—Ruadhan, he held them, run all the way, he told us, and he stayed, him and ten of the bowmen—Lead them back, he told me; the old men and Ruadhan, they bid us go—"

"Let us get up there," Rhys said.

"There be all the Bradhaeth behind us," Blian said. Tears made tracks through blood and grime. "Lord Rhys, there was no holding that—" He twisted about in his saddle, casting a look backward, looked toward them yet again. "We be the first— break the way, Ruadhan said, if need be; the farmer-lads come after, them as could double up on horses; and Tuathal and his lot to put a shield behind them; and since yesterday we've been battered at—they've broken through, the Bradhaeth has, and four, five times we've had to fight them since yestereve."

There was silence, only the blowing of exhausted horses.

"Go," Beorc said heavily. "Get behind us. Move easier. From now the road is safer."

"Aye," Blian said. He drew his horse's head up. He rode through their midst, he and the men with him, slowly now; but then he stopped, and came back, and all his men with him. "We are not cowards," Blian said.

"No," said Beorc. "You are not."

"My cousin was right," Rhys said, riding near, with Owein and Madawc beside him. "Go back, all you Caer Wiell folk. Part of us will scatter through these hills, part of us go west and south; we can at least delay them."

"And what after?" Beorc said. "No. There is no hope in that. We gather those we can save. Then we go home—and quickly."

A cry sounded through the hills, a singing they had heard before at Caerbourne. Horses shied. Men swore.

"Wail all you like!" Rhys shouted at it, lifting his sword. "Here's iron for you!"

The wailing died away; the grass whispered.

"A horse," Blian said, looking to the right of them.

There was no horse there. The hoofbeats came and vanished into distance, both unnaturally swiftly.

They gathered at the gate and outside it, a great confusion of horses and people with bundles; but Meadhbh had none, like her mother, like her brother, like all of them who had had most and now were leaving it. She had lost too much to care for any part of it; only she had brought her tiny box of treasures in her pocket, the bright bird's feather, the river-smoothed stones, the things that she had gathered in her walks and rides with her father. Having lost him she had little longing even for these things, but thought she might want them and regret them too late, these small strange objects; the rest she left uncaring, though she had silver pins and gold, and fine clothes and a silver ring. She went empty handed down the stairs, and so did Ceallach, with their mother, with Muirne, with her bundle of clothes; but they had their Sidhe gifts about their necks, and the stones of Caer Wiell under their feet, and the memory of the tower hall and all its days and nights in their minds: that was what they took away that mattered.

There would be a guide, their mother had said: if it had been their father come home, their mother would have said that first, so they went without real interest in questions. Their thoughts were all to what was behind them, to feathers and stones and the thought of their father sitting in his corner. Now that they were out of the rooms it seemed to Meadhbh he might indeed come home, a memory sitting in hall, the Cearbhallain's great sword on his knees, his hands tending it, the light golden and flickering on his face. The hall was his now, lost like him, once the door was shut behind them.

They came down the last steps, where already the air seemed to tingle with perhaps and might be. The Sidhe-gifts burned. They looked up: they knew the small brown creature that turned up in their way without being there the moment before. "It's the Gruagach," Ceallach exclaimed; but it seemed their mother knew this: nothing today seemed to daunt their mother, not even a Sidhe before them.

"Gruagach," Meadhbh said; all at once the Sidhe-gift at her throat ached the more, or her heart did. She thought of her father and it was as if the world had started moving again, or she had; as if she had come alive again—her heart hurt, but she lifted her head and knew that she had not truly lived between that night and this, though the world had gone on. Suddenly she felt surrounded by secrets, finding her mother—her mother!—meshed with the Sidhe.

Her father had a hand in this. He must have. The world was bending round them like water round a rock, disasters flowing past them, and somehow *he* was in it.

"Come," the Gruagach said, motioning with long, lank hands. "O hurry, hasten. The ponies will come, the fine horses, all, all."

"Gruagach," their mother said, sharp as she spoke in hall. "Gruagach, there are more of us—up on the road by Hlowebourne."

It stopped. It hugged itself and rocked, its dark eyes wrinkled up in pain. "O gold lady, the Gruagach cannot reach them. They come as they can. The big red Man, the small dark one: the Gruagach has known them, the Sidhe has touched them, no more, no more can help them. Come! Come! Come! The people, the fine, polite people—no, no delay, come, hurry. It comes, it comes, dark up the dale; I cannot say its name, but the river cannot stop it." It turned, hopped a few paces away, clambered long-armed up the side of a shaggy brown pony. "Haste. O haste!"

They heard Domhnull's voice above the others, shouting at folk to move; he came with Leannan and Cein and Cobhan, a whole troop of the boys leading their father's horse and their ponies and horses for themselves through the press. They stopped suddenly; all about them silence fell, and then cries, as if only then folk had seen the Brown Man and his pony.

"Come," the Gruagach said, beckoning, "o Man, the Gruagach knows you, far we rode together—come, come, come, the horses too, o hurry! From north and west they come, the dark things, the shadow. Ride, ride, all who can: the Gruagach will lead you!"

Some magic fell on them all: the air was full of it. Folk scrambled for unsaddled horses that did not shy, handed children up that stared wide-eyed, bewildered. Meadhbh took Floinn's mane, trying to get up, and Floinn never flinched when she clambered belly-down and awkward. Her brother was up on Flann. Domhnull helped their mother and Muirne up to a white nosed mare and gave her mother the halter-rope.

"My husband," a woman said; "my son," said another. "How will they find us? Where are we going?"

"To safety!" their mother said, all sharp. "Where they would want you."

"Give me leave," said Domhnull, delaying, holding Iolaire's halter. "I will find the rest of us."

"You have a duty," their mother said sharply. "You have a lord—still; come with us."

"*Now!*" the Gruagach cried—like some part of the brown pony itself he was, atop its back with knees drawn up. It waved shaggy arms. The air wavered about them; the murky dawn became gray mist, and the gates were naught but shadow.

A forest lay before them. The Gruagach rode out with his pony and all at once they were moving: Domhnull walked, caught all unwilling and desperate, leading Iolaire beside them. Then he seized Iolaire's mane and swung up, settling himself. He rode a distance in front and then rode back past them, his face showing no sign of the grief that ached in the Sidhe—gift when he was near. "Keep together," they heard him call. "Come, come on, my lady gave her orders. The luck is on us; it always was. Keep sight of one another, call out if anyone should falter."

We have left Beorc, Meadhbh thought. *And Rhys and all the men. I might go to him.* She clutched the Sidhe-gift at her throat, and wondered if she could go so far as a border she had never seen. But *no*, she thought, oddly sure of something with so much pain in it; the way streamed ahead of them, and she was bound with Ceallach: it was no less dire a way, no less perilous than that their men took. It was their way, and she must not leave it.

Beyond the trees soon other creatures followed. Deer moved, ghostly through the mist and darkness; a fox trotted; there were other creatures, as if even Caer Wiell's wild things were going, as if all life were leaving the land. Meadhbh turned and looked back at the column they made, the end of it lost in mist, horses, riders, a few of the men walking, carrying children on their backs. The great oxen and even the cattle were with them, loose, moving with patient care; a flock of sheep walked along beside, quite un-sheeplike sure where they were going. There was the old spotted hound that was almost blind; there were foals and yearlings following after the mares. Domhnull rode back out of the mist, shepherding the line; he had taken a child up in front of him.

The Sidhe-gift burned. Meadhbh held it in her hand, and felt Ceallach near, knee to knee with her as she looked again to the forest ahead. The way grew dark. Trees towered up, and the mist threatened them; but always just in front of them rode her mother with Muirne, and the swishing tail of the Gruagach's brown pony. She shrugged her cloak about her, feeling cold and glad that her mother had thought of warmer clothing.

Father, she thought. The thought kept growing in her, not a hope, but a certainty. She looked back again: she saw Leannan. The harper rode by Domhnull, and a doe and fawn walked soberly beside him. A pony carried Ruadhan's Seamaire, who had someone's baby in her arms and a little girl behind her. There was Cook afoot, still in her apron, with two of the scullery maids and a cluster of the pages. The mist gave them up and took them back again, and they were there and not there, all of Caer Wiell. She looked about in fright, relieved to find her mother still in front of her, with Muirne, the mare padding along with soundless steps, tame like all the others. The Gruagach sat backwards on his pony, watching them all with dark and sober eyes.

The grove had suffered. More leaves had fallen; dark things had crept close but there was still power here: Cinniuint still lived, though his leaves were dimmed; so did Miadhail, and the others. So Arafel came to it afoot from Airgiod, where Fionnghuala waited. She gathered what she wanted, took up the armor that was hers, her weapons. She looked about her, touched Miadhail's leaves. She wove protection then, a patient spell of different sort, with all her strength, for she was leaving, not to see this place again: she whispered names, and drew on all they held; she set the stones to singing, a bright clashing in the breeze. It was exchange, strength pouring into the earth, the air, consuming itself at last: its duration would be brief, after so long ages, a brightness soon to fade. Flowers bloomed again. Cinniuint budded, blossomed; Miadhail put forth new leaves; Ciataich greened again, and the air was fresh and good. The grove became what it had been. She gazed on it, fit to break her heart, and turned then and walked away. One backward look: her kind had ever been flawed, and so elves had fallen to fair voices whispering of what had been, what might have been. But it was time to go.

She turned her face to Airgiod, to shadows Fionnghuala held at bay. "Begone," she said, powerful in this place, a voice so still the breeze might have drowned it and so sure it could be heard through thunder. Light shone about her; it reflected in the waters, moon-cold and having the sun about it: elvish armor, elvish weapons.

Duilliath advanced, and summoned other allies. From Dun Gol they came, streamed through the hills on horses fleet as nightmares. But there was worse than Duilliath; there was the Voice that moved them all, and that was what she sought, to keep its attention on herself, to threaten with what fading might she had, so long as it should last.

She swung up to Fionnghuala's back. The elf horse trembled, threw her head.

Now the whisper reached her, as it reached the drow, coming softly through ghostly trees. It sang battle-joy and madness, tempted to glory and abandon—but that too was temptation, calling her forward as the grove called her to return, to wrap herself in safety, to fall asleep with it when the end should come.

So they had erred once, to turn to the dragons in their wars, the ancient, the long-remembering; and this one was oldest, most persuasive, having spells within his voice.

This one they had never tamed. This one had seduced them. *Follow me,* it had said, *drive out Men, yield nothing. Remember pride. Take what is yours. I am power, more than all my kind; listen to me. Listen.*

"Not I, old Worm," she answered it. "Come find me if you can . . . if you can break my binding."

The dark rider was there again before them, as he had been since Hlowebourne, in this day that was no day, with the sun wrapped in cloud. They had gathered what of their folk they could, and now they came southward, daring no pause now, for the Bradhaeth came behind them; Damh's horsemen scoured the land and columns of smoke went up from steadings all about the hills.

But that rider was no man of Damh, no Man at all: Beorc knew him for what he was; and doubtless Rhys did. As for Owein and Madawc, they lay dead beyond Hlowebourne ford, and Blian had fallen with them, with no few others in that hail of Bradhaeth arrows. So it was not surprising that this rider had joined them, went with them, behind, before them.

My lady foreknew this, Beorc thought, not for the first time; and now he dreaded worse, that all else she had foreseen might have fallen on Caer Wiell, Donnchadh moving up the dale with fire and slaughter.

Rhys said no word. The small man's lips were set and hard; he had no curse for the enemy, no threat but his look, which was black and baneful. From wildness he had gone to a fey dark rage, and never spoke, not since Owein fell beside him.

But now the rider paced close beside them, a shadow on the day, darker than the southron banners.

"You!" Beorc cried, having had enough and caring nothing whether others thought him mad. "Be off with you! We have no more to give you!"

He could not see the face; but he saw others looking, saw

haggard southrons half-draw swords, letting them fall back in uncertainty; but Rhys reined aside, his blade full-drawn; and then he stopped cold, for other riders waited in the shadow of the trees beside the road. His face went gray. The sword-point wavered.

"No," Beorc said. "Rhys, stay back."

"It's Madawc."

"Caer Wiell," Beorc said, "Rhys, *Caer Wiell*. Remember."

The southron backed his horse. Its ears were flattened; its eyes were white-edged, its nostrils wild: it fought the rein and shied, stumbling in exhaustion. The column broke in rout; the day dimmed; the rain broke on them in heavy spatters as they ran.

Still Death stayed with them; and their horses that had leapt forward in panic ran now with strange slowness. Hounds coursed beside them, loping dark shapes; in the hills the Bain Sidhe wailed. Death rode next to them, the black horse showing bone dimly through its shadow flesh: the rider turned his cowled head, almost, almost facing them.

"Death," Beorc shouted at it, rash in desperation, "do you make bargains?"

"Sometimes."

"Then give my lord back to us!"

"Would you find him?" The pace quickened, and somehow their horses kept it. The way darkened still, into night and terror. "Then follow: my way, iron can pass. You should remember that, Skaga's-son."

"Beorc!" It was Rhy's voice behind him. "Beorc—gods—"

"Do not falter," the dark rider said beside him, and sped then before them like some eclipse of light and life. "Caer Wiell stands empty; your lady has gone before you to find your lord— Would you have battle? I shall give you that: blood and vengeance!"

Beorc followed; he kept the shadow before him, heard the baying hounds, and Blaze never faltered, dodging along a track of dead trees and desolation, under a moon red and leprous. No stars shone in this night. No wind blew but carried despair with it.

"*Beorc—*" Riders overtook him, his own folk, Rhys, riders shining with pale banners which were the black banners of the sons of Dryw, the darkest hue of the world above made pale by this night.

White things fluttered; something deerlike raced beside them, pursued by the likeness of hounds.

"Stay," voices whispered from the trees, the thickets. "Ahead is pain and wounds. This forest is less dire than the way ahead."

"Your lady will join you here," whispered others. "Your lord has thrown away his chance of worlds to come. Turn aside, follow no more. There is peace in darkness."

"No!" Beorc cried, a voice that had carried across battlefields, but here it seemed wan and weak. "Pay no heed to the voices!"

Then other riders joined them, pale-faced, on horses that moved with soundless stride.

"Madawc!" Rhys cried. "Owein!" A third came close.

"You see I did not leave," Blian Cein's-son said, riding by them.

And others were there, a shadowy band of riders; a plain-faced man rode at their head.

"Ruadhan," Beorc named him.

"You cannot pace us now," Ruadhan said. "We go ahead of you. Look for us at Aescford."

The riders passed them then, pouring ahead of them like shadows in the dark.

Lord Death stayed before them. From Caer Wiell folk rose a shout that shook the shadows. "Follow!" Beorc cried; "Follow!" Rhys shouted. They knew their way now; a madness had fallen on them, that they raced side by side, given a second chance, a hope, a tryst there was no failing.

Before them in the night were fences, sheds, a rambling house with its windows still alight, under a huge old tree. A heron watched them ride by, solemn sentinel along a streambank, water glinting in the starlight—for here were only scattered clouds. Ahead of them the Gruagach slid off his pony and the two ran side by side, the pony jogging, the small Sidhe capering and dancing as if walking were too ordinary for him.

The deer scampered off, with the moonlight on their backs; the fox left them; the sheep went straying, the great oxen too. Only the horses and the ponies kept on their steady pace, and folk began to murmur and to call out to one another as the spell unraveled.

Meadhbh and Ceallach rode up by their mother and Muirne; Leannan joined them with a drowsing rider at his back, one of the youngest pages. Domhnull came up beside them, on Iolaire, and the stallion snuffed the wind and called a greeting to the valley and the barns.

A greeting came back to them. And the doors of the steading opened, pouring out light and people.

"Where can we be?" asked Muirne. "Are they Caer Wiell folk?"

"No," Meadhbh said. There was a shiver in this place, like air before a rain. "It is Sidhe. O mother—"

"We are safe," their mother said, in a faint, faded voice. "I heard once of such a place—Skaga told me of it, when I was young—We are safe here. We must be."

All the people poured after them, up the hill between the fences; and folk met them there at the fence. The foremost of them was a huge man with hair and beard glowing ruddy as the torch he carried.

"I am Beorc," that one said. "And you are welcome."

SIXTEEN
Light and Dark

Something dire came near. Arafel lifted her head, hearing the difference in the wind, the stillness of the trees. Beneath her Fionnghuala fretted, anxious. "Hush," whispered Arafel.

A darkness drifted close to her in the midst, growling, threatening her a moment, then sinking down to wait. She ignored it. It was not what she had felt.

Other small things had stalked her along Caerbourne. Most of the ill went two-footed, humankind, Men the like of which she had long known, robbers, bandits. She wasted no time on the likes of An Beag. Their ambush, which they had set for Caer Wiell, caught them nothing but a sleepy shellycoat come rattling up out of Death's dark river into Caerbourne's willowed banks, and she had laughed to see them run. A tree had flourished at that laughter, put forth buds, tried life. As for the shellycoat it dived back again, rattling and grumbling; and the Men had run for walls and safety.

But other men had worked their malice. When she looked into the mortal world she saw the north asmoke, and some of that smoke came from Caer Wiell. In that sight she had no joy at all, in the ruin of the land, the orchards, the place to which she had set her own hand, greening it and loving it—less than her own woods, but greatly even so, respecting the Men who had poured love on that iron—sown earth. They had coaxed growth there, where forest had failed, in the land Dun Gol had ruined. Now it burned. Now its folk were homeless. Those who still strayed, she guided where she could, with what thought she could spare: *West,* she whispered, *go westward through the hills;* and scattered fugitives kept running, abandoning everything but hope of Eald—Men from the border, hurt and lost; a steader's fleet-footed daughter . . . such found the paths, following will o' wisps and wishes, while things darker than they knew how to fear coursed over the hills and under. They were the drow's dark dogs, hastening to a summons too great for them to wait for such small prey, to a border that was forming.

"Come," she said to Fionnghuala, and they trod their careful way farther—far more slowly than Fionnghuala might have carried her, but no more quickly could she work—touching here a tree that still had strength, drawing constantly on what remained of Eald, deep-rooted in Cinniuint. They were not great magics. She had done as much for Caer Wiell once, in the greening of its fields; but they were deep magics, all the same. They had needed all the might of Dun Gol to overcome them thus far and they were, with Cinniuint, the binding on Lioslinn's chill depths. She drew a tide of life in her wake, bringing her Eald with her. Sometimes her workings were fragile as a flower springing up where the elf-horse had trod; or a seed's bursting its shell; or a failing tree's few leaves given strength to cling. Her work widened from that beginning, taking its own course east and west, flowed wide, dimming Duilliath's ghostly trees and giving place to smaller, truer growth. Across the waters of Airgiod lilies bloomed; on Caerbourne's banks an old willow drank a bit and ventured all his fading strength in a few new leaves, and an old oak did the same, mistaking the touch for sunlight. Even beside Death's river unaccustomed flowers bloomed, ghostly white.

Drow could not cross this advancing tide. They fled before it.

But now the ill came near, appearing just before her: drow, pale and slim and having shadow and fire about them, so that looking at them was like looking beyond the sunset. A wind obeyed them, chill and killing; it warred with life. Even so a small gold flower bloomed, and threatened all their magic. They yielded backward, wishing to regroup, but she fought them, step by step in her advance.

"Such struggle costs you," one said, whose name had been Suileach.

"There is Cinniuint," the other said. "His roots are deep, but even there things delve."

"Lord Death will perish soon," said the first. "He prospers now. But he will pass when Men do."

"You are corrupt, o Arafel, to cherish such allies as Men and Death. You are Sidhe. It is unnatural."

"Your magic fails. It has Death at its roots. Look on us; remember what you are. No more of war." Suileach drew close. "The green shade might come again to Dun Gol. We might call it again Airgiodach, of silver leaves and stars."

"Do you remember? We were friends."

Against that one she drew the sword; and it vanished, but Suileach remained.

"Like the leaves in the forest," said Suileach, "are our numbers. And this Man—Ciaran is his name. Do you seek him? We have not forgotten him. We can show you where he is."

"Be gone, Suileach!" She extended not her sword but her left hand toward him, with the magic that she wove. "Or yield to *me*—you know what I offer. Memory. Green shade, fair sun—"

It cried aloud, cold as it had grown; it could still feel torment, and the green magic burned it. "We will have these things. We are wiser than we were. Peace, Aoibheil! Who now makes strife, but you?"

"Cold jewels, lifeless wealth, the fall of Caer Righ—these things you wrought! You serve a dark thing that hates us—have you never seen that?"

"Hates us—do Men not hate us? You would have shared the world with them and look how they repaid you."

"Men the Worm corrupted—O Suileach, think! if thought is left you. The dragon used you; it never loved elves or Men. It set one against the other."

"O Aoibheil, does that stone of yours remember? Of Caer Righ you made Dun Gol." Malice came through the voice, so great a malice it almost overthrew her. "*Come closer.*"

She had flung up her hand to shield herself; her sword was dimmed; the stone at her breast went cold.

"Lioslinn," it whispered, and not Suileach, but another thing speaking through him, in the face of which she shivered. "*Hail, Arafel.* Come, Arafel; you must keep coming. Others will attend this Man. You and I must meet. The bindings—o weave them with all your strength: with all your strength—come, spend it. Mine will not diminish in the least and yours is fading."

Even Suileach had faltered. The drow retreated in disorder,

recovering them with distance. "Ciaran," it called back spitefully. "Ciaran, Ciaran Cuilean."

She ventured no attack, no answer. She only stood still, and that itself was effort, in the dread that blew about her. "You cannot touch him," she cried to the empty air. "Try, Suileach. *Try*. When one of us goes *that* way, neither you nor I can hold him."

"Because he desires nothing—recalls nothing." Malice leapt and crackled like fire in the voice from among Duilliath's black trees. "But for you to use him he must keep something of himself—and by that something we can hold him, by that something bind him, in pain and torment, o Aoibheil, as long as yours will be— Revenge, Aoibheil—revenge and patience—these we know. We will give you to the dragon."

"Begone!"

"To this Man of yours?"

It vanished. But the voice was slow to fade.

Something touched him, faint and far away. He remembered, then: sometimes he wandered, and even Aodan lost the way, in the woods that were everywhere across the face of the world, in the maze of his thoughts, the tangle of his desires. Going anywhere was difficult; going the way that he must made his heart ache. But that voice spoke now in a tremor of the ground, in small shudderings as if the earth itself knew pain.

He looked over his shoulder, toward the darker trees, and there were elves.

"Brother," they hailed him kindly, "what do you here, astray?"

He had seen them before. They had never come so close. He gazed on them, on faces fair and perilous, into the eyes of Sidhe. They were not Sidhe of the kind he knew. He read cold power there and lust for a thousand things to which elves might be tempted.

"Let go the stone," they whispered. "It hinders you."

Aodhan shied, breaking the spell. Then he could look away, desperately toward the west.

"Let it go, Ciaran Cuilean!"

He clutched the stone within his hands; they held his Name in theirs, and it was hard, hard, not to hear them. There had been a place, a hall, faces that he loved. They wished to show him these things, to bind him to the name that once had been enough for him; they offered these things, and his heart ached, somewhere in the stone.

"Ciaran," they called behind him. "Ciaran!"

Aodhan ran, ran toward the west, spurning the earth beneath him. Small darknesses leapt at him. The dark elves pursued. On and on he fled in his despair, seeming at last to gain a little.

But there was worse ahead. He felt it, like a rift in the world itself, a blight on all that was.

He broke from the woods on a hillcrest, and it was there, in the plain that stretched before him, a darkness the like of which he had never seen, not in the world and not in Death's domain. It lay from hill to hill, and reached toward the sea, casting a pall everywhere, from Caerbourne to the north. The likeness of horses moved in it; it glittered with spears and arms.

He had never felt so naked as on that hillside, where distance meant nothing and that darkness might see as well as be seen. The stone burned with icy cold, and Aodhan faltered, shivering, coming to a standstill. Love, duty, all these things seemed small and far and fleeting against such a thing. The hills lay broken, having given up the secrets at their roots; every tree was slain; every blade of grass had perished in that darkness.

"No, go on," he urged Aodhan, though all the fear that was gathered in him counseled otherwise. "They are at our heels—*go on!*"

You will perish, the doubts assailed him.

And an attention which he had felt but slightly until now turned full upon him.

There, it said, *he is there*, and the hills themselves quaked with it. He was shaken; his bones ached; he looked behind him for retreat, and Aodhan broke stride and turned.

But: "No!" he cried then; and the elf horse veered back to westward. He kept going, into the darkening wind. His substance blew in tatters. He heard his name called behind him and before, but it was not all his Name. They thrust at him with weapons, but those nearest him were shadows to him: iron pained but could not touch him. Drow sought him with their cold power: they named Aodhan, and Arafel; and at every naming the stone burned, until there seemed nothing more desirable in that maelstrom than to cast it away, to have relief of pain.

There was another voice. He could not hear what it said, but it reminded him of life.

But, *Ciaran*, the wind sang, *Ciaran Cuilean—what do you here, astray?*

He went forward. Over all that distance, he heard the gulls.

"It is your brother coming," the Dark Man whispered calmly; and Donnchadh, the body that was Donnchadh's, lifted its face from the plain before them. There was little left that answered to that name. That which did remain remembered kinship, and a shiver passed through the flesh, a remnant of fear for vanished reasons, a remnant of jealousy and regret.

She still drives him, said Duilliath. *She moves other things, in other realms. But these are thin shields, King-of-Men, unlike ours. I speak of dragons. Come, let us deal with him.*

My nephew, Donnchadh remembered the reason of his fear, recalling that this was not the direction that they had begun, not the thing the Dark Man had offered him when first he let him in. *O gods, what have you done?*

O, sweet self, it is late to ask, is it not? You must meet him. Think, think, how to name him—think of him, and show me that.

The host advanced. They moved slowly, being great in number, being in this world and others. They shed small groups which sped as things could which traveled one realm only, one band toward the south, to the siege of Dryw in his mountain fastness; another by An Beag toward Caer Wiell, but these were nothing to the numbers that remained. They had crossed the Caerbourne, and some had drowned in that flood, but advanced the more swiftly in Death's dark realm, yet another front, a portion of the whole.

A pair of youths climbed a hill outside Caer Donn, one fair, one dark, but the hill was hollow and full of promises.

You are not afraid now, the voice told him. *You are Sidhe the same as he, no, more—old as the world and direr than Death.*

A pair of brothers embraced outside the King's tent at Dun na h-Eoin. But he was the King now; and his brother—out there beyond the lines.

An Beag has served you well, the dark Sidhe whispered, *even by being there. Caer Wiell has come to us; we have no need to seek it. They have found a place: Men could never take it—but we shall. Your brother's elvish ally . . . her name is Arafel. Remember it. She has favored this haven. But we shall have it. And the last of her will fade.*

Donnchadh's visions faded; he remembered such a valley as he began to remember darker things, prison beneath the hills, elvish dead . . . cold and heartless hate, smothered under bindings and hatred of Men and all their doings.

That which had been Donnchadh winked out, lost in that gale of wrath. Those about him had another aspect than they had had, having gone pale and strange; and the horses that bore them had brought their other aspect into this world. Some of his followers had sought to flee, but these were hunted, and no more tried after them. Most had ambition only to be the hunters, which was all they had ever wanted, to give pain and not to feel it. Breandan, one had been, seneschal of Donn; Geannan another; Wulf, new lord of Ban, murderer of the last. They had acquired the calm, cold grace of elves; they had become beautiful, but no Man met their eyes.

Duilliath looked out on the world unhindered now; he smiled with Donnchadh's lips as the black horse leapt forward, a fuath of shifting shape, speeding with speed no horse could match. He drew his tainted sword.

"I know why you have come," said Beorc, the stranger who was so like their own, as they shared his table in the yard beneath the tree, "and I know where you hope to go, lady. You will ask have I seen him; I will tell you no. And all of that is too simple. I will tell you you must not go, and I know you will never heed. You cannot. Your luck is on you. And on all your house. Against that I have no power. I fare as you do. No more will I say than that."

"Riddles," said their mother. She was not wont to raise her voice. It trembled now, so that Meadhbh clenched her hands and stared at this Beorc at whose table they were guests.

"My mother deserves more than that, sir," Ceallach said, who was never wont to say anything at all. He stood up from the table beside Meadhbh, tall as he could. "If you do know—"

"Young lord," said Domhnull.

"I am not any lord," Ceallach returned. "My father is."

"You are King," said Beorc quite gravely, and Meadhbh's heart turned in her, for there was a great silence down the table, among the steaders and those of Caer Wiell who had found seats. Others moved about the yard, children shouted, horses called to each other down at stable, being in a strange place; Beorc's own folk went to and fro with baskets and baskets of bread and plates of cheese for their guests and they had breached a cider-keg on the porch of the rambling house where folk gathered, finding heart to laugh. But at the table no one stirred.

"Ceallach," their mother said, "sit down, please." And Ceallach did that, quietly, but he was not quiet, not inside: Meadhbh knew. The elf-gift burned, and the master of the steading gazed at them in a way that made it worse. *He is Sidhe himself*, Meadhbh thought, *or something very like; but there is iron in this place, if not in getting to it. We would not be safe if this man were angry.*

But he was not angry. He gazed at them quietly, holding his

secrets, his beard and hair stirring in the wind which came on them then. His wife beside him, Aelfraeda, he called her, who was crowned with gold braids that shone in the torchlight—she sat still and wise-looking—*Like some king,* Meadhbh thought, *and queen. One wants to call them lord and lady. And our father would like them—he always talked with our farmers, of horses and weather and grain*— She found herself remembering all in one tumbling moment, and gathering up the pieces of everything that had shattered; but sadness came with it too, a different kind of sadness than she had ever felt, a sureness of loss, of change imminent that could not be called back.

He was looking straight at her, in that way the Sidhe had done, and that gaze passed on to all of them.

"Here is shelter," he said, "young King, lady of Caer Wiell, and all who come with you—but outside, all about us, there is evil gathered. This is truly what it is, not as Men measure it, wanting this and that and naming their enemies evil, who also have desires. This wants nothing. It *is*. What it does it does because of itself." He rose from his place, towering above them. "Once upon a time, my friends—is that not a fair beginning? —the Sidhe came into the world; they came, and loved it, and would not see it change.

"They had wars. They were not without ambition. There were older things in the world. With most of them they warred—but not the dragons. The dragons seemed fair and wise; they shone beneath the sun like gold and brass together. Their wings—ah, their wings, like sun through ice, their wings.

"But they hated change themselves, and the Sidhe to them were change. The oldest of them was fairest, but no Sidhe could master him—he was too great, he said. But he would give advice to any who would seek him out.

"After all, he said—the world might change again, and who knew what way his folk would go? Even then a folk arose who shifted from day to day, who brought iron and mortality. Perhaps the dragons would go and serve humankind instead.

"There was nothing fairer than Nathair Sgiathach, prince of dragons.

"There was a prince of the Daoine Sidhe; Duilliath was his name, and of all Sidhe his was the proudest, quickest temper.

" 'Come,' said the winged Worm. 'I shall bear you on my back and show you what Men and Death are.' "

The way grew darker, the chaos roiled, and still they cried his name. Aodhan flew, spurning Aescbourne's flood, striding long past mortal steeds. But those came that were not mortal, that were nightmares and worse.

"Brother," he heard. "Ciaran, my brother—" shouted across the tumult.

Then he looked. He must. A Man rode toward him; and he knew this Man, through all the toll of years and other changes too. "Donnchadh," he said. He faced this rider, weaponless.

A darkness passed between, a sheet of darkness, a torrent of horned things and hounds, a rider on a horse that gleamed with bone.

"Lord Ciaran!" someone cried. "Run!"

It was Ruadhan, from the border; it was Madawc and Owein the southrons, and others come besides, a rush of shadowed riders. There were border archers—a black sleet of arrows fell into the press; they were figures that moved like dream, arrows that fell with deceptive swiftness.

"Lord!" cried other voices: it was Beorc and Rhys, not dead—arrived on lathered horses, with haggard faces, and their weapons solid iron. A troop of riders was with them, coming from darkened air. "Lord, wait for us!"

Aodhan turned beneath him, leapt forward, bearing him away. Tears were on his face, blinding him; there was pain again, of loss and grief. But: "*Go!*" he shouted, consenting, and now the elf horse flew, faster, faster, faster, till all the world blurred about them to a dim gray light, til the air smelled of sea and they found the sun. Water scattered from Aodhan's hooves, splashing droplets that seemed to fall and fall.

The pain stopped then. "Liosliath!" he cried, flinging out his hands. "Liosliath! *Liosliath! I have come as far as I can! Come to me now—the rest is yours!*"

He ceased. That was all.

The elf horse threw its head, it danced and turned; its rider straightened and lifted his face again toward the shadowed east where riders clashed and died.

He had brought little with him; he touched the stone about his neck and shut his eyes and came more fully into this world. He had neither weapon nor armor; he had not even fully his own shape: but one thing he drew with him by the power in the stone—a silver horn: Daybreak was its name: Camhanach. He had no strength as yet to sound it; he was still mazed in the change, mazed as battle swept the plain.

"—Duilliath," he said. And louder: "Duilliath!"

He rode forward, as far as Aescbourne's banks. Men were

being pressed back and back toward him, behind their shield of ghosts; drow came at them, fuaths, every sort of ill amid the darkness. He felt the world different than he had known and dimmer; but from the stone a thousand memories came flooding, a Man's memories, his love, his life, his understanding of the world. He knew all of these Men, the allies of Lord Death. Love welled up in him, and pride, from somewhere in the stone. Hard-pressed, mortal men and ghosts made a wall about him, taking him for their lord: with iron and lives the living defended him; with courage, the human dead.

He lifted the horn and sounded it.

The earth quaked. The drow shrieked one awful cry. "No," one shouted, who lifted a venomed sword. "Fall back—O cousin, you do not defeat us! You only draw new battlelines. And she is there, our cousin, when you release the Worm—A world divided, Liosliath! That is what you win—but Aoibheil is ours!"

They retreated; the lesser evils flowed after them, less swift, leaving mortal allies in confusion and panic on Aescbourne's wooded shores.

"Lord!" Beorc cried. "O gods, my lord—"

A second time he set the horn to his lips and pealed out a note wilder and louder than the first.

The meal was done, the tale ended. Beorc turned down his cup and looked at them all. There was a scurrying beside him. The Gruagach scrambled up on the bench.

"A thing has happened," said Beorc gazing at them all. Aelfraeda rose and took his hand. The wind increased. Leaves began to fly from the tree above them as if autumn had come in an instant. They fell onto the table, among the dishes. Meadhbh's heart was beating hard with a fear she could put no name to, but some spell had been on them all the while Beorc was speaking. And now the Gruagach was staring at them with round dark eyes, and her mother's hand sought hers on one side, and Ceallach's on the other. "Lady," Beorc said, "you brought your folk for refuge. But no on can claim it who does not wish, for whom it is not the last of hopes. And you cherish others. So good night to you. Farewell. A horn has blown in Eald; and that summons we may not deny."

Their mother rose; and they stood, dismayed to see the tall steader walk away from them, and all their folk withdrawing. He turned again toward them, lifted his hand as if he would bid them farewell.

Then everything ceased to be—the house, the fences—all the

tumult of people. They stood alone, they, their mother, Domhnull— beneath a dead and leafless tree, on a hillside whispering
with grass.

"Domhnull!" their mother cried. "O Muirne—!"

Meadhbh shivered. The elfgift burned and dazed her. There
was ill all about them, except in one direction.

A horn sounded across the hills. Yet again the air thickened
about them and they stood in twilight, on a riverside littered with
the dead, where a rider on a white horse stood amid a knot of
Caer Wiell and southron riders—

That one slid down from the horse and came to them as others
dismounted there in this dreadful place. Their mother stood still,
by them and Domhnull—*not our father*, Meadhbh thought, with
a new and more terrible ache within her heart. She felt Ceallach's
hand clench hers.

He came to their mother, this tall elf with so much like their
father and so smooth-faced young: he took her hand and knelt
and kissed it as if she were some queen. Then he rose again, and
their mother's hand left his slowly, with such sorrow as she drew
away. Domhnull moved at once to take her arm; Beorc was there
glowering, and Rhys—but Meadhbh could never stir from where
she stood, gone cold inside as the stranger turned to her.

"Meadhbh, Ceallach," said the elf prince—only that; but
when he bent a look on them it felt—there was no word for what
it was: the elf-gifts ached with it, with all the world was not and
she wanted it to be again.

He walked away; the elf horse came to him. He swung up to
its back and it leapt away with him, so swiftly only the heart
could see it, away from them, across the river where there were
things she never wanted to see. *He is in danger*, Meadhbh
thought. Nothing was what it ought to be; there were men lying
dead, blood everywhere and such a poison of iron—She wanted
to run, run, run, where none of this was true; she wanted to
strike and make things what they were again, wanted, wanted,
wanted—

Lost, a voice wailed from the river. *O lost, lost—the kind
children. I follow, follow through the waters—I hear; o come!
come! o help—"*

She went; it was so easy. Her brother came with her—or
perhaps he had gone before. They were *there* on the banks deep
within the trees. They heard their mother calling. "Meadhbh!
Ceallach!—o gods—Beorc—"

"*Caolaidhe!*" Meadhbh called.

A horse snorted, close by their feet. They looked and it was a young man clad in nothing but the shadow, with red and dreadful eyes.

"Seaghda am I," said that one. "Caolaidhe is afraid. Camhanach has sounded and the world is in danger of it. Come! I will carry you. I have no master. But I will take you up."

The water stirred and sang: a fair face drifted in muddy water, in flood and rapid current. "Where river runs, run I. O children, trust me, trust Seaghda—where river runs, run I. Seaghda is frightened too, but he will never say it. Come with us, kind children; come, o come—keep us free, no slave to Sidhe or dragon."

"Help us," Ceallach said. "Help us if you can.

Water splashed; a branch snapped. The each-uisge was coming up, trailing weed and water; the pooka came to Ceallach, moving through the brush. "Meadhbh!" came their mother's voice. "O Ceallach—"

Meadhbh seized the each-uisge's mane. Here was help and power, if she could only tame it. She climbed and it was easy: all at once she was up and the each—uisge was moving, not like a horse, but like the river itself, smooth and dreadful; and Ceallach raced beside her.

They ran along the river south, so swiftly—"No!" Meadhbh cried; "Wait, turn back!" cried Ceallach; but the fuaths never heeded. Black and dreadful they ran the rivercourse, turning into another; and now toward the sea, where other horses came, white horses out of the foam, in the breaking of thunder.

Then ships came from nowhere, from the sunlight, wide-sailed, gliding swift as gulls before the wind; and light was all about them.

"They're the Sidhe!" Ceallach cried; and it was as sure in them as their own names. "O Meadhbh, the Sidhe have come to help us!"

A stormwind swept the weary men that held a hill at Aescbourne. It scoured their faces, cracked in the tattered banners, brought the smell of green things where was the stench of blood and death. Men swore. "Hush," said Domhnull, getting to his feet. And Branwyn lifted her head, hearing something—feeling it, who lost too much to feel any hope at all: her heart beat faster—it was the wind, and thunder, and something passed them, skirled about them, raced off eastward, like storm. The sound of horns came pealing, pealing off the hills; and it set a faint cold tingling in her veins, like nothing else she had ever felt. It was Eald; it was brightness, and something of her own, sped safely—*O run*, she wished them, *O run, run, my children!*

"My lady—" Domhnull was by her, gathering her cloak about her. He had armed himself: there was no dearth of weapons on this littered ground. They stood in stormlight now, in thickening murk as sunset faded; perhaps he had seen what had passed him—there was that look within his eyes. "The Sidhe," she said. "Domhnull, did you hear them?"

"I heard it," said Beorc, who came up from the shoulder of the rise. "Something went past, at least. They know it out there too, and they'll move." He pointed into the dark, by the trees along the river. "They're gathering. It's getting dark fast, and that wind on whatever side won't help our archers. I'd advise the horses loosed. They'll only be confusion. And gods know we've nowhere to be riding to."

She looked at him. If there was any fear in Beorc, if there was grief or weariness or any other thing, he showed none of it. When they had not found the children he had set about ordering this and that calmly, choosing this place, this sandy hill halfway to the sea. He and Rhys and Domhnull—*Hold here*, he claimed his orders were; and none of them gave any hint in voice or look that they could not hold this place forever.

"Do that then," she said. She wrapped her cloak about her. She felt the earth tremble, heard the baying of hounds.

SEVENTEEN
Nathair Sgiathach

The earth trembled beneath a darkened sky in this edge where magic met desolation. The chill air shook to the peal of a distant horn, and in that moment Arafel's heart leapt in startlement, in joy turned swiftly bittersweet—for this hope came at cost, and she knew that cost. It came at direst risk, wide and wild and shaking the world in its path. Liosliath! A friend had reached the sea and brought hope with the leaving of his life. That was Camhanach sounding, to the peril of the earth.

Eald waked from slumber. Every pact and vow the Sidhe had shaped in their parting from the world unsealed itself, for that was the undoing of it, that horn, sounding Daybreak after dark.

An elf had crossed all the barriers with Camhanach in his hand and now the ships themselves might come, the great silver ships, and the herds from behind the wind. She might have wept for terror; she shouted instead for joy, at the threatening hills. "Ceud Failte!" she cried as the elf horse danced beneath her. "*O Welcome! Welcome home!*"

The green magic surged. Fionnghuala leapt forward as the echoes of that horn still rang among the hills. The dark Sidhe fled in panic from the hooves, the small ones scuttled under stones and into any shadow they could find. Harpsong sounded. It was memory and magic, echoing across the land in every place that had ever held Harp and harper . . . from Dun na h-Eoin and the ruins of Caer Wiell to the heart of Eald itself, bound in elvish jewels and the wind that stirred the trees.

But Dun Gol lay before her now, the way to Lioslinn. She saw the drow massing like shadow on the hills and that shadow grew, turning all her power. "Turn," she urged Fionnghuala, "turn now! No farther. We have delayed it all we can."

The elf horse obeyed at once, whirling back in the direction they had come, flying now, striking thunders from the air, shaking lightning from her mane. There was hope now: they went to find it. They sped along the path they themselves had made, through land she had shaped and healed.

But: *Ruin,* the dragon whispered, away to the east, in the depths of Lioslinn. *Ruin, o Arafel—for all bindings are undone now—and it was Cinniuint bound me. The tree is dying, do you not feel it? Camhanach has slain it, and I am free! Your magic fails. Stay and meet me, Arafel.*

She put a hand to the stone, even while she rode; but in nothing could she tell whether the dragon lied. Her magic, Cinniuint's, they were both the same, woven deep into land and air and running rivers.

Despair, the dragon said. *Your magic is failing, failing, Arafel.*

Then a darkness swept before her in this land she had reclaimed. Drow flooded the way before her to cut her off, between her and Airgiod. They streamed down from the hills, a host with banners, the standard of the King.

It is your cousin, the dragon said. *Duilliath has found you. And Cinniuint is dead.*

Fionnghuala checked her pace, turned westward—but on those hills too were shadows; and from north and eastward—from the north came drow from Dun Gol; from eastward the dragon began his slow advance, shaping the land in his turn, binding what he had made until his path was sure.

"Stay, stay," said Arafel, patting Fionnghuala's neck, seeking some way among the hills. The elf horse turned this way, that way, striking thunder from her hooves, shaking herself and throwing her head. Nothing yet had dismayed Fionnghuala: but now they were well ensnared, now the circle narrowed, and to the east they must not go. Arafel took her sword in hand. There was mist about them. The air grew chill and hushed.

"O Arafel," the sweet Voice said, far nearer now, "Arafel, now do you believe? In this little valley neither of us may win—all that we would wish. But is that not the way of things in this wicked world? Turn from them and come to me. I will treat you well, with honor. I will give you place with me, among my servants. Only Duilliath will be greater."

It did not deserve an answer. Fionnghuala turned as she looked about her. The east lay open, blank with mist, inviting her to try it: Nathair Sgiathach hoped for that, in his ambush in the hills. On other sides the drow advanced, riders on fuaths and black beasts, with smaller evils trailing.

"These Men of yours," the silken Voice went on, deep as thunder, soft as summer rain. "O Arafel, did you truly think yourself Men's warden? Bindings you laid on me, but I was not asleep. There was the lord of Damh, my neighbor—it took so little, a whisper in his dreams; then was massacre at Aescbourne Ford, an end of one King of Men, the makings of another."

She looked south, gazing on the hate that spoiled the land, on Duilliath and those beside him, who rode on horned beasts beneath their glowing banners.

"Murder and murder," the dragon mocked her, still chuckling at her back. "Evald served me well. Yours the Cearbhallain, the harper, perhaps; surely Ciaran Cuilean; but mine were Laochailan, Donnchadh—and Evald's tainted line. The children, the fine fair children—of Evald's blood, of murderer and thief and king—O Arafel, what might I yet make of them?"

"Duilliath," she shouted, ignoring that silken voice. "I weary of you!"

"Put away your sword, cousin," the cry came back. "There is no use in this."

"Something must keep the magic," the dragon whispered. "Duilliath knows well that we have gained a prize in you. Any small Sidhe might we have bound—for our Cinniuint; but you will serve far better, willing or unwilling. Tell me, what would the Daoine Sidhe not venture—knowing you within our hands?"

It was truth: of her a great binding could be made, as great as that which had flourished about the elvish tree, herself and the stone that was her heart, to bind the realms together and govern all their magic. She had made herself like the tree himself, rooted in all realms, gathered too much of power here within her hands, and she stood within their reach.

"Come," said Nathair Sgiathach, "cast down your weapons. Do you still hope for Liosliath—and the Daoine Sidhe? I have called him for you. And he has come this way—alone. If one of you will serve us, well, what might we make of two? *Then* let the others come. Dun Gol will be avenged."

Still the circle narrowed. She saw the green land die, saw leaves blacken. Fionnghuala laid back her ears and paced and fretted, leapt forward as they came—but there was here no shifting, no escaping from realm to realm: they were deep in Eald already and there was nowhere left to run.

It was the harping that had guided him, the song within the stone. And now it was stilled. "*Arafel!*" he cried, and Aodhan ran the harder, ran with all his heart for him, taking risks, finding ways even when trees sprang out of mist, when roots impeded and branches raked and clung. The elf horse was wise: his rider knew this—when magic failed and every trial of it let some green thing die. It was Arafel all efforts bled, Arafel whose strength now held Eald, as much of it survived.

He rode with nothing, nothing but Camhanach and the stone; the Man had worn no armor, carried even less; and the Man haunted him. He remembered the lady's careworn face at Aescbourne, the bright eyes of the children—so rich this Man had been. He could never now forget them, this kind he had despised, though he had fought them once, no less than Duilliath; had slain them, had warred against their iron and their changing of the land.

He had fought for them at the end, when he had no other choice. He had made Dun Gol of Airgiodach, after which no elf found joy in remembering. One by one the others had hung the stones on Cinniuint's boughs and passed from Eald, when they could no longer love the world that Men would make or the thing that they had done.

He had been last but Arafel, an age of the world ago: for pride he stayed, for duty—that Cinniuint should hold.

But what care we? he had asked her. *What matter, if Cinniuint should perish, if this world should pass away? There is no restoring, Arafel, only waiting—We have shut that door and sealed it. What gain is left?*

But a Man had shown him that, shown him in brief bright fire, a life so blinding swift in days and nights he had hardly understood it, who had never yet grown old. An elf had learned something in this land of seasons: an elf sped now with a Man's knowledge, and faithfulness and fear; he should never be free of these things, would never wish to be.

"Arafel!" he cried. He went as wildly as Ciaran would have done, hearing the dragon-whisper threatening all that he had loved.

Aodhan leapt the lesser darknesses, dodged the greater, evaded roots and branches in the flicker of an eye. Drow loomed before him on beasts of glowing fire, of watery shifting shapes and every sort of horror. They wished to hold him, but he would not be held: the elf horse overrode them as they caught and clawed at him, outraced them in wind and moon-green light.

Life struggled all about him. Now there was grass beneath, now barrenness and dead trees about them, now clear air, now mist, and the rushing shapes of riders on black beasts that constantly shifted aspect. Fear was the venom of their swords, poisoning the Man with the dread of death, the Elf with doubt and hate at the kiss of their tarnished blades; but the Man was dead already and the elf had no doubts to use. "Go!" he urged Aodhan, and the elf horse flew beneath him, finding ways through ambushes, through mist and shadows. He felt battle through the stone, felt danger and desperation. "O Arafel, *hold fast!*"

A mass of shadows gave way before him. He saw a clearing, a snarling horde that circled Arafel. She was afoot and bleeding, her brightness dimmed with dark; Fionnghuala struggled to rise again from falling, dark-streaked with blood, sent a horror flying, lightning-struck, while Arafel used her sword.

Aodhan never stopped: the dark Sidhe scattered from his hooves, scattered from his lightningbolts, and the elf horses circled, herding all the shadows, striking and harrying them in retreat until there was space within the grove.

Then Arafel sank down on one knee, her hand upon the ground, her head drooping, for her hurts were many and deep. There was pain within the stone, great pain and weariness; he took it such as he could, sliding down from Aodhan between her and the dark.

"Liosliath," said a voice from among the shadows. It touched Ciaran's self, deep within the stone.

Donnchadh, that memory said.

But his own: *Duilliath*.

*   *   *

The wind streamed past, but there was no chance of falling: that was the nature of what they rode, with neither rein nor saddle: There was no need of clinging as the fuaths ran, matching strides with the Sidhe host's elvish mounts, black amid their light.

They had left the shore behind, and Meadhbh wept for her mother, for Beorc and Domhnull, Rhys and all the others—"Stop!" she had cried; and Ceallach: "Help us!"

But nothing would stop the rush that swept them on, and nothing stopped the fuaths.

Now they came up beside the first, the elvish captain. Unarmored he was, like the rest a bowman, his arrows fletched with light. His white horse ran because it would, reinless as the fuaths. He seemed young: there was none of the Sidhe but looked both young and fair: there was no age among them. They were all cold light and dreadful and there was terror about them as they came.

"Turn back," Ceallach pleaded still. "At least leave someone behind to help them!"

"It is not our people," said the elf, "not our war."

"Then let us go!" Meadhbh cried.

"It is what you bear that draws you," said the elf, "not what bears you."

Meadhbh touched the gift that she wore. *A virtue of finding,* she remembered.

They have no hearts, a whisper came to her. *They hung them all on trees, to forget this land, to forget all that they have done here.*

"That is the dragon speaking," said the captain staring straight ahead. "Do not heed it; shut your ears—"

That one's name is Nearachd. He has no love of Men. He covets what you bear—would have it if he could. Beware him.

"Be still, old Worm!" Nearachd cried into the air.

What are you to them? What was your father? They killed him. Your mother left to die—

They rode suddenly into mist and trees, shifting and turning now; branches came between. "Keep with us!" Nearachd called. "Keep with us, young Sidhe! Do not listen to that voice!"

"*King without a kingdom, queen born of thieves and murderers—o hear me, young ones: see what virtue brings—what it brought your father.*"

Be still, be still, Meadhbh told it. She clenched the elf-gift in her hand and thought of Ceallach beside her, only, only Ceallach, made a wall with him, to shield them from the dragon.

She grew calm and still inside: perhaps it was her doing; perhaps Caolaidhe's cold heart. Beside them the pooka ran, at home in this shadow. She saw her brother's face, that it had shed its grief, that it grew very like the Sidhe. Dark things took shape before them: elvish arrows flew with light no less dreadful than the shadow.

It is not a place for us, she thought, despairing, and then cast despair away, remembering Liosliath, and the kindness in his eyes. She felt a strength within her hand, imagining a tree— young it was and few its leaves and yet it lived, lent something of warmth and life.

Find them, came a voice within her heart, bubbling like waters. *O hold, hold, hold, the precious thing I bear upon my back. Dark water, dark paths, no fuath fears them.*

She feared, feared for all the world, for what was left worth loving, for the least light and the last beauty and the small band standing against the dark somewhere behind them. *Home*, she kept thinking, remembering the faces. *Home, home, home.*

Her brother rode beside her. There was a light about him, about her, and the elf-gifts were that brightness.

The drow's sword was in his hand, tarnished silver, poisoned. His comrades made now a ring about the grove, a darkness cold with hate.

"I would not fight you," said Duilliath, "either one. There is nothing more to gain but wounds—on either side. Give up, cousins."

Liosliath stood watching, every shift of eye; and at their backs the two horses moved, circling, small mutters of thunder, pacing the ring that was all that remained of Eald on the earth, protecting Arafel.

Arafel gained her feet, such as she could. But the circle diminished more, grass curling black. "Liosliath," she said. A sword-hilt touched his hand. He took it, lifted it; the blade shone bright against the dark.

"We have done this before," Duilliath reminded him.

"Not well enough," he said.

More grass perished. A flower died. The drow came nearer, and there was about him the gleam of sullen fires. The blades lifted, crossed, flickered with subtle passes, feigning ease, feigning movements that led to this side and that.

Faster, then and faster. The line of green drew inward, held. They battled back and forth on that line which he could cross and

drow could not; and the wind was blowing, with chill that grew
and grew. He heard his name called, heard the dragon-voice.

"Ware!" cried Arafel.

The border yielded all at once, a falling inward. Grass blackened,
a flower died and went to dust: Duilliath thrust forward on the
instant and Liosliath flung up a hand, took the point, unarmored
as he was. The blade slid through, venomed, cold and keen. His
own moonbright point touched armor, found a hold, went deep,
and snapped within the wound.

"Brother!" wailed what had been Donnchadh.

It perished. The drow lingered longer, fading even so, a fair
cold face, a wail, a passing chill. Horns were sounding, riders
were coming; the drow sped in retreat, racing for Dun Gol.

The trees faded; the mist remained. The riders came in sudden
pallor, and two that rode on fuaths, hair red as sunrise; two
steeds black and sleek. Thunder muttered; elf horses neighed and
stamped. There was light within the grove.

"Arafel!" cried Nearachd, leaping to the ground. "Liosliath!"

Then he felt his wound, the cold within his arm, felt the
strength ebbing from him with a flow of blood dark as the night
about them. He wavered on his feet, and there were friends
about him; there was Arafel before him, after so many ages—
face to face.

"Stay," came a Voice through the earth itself, soothing and
seducing. "O stay, Daoine Sidhe. Do not think to go."

"Do not listen," said Nearachd. "The ships are waiting,
Aoidheil. And it will never take us. Come. There is nothing
more to gain."

"Nothing more," said Liosliath. He looked at her with ages
stored up of hope, of waiting, but something came into the stone
that dimmed it all at once. She looked sadly faded, streaked with
darkness that was blood; there was sorrow in her eyes and
heartbreak in the stone.

"You understand," she said. "You would understand."

"Haste!" cried Nearachd.

"No," said Arafel.

"Hold to this?" Liosliath asked. "O Aoibheil, no more."

"But there are Men," she said. "If we quit this world to
safety—we leave them to the Worm. We have weapons. We are
not done. —O cousins, have we learned nothing? What happens
here matters."

"If we should fall to it," said Gliadrachan, "o Arafel, the
risk—"

"It matters," Liosliath said. He still held the broken sword, hear the dragon coming, felt cold steal up his arm. He touched the stone he wore, that all the others lacked. "I *remember*. I remember Caer Righ before it was Dun Gol. We made both. Myself—I stand with Arafel."

"Not alone," said Gliadrachan, leaping from her horse.

"Not alone," said Nearachd, and others leaped down, setting arrows to their bows.

So they set themselves and waited, and now they heard its tread, felt the shiver in the air. Arafel stood with them, nocked the last arrow that she had. "Stay back from it," Liosliath said, standing by her. "It aim's most at you."

She said nothing.

Foolish, said the Worm. *Why struggle? You have seen the world changed from all it was. Would you have it back again? We can remake it. It can be anything we will.*

Then was cold and a time that passed measureless, when nothing stirred at all. It was with them, how they had not seen, came glittering like bronze and gold, moving slowly as in some dream, and it seemed the sun had come into that darksome place, glowing on its scales. Its wings blew away the mist and fire coursed the veins that webbed them. Most of all its eyes—its eyes were no color at all. They drew the eye that tried to see what in truth that color was, and nothing was there at all.

No need of weapons, said Nathair Sgiathach. *No need of struggle. The leaves will grow again, the lakes be pure, all things that you desire.*

Bows unbent, strings eased. The Sidhe stood mazed and lost.

The last green perished.

Meadhbh held her gift within her hand; it burned, it had warmth when all had failed, when the each-uisge's trembling stilled, as spellbound as the elves. It loomed, this dreadful thing—it wanted them; and the thing she had, that Ceallach had, it spied this now and drew them.

"No," she said, and louder yet: "*No!*" cried Ceallach.

One Sidhe moved. It was Arafel, who fell to one knee, who bent her bow; it shook and faltered.

The dragon lunged, the arrow sped, into its numbing eye. It wailed, it reared, its wings beat in storm and whirlwind as it rose into the air.

It rose and rose, a shadow now, like a plume of smoke above them; it hovered, plunged—somewhere beyond the hills. The earth shuddered. There was silence.

Then the world began dissolving, blown on winds that blew it all in shreds of light and dark.

There was quiet on Aescbourne's banks, on the sandy hill, quiet in the midst of battle—the enemy fell back, yet another time.

Death was there again. Branwyn had seen him. Rhys had told her who he was, the dark ally who was sometimes here and sometimes not—she saw ghosts; and horrors. There were things horned like stags, clawed like bears, with wolvish eyes, worse even than the enemy. She huddled there behind a wall of shields, of men she loved, of all the world left to her. Weapons flew; arrows struck shields—

And then the silence, as if the world had held its breath. She rose, gazing outward past a sudden gap, for shields had dropped. The air felt strange and cold, the very earth seemed wavering in shadow and in light like light through thickest cloud.

"Where are they?" someone asked. "Where have they gone?"

There were hoofbeats, drawing near. The dark rider had come among them; and suddenly there was nothing else—the hill, their little band, the rider who beckoned.

"Come," Death said. "Your battle now is ended. You must leave this place, and quickly. Trust me now and come."

Branwyn was held then. Her breaths seemed slowed or her life went quicker: she saw—everything, as if the day had come, when yet there was no color. The rider beckoned yet again.

"Traitor," said Beorc. Shields moved slowly; Domhnull brought his up: she saw this, saw Rhys on his feet again, the Boglach shaft still in his side; but he held his sword, left-handed. "There were bargains, and you failed."

"All the world is failing. You have no part in what will be. Lady Branwyn: come to me. Come now. Come first and bring the others."

"No," she said, said it softly, with all her heart; and cried out, for it seemed he tried to reach them. *"No!"* The world quaked. "Go away! Let my people be!"

"You are mine. These folk belong to me." He came closer; his sword was drawn. It shone with baleful fires. "Rhys, Beorc, and Domhnull—"

"Let be!" Branwyn cried. She was cold coming down the hill. Men moved slowly about her, in the colorless, dreadful light. They wished to stop her, held out their hands, fading like the world. "Let them go, let them all go and I will come."

"Gods, no!" said Beorc. He thrust up his sword, met Death's. The iron parted, left him weaponless. The world swirled about them all.

And color came, pale at first, like mist on meadows, a touch of green and coolness. The mist gave way to sun, to trees about them, silver-leaved, hills folding about them.

"Beorc!" Domhnull cried. But of all of them, only Beorc was not there, and all the ghosts had gone. They stood few and tattered, bewildered in this place. There was silence, but for the wind.

"*Welcome,*" piped a voice. "*O welcome, gold lady! O come, come, come!*"

It was the Gruagach, perched upon a stone. Three ponies waited near him, and a tall piebald mare.

"Gruagach," said Branwyn, "o Gruagach—Come where?"

"You *are* there already. Follow, follow now. Some ride, some walk, not far, not far, o my Men, my gold lady, follow as you can."

Rhys thought to walk; he could not. His men caught him in their arms and set him on the horse. So they did for others that were hurt too much to walk, and the ponies bore them gently.

The Gruagach went before them, dancing as he went, up, up the vale while the hills unfolded. They went with all their strength, with hope in what they should find.

The steading lay before them, just as it had been before—if anything, more rambling.

They came as quickly as they could, some even running at the last, for Caer Wiell folk were streaming down the hill to meet them, and foremost, two red-haired children.

"Meadhbh!" Ceallach!" Branwyn cried, and ran to catch them in her arms. Muirne came, and Cein, Cook and Seamaire, Cobhan and Smith and Domhnull's kin—there was no lack of tears; and laughter mingled with them, for all that they had saved.

"The elves brought us," Meadhbh said. "They're here."

Last the steaders came, with the tall, red-haired master and his gold-braided wife.

"Come," said this Beorc, who was very like their own. "Welcome here, three times welcome. Here is a place better than the last, for as long as you want to stay."

EIGHTEEN

Farewells

Autumn came and winter, and the Sidhe who had passed near the Steading in their riding appeared less frequently and not so near, appearing sometimes in the distance and sometimes passing by night in wind and rush of thunder like some wintry storm.

But with snow deep on Steading fields, there still was warmth and crowded comfort, for somehow they had found a place and nook for everyone. The storage on the west of the house was warm and snug; and barnloft held some: they nested everywhere, did Caer Wiell folk, like sheltering birds, and began to laugh again now that dread was past and griefs were healing. Children began to play with Steading children and make snowball ambushes, while farmers talked of spring.

And spring came. The snow melted straightway under a pale fair sun, the nights seemed warmer with gentle winds and a strangely greenish moon.

"Planting time," the farmers said; and the plows turned up sharpened and the tools set on the porch.

"Who did that?" Caer Wiell folk asked.

And the Gruagach looked wise.

There was an evening the fuaths came, down by the little stream that wandered by the steading; they were two black horses grazing on the margin; and on another evening a black horse bounded the fences just for sport and raced across the fields.

"That would be Seaghda," said Ceallach, and felt a longing in his heart that was cramped by fences.

So Meadhbh felt a longing too, a restlessness beneath this open sky; at night she heard the forest singing, and she thought of the Daoine Sidhe—for they had never left her heart. Indeed a thing had happened with the elf-gifts, and they were never still, so she was never much distressed at the absence of the Sidhe. *Not yet, not yet*, they said within their hearts.

And there was much to do here, with Caer Wiell folk, with

245

their mother, with Muirne and Domhnull, and Rhys as he healed.
There was all the Steading to find out about, and riding to be
done, with Flann and Floinn to carry them again. The Gruagach
kept them company on the piebald mare, or on the brown pony,
and was sometimes there and sometimes not, according to his
whims. They learned the heron's name from him, and what the
owls were like, who hunted in the barn; they learned all the
horses' true names, and where the brook came from, high up in
the hills, and where the brook went, which was down to the sea
if one followed it.

We shall go there someday, Meadhbh thought, as she planned
other things. And always in her heart she knew the world alive
and all about them: she knew when Sidhe were near that no one
saw; and that there were two most near them who would come
when hearts were healed.

Rhys for his part began to fret about, now that he was healed;
one found him sitting on the steading porch and staring forestward.
And one evening:

"I shall ride south," he said. "The Sidhe said all was well
there, but my folk and I—we've been too long from home. The
road at least should be safer."

"I shall ride with you," said Domhnull. "To see these mountains of yours." So Muirne looked up from her spinning by
the fire, saying nothing, but with anxiousness.

And Branwyn said nothing, thinking only that such partings
were inevitable. That was what she had learned in life. She saw
Meadhbh and Ceallach, that silence that came on them in winter
and lingered into spring. She marked how grave they could
become, how wise their eyes had grown. *Ceallach* the folk called
her son, quite simply, for he was still a boy; but *the young King*
Beorc named him when he spoke of him. King he was, but of
what she did not know; and what her daughter was she hardly
dared to guess—*Meadhbh* Beorc called her, just Meadhbh and
nothing more, but with that tone he used on *King*. Meadhbh rode
where she liked and nothing harmed her; the ponies came when
she wanted and the owls answered when she called to them.

Branwyn did not hope to keep them, or anything else. But she
cherished what she had, which was the warmth of friends about
her, a hearth to sit by, fences that kept things generally where
they belonged . . . but they could keep nothing in nor out that
tried. And this was the way of things. Spring came. Her children
strayed; Leannan went walking in the hills and sometimes they
heard his harping where he played alone, harpsong drifting like
magic down the hills, sweeter than the songs he played for them.

And most of all the Sidhe came back with the greening of the land. They would pass on their white horses, usually in the morning, riding from the south.

So Branwyn sat on the porch this morning, while Rhys and Domhnull were about whatever preparations they made, and Smith was hammering away down beside the barn. She counted all her memories and wished—so many things.

"They are coming," said the Gruagach, sitting on the step where he had not been before, and then he was gone again.

So Branwyn stood up, glancing to the south; and her heart lifted with the sight of elvish riders by the stream.

And the whole Steading stopped its business when the riders turned up toward the yard.

"Bring food," Beorc called, "and drink! Visitors have come!"

Meadhbh and Ceallach arrived from wherever they had been; Domhnull came, all out of breath, and Rhys; and Muirne from the house. But Branwyn stood still, her heart beating hard, her hands clenched together, for it was Arafel, with Liosliath.

The riders came up by the fence. All clad in green they were, with gray cloaks, and a light seemed to go about them, like the sun upon far hills. They carried bows and swords, rode reinless, and when they slid down by the gate the white horses vanished in that way those horses had.

Folk gathered, making a ring about them—it was always like that, that folk wanted to see, and somehow felt a silence on them and a dread.

"Rhys," said Liosliath, offering his hand. "Domhnull." It was a familiar gesture, like one they had known and lost. He embraced the children, touched their faces; and on his left hand was a mark like a pale smooth star. They kissed him on the cheek and he touched his lips to each brow.

Branwyn clenched her hands. But then he looked at her, and came to the porch step where she stood. His eyes were gray, not like Ciaran's; nothing about him recalled the Man that she had loved—except a gentleness as he took her hand and touched it to his lips, the look within his eyes: *I was his friend*, it said. *He loved you; loves you still.* "Branwyn," he said. So it was duty that he paid, this prince of the Daoine Sidhe, who was older than the hills about them and younger than the dawn. She was earth and knew it. But he had to love them. It was Ciaran's heart he had, buried deep within his own.

"Come," said Beorc, "come, sit and drink. Leannan, where is your harp? Be welcome, all who come."

So they went to the great table in the yard. The Gruagach had snatched a cake; he had a pot of ale and perched on the fence to watch. A fox rested near, his long eyes dark and wise. There was milk and honey, cakes and ale and cider and mounds of butter yellow as the flowers that bloomed down by the stream. Her children were there, her friends about her, all that mattered in the world; and she felt fortunate again.

"Is it well with you?" asked Liosliath.

"Well enough," she said, "lord elf."

"The fuaths are back," said Meadhbh at once.

"Oh, well," said Arafel, "that was certain." She sipped at the cider and a smile touched her face. "Tame trees," she said.

"We like them," said Beorc. "And tend them."

"Fences," said Arafel.

"They have stood you in good stead, elf."

"That they have." A light was in her eye and dancing in the stone that hung upon her breast. "I shall bring you wild honey when next we come. The Gruagach likes his saucer and his cup of ale, but most of all he likes the fields, o Man. For that he labors. And still your fences stand; and shall. But there will be singing in your brook come moonrise. And that will take no saucers and respect no fences." She set the cup aside. "May your tame trees flourish, neighbor. And those who care for them. The luck is on this place and rests on all who find it."

"On our friends," said Liosliath, whose way was to say little. "When you go south, I shall go, and show you wonders."

"Might we?" asked Meadhbh at once.

"Not yet," said Arafel. "But someday soon—The gifts I gave you: how do they fare?"

Meadhbh looked distressed then, looked at Branwyn, and Ceallach did, in a way that boded something, that foretold secrets and Sidhe things long kept from her. Her heart ached without knowing why at the look in her daughter's eyes. *I love you*, she thought at her children: she was doomed to love the Sidhe, at last, the green magic, the things that would not be held. "I love you," she shaped with her lips, and thought: *even if I lose you now.*

They brought out the gifts, but no longer leaves—they were stones, filled with light. "They changed," said Ceallach to the Sidhe. "They changed that day."

"So did Miadhail," said Arafel. "He was the only tree born within Man's age. They were his life you bore; no one else could have borne it but Sidhe born within this age. Your burden was more precious than even your father knew. Now they hold your hearts; be careful of them, to keep them what they are."

She looked at Branwyn, a long, gray glance in which the wind forgot to breathe and nothing stirred. "This place will hold you while you will. Forever if you like. But take my counsel—go."

"Go where?" asked Branwyn. "Where should we go? Our enemies have Caer Wiell—do they not?"

"Do you not know by now," asked Beorc beside her, "that you are beyond the sea—that the land has left the world?"

"Then my father—" said Rhys. "My home—"

"Oh, your mountains are here," said Liosliath. "The forest, the plain—all, wherever Camhanach sounded in Men's hearts. The world goes on much as it was. It will not miss this little corner of it. Your mountains, Caer Wiell and Donn—Dun na h-Eoin of the Kings—Men might till the fields, heal old scars, live in peace with Eald—Have you not seen gulls fly here? They come from behind the wind."

"The realms are divided now," said Arafel. "The dark things and the brighter—we could not take the bright and leave the dark to Men. Caer Wiell *might* be; many things might be, Branwyn of Caer Wiell."

"Go there," said Liosliath.

Tears burned in Branwyn's eyes so that the Sidhe's brightness wavered. "If *he* were here, lord elf—"

"Do what pleases you. He would say that if he were here."

She thought on it, on fields golden in the sun, on steadings far and wide, and something widened in her heart, forever.

They rode out into the morning and Arafel looked back as the Gruagach capered along the fence rail a little distance, as earth-born horses paced them and whinnied salutation to their own.

"Care for them!" Liosliath called. "Take care for them all!"

"The Gruagach is with them," the Brown Man called. "Fair, o fair the morning, Daoine Sidhe, and the spring will be long, o long—fare well, fare back, light shine on you, Daoine Sidhe!"

The Steading fields lay brown beneath the plow; the hills were turning green and Men had their work before them. Liosliath loved these human folk; there was no helping that.

And if Arafel searched her heart she found a certain joy in seeing the works of Men, neat fields, well cared for, folk keeping their boundaries and observing such swift change within them. They were scattered far, from Dryw in the south to these folk of the Steading. At Dun Gol the drow slept fast. In Lioslinn, in those dark waters—no one knew what slept. But Men would wonder. They would be faring here and there through Eald, and dreaming dreams of things not yet done; but that was the way of Men.

They were chance, and risk and change.

And sometimes there was greatness about them. Liosliath could say so.

If one thing was certain, thought Arafel on this morning of the world, it was that change might happen; and the Daoine Sidhe rode through the land in hope of things unfound.

On Names

Ealdwood is a place in faery and has like all such places an indefinite geography. The nomenclature is Celtic and Welsh, with a touch of the Old English, so this particular corner of faery in language and in spirit sits at some juncture of lands where there has been much coming and going of various peoples, likeliest some corner just above Wales.

In this world the speakers of the English are farthest east; the Welsh to the south; and the speakers of the Celtic tongues have their homes farthest seaward; but they mix at Caer Wiell.

As for the elves, they have generally Celtic names, or the Celtic is very like elvish: or what it once was.

Certain of the names like Arafel and Evald which appear early and often, show a different orthography, being somewhat older in the story, and here retained in mercy to the reader. In further sympathy for the reader who may never have dealt with any of these tongues, the following table may provide some aid, and some delight as well, since the names of Eald are, if one knows how to look at them, our own.

There are many sounds to be passed over very lightly: the reader skilled in languages may come closest to the ancient way of saying them just by the hint of them passing over the tongue. But this was very long ago and accents change even over one hill and the other, let alone in and out of faery. For the sake of those readers who only wish to read without tripping on the words, this table will give little hint of these almost silent sounds, paring them away until only the simplest version is left. C will denote the words that are Celtic; W the Welsh; OE the English.

In general, in the Celtic words, be it noted, mh and bh are the sound we call v; ch is breathed, if possible, as in the familiar lo*ch*, a word for lake (but k will do); -gach has often by our day gone to the sound of a hard -gy; and the profusion of vowels has generally a single simple sound at the heart.

In the Welsh most notably -dd- is -th-.

In the English, easiest to render ae- as simple e-.

Where a name has a more familiar form, it will be given in capitals.

And if for any reader this small list provokes further curiosity, Celtic, Welsh, and Old English reference works are not that difficult to find. A good place to begin is, after all, with names, the -nesses and -hams and -denes and -eys that come off modern tongues as if they had no meaning in themselves. Names do have power, after all, that of conjuring images of places we have not seen.

aelf (elf) OE an elf
Aelfraeda (elf red a) OE from aelf [elf] and raeda [counsel]
aesc (esh) OE ash
Aescbourne (esh burn) OE ash brook: ASHBURN
Aescford (esh ford) OE ash ford: ASHFORD
Aesclinn (esh linn) OE ash pool: ASHLIN
Airgiod (ar gi ud) C silver
Airgiodach (air gyud y) C silver leaves
Alhhard (al ard) OE sacred courage: ALLARD
An Beag (an beg) C small
Aodhan (a o dan) C rascal: AIDAN
Aogail (a ogel) C deathshead
Aoibheil (a o vel) C joy: ARAFEL
ap (ap) W son of
Arafel (ar a fel) C from AOIBHEIL, qv.
Ban (ban) C fair, pale
Bainbourne (ban burn) OE fair brook: BANBURN
Bain Sidhe (ban shee) C a Sidhe whose wail portends death; usually appears near water, usually in the shape of a woman washing bloody clothes; lit. White Sidhe: BANSHEE
Beorc (burk) OE birch: BURKE
Blian (blin) OE slender: BLINN; BLYNN
Boc (bok) OE deer: BUCK
Boda (boda) OE herald: BODE
Boglach (bog lach) C marsh

Bourne (burn) OE stream
brad (brad) OE broad
Bradhaeth (brad heath) OE broad heath
Branwyn (bran win) W from BRANGWEN (bron win) white breast
Breandan (brendan) C raven: BRENDAN
Brom (brom) OE broom plant: BROM
caer (ker) W stronghold
Caer Damh (ker dav) C stag keep
Caer Glas (ker glas) C gray castle
Caer Luel (ker lel) OE castle keep: CARLISLE
Caer Wiell (ker well) OE spring keep
Caerbourne (ker burn) OE castle brook
Caerdale (ker dale) OE castle dale
Caith (kaith) C battleground: KEITH
Camhanach (kavanak) C daybreak
Caoimhin (ku EV in) C kindly: KEVIN
Caolaidhe (keely) C thin: KEELY
Ceallach (kelly) C warrior: KELLY
Cearbhallain (KER va len) C fr. Spearthrower: victor: CAR-ROLLAN; CAROLYN
Cein (shawn) C old: SEAN; SHAWN
Ceud failte! (ked faly-tya) C a hundred welcomes!—hail!
Ciaran (kiran) C twilight: KIERAN
Ciataich (ketik) C delight
Cinniuint (kennent) C fate, luck
Cobhan (kovan) C hill: COWAN
Coille (cully) C woodland: CULLY
Cuilean (kul an) C cub: QUILLAN
damh (dav) C stag; horned beast
Daoine Sidhe (thee na Shee) C the People of Peace; the folk of Faery. Often powers felt to be dangerous and perhaps ill-wishing are named by names felt to be quite contrary to their natures, to avoid calling them up accidentally or offending them by mentioning their true names; again, the feeling is that the true name is not for using. And of course the Daoine Sidhe are not likely to give the true name of all their kin for common use. Other names are the FAIR FOLK, for much the same reason. SIDHE applies to many kinds of creature: the Gruagach by some extension is one of the Sidhe and so are some things very much worse to look on. But the Daoine Sidhe are the highest of their kind.
Domhnull (donal) C ruler: DONAL; DONALD
Donn (don) C brown
Donnchadh (don chad) C brown tartan: DUNCAN
drow (drow) C fr. drough; dark elf

Dryw (drew) W sight: DREW

Dubh (du) C black

Dubhlaoch (dooley) C dark fighter: DOOLEY

Duilliath (dul yeth) C shadowleaf

Duine Sidhe (dena shee) sing, of DAOINE SIDHE, qv.

Dun na h-Eoin (doon na hey win) C tower of birds

Dun Gol (doon goal) C hill of weeping

each (ek) C horse

each-uisge (ek-wiskey) C water horse; a type of fuath, which entices one to ride and then drowns the victim who is stuck to the each-uisge's back. See: fuath.

Eada (ed) OE noble: ED-

eald (eld) OE old

Evald (ev ald) OE fr. ÆCWEALD, oak wood

Feochadan (fo ka dan) C thistle

Fionn (fee an) C fair: FINN

Fionnbhar (fin var) C fairhair

Fionnghuala (fin el a) C white shoulder: FINELLA

Flann (flan) C red: FLANN

Floinn (floin) C red: FLYNN

fuathas (fyath-as) C hate, spite; also, a water-dwelling Sidhe such as the each-uisge or pooka. Many baneful Sidhe appear as black animals.

Gaelbhan (gelven) C white

Geannan (gennon) C pale

Gearr (gear) C spear; also CEAR: GEAR-; GER-

Glas (glass) C gray

Gliadrachan (li-ad-ran) C lightsome

Gruagach (gru gy) fr. C: hairy. The word has scattered meanings. As one of the Sidhe, this is one of the working sort who performs homely tasks.

Gwernach (gwer nak) alder stream: GARNOCK

haeth (heath) OE heath: HEATH

Hagan (ha gen) C little: HAGEN

Haraleah (harley) OE haremeadow: HARLEY

Hlowebourne (lowburn) OE low water

Hugi (hu (g) i) OE wise: HUGH

Laochailan (la ok lan) C hero: LACHLANN

Leannan (lennon) C cloak: LENNON

linn (lin) OE pool: LYNN

lios (li-ess) C Sidhe fort

Liosliath (liess-lia) C Sidhe fortress: LESLEY

Lioslinn (liess-lin) C Sidhe fort lake

Madawc (maddock) W good: MADDOCK; MADOC

Meadhbh (mev) C: laughter: MAEVE; MAB
Meara (mer a) C wild laughter.
Meredydd (me re dith) W sea; MEREDITH
Miadhail (mithil) C precious
Muirne (murn a) C hospitality; MYRNA
Nathair Sgiathach (nayer skey-ak) C lit.: winged serpent; dragon
Nearachd (ńyerakt) C fortunate
Niall (ne al) C hero: NEAL
Odhran (odrin) C pale
Owein (owen) W noble: OWEN
pooka (pooka) C a fuath which appears in the form of a black horse, and which entices one to ride it—to (as the legend runs) disaster: POOKA, also PHOOKA
Raghallach (rahkly) C brave: RIDDOCK; RIDLEY
Rhys (reese) W burning; glory: REECE; REESE
Riagan (regan) C little king: REGAN
righ (ree) C king
Ronan (ronan) C seal ring: RONAN
ruadh (ro ak) C red; red deer
Ruadhan (ro an) C red; rowan: ROWAN
Seaghda (shea) C kingly: SHEA
Seamaire (sha-mare) C shamrock
shellycoat a type of fuath which has no skin, but is covered with rocks and shells and debris from river and lake bottoms which rattle as it moves. It drowns its victims.
Sidhe (shee) See: Daoine Sidhe
Siodhachan (sheehan) C peace: SHEEHAN
Skaga (s(k)a(g)a) ( ) = soft; stand of trees: SHAW
Sobhrach (sov rak; sovry) C primrose
Suileach (sullak) C darkeye
Tuathal (tu-aly) C northerner: TULLY
Tiamhaidh (tiv ak) C drear
wiell (well) OE spring
Wulf (wolf) OE wolf

DAW sf BOOKS

Presenting ANDRE NORTON in DAW editions:

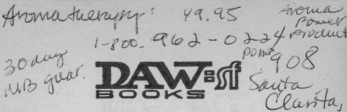

DAW BOOKS

Presenting C. J. CHERRYH